WITHDRAW
FROM
STOCK

THIS
BOOK
BELONGS
TO

LORNA DOONE

R. D. Blackmore

André Deutsch Classics

386 776.

André Deutsch Classics

Published by André Deutsch Classics

André Deutsch Ltd, 106 Great Russell Street, London WC1B 3LJ, England

First published 1869

First published by André Deutsch Classics 1997

ISBN 0 233 99076 3

This setting copyright © André Deutsch Classics 1997

All rights reserved. This book is sold subject to the condition that it may not be
reproduced, stored in a retrieval system, or transmitted, in any form or by any
means, electronic, mechanical, photocopying, recording or otherwise, without
the publisher's prior consent.

Typeset by CentraCet Ltd, Cambridge

Printed in Great Britain by WBC, Bridgend

Contents

1

Elements of Education

If anybody cares to read a simple tale told simply, I, John Ridd, of the parish of Oare, in the county of Somerset, yeoman and churchwarden, have seen and had a share in some doings of this neighbourhood, which I will try to set down in order, God sparing my life and memory. And they who light upon this book should bear in mind, not only that I write for the clearing of our parish from ill-fame and calumny, but also a thing which will, I bow, appear too often in it, to wit – that I am nothing more than a plain unlettered man, not read in foreign languages, as a gentleman might be, nor gifted with long words (even in mine own tongue), save what I may have won from the Bible, or Master William Shakespeare, whom, in the face of common opinion, I do value highly. In short, I am an ignoramus, but pretty well for a yeoman.

My father being of good substance, at least as we reckon in Exmoor, and seized in his own right, from many generations, of one, and that the best and largest, of the three farms into which our parish is divided (or rather the cultured part thereof), he, John Ridd, the elder, churchwarden and overseer, being a great admirer of learning, and well able to write his name, sent me his only son to be schooled at Tiverton, in the county of Devon. For the chief boast of that ancient town (next to its woollen-staple) is a worthy grammar-school, the largest in the west of England, founded, and handsomely endowed in the year 1604, by Master Peter Blundell, of that same place, clothier.

Here, by the time I was twelve years old, I had risen into the upper school, and could make bold with Eutropius and Caesar – by aid of an English version – and as much as six lines of Ovid. Some even said that I might, before manhood, rise almost to the third form, being of a persevering nature; albeit, by full consent of all (except my mother), thick-headed. But that would have been, as I now perceive, an ambition beyond a farmer's son; for there is but one form above it, and that made of masterful scholars, entitled rightly 'monitors.' So it came to pass, by the grace of God, that I was called away from learning, whilst sitting at the desk of the junior first in the upper school, and beginning the Greek verb τύπτω.

But if you doubt of my having been there, because now I know so little, go and see my name, 'John Ridd,' graven on that very form. Forsooth, from the time I was strong enough to open a knife and to spell my name, I began to grave it in the oak, first of the block whereon I sate, and then of the desk in front of it, according as I was promoted from one to other of them: and there my grandson reads it now, at this present time of writing, and hath fought a boy for scoffing at it – 'John Ridd his name.'

But, lo! I am dwelling on little things and the pigeons' eggs of infancy, forgetting the bitter and heavy life gone over me since then. If I am neither a hard man nor a very close one, God knows I have had no lack of rubbing and pounding, to make stone of me. Yet can I not somehow believe that we ought to hate one another, to live far asunder, and block the mouth each of his little den; as do the wild beasts of the wood, and the hairy outangs now brought over, each with a chain upon him. Let that matter be as it will. It is beyond me to unfold, and mayhap of my grandson's grandson. All I know is that wheat is better than when I began to sow it.

Now the cause of my leaving Tiverton school, and the way of it, were as follows. On the 29th day of November, in the year of our Lord 1673, the very day when I was twelve years old, and had spent all my substance in sweetmeats, with which I made treat to the little boys, till the large boys ran in and took them, we came out of school at five o'clock, as the rule is upon Tuesdays.

A certain boy, Robin Snell by name, would not allow my elbow room, and struck me very sadly in the stomach part, though his own was full of my parliament. And this I felt so unkindly, that I smote him straightway in the face without tarrying to consider it, or weighing the question duly. Upon this he put his head down, and presented it so vehemently at the middle of my waistcoat, that for a minute or more my breath seemed dropped, as it were, from my pockets, and my life seemed to stop from great want of ease. Before I came to myself again, it had been settled for us that we should move to the 'Ironing-box,' as the triangle of turf is called, where the two causeways coming from the school-porch and the hall porch meet, and our fights are mainly celebrated; only we must wait until the convoy of horses had passed, and then make a ring by candlelight, and the other boys would like it. But suddenly there came round the post where the letters of our founder are, not from the way of Taunton, but from the side of Lowman bridge, a very small string of horses, only two indeed (counting for one the pony), and a red-faced man on the bigger nag.

'Praise ye, worshipful masters,' he said, being feared of the gateway, 'carn 'e tull whur our Jan Ridd be?'

'Hyur a be, ees fai, Jan Ridd,' answered a sharp little chap, making game of John Fry's language.

'Zhow un up, then,' says John Fry, poking his whip through the bars at us; 'Zhow un up, and putt un aowt.'

The other little chaps pointed at me, and some began to holla: but I knew what I was about.

'Oh, John, John,' I cried; 'what's the use of your coming now, and Peggy over the moors, too, and it so cruel cold for her? The holidays don't begin till Wednesday fortnight, John. To think of your not knowing that!'

John Fry leaned forward in the saddle, and turned his eyes away from me; and then there was a noise in his throat, like a snail trawling on a window-pane.

'Oh, us knaws that wull enough Maister Jan; reckon every Oare-man knew that, without go to skoo-ull, like you doth.

Your moother have kept arl the apples up, and old Betty toorned the black puddens, and none dare set trap for a blagbird. Arl for thee, lad; every bit of it now for thee!'

He checked himself suddenly, and frightened me. I knew that John Fry's way so well.

'And father, and father – oh, how is father?' I pushed the boys right and left as I said it. 'John, is father up in town! He always used to come for me, and leave nobody else to do it.'

'Vayther 'll be at the crooked post, t'other zide o' telling-house.[1] Her coodn't lave 'ouze by raison of the Christmas bakkon comin' on, and zome o' the cider welted.'

He looked at the nag's ears as he said it; and, being up to John Fry's ways, I knew that it was a lie. And my heart fell like a lump of lead, and I leaned back on the stay of the gate and longed no more to fight anybody. A sort of dull power hung over me, like the cloud of a brooding tempest, and I feared to be told anything. I did not even care to stroke the nose of my pony Peggy, although she pushed it in through the rails, where a square of broader lattice is, and sniffed at me, and began to crop gently after my fingers. But whatever lives or dies, business must be attended to; and the principal business of good Christians is, beyond all controversy, to fight with one another.

'Come up, Jack,' said one of the boys, lifting me under the chin; 'he hit you, and you hit him, you know.'

'Pay your debts before you go,' said a monitor, striding up to me, after hearing how the honour lay; 'Ridd, you must go through with it.'

I marvel how Robin Snell felt. Very likely he thought nothing of it, always having been a boy of an hectoring and unruly sort. But I felt my heart go up and down, as the boys come round to strip me; and greatly fearing to be beaten, I blew hot upon my knuckles. Then pulled I off my little cut jerkin, and laid it down on my head cap, and over that my waistcoat; and a boy was proud to take care of them, Thomas Hooper was his name, and I remember how he looked at me.

---

[1] The 'telling-houses' on the moor are rude cots where the shepherds meet, to 'tell' their sheep at the end of the pasturing season.

Then up to me came Robin Snell (mayor of Exeter thrice since that), and he stood very square, and looked at me, and I lacked not long to look at him. Round his waist he had a kerchief, busking up his small-clothes, and on his feet light pumpkin shoes, and all his upper raiment off. And he danced about, in a way that made my head swim on my shoulders, and he stood some inches over me. But I, being muddled with much doubt about John Fry and his errand, was only stripped of my jerkin and waistcoat, and not comfortable to begin.

'Come now, shake hands,' cried a big boy, jumping in joy of the spectacle, a third-former nearly six feet high; 'shake hands, you little devils. Keep your pluck up, and show good sport, and Lord love the better man of you.'

Robin took me by the hand, and gazed at me disdainfully, and then smote me painfully in the face, ere I could get my fence up.

'Whutt be 'bout, lad?' cried John Fry; 'hutt un again, Jan, wull 'e? Well done then, our Jan boy.'

For I had replied to Robin now with all the weight and cadence of penthemimeral cæsura (a thing, the name of which I know, but could never make head nor tail of it), and the strife began in a serious style, and the boys looking on were not cheated. Although I could not collect their shouts when the blows were ringing upon me, it was no great loss; for John Fry told me afterwards that their oaths went up like a furnace fire. But to these we paid no heed or hap, being in the thick of swinging, and devoid of judgement. All I know is, I came to my corner, when the round was over, with very hard pumps in my chest, and a great desire to fall away.

'Finish him off, Bob,' cried a big boy, and that I noticed especially, because I thought it unkind of him, after eating of my toffee as he had that afternoon; 'finish him off, neck and crop; he deserves it for sticking up to a man like you.'

But I was not so to be finished off, though feeling in my knuckles now as if it were a blueness and a sense of chilblain. Nothing held except my legs, and they were good to help me. So this bout, or round, if you please, was foughten warily by me, with gentle recollection of what my tutor, the clever boy had told me, and some resolve to earn his praise before I came back to his knee again. And never, I think, in all my life, sounded sweeter words in my ears (except when my love loved me) than when my second and backer, who had made himself part of my doings now, and would have wept to see me beaten said –

'Famously done, Jack, famously! Only keep your wind up, Jack, and you'll go right through him!'

Meanwhile John Fry was prowling about, asking the boys what they thought of it, and whether I was like to be killed, because of my mother's trouble. But finding now that I had foughten three-score fights already, he came up to me woefully, in the quickness of my breathing, while I sat on the knee of my second, with a piece of spongious coralline to ease me of my bloodshed, and he says in my ears, as if he was clapping spurs into a horse –

'Never thee knack under, Jan, or never coom naigh Hexmoor no more.'

With that it was all up with me. A simmering buzzed in my heavy brain, and a light came through my eye-places. At once I set both fists again, and my heart stuck to me like cobbler's wax. Either Robin Snell should kill me, or I would conquer Robin Snell. So I went in again, with my courage up; and Bob came smiling for victory, and I hated him for smiling. He let at me with his left hand, and I gave him my right between his eyes, and he blinked, and was not pleased with it. I feared him not, and spared him not, neither spared myself. My breath came again, and my heart stood cool, and my eyes struck fire no longer. Only I knew that I would die, sooner than shame my birthplace. How the rest of it was I know not; only that I had the end of it, and helped to put Robin in bed.

2

The Warpath of
the Doones

From Tiverton town to the town of Oare is a very long and painful road, and in good truth the traveller must make his way, as the saying is; for the way is still unmade, at least, on this side of Dulverton.

We left the town of the two fords, which they say is the meaning of it, very early in the morning, after lying one day to rest, as was demanded by the nags, sore of foot and foundered. For my part, too, I was glad to rest, having aches all over me, and very heavy bruises; and we lodged at the sign of the White Horse Inn, in the street called Gold Street, opposite where the souls are of John and Joan Greenway, set up in gold letters, because we must take the homeward way at cockcrow of the morning.

It was high noon before we were got to Dulverton that day, near to which town the river Exe and its big brother Barle have union. My mother had an uncle living there, but we were not to visit his house this time, at which I was somewhat astonished, since we needs must stop for at least two hours, to bait our horses thorough well, before coming to the black bogway.

John had been rather bitter with me, which methought was a mark of ill-taste at coming home for the holidays; and yet I made allowance for John, because he had never been at school, and never would have chance to eat fry upon condition of spelling it; therefore I rode on, thinking that he was hard-set, like a saw, for his dinner, and would soften after tooth-work. And yet at his most hungry times, when his mind was far gone upon bacon, *certes* he seemed to check himself and look at me as if he were sorry for little things coming over great.

But now, at Dulverton, we dined upon the rarest and choicest victuals that ever I did taste. Even, now, at my time of life, to think of it gives me appetite, as once and awhile to think of my first love makes me love all goodness. Hot mutton pasty was a thing I had often heard of from very wealthy boys and men, who made a dessert of dinner; and to hear them talk of it made my lips smack, and my ribs come inwards.

When the mutton pasty was done, and Peggy and Smiler had dined well also, out I went to wash at the pump, being a lover of soap and water, at all risk, except of my dinner. And John Fry, who cared very little to wash, save Sabbath days in his own soap, and who had kept me from the pump by threatening loss of the dish, out he came in a satisfied manner, with a piece of quill in his hand, to lean against a door-post, and listen to the horses feeding, and have his teeth ready for supper.

Then a lady's-maid came out, and the sun was on her face, and she turned round to go back again; but put a better face upon it, and gave a trip and hitched her dress, and looked at the sun full body, lest the hostlers should laugh that she was losing her complexion. With a long Italian glass in her fingers very daintily, she came up to the pump in the middle of the yard, where I was running the water off all my head and shoulders, and arms, and some of my breast even, and though I had glimpsed her through the sprinkle, it gave me quite a turn to see her, child as I was, in my open aspect. But she looked at me, no whit abashed, making a baby of me, no doubt, as a woman of thirty will do, even with a very big boy when they catch him on a hayrick, and she said to me, in a brazen manner, as if I had been nobody, while I was shrinking behind the pump, and craving to get my shirt on, – 'Good leetle boy, come hither to me. Fine heaven! how blue your eyes are, and your skin like snow; but some naughty man has beaten it black. Oh, leetle boy, let me feel it. Ah, how then it must have hurt you! There now, and you shall love me.'

'If you please, madam, I must go. John Fry is waiting by the tapster's door, and Peggy neighing to me. If you please, we must get home to-night; and father will be waiting for me this side of the telling-house.'

'There, there, you shall go, leetle dear, and perhaps I will go after you. I have taken much love of you. But the Baroness is hard to me. How far you call it now to the bank of the sea at Wash – Wash – '

'At Watchett, likely you mean, madam. Oh, a very long way, and the roads as soft as the road to Oare.'

'Oh-ah, oh-ah, – I shall remember; that is the place where my leetle boy live, and some day I will come seek for him. Now make the pump to flow, my dear, and give me the good water. The Baroness will not touch, unless a nebule be formed outside the glass.'

I did not know what she meant by that; yet I pumped for her very heartily, and marvelled to see her for fifty times throw the water away in the trough, as if it was not good enough. At last the water suited her, with a likeness of fog outside the glass, and the gleam of a crystal under it, and then she made a courtesy to me, in a sort of mocking manner, holding the long glass by the foot, not to take the cloud off; and then she wanted to kiss me; but I was out of breath, and have always been shy of that work, except when I come to offer it; and so I ducked under the pump-handle, and she knocked her chin on the knob of it; and the hostlers came out, and asked whether they would do as well.

Upon this, she retreated up the yard, with a certain dark dignity, and a foreign way of walking, which stopped them at once from going further, because it was so different from the fashion of their sweethearts.

Now, up to the end of Dulverton town, on the northward side of it, where the two new pigsties be, the Oare folk and the Watchett folk must trudge on together, until we come to a broken cross, where a murdered man lies buried. Peggy and Smiler went up the hill, as if nothing could be too much for them, after the beans they had eaten, and suddenly turning a corner of trees, we happened upon a great coach and six horses labouring very heavily. John Fry rode on with his hat in his hand, as became him towards the quality; but I was amazed to that degree that I left my cap on my head, and drew bridle without knowing it.

For in the front seat of the coach, which was half-way open, being of new city-make, and the day in want of air, sate the foreign lady, who had met me at the pump and offered to salute me. By her side was a little girl, dark-haired and very wonderful, with a wealthy softness on her, as if she must have her own way. I could not look at her for two glances, and she did not look at me for one, being such a little child, and busy with the hedges. But in the honourable place sate a handsome lady, very warmly dressed, and sweetly delicate colour. And close to her was a lively child, two or it may be three years old, bearing a white cockade in his hat, and staring at all and everybody.

Then I took off my cap to the beautiful lady, without asking whereof; and she put up her hand and kissed it to me, thinking perhaps, that I looked like a gentle and good little boy; for folk always called me innocent, though God knows I never was that. But now the foreign lady, or lady's-maid, as it might be, who had been busy with little dark-eyes, turned upon all this going on, and looked me straight in the face. I was about to salute her, at a distance, indeed, and not with the nicety she had offered to me, but, strange to say, she stared at my eyes as if she had never seen me before, neither wished to see me again. At this I was so startled, such things being out of my knowledge, that I startled Peggy also with the muscle of my legs, and she being fresh from stable, and the mire scraped off with cask-hoop, broke away so suddenly that I could do no more than turn round and lower my cap, now five months old, to the beautiful lady.

We saw no more of them after that, but turned into the sideway, and soon had the fill of our hands and eyes to look to our own going. For the road got worse and worse, until there was none at all, and perhaps the purest thing it could do was to be ashamed to show itself. But we pushed on as best we might, with doubt of reaching home any time, except by special grace of God.

The fog came down upon the moors as thick as ever I saw it; and there was no sound of any sort, nor a breath of wind to guide us.

John Fry was bowing forward with sleep upon his saddle. and now I could no longer see the frizzle of wet upon his beard. But still I could see the jog of his hat – a Sunday hat with a top to it – and some of his shoulder bowed out in the mist, so that one could say, 'Hold up, John,' when Smiler put his foot in.

'Mercy of God! Where be us now?' said John Fry, waking suddenly; 'us ought to have passed hold hash, Jan. Zeen it on the road, have 'ee?'

'No indeed, John; no old ash. Nor nothing else to my knowing; nor heard nothing, save thee snoring.'

'Hould thee tongue, lad,' he said sharply; 'us be naigh the Doone-track now, two maile from Dunkery Beacon hill, the haighest place of Hexmoor. So happen they be abroad to-naight, us must crawl on our belly-places, boy.'

I knew at once what he meant, – those bloody Doones of Bagworthy, the awe of all Devon and Somerset, outlaws, traitors, murderers.

'But, John,' I whispered, warily, sidling close to his saddle-bow; 'dear John, you don't think they will see us in such a fog as this?'

'Never God made vog as could stop their eyesen,' he whispered in answer, fearfully; 'here us be by the hollow ground. Zober, lad, goo zober now, if thee wish to see thy moother.'

For I was inclined, in the manner of boys, to make a run of the danger, and cross the Doone-track at full speed; to rush for it, and be done with it. But even then I wondered why he talked of my mother so, and said not a word of father.

We were come to a long deep 'goyal,' – to wit, a long trough among wild hills, falling towards the plain country, rounded at the bottom, perhaps, and stiff, more than steep, at the sides of it. Whether it be straight or crooked, makes no difference to it.

We rode very carefully down our side, and through the soft grass at the bottom, and all the while we listened as if the air was a speaking-trumpet. Then gladly we breasted our nags to the rise, and were coming to the comb of it, when I heard something, and caught John's arm, and he bent his hand to the shape of his ear. It was the sound of horses' feet, knocking up through splashy ground, as if the bottom sucked them. Then a grunting of weary men, and the lifting noise of stirrups, and sometimes the clank of iron mixed with the wheezy croning of leather, and the blowing of hairy nostrils.

'God's sake, Jack, slip round her belly, and let her go where she wull.'

As John Fry whispered, so I did, for he was off Smiler by this time; but our two pads were too fagged to go far, and began to nose about and crop, sniffing more than they need have done. I crept to John's side very softly, with the bridle on my arm.

'Let goo braidle; let goo, lad. Plaise God they take them for forest-ponies, or they'll zend a bullet through us.'

I saw what he meant, and let go the bridle; for now the mist was rolling off, and we were against the sky-line to the dark cavalcade below us. John lay on the ground by a barrow of heather, where a little gullet was, and I crept to him, afraid of the noise I made in dragging my legs along, and the creak of my cord breeches. John bleated like a sheep to cover it – a sheep very cold and trembling.

Then just as the foremost horseman passed, scarce twenty yards below us, a puff of wind came up the glen, and the fog rolled off before it. And suddenly a strong red light, cast by the cloud-weight downwards, spread like fingers over the moorland, opened the alleys of darkness, and hung on the steel of the riders.

'Dunkery Beacon,' whispered John, so close into my ear, that I felt his lips and teeth ashake; 'dursn't fire it now, no more than to show the Doones way home again, since the naight as they went up, and throwed the watchman atop of it. Why, wutt be 'bout, lad? God's sake – '

For I could keep still no longer, but wriggled away from his arm, and along the little gullet, still going flat on my breast and thighs, until I was under a grey patch of stone, with a fringe of dry fern round it; there I lay, scarce twenty feet above the heads of the riders, and I feared to draw my breath, though prone to do it with wonder.

For now the beacon was rushing up, in a fiery storm to heaven, and the form of its flame came and went in the folds, and the heavy sky was hovering. All around it was hung with red, deep in twisted columns, and then a giant beard of fire streamed throughout the darkness. The sullen hills were flanked with light, and the valleys chined with shadow, and all the sombrous moors between awoke in furrowed anger.

But most of all, the flinging fire leaped into the rocky mouth of the glen below me, where the horsemen passed in silence, scarcely deigning to look round. Heavy men, and large of stature, reckless how they bore their guns, or how they sate their horses, with leathern jerkins, and long boots, and iron plates on breast and head, plunder heaped behind their saddles, and flagons slung in front of them; more than thirty went along, like clouds upon red sunset. Some had carcases of sheep swinging with their skins on, others had deer, and one had a child flung across his saddle-bow. Whether the child were dead, or alive, was beyond my vision, only it hung head downwards there, and must take the chance of it. They had got the child, a very young one, for the sake of the dress, no doubt, which they could not stop to pull off from it, for the dress shone bright, where the fire struck it, as if with gold and jewels. I longed in my heart to know most sadly, what they would do with the little thing, and whether they would eat it.

It touched me so to see that child, a prey among those vultures, that in my foolish rage and burning I stood up, and shouted to them, leaping on a rock, and raving out of all possession. Two of them turned round, and one set his carbine at me, but the other said it was but a pixie, and bade him keep his powder. Little they knew, and less thought I, that the pixie then before them would dance their castle down one day.

Soon we found Peggy and Smiler in company, well embarked on the homeward road, and victualling where the grass was good. Right glad they were to see us again, – not for the pleasure of carrying, but because a horse (like a woman) lacks, and is better without, self-reliance.

My father never came to meet us, at either side of the telling-house, neither at the crooked post, nor even at home-linhay, although the dogs kept such a noise that he must have heard us. Home-side of the linhay, and under the ashen hedge-row, where father taught me to catch blackbirds, all at once my heart went down, and all my breast was hollow. There was not even the lanthorn light on the peg against the cow's house, and nobody said 'Hold your noise!' to the dogs, or shouted 'Here our Jack is!'

I looked at the posts of the gate, in the dark, because they were tall, like father, and then at the door of the harness-room, where he used to smoke his pipe and sing. Then I thought he had guests perhaps – people lost upon the moors – whom he could not leave unkindly, even for his son's sake. And yet about that I was jealous, and ready to be vexed with him, when he should begin to make much of me. And I felt in my pocket for the new pipe which I had brought him from Tiverton, and said to myself, 'He shall not have it until to-morrow morning.'

Woe is me! I cannot tell. How I knew I know not now – only that I slunk away, without a tear, or thought of weeping, and hid me in a saw-pit. There the timber, over-head, came like streaks across me; and all I wanted was to hide, and none to tell me anything.

By and by, a noise came down, as of woman's weeping; and there my mother and sister were, choking and holding together. Although they were my dearest loves, I could not bear to look at them, until they seemed to want my help, and turned away, that I might come.

3

A Rash Visit

My dear father had been killed by the Doones of Bagworthy, while riding home from Porlock market, on the Saturday evening. With him were six brother-farmers, all of them very sober; for father would have no company with any man who went beyond half-a-gallon of beer, or a single gallon of cider. The robbers had no grudge against him; for he had never flouted them, neither made overmuch of outcry, because they robbed other people. For he was a man of such strict honesty, and due parish feeling, that he knew it to be every man's own business to defend himself and his goods; unless he belonged to our parish, and then we must look after him.

These seven farmers were jogging along, helping one another in the troubles of the road, and singing goodly hymns and songs, to keep their courage moving, when suddenly a horseman stopped in the starlight full across them.

By dress and arms they knew him well, and by his size and stature, shown against the glimmer of the evening star; and though he seemed one man to seven, it was in truth one man to one. Of the six who had been singing songs and psalms, about the power of God, and their own regeneration – such psalms as went the round, in those days, of the public-houses – there was not one but pulled out his money, and sang small beer to a Doone.

But father had been used to think, that any man, who was comfortable inside his own coat and waistcoat, deserved to have no other set, unless he would strike a blow for them. And so, while his gossips doffed their hats, and shook with what was left of them, he set his staff above his head, and rode at the Doone robber. With a trick of his horse, the wild man escaped the sudden onset; although it must have amazed him sadly, that any durst resist him. Then when Smiler was carried away with the dash and the weight of my father (not being brought up to battle, nor used to turn, save in plough harness), the outlaw whistled upon his thumb, and plundered the rest of the yeomen. But father, drawing at Smiler's head, to try to come back and help them, was in the midst of a dozen men, who seemed to come out of a turf-rick, some on horse, and some afoot. Nevertheless, he smote lustily, so far as he could see; and being of great size and strength, and his blood well up, they had no easy job with him. With the play of his wrist, he cracked three or four crowns, being always famous at singlestick; until the rest drew their horses away, and he thought that he was master, and would tell his wife about it.

But a man beyond the range of staff was crouching by the peat-stack, with a long gun set to his shoulder, and he got poor father against the sky, and I cannot tell the rest of it. Only they knew that Smiler came home, with blood upon his withers, and father was found in the morning dead on the moor, with his ivy-twisted cudgel lying broken under him. Now, whether this were an honest fight, God judge betwixt the Doones and me.

It was more of woe than wonder, being such days of violence, that mother knew herself a widow, and her children fatherless. Of children there were only three, none of us fit to be useful yet, only to comfort mother, by making her to work for us. I, John Ridd, was the eldest, and felt it a heavy thing on me; next came sister Annie, with about two years between us; and then the little Eliza.

Now, before I got home and found my sad loss – and no boy ever loved his father better than I loved mine – mother had done a most wondrous thing, which made all the neighbours say that she must be mad, at least. Upon the Monday morning, while her husband lay unburied, she cast a white hood over her hair, and gathered a black cloak round her, and, taking counsel of no one, set off on foot for the Doone-gate.

In the early afternoon she came to the hollow and barren entrance; where in truth there was no gate, only darkness to go through. If I get on with this story, I shall have to tell of it by and by, as I saw it afterwards; and will not dwell there now. Enough that no gun was fired at her, only her eyes were covered over, and somebody led her by the hand, without any wish to hurt her.

A very rough and headstrong road was all that she remembered, for she could not think as she wished to do, with the cold iron pushed against her. At the end of this road they delivered her eyes, and she could scarce believe them.

For she stood at the head of a deep green valley, carved from out the mountains in a perfect oval, with a fence of sheer rock standing round it, eighty feet or a hundred high; from whose brink black wooded hills swept up to the sky-line. By her side a little river glided out from underground with a soft dark babble, unawares of daylight; then growing brighter, lapsed away, and fell into the valley. There, as it ran down the meadow, alders stood on either marge, and grass was blading out upon it, and yellow tufts of rushes gathered, looking at the hurry. But further down, on either bank, were covered houses, built of stone, square and roughly cornered, set as if the brook were meant to be the street between them. Only one room high they were, and not placed opposite each other, but in and out as skittles are; only that the first of all, which proved to be the captain's, was a sort of double house, or rather two houses joined together by a plank-bridge over the river.

Fourteen cots my mother counted, all very much of a pattern, and nothing to choose between them, unless it were the captain's. Deep in the quiet valley there, away from noise, and violence, and brawl, save that of the rivulet, any man would have deemed them homes of simple mind and inno-cence. Yet not a single house stood there but was the home of murder.

Two men led my mother down a steep and gliddery

stairway, like the ladder of a hay-mow; and thence, from the break of the falling water, as far as the house of the captain. And there at the door, they left her trembling, strung as she was, to speak her mind.

A tall old man, Sir Ensor Doone, came out with a bill-hook in his hand, and hedger's gloves going up his arms, as if he were no better than a labourer at ditch-work. Only in his mouth and eyes, his gait, and most of all his voice, even a child could know and feel, that here was no ditch-labourer. Good cause he has found since then, perhaps, to wish that he had been one.

With his white locks moving upon his coat, he stopped and looked down at my mother, and she could not help herself but courtesy under the fixed black gazing.

'Good woman, you are none of us. Who has brought you hither? Young men must be young – but I have had too much of this work.'

And he scowled at my mother, for her comeliness; and yet looked under his eyelids, as if he liked her for it. But as for her, in the depth of love-grief, it struck scorn upon her womanhood; and in the flash she spoke.

'What you mean, I know not. Traitors! cut-throats! cowards! I am here to ask for my husband.' She could not say any more, because her heart was now too much for her, coming hard in her throat and mouth; but she opened up her eyes at him.

'Madam,' said Sir Ensor Doone – being born a gentleman, although a very bad one – 'I crave pardon of you. My eyes are old, or I might have known. Now, if we have your husband prisoner, he shall go free without ransom, because I have insulted you.'

'Loth would I be,' said mother, sobbing with her new red handkerchief, and looking at the pattern of it, 'loth indeed, Sir Ensor Doone, to accuse any one unfairly. But I have lost the very best husband God ever gave to a woman; and I knew him when he was to your belt, and I not up to your knee, sir; and never an unkind word he spoke, nor stopped me short in speaking.'

'This matter must be seen to; it shall be seen to at once,'

the old man answered, moved a little in spite of all his knowledge. 'Madam, if any wrong has been done, trust the honour of a Doone; I will redress it to my utmost. Come inside and rest yourself, while I ask about it. What was your good husband's name, and when and where fell this mishap?'

'Deary me,' said mother, as he set a chair for her very polite, but she would not sit upon it; 'Saturday morning I was a wife, sir; and Saturday night I was a widow, and my children fatherless. My husband's name was "John Ridd," sir, as everybody knows; and there was not a finer or better man, in Somerset or Devon. He was coming home from Porlock market, and a new gown for me on the crupper, and a shell to put my hair up, – oh, John, how good you were to me!'

Of that she began to think again and not to believe her sorrow, except as a dream from the evil one, because it was too bad upon her, and perhaps she would awake in a minute, and her husband would have the laugh of her. And so she wiped her eyes and smiled, and looked for something.

'Madam, this is a serious thing,' Sir Ensor Doone said graciously, and showing grave concern: 'my boys are a little wild, I know. And yet I cannot think that they would willingly harm any one. And yet – and yet, you do look sad. Send Counsellor to me,' he shouted, from the door of his house; and down the valley went the call, 'send Counsellor to Captain.'

Counsellor Doone came in, ere yet my mother was herself again; and if any sight could astonish her, when all her sense of right and wrong was gone astray with the force of things, it was the sight of the Counsellor. A square-built man of enormous strength, but a foot below the Doone stature (which I shall describe hereafter), he carried a long grey beard descending to the leather of his belt. Great eyebrows overhung his face, like ivy on a pollard oak, and under them two large brown eyes, as of an owl when muting. And he had a power of hiding his eyes, or showing them bright, like a blazing fire. He stood there with his beaver off, and mother tried to look at him; but he seemed not to descry her.

'Counsellor,' said Sir Ensor Doone, standing back in his height from him, 'here is a lady of good repute – '

'Oh, no sir; only a woman.'

'Allow me, madam, by your good leave. Here is a lady, Counsellor, of great repute in this part of the country, who charges the Doones with having unjustly slain her husband – '

'Murdered him! murdered him!' cried my mother; 'if ever there was a murder. Oh, sir! oh, sir! you know it.'

'Put the case,' said the Counsellor.

'The case is this,' replied Sir Ensor, holding one hand up to mother: 'This lady's worthy husband was slain, it seems, upon his return from the market at Porlock, no longer ago than last Saturday night.'

'Cite his name,' said the Counsellor, with his eyes still rolling inwards.

'"Master John Ridd," as I understand. Counsellor, we have heard of him often; a worthy man and a peaceful one, who meddled not with our duties. Now, if any of our boys have been rough, they shall answer it dearly. And yet I can scarce believe it. For the folk about these parts are apt to misconceive of our sufferings, and to have no feeling for us. Counsellor, you are our record, and very stern against us; tell us how this matter was.'

The square man with the long grey beard, quite unmoved by any thing, drew back to the door, and spoke, and his voice was like a fall of stones in the bottom of a mine.

'Few words will be enow for this. Four or five of our best-behaved and most peaceful gentlemen went to the little market at Porlock, with a lump of money. They bought some household stores and comforts at a very high price, and pricked upon the homeward road, away from vulgar revellers. When they drew bridle to rest their horses, in the shelter of a peat-rick, the night being dark and sudden, a robber of great size and strength rode into the midst of them, thinking to kill or terrify. His arrogance, and hardihood, at the first amazed them, but they would not give up without a blow goods which were on trust with them. He had smitten three of them senseless, for the power of his arm was terrible; whereupon the last man tried to ward his blow with a pistol.

26

Carver, sir, it was, our brave and noble Carver, who saved the lives of his brethren and his own; and glad enow they were to escape. Notwithstanding, we hoped it might be only a flesh-wound, and not to speed him in his sins.'

As this atrocious tale of lies turned up joint by joint before her, like a 'devil's coach-horse,'[1] mother was too much amazed to do any more than look at him, as if the earth must open. But the only thing that opened was the great brown eyes of the Counsellor, which rested on my mother's face, with a dew of sorrow, as he spoke of sins.

She, unable to bear them, turned suddenly on Sir Ensor, and caught (as she fancied) a smile on his lips, and a sense of quiet enjoyment.

'All the Doones are gentlemen,' answered the old man, gravely, and looking as if he had never smiled since he was a baby. 'We are always glad to explain, madam, any mistake which the rustic people may fall upon about us; and we wish you clearly to conceive, that we do not charge your poor husband with any set purpose of robbery; neither will we bring suit for any attainder of his property. Is it not so, Counsellor? '

'Without doubt his land is attainted; unless in mercy you forbear, sir.'

'Counsellor, we will forbear. Madam, we will forgive him. Like enough he knew not right from wrong, at that time of night. The waters are strong at Porlock, and even an honest man may use his staff unjustly, in this unchartered age of violence and rapine.'

The Doones to talk of rapine! Mother's head went round so, that she courtesied to them both, scarcely knowing where she was, but calling to mind her manners. All the time she felt a warmth, as if the right was with her, and yet she could not see the way to spread it out before them. With that, she dried her tears in haste, and went into the cold air, for fear of speaking mischief.

But when she was on the homeward road, and the sentinels had charge of her, blinding her eyes, as if she were not blind

---

[1] The cock-tailed beetle has earned this name in the West of England.

enough with weeping, some one came in haste behind her, and thrust a heavy leathern bag into the limp weight of her hand.

'Captain sends you this,' he whispered; 'take it to the little ones.'

But mother let it fall in a heap, as if it had been a blind worm; and then for the first time crouched before God, that even the Doones should pity her.

4

An Illegal Settlement

Good folk, who dwell in a lawful land, if any such there be, may, for want of exploration, judge our neighbourhood harshly, unless the whole truth is set before them. In bar of such prejudice, many of us ask leave to explain how, and why, the robbers came to that head in the midst of us. We would rather not have had it so, and were wise enough to lament it; but it grew upon us gently, in the following manner. Only let all who read observe that here I enter many things which came to my knowledge in later years.

In or about the year of our Lord 1640, when all the troubles of England were swelling to an outburst, great estates in the north country were suddenly confiscated, through some feud of families, and strong influence at Court, and the owners were turned upon the world, and might think themselves lucky to save their necks. These estates were in co-heirship, joint tenancy I think they called it, although I know not the meaning, only so that if either tenant died, the other living, all would come to the live one, in spite of any testament.

One of the joint owners was Sir Ensor Doone, a gentleman of brisk intellect; and the other owner was his cousin, the Earl of Lorne and Dykemont.

Lord Lorne was some years the elder of his cousin Ensor Doone, and was making suit to gain severance of the cumbersome joint-tenancy, by any fair apportionment, when suddenly this blow fell on them, by wiles and woman's meddling; and instead of dividing the land, they were divided from it.

The nobleman was still well-to-do, though crippled in his expenditure; but as for the cousin, he was left a beggar, with many to beg from him. He thought that the other had wronged him, and that all the trouble of law befell through his unjust petition. Many friends advised him to make interest at Court; for, having done no harm whatever, and being a good Catholic, which Lord Lorne was not, he would be sure to find hearing there, and probably some favour. But he, like a very hot-brained man, although he had long been married to the daughter of his cousin (whom he liked none the more for that), would have nothing to say to any attempt at making a patch of it, but drove away with his wife and sons, and the relics of his money, swearing hard at everybody. In this he may have been quite wrong; probably, perhaps he was so; but I am not convinced at all, but what most of us would have done the same.

Some say that, in the bitterness of that wrong and outrage, he slew a gentleman of the Court, whom he supposed to have borne a hand in the plundering of his fortunes. Others say that he bearded King Charles the First himself, in a manner beyond forgiveness. One thing, at any rate, is sure – Sir Ensor was attainted, and made a felon outlaw, through some violent deed ensuing upon his dispossession.

In great despair at last, he resolved to settle in some outlandish part, where none could be found to know him; and so, in an evil day for us, he came to the West of England. Not that our part of the world is at all outlandish, according to my view of it (for I never found a better one), but that it was known to be rugged, and large, and desolate. And here, when he had discovered a place which seemed almost to be made for him, so withdrawn, so self-defended, and uneasy of access, some of the country-folk around brought him little offerings – a side of bacon, a keg of cider, hung mutton, or a brisket of venison; so that for a little while he was very honest. But when the newness of his coming began to wear away, and our good folk were apt to think, that even a gentleman ought to work, or pay other men for doing it, and many farmers were grown weary of manners without discourse to them, and all cried out to one another, how unfair it was that owning such a fertile valley, young men would not spade or plough by reason of noble lineage – then the young Doones, growing up, took things they would not ask for.

There were not more than a dozen of them, counting a few retainers, who still held by Sir Ensor; but soon they grew and multiplied in a manner surprising to think of. Whether it was the venison, which we call a strengthening victual, or whether it was the Exmoor mutton, or the keen soft air of the moorlands, anyhow the Doones increased much faster than their honesty. At first they had brought some ladies with them, of good repute with charity; and then, as time went on, they added to their stock by carrying. They carried off many good farmers' daughters, who were sadly displeased at first; but took to them kindly after awhile, and made a new home in their babies. For women, as it seems to me, like strong men more than weak ones, feeling that they need some staunchness, something to hold fast by.

Perhaps their den might well have been stormed, and themselves driven out of the forest, if honest people had only agreed to begin with them at once, when first they took to plundering. But having respect for their good birth, and pity for their misfortunes, and perhaps a little admiration at the justice of God, that robbed men now were robbers, the squires, and farmers and shepherds, at first did nothing more than grumble gently, or even make a laugh of it, each in the case of others. After awhile they found the matter gone too far for laughter, as, violence and deadly outrage stained the hand of robbery, until every woman clutched her child, and every man turned pale, at the very name of 'Doone.' For the sons, and grandsons, of Sir Ensor, grew up in foul liberty, and haughtiness, and hatred, to utter scorn of God and man, and brutality towards dumb animals. There was only one good thing about them if indeed it were good, to wit, their faith to one another, and truth to their wild eyry. But this only made them feared the more, so certain was the revenge they wreaked upon any who dared to strike a Doone. And now they had so entrenched themselves, and waxed so strong in number, that nothing less than a troop of soldiers could wisely enter their premises; and even so it might turn out ill, as perchance we shall see by and by.

For not to mention the strength of the place, which I shall describe in its proper order, when I come to visit it, there was not one among them but was a mighty man, straight and tall, and wide, and fit to lift four hundred-weight. If son or grandson of old Doone, or one of the northern retainers, failed at the age of twenty, while standing on his naked feet, to touch with his forehead the lintel of Sir Ensor's door, and to fill the door-frame with his shoulders from sidepost even to sidepost, he was led away to the narrow pass, which made their valley so desperate, and thrust from the crown with ignominy, to get his own living honestly. Now, the measure of that doorway is, or rather was, I ought to say, six feet and one inch lengthwise, and two feet all but two inches taken crossways in the clear. Yet I not only have heard, but know, being so closely mixed with them, that no descendant of old Sir Ensor, neither relative of his (except, indeed the Counsellor, who was kept by them for his wisdom), and no more than two of their following, ever failed of that test, and relapsed to the difficult ways of honesty.

Now, after all this which I have written, and all the rest which a reader will see, being quicker of mind than I am (who leave more than half behind me, like a man sowing wheat, with his dinner laid in the ditch too near his dog), it is much but what you will understand the Doones, far better than I did, or do even to this moment; and therefore none will doubt, when I tell them that our good justitiaries feared to make an ado, or hold any public enquiry about my dear father's death. They would all have had to ride home at night, and who could say what might betide them? Least said soonest mended, because less chance of breaking.

So we buried him quietly – all except my mother, indeed, for she could not keep silence – in the sloping little church-yard of Oare, as meek a place as need be, with the Lynn brook down below it.

5

Hard It Is To Climb

Almost everybody knows, in our part of the world at least, how pleasant and soft the fall of the land is round about Plover's Barrows farm. All above it is strong dark mountain, spread with heath, and desolate, but near our house the valleys cove, and open warmth and shelter. Here are trees, and bright green grass, and orchards full of contentment, and a man may scarce espy the brook, although he hears it everywhere. And indeed a stout good piece of it comes through our farm-yard, and swells sometimes to a rush of waves, when the clouds are on the hill-tops. But all below, where the valley bends, and the Lynn stream goes along with it, pretty meadows slope their breast, and the sun spreads on the water. And nearly all of this is ours, till you come to Nicholas Snowe's land.

But about two miles below our farm, the Bagworthy water runs into the Lynn, and makes a real river of it. Thence it hurries away, with strength and a force of wilful waters, under the foot of a barefaced hill, and so to rocks and woods again, where the stream is covered over, and dark, heavy pools delay it.

When I was turned fourteen years old, and put into good small-clothes, buckled at the knee, and strong blue worsted hosen, knitted by my mother, it happened to me without choice, I may say, to explore the Bagworthy water. And it came about in this wise.

Being resolved to catch some loaches, whatever trouble it

cost me, I set forth without a word to any one, in the forenoon of St Valentine's day, 1675–6, I think it must have been. I never could forget that day, and how bitter cold the water was. For I doffed my shoes and hose, and put them into a bag about my neck; and left my little coat at home, and tied my shirt-sleeves back to my shoulders. Then I took a three-pronged fork firmly bound to a rod with cord, and a piece of canvas kerchief, with a lump of bread inside it; and so went into the pebbly water, trying to think how warm it was. For more than a mile all down the Lynn stream, scarcely a stone I left unturned, being thoroughly skilled in the tricks of the loach, and knowing how he hides himself. When I had travelled two miles or so, conquered now and then with cold, and coming out to rub my legs into a lively friction, and only fishing here and there because of the tumbling water; suddenly, in an open space, where meadows spread about it, I found a good stream flowing softly into the body of our brook. And it brought, so far as I could guess by the sweep of it under my knee-caps, a larger power of clear water than the Lynn itself had; only it came more quietly down, not being troubled with stairs and steps, as the fortune of the Lynn is, but gliding smoothly and forcibly, as if upon some set purpose.

I buckled my breeches far up from the knee, expecting deeper water, and crossing the Lynn, went stoutly up under the branches which hang so dark on the Bagworthy river.

I found it strongly over-woven, turned, and torn with thicket-wood, but not so rocky as the Lynn, and more inclined to go evenly. There were bars of chafed stakes stretched from the sides half-way across the current, and light outriders of pithy weed, and blades of last year's water-grass trembling in the quiet places, like a spider's threads, on the transparent stillness, with a tint of olive moving it; and here and there the sun came in, as if his light were sifted, making dance upon the waves, and shadowing the pebbles.

Here, although affrighted often by the deep, dark places, and feeling that every step I took might never be taken backward, on the whole I had very comely sport of loaches, trout, and minnows, forking some, and tickling some, and driving others to shallow nooks, whence I could bail them ashore.

Now the day was falling fast behind the brown of the hill-tops; and the trees, being void of leaf and hard, seemed giants ready to beat me. And every moment, as the sky was clearing up for a white frost, the cold of the water got worse and worse, until I was fit to cry with it. And so, in a sorry plight, I came to an opening in the bushes, where a great black pool lay in front of me, whitened with snow (as I thought) at the sides, till I saw that it was only foam-froth.

Now, though I could swim with great ease and comfort, and feared no depth of water, when I could fairly come to it, yet I had no desire to go over head and ears into this great pool, being so cramped and weary, and cold enough in all conscience, though wet only up to the middle, not counting my arms and shoulders. And the look of this black pit was enough to stop one from diving into it, even on a hot summer's day with sunshine on the water; I mean, if the sun ever shone there. As it was, I shuddered and drew back; not alone at the pool itself, and the black air there was about it, but also at the whirling manner, and wisping of white threads upon it, in stripy circles round and round; and the centre still as jet.

But soon I saw the reason of the stir and depth of that great pit, as well as of the roaring sound which long had made me wonder. For skirting round one side, with very little comfort, because the rocks were high and steep, and the ledge at the foot so narrow, I came to a sudden sight and marvel, such as I never dreamed of. For, lo! I stood at the foot of a long pale slide of water, coming smoothly to me, without any break or hindrance, for a hundred yards or more, and fenced on either side with cliff, sheer, and straight, and shining. The water neither ran nor fell, nor leaped with any spouting, but made one even slope of it, as if it had been combed or planed, and looking like a plank of deal laid down a deep black staircase. However there was no side-rail, nor any place to walk upon, only the channel a fathom wide, and the perpendicular walls of crag shutting out the evening.

Seeing hard strife before me, I girt up my breeches anew,

with each buckle one hole tighter, for the sodden straps were stretching and giving, and mayhap my legs were grown smaller from the coldness of it. Then I bestowed my fish around my neck more tightly, and not stopping to look much, for fear of fear, crawled along over the fork of rocks, where the water had scooped the stone out; and shunning thus the ledge from whence it rose, like the mane of a white horse, into the broad black pool, softly I let my feet into the dip and rush of the torrent.

And here I had reckoned without my host, although (as I thought) so clever; and it was much but that I went down into the great black pool, and had never been heard of more; and this must have been the end of me, except for my trusty loach-fork. For the green wave came down, like great bottles upon me, and my legs were gone off in a moment, and I had not time to cry out with wonder, only to think of my mother and Annie, and knock my head very sadly, which made it go round so that brains were no good, even if I had any. But all in a moment, before I knew aught, except that I must die out of the way, with a roar of water upon me, my fork, praise God, stuck fast in the rock and I was borne up upon it. I felt nothing, except that here was another matter to begin upon; and it might be worth while, or again it might not, to have another fight for it. But presently the dash of the water upon my face revived me, and my mind grew used to the roar of it; and meseemed I had been worse off than this, when first flung into the Lowman.

Therefore I gathered my legs back slowly, as if they were fish to be landed, stopping whenever the water flew too strongly off my shin-bones, and coming along, without sticking out to let the wave get hold of me. And in this manner I won a footing, leaning well forward like a draught-horse, and balancing on my strength as it were, with the ashen stake set behind me. Then I said to myself, 'John Ridd, the sooner you get yourself out by the way you came, the better it will be for you.' But to my great dismay and affright, I saw that no choice was left me now, except that I must climb somehow up that hill of water, or else be washed down into the pool, and whirl around till it drowned me. For there was no chance of fetching back, by the way I had gone down into it; and further up was a hedge of rock on either side of the water-way, rising a hundred yards in height, and for all I could tell five hundred, and no place to set a foot in.

Having said the Lord's Prayer (which was all I knew), and made a very bad job of it, I grasped the good loach-stick under a knot, and steadied me with my left hand, and so with a sigh of despair began my course up the fearful torrent-way. To me it seemed half a mile at least of sliding water above me, but in truth it was little more than a furlong, as I came to know afterwards. It would have been a hard ascent, even without the slippery slime, and the force of the river over it, and I had scanty hope indeed of ever winning the summit.

The water was only six inches deep, or from that to nine at the utmost, and all the way up I could see my feet looking white in the gloom of the hollow, and here and there I found resting place, to hold on by the cliff and pant awhile. And gradually as I went on, a warmth of courage breathed in me, to think that perhaps no other had dared to try that pass before me, and to wonder what mother would say to it. And then came thought of my father also, and the pain of my feet abated.

How I went carefully, step by step, keeping my arms in front of me, and never daring to straighten my knees, is more than I can tell clearly, or even like now to think of, because it makes me dream of it. Only I must acknowledge, that the greatest danger of all was just where I saw no jeopardy, but ran up a patch of black ooze-weed in a very boastful manner, being now not far from the summit.

Here I fell very piteously, and was like to have broken my knee-cap, and the torrent got hold of my other leg, while I was indulging the bruised one. And then a vile knotting of cramp disabled me, and for a while I could only roar, till my mouth was full of water, and all of my body was sliding. But the fright of that brought me to again, and my elbow caught in a rock-hole; and so I managed to start again, with the help of more humility.

Now being in the most dreadful fright, because I was so

near the top, and hope was beating within me, I laboured hard with both legs and arms, going like a mill, and grunting. At last the rush of forked water, where first it came over the lips of the fall, drove me into the middle, and I stuck awhile with my toe-balls on the slippery links of the pop-weed, and the world was green and gliddery, and I durst not look behind me. Then I made up my mind to die at last; for so my legs would ache no more, and my breath not pain my heart so; only it did seem such a pity, after fighting so long to give in, and the light was coming upon me, and again I fought towards it; then suddenly I felt fresh air, and fell into it headlong.

6

A Boy and a Girl

When I came to myself again, my hands were full of young grass and mould; and a little girl kneeling at my side was rubbing my forehead tenderly, with a dock-leaf and a handkerchief.

'Oh, I am so glad,' she whispered softly, as I opened my eyes and looked at her; 'now you will try to be better, won't you?'

I had never heard so sweet a sound as came from between her bright red lips, while there she knelt and gazed at me; neither had I ever seen anything so beautiful as the large dark eyes intent upon me, full of pity and wonder.

I sate upright, with my little trident still in one hand, and was much afraid to speak to her, being conscious of my country-brogue, lest she should cease to like me. But she clapped her hands, and made a trifling dance around my back, and came to me on the other side, as if I were a great plaything.

'What is your name?' she said, as if she had every right to ask me; 'and how did you come here, and what are these wet things in this great bag?'

'You had better let them alone,' I said; 'they are loaches for my mother. But I will give you some, if you like.'

'Dear me, how much you think of them! Why they are only fish. But how your feet are bleeding! Oh, I must tie them up for you. And no shoes nor stockings! Is your mother very poor, poor boy?'

'No,' I said, being vexed at this; 'we are rich enough to buy all this great meadow, if we chose; and here my shoes and stockings be.'

'Why they are quite as wet as your feet; and I cannot bear to see your feet. Oh, please to let me manage them; I will do it very softly.'

'Oh, I don't think much of that,' I replied; 'I shall put some goose-grease to them. But how you are looking at me! I never saw any one like you before. My name is John Ridd. What is your name?'

'Lorna Doone,' she answered, in a low voice, as if afraid of it, and hanging her head, so that I could see only her forehead and eyelashes; 'if you please, my name is Lorna Doone: and I thought you must have known it.'

Then I stood up, and touched her hand, and tried to make her look at me; but she only turned away the more. Young and harmless as she was, her name alone made guilt of her. Nevertheless I could not help looking at her tenderly, and the more when her blushes turned into tears, and her tears to long, low sobs.

'Don't cry,' I said, 'whatever you do, I am sure you have never done any harm. I will give you all my fish, Lorna, and catch some more for mother; only don't be angry with me.'

She flung her little soft arms up, in the passion of her tears, and looked at me so piteously, that what did I do but kiss her. It seemed to be a very odd thing, when I came to think of it, because I hated kissing so, as all honest boys must do. But she touched my heart with a sudden delight, like a cowslip-blossom (although there were none to be seen yet) and the sweetest flowers of spring.

Now, seeing how I heeded her, and feeling that I had kissed her, although she was such a little girl, eight years old or thereabouts, she turned to the stream in a bashful manner, and began to watch the water, and rubbed one leg against the other.

I for my part, being vexed at her behaviour to me, took up all my things to go, and made a fuss about it; to let her know I was going. But she did not call me back at all, as I had made sure she would do; moreover, I knew that to try the descent was almost certain death to me, and it looked as dark as pitch; and so at the mouth I turned round again, and came back to her, and said, 'Lorna.'

'Oh, I thought you were gone,' she answered; 'why did you ever come here? Do you know what they would do to us, if they found you here with me?'

'Beat us, I dare say, very hard, or me at least. They could never beat you.'

'No. They would kill us both outright, and bury us here by the water; and the water often tells me that I must come to that.'

'But what should they kill me for?'

'Because you have found the way up here, and they never could believe it. Now, please to go; oh please to go. They will kill us both in a moment. Yes, I like you very much' – for I was teasing her to say it – 'very much indeed, and I will call you John Ridd, if you like; only please to go, John. And when your feet are well, you know, you can come and tell me how they are.'

'But I tell you, Lorna, I like you very much indeed, nearly as much as Annie, and a great deal more than Lizzie. And I never saw any one like you; and I must come back again tomorrow, and so must you, to see me; and I will bring you such a maun of things – there are apples, still, and a thrush I caught with one leg broken, and our dog has just had puppies – '

'Oh dear, they won't let me have a dog. There is not a dog in the valley. They say they are such noisy things – '

A shout came down the valley; and all my heart was trembling, like water after sunset, and Lorna's face was altered from pleasant play to terror. She shrank to me, and looked up at me, with such a power of weakness, that I at once made up my mind, to save her, or to die with her.

'Come with me down the waterfall. I can carry you easily; and mother will take care of you.'

'No, no,' she cried, as I took her up: 'I will tell you what to do. They are only looking for me. You see that hole, that hole there?'

She pointed to a little niche in the rock, which verged the

meadow, about fifty yards away from us. In the fading of the twilight I could just descry it.

'Yes, I see it; but they will see me crossing the grass to get there.'

'Look! look!' She could hardly speak. 'There is a way out from the top of it; they would kill me if I told it. Oh, here they come; I can see them. '

I drew her behind the withy-bushes, and close down to the water, where it was quiet, and shelving deep, ere it came to the lip of the chasm.

Crouching in that hollow nest, as children get together in ever so little compass, I saw a dozen fierce men come down, on the other side of the water, not bearing any firearms, but looking lax and jovial, as if they were come from riding and a dinner taken hungrily. 'Queen, queen!' they were shouting, here and there, and now and then: 'where the pest is our little queen gone?'

'They always call me "queen," and I am to be queen by and by,' Lorna whispered to me, with her soft cheek on my rough one, and her little heart beating against me: 'oh, they are crossing by the timber there, and then they are sure to see us.'

'Stop,' said I; 'now I see what to do. I must get into the water, and you must go to sleep.'

'To be sure, yes, away in the meadow there. But how bitter cold it will be for you!'

She saw in a moment the way to do it, sooner than I could tell her; and there was no time to lose.

'Now mind you never come again,' she whispered over her shoulder, as she crept away with a childish twist, hiding her white front from me; 'only I shall come sometimes – oh, here they are, Madonna!'

Daring scarce to peep, I crept into the water, and lay down bodily in it, with my head between two blocks of stone, and some flood-drift combing over me. She was lying beneath a rock, thirty or forty yards from me, feigning to be fast asleep, with her dress spread beautifully, and her hair drawn over her.

Presently one of the great rough men came round a corner

upon her; and there he stopped, and gazed awhile at her fairness and her innocence. Then he caught her up in his arms, and kissed her so that I heard him; and if I had only brought my gun, I would have tried to shoot him.

'Here our queen is! Here's the queen, here's the captain's daughter!' he shouted to his comrades; 'fast asleep, by God, and hearty! Now I have first claim to her; and no one else shall touch the child. Back to the bottle, all of you!'

He set her dainty little form upon his great square shoulder, and her narrow feet in one broad hand; and so in triumph marched away.

Going up that darkened glen, little Lorna, riding still the largest and most fierce of them, turned and put up a hand to me; and I put up a hand to her, in the thick of the mist and the willows.

I crept into a bush for warmth, and rubbed my shivering legs on bark, and longed for mother's fagot. Then, as daylight sank below the forget-me-not of stars, with a sorrow to be quit, I knew that now must be my time to get away.

7

A Man Justly Popular

It happened upon a November evening (when I was about fifteen years old, and out-growing my strength very rapidly, my sister Annie being turned thirteen, and a deal of rain having fallen, and all the troughs in the yard being flooded, and the bark from the wood-ricks washed down the gutters, and even our water-shoot going brown) that the ducks in the court made a terrible quacking, instead of marching off to their pen, one behind another. Thereupon Annie and I ran out to see what might be the sense of it. A man on horseback came suddenly round the corner of the great ash-hedge. The gentleman turned round to us, with a pleasant smile on his face, as if he were lightly amused with himself; and we came up and looked at him. He was rather short, about John Fry's height, or maybe a little taller, but very strongly built and springy, as his gait at every step showed plainly, although his legs were bowed with much riding, and he looked as if he lived on horseback. To a boy like me he seemed very old, being over twenty, and well-found in beard; but he was not more than four-and-twenty, fresh and ruddy-looking, with a short nose, and keen blue eyes, and a merry waggish jerk about him, as if the world were not in earnest. Yet he had a sharp, stern way, like the crack of a pistol, if anything misliked him; and we knew (for children see such things) that it was safer to tickle than tackle him.

'Well, young uns, what be gaping at?' He gave pretty Annie a chuck on the chin, and took me all in without winking.

'Your mare,' said I, standing stoutly up, being a tall boy now; 'I never saw such a beauty, sir.'

'I am thy mother's cousin, boy, and am going up to house. Tom Faggus is my name, as everybody knows; and this is my young mare, Winnie.'

What a fool I must have been not to know it at once! Tom Faggus, the great highwayman, and his young blood-mare, the strawberry! Already her fame was noised abroad, nearly as much as her master's.

Tom Faggus stopped to sup that night with us, and took a little of everything; a few oysters first, and then dried salmon, and then ham and eggs, done in small curled rashers, and then a few collops of venison toasted, and next to that a little cold roast-pig, and a woodcock on toast to finish with, before the Schiedam and hot water. And having changed his wet things first, he seemed to be in fair appetite, and praised Annie's cooking mightily, with a relishing noise like a smack of his lips, and a rubbing of his hands together, whenever he could spare them.

Now although Mr Faggus was so clever, and generous, and celebrated, I know not whether, upon the whole, we were rather proud of him as a member of our family, or inclined to be ashamed of him. And indeed I think that the sway of the balance hung upon the company we were in. For instance, with the boys at Brendon – for there is no village at Oare – I was exceeding proud to talk of him, and would freely brag of my Cousin Tom. But with the rich parsons of the neighbourhood, or the justices (who came round now and then, and were glad to ride up to a warm farm-house), or even the well-to-do tradesmen of Porlock – in a word, any settled power, which was afraid of losing things – with all of these we were very shy of claiming our kinship to that great outlaw.

He came again, about three months afterwards, in the beginning of the spring-time, and brought me a beautiful new carbine, having learned my love of such things, and my great desire to shoot straight. But mother would not let me have the gun, until he averred upon his honour that he had bought it honestly. And so he had, no doubt, so far as it is honest to buy with money acquired rampantly. Scarce could I stop to make my bullets in the mould which came along with it, but must be off to the Quarry hill, and new target I had made there. And he taught me then how to ride bright Winnie who was grown since I had seen her, but remembered me most kindly. After making much of Annie, who had a wondrous liking for him – and he said he was her godfather, but God knows how he could have been, unless they confirmed him precociously – away he went, and young Winnie's sides shone like a cherry by candlelight.

8

Master Huckaback
Comes In

Mr Reuben Huckaback, whom many good folk in Dulverton
will remember long after my time, was my mother's uncle,
being indeed her mother's brother. He owned the very best
shop in the town, and did a fine trade in soft ware, especially
when the pack-horses came safely in at Christmas-time. And
we being now his only kindred (except indeed his granddaughter, little Ruth Huckaback, of whom no one took any
heed), mother beheld it a Christian duty to keep as well as
could be with him, both for love of a nice old man, and for
the sake of her children. And truly, the Dulverton people
said that he was the richest man in their town, and could buy
up half the county armigers; ay, and if it came to that, they
would like to see any man, at Bampton, or at Wivelscombe,
and you might say almost Taunton, who could put down
golden Jacobus and Carolus against him.

Now this old gentleman – so they called him, according to
his money; and I have seen many worse ones, more violent
and less wealthy – he must needs come away that time to
spend the New Year-tide with us; not that he wanted to
do it (for he hated country life), but because my mother
pressing, as mothers will do to a good bag of gold, had
wrung a promise from him; and the only boast of his life
was, that never yet had he broken his word, at least since he
opened business. It had been settled between us, that we
should expect him soon after noon, on the last day of
December.

Now when I came in, before one o'clock, after seeing to the cattle – for the day was thicker than ever, and we must keep the cattle close at home, if we wished to see any more of them – I fully expected to find Uncle Ben sitting in the fireplace, lifting one cover and then another, as his favourite manner was, and making sweet mouths over them; for he loved our bacon rarely, and they had no good leeks at Dulverton; and he was a man who always would see his business done himself.

'Oh Johnny, Johnny,' my mother cried, running out of the grand show-parlour, where the case of stuffed birds was, and peacock-feathers, and the white hare killed by grandfather: 'I am so glad you are come at last. There is something sadly amiss, Johnny.'

'Well, mother, what is the matter, then?'

'I am sure you need not be angry, Johnny. I only hope it is nothing to grieve about, instead of being angry, but what would you say if the people there' – she never would call them 'Doones' – 'had gotten your poor Uncle Reuben, horse, and Sunday coat, and all?'

'Why, mother, I should be sorry for them. He would set up a shop by the river-side, and come away with all their money.'

'That all you have to say, John! And my dinner done to a very turn, and the supper all fit to go down, and no worry, only to eat and be done with it. And all the new plates come from Watchett, with the Watchett blue upon them, at the risk the lives of everybody, and the capias from good Aunt Jane for stuffing a curlew with onion before he begins to get cold, and make a wood-cock of him, and the way to turn the flap over in the inside of a roasting pig – '

'Well, mother dear, I am very sorry. But let us have our dinner. You know we promised not to wait for him after one o'clock; and you only make us hungry. Everything will be spoiled, mother, and what a pity to think of! After that I will go to seek for him in the thick of the fog, like a needle in a hay-band. That is to say, unless you think' – for she looked very grave about it – 'unless you really think, mother, that I ought to go without dinner.'

'Oh no, John, I never thought that, thank God! Bless Him for my children's appetites; and what is Uncle Ben to them?'

So we made a very good dinner indeed, though wishing that he could have some of it, and wondering how much to leave for him; and then, as no sound of his horse had been heard, I set out with my gun to look for him.

I followed the track on the side of the hill, from the farm-yard, where the sledd-marks are – for we have no wheels upon Exmoor yet, or ever shall, I suppose; though a dunder-headed man tried it last winter, and broke his axle piteously, and was nigh to break his neck – and after that I went all along on the ridge of the rabbit-cleve, with the brook running thin in the bottom; and then down to the Lynn-stream, and leaped it, and so up the hill and the moor beyond. The fog hung close all around me there, when I turned the crest of the highland, and the gorse, both before and behind me, looked like a man crouching down in ambush. But still there was a good cloud of daylight, being scarce three of the clock yet, and when a lead of red deer came across, I could tell them from sheep even now. I was half inclined to shoot at them, for the children did love venison; but they drooped their heads so, and looked so faithful, that it seemed hard measure to do it. If one of them had bolted away, no doubt I had let go at him.

After that I kept on the track, trudging very stoutly, for nigh upon three miles, and my beard (now beginning to grow at some great length) was full of great drops and prickly, whereat I was very proud. I had not so much as a dog with me, and the place was unkind and lonesome, and the rolling clouds very desolate; and now if a wild sheep ran across, he was scared at me as an enemy; and I for my part could not tell the meaning of the marks on him. We called all this part 'Gibbet-moor,' not being in our parish; but though there were gibbets enough upon it, most part of the bodies was gone, for the value of the chains, they said, and the teaching of young chirurgeons.

But of all this I had little fear, being no more a school-boy now, but a youth well acquaint with Exmoor, and the wise art of the sign-posts, whereby a man, who barred the road, now leads us along it with his finger-bones, so far as rogues allow him. My carbine was loaded and freshly primed, and I knew myself to be even now a match in strength for any two men of the size around our neighbourhood, except in the Glen Doone.

Now when I came to an unknown place, where a stone was set up endwise, with a faint red cross upon it, and a polish from some conflict, I gathered my courage to stop and think, having sped on the way too hotly. Against that stone I set my gun, trying my spirit to leave it so, but keeping with half a hand for it; and then what to do next was the wonder. As for finding Uncle Ben – that was his own business, or at any rate his executor's; first I had to find myself, and plentifully would thank God to find that self at home again, for the sake of all our family.

The volumes of the mist came rolling at me (like great packs of wool, pillowed up with sleepiness), and between them there was nothing more than waiting for the next one. Then everything went out of sight, and glad was I of the stone behind me, and view of mine own shoes. Anon a distant noise went by me, as of many horses galloping, and in my fright I set my gun, and said, 'God send something to shoot at.' Yet nothing came and my gun fell back, without my will to lower it.

But presently, while I was thinking 'What a fool I am!' arose as if from below my feet, so that the great stone trembled, a long lamenting lonesome sound, as of an evil spirit not knowing what to do with it. For the moment I stood like a root, without either hand or foot to help me; and the hair of my head began to crawl, lifting my hat, as a snail lifts his house; and my heart, like a shuttle, went to and fro. But finding no harm to come of it, neither visible form approaching, I wiped my forehead, and hoped for the best, and resolved to run every step of the way, till I drew our big bolt behind me.

Yet here again I was disappointed, for no sooner was I come to the crossways by the black pool in the hole, but I heard through the patter of my own feet a rough low sound, very close in the fog, as of a hobbled sheep a-coughing. I listened, and feared, and yet listened again, though I wanted not to hear it. For being in haste of the homeward road, and all my heart having heels to it, loth I was to stop in the dusk, for the sake of an aged wether. Yet partly my love of all animals, and partly my fear of the farmer's disgrace, compelled me to go to the succour, for the noise was coming nearer. A dry short wheezing sound it was, barred with coughs, and want of breath; but thus I made the meaning of it.

'Lord have mercy upon me! O Lord, upon my soul have mercy! An' if I cheated Sam Hicks last week, Lord knowest how well he deserved it, and lied in every stocking's mouth – oh Lord, where be I a-going?'

These words, with many jogs between them, came to me through the darkness, and then a long groan, and a choking. I made towards the sound, as nigh as ever I could guess, and presently was met, point-blank, by the head of a mountain-pony. Upon its back lay a man, bound down, with his feet on the neck and his head to the tail, and his arms falling down like stirrups. The wild little nag was scared of its life by the unaccustomed burden, and had been tossing and rolling hard, in desire to get ease of it.

Before the little horse could turn, I caught him, jaded as he was, by his wet and grizzled forelock, and he saw that it was vain to struggle, but strove to bite me none the less, until I smote him upon the nose.

'Good and worthy sir,' I said to the man who was riding so roughly; 'fear nothing; no harm shall come to thee.'

'Help, good friend, whoever thou art,' he gasped, but could not look at me, because his neck was jerked so; 'God hath sent thee; and not to rob me, because it is done already.'

'What, Uncle Ben!' I cried, letting go the horse, in amazement that the richest man in Dulverton – 'Uncle Ben here in this plight! What, Mr Reuben Huckaback!'

Not to make a long story of it, I cut the thongs that bound him, and set him astride on the little horse; but he was too weak to stay so. Therefore I mounted him on my back, turning the horse into horse-steps; and leading the pony by the cords, which I fastened around his nose, set out for Plover's Barrows.

My mother made a dreadful stir, to see Uncle Ben in such a sorry plight as this; so I left him to her care and Annie's; and soon they fed him rarely, while I went out to look to the comfort of the captured pony.

Of course, the Doones, and nobody else, had robbed good Uncle Reuben; and then they grew sportive, and took his horse, an especially sober nag, and bound the master upon the wild one, for a little change as they told him. For two or three hours they had fine enjoyment, chasing him through the fog, and making much sport of his groanings; and then waxing hungry they went their way, and left him to opportunity. Now, Mr Huckaback, growing able to walk in a few days' time, became thereupon impatient, and could not be brought to understand why he should have been robbed at all.

Thereupon, we would kindly tell him, how truly thankful he ought to be, for never having been robbed before, in spite of living so long in this world; and how he was taking a very ungrateful, not to say ungracious, view, in thus repining and feeling aggrieved; when any one else would have knelt and thanked God, for enjoying so long an immunity. But say what we would, it was all as one; Uncle Ben stuck fast to it, that he had nothing to thank God for.

On the following day Master Huckaback, with some show of mystery, demanded from my mother an escort into a dangerous part of the world, to which his business compelled him. My mother made answer to this, that he was kindly welcome to take our John Fry with him; at which the good clothier laughed, and said that John was nothing like big enough, but another John must serve his turn, not only for his size, but because if he were carried away, no stone would be left unturned upon Exmoor, until he should be brought back again.

'My condition is this, Jack,' he said, 'that you shall guide me to-morrow, without a word to any one, to a place where I may well descry the dwelling of these scoundrel

Doones, and learn the best way to get at them, when the time shall come. Can you do this for me? I will pay you well, boy.'

I promised very readily to do my best to serve him; but vowed I would take no money for it, not being so poor as that came to. Accordingly, on the day following, I managed to set the men at work on the other side of the farm, especially that inquisitive and busy-body John Fry, who would pry out almost anything, for the pleasure of telling his wife; and then, with Uncle Reuben mounted on my ancient Peggy, I made foot for the westward, directly after breakfast. There was very little said between us, along the lane and across the hill, although the day was pleasant.

I thought of Lorna Doone, the little maid of so many years back, and how my fancy went with her. Could Lorna ever think of me? Was I not a lout gone by, only fit for loach-sticking? Had I ever seen a face fit to think of near her? The sudden flash, the quickness, the bright desire to know one's heart, and not withhold her own from it, the soft withdrawal of rich eyes, the longing to love somebody, any body, any thing, not imbrued with wickedness

My uncle interrupted me, misliking so much silence now, with the naked woods falling over us. For we were come to Bagworthy forest, the blackest and the loneliest place of all that keep the sun out. Even now in winter-time, with most of the wood unriddled, and the rest of it pinched brown, it hung around us, like a cloak containing little comfort. I kept quite close to Peggy's head, and Peggy kept quite close to me, and pricked her ears at everything. However, we saw nothing there, except a few old owls and hawks, and a magpie sitting all alone, until we came to the bank of the hill, where the pony could not climb it. Uncle Ben was very loth to get off, becanse the pony seemed company, and he thought he could gallop away on her, if the worst came to the worst; but I persuaded him that now he must go to the end of it. Tberefore we made Peggy fast, in a place where we could find her; and speaking cheerfully, as if there was nothing to be afraid of, he took his staff, and I my gun to climb the thick ascent.

There was now no path of any kind; which added to our courage all it lessened of our comfort, because it proved that the robbers were not in the habit of passing there. And we knew that we could not go astray, so long as we breasted the hill before us; inasmuch as it formed the rampart, or side-fence of Glen Doone. But in truth I used the right word there for the manner of our ascent, for the ground came forth so steep against us, and withal so woody, that to make any way we must throw ourselves forward, and labour, as at a breast-plough. Rough and loamy rungs of oak-root bulged, here and there, above our heads; briars needs must speak with us, using more of tooth than tongue; and sometimes bulks of rugged stone, like great sheep, stood across us. At last, though very loth to do it, I was forced to leave my gun behind, because I required one hand to drag myself up the difficulty, and one to help Uncle Reuben. And so at last we gained the top, and looked forth the edge of the forest, where the ground was very stony, and like the crest of a quarry; and no more trees between us and the brink of cliff below, three hundred yards below it might be, all strong slope and gliddery. And now for the first time I was amazed at the appearance of the Doones' stronghold, and understood its nature. For when I had been even in the valley, and climbed the cliffs to escape from it, about seven years agone, I was no more than a stripling boy, noting little, as boys do, except for their present purpose, and even that soon done with. But now, what with the fame of the Doones, and my own recollections, and Uncle Ben's insistence, all my attention was called forth, and the end was simple astonishment.

The chine of highland, whereon we stood, curved to the right and left of us, keeping about the same elevation, and crowned with trees and brushwood. At about half a mile in front of us, looking as if we could throw a stone to strike any man upon it, another crest, just like our own, bowed around to meet it; but failed, by reason of two narrow clefts, of which we could only see the brink. One of these clefts was the Doone-gate, with a portcullis of rock above it; and the other was the chasm, by which I had once made entrance. Betwixt them, where the hills fell back, as in a perfect oval, traversed by the winding water, lay a bright green valley, rimmed with sheer black rock, and seeming to have sunken bodily from the bleak rough heights above. It looked as if no frost could enter, neither winds go ruffling: only spring, and hope, and comfort, breathe to one another. Even now the rays of sunshine dwelt, and fell back on themselves, whenever the clouds lifted; and the pale blue glimpse of the growing day seemed to find young encouragement.

But for all that, Uncle Reuben was none the worse nor better. He looked down into Glen Doone first, and sniffed as if he were smelling it, like a sample of goods from a wholesale house; and then he looked at the hills over yonder, and then he stared at me.

'See what a pack of fools they be? '

'Of course I do, Uncle Ben. "All rogues are fools," was my first copy, beginning of the alphabet.'

'Pack of stuff, lad. Though true enough, and very good for young people. But see you not, how this great Doone valley may be taken in half-an-hour?'

'Yes, to be sure I do, uncle; if they like to give it up, I mean.'

'Three culverins on yonder hill, and three on top of this one – and we have them under a pestle. Ah, I have seen the wars, my lad, from Keinton up to Naseby; and I might have been a General now, if they had taken my advice – '

But I was not attending to him, being drawn away on a sudden by a sight which never struck the sharp eyes of our General. For I had long ago descried the little opening in the cliff, through which I made my exit, as before related, on the other side of the valley. No bigger than a rabbit-hole it seemed from where we stood; and yet of all the scene before me, that (from my remembrance perhaps) had the most attraction. Now gazing at it, with full thought of all that it had cost me, I saw a little figure come, and pause, and pass into it. Something very light and white, nimble, smooth, and elegant, gone almost before I knew that any one had been there. And yet my heart came to my ribs and all my blood was in my face, and pride within me fought with shame, and vanity with self-contempt; for though seven years were gone, and I from boyhood come to manhood, and she must have forgotten me, and I had half-forgotten; at that moment, once for all, I felt that I was face to face with fate (however poor it might be), weal or woe, in Lorna Doone.

9

Lorna Growing Formidable

Now Master Reuben Huckaback being gone, as he went next day, to his favourite town of Dulverton, and leaving behind him shadowy promise of the mountains he would do for me, my spirit began to burn, and pant, for something to go on with; and nothing showed a braver hope of movement, and adventure, than a lonely visit to Glen Doone, by way of the perilous passage discovered in my boyhood. Therefore I waited for nothing more than the slow arrival of new small-clothes, made by a good tailor at Porlock, for it seemed a pure duty to look my best; and when they were come and approved, I started, regardless of the expense, and forgetting (like a fool) how badly they would take the water.

What with urging of the tailor, and my own misgivings, the time was now come round again to the high-day of St Valentine, when all our maids were full of lovers, and all the lads looked foolish. And none of them more sheepish, or more innocent, than I myself, albeit twenty-one years old, and not afraid of men much, but terrified of women, at least, if they were comely. And what of all things scared me most was the thought of my own size, and knowledge of my strength, which came, like knots, upon me daily. In honest truth I tell this thing (which often since hath puzzled me, when I came to mix with men more), I was to that degree ashamed of my thickness, and my stature, in the presence of a woman, that I would not put a trunk of wood on the fire in the kitchen, but let Annie scold me well, with a smile to follow, and with her own plump hands lift up a little log, and fuel it. Many a time, I longed to be no bigger than John Fry was; whom now (when insolent) I took with my left hand by the waist-stuff, and set him on my hat, and gave him little chance to tread it; until he spoke of his family, and requested to come down again.

Now taking for good omen this, that I was a seven-year Valentine, though much too big for a Cupidon, I chose a seven-foot staff of ash, and fixed a loach fork in it, to look as I had looked before; and leaving words upon matters of business, out of the back door I went, and so through the little orchard, and down the brawling Lynn-brook. Not being now so much afraid, I struck across the thicket land between the meeting waters, and came upon the Bagworthy stream near the great black whirlpool. Nothing amazed me so much as to find how shallow the stream now looked to me, although the pool was still as black, and greedy, as it used to be. And still the great rocky slide was dark and difficult to climb; though the water, which once had taken my knees was satisfied now with my ankles. After some labour, I reached the top; and halted to look about me well, before trusting to broad daylight.

The winter had been a very mild one; and now the spring was toward, so that bank and bush were touched with it. The valley into which I gazed was fair with early promise, having shelter from the wind, and taking all the sunshine. The willow-bushes over the stream hung as if they were angling, with tasselled floats of gold and silver, bursting like a bean-pod. Between them came the water laughing, like a maid at her own dancing, and spread with that young blue which never lives beyond the April. And on either bank, the meadow ruffled, as the breeze came by opening (through new tufts of green) daisy-bud or celandine, or a shy glimpse now and then of the love-lorn primrose.

Though I am so blank of wit, or perhaps for that same reason, these little things come and dwell with me; and I am happy about them, and long for nothing better. I feel with every blade of grass, as if it had a history; and make a child of every bud, as though it knew and loved me. And being so, they seem to tell me of my own oblivions, how I am no more than they, except in self-importance.

While I was forgetting much of many things that harm one, and letting of my thoughts go wild to sounds and sights of nature, a sweeter note than thrush or ouzel ever wooed a mate in, floated on the valley breeze, at the quiet turn of sundown. The words were of an ancient song, fit to cry or laugh at.

But all the time, I kept myself in a black niche of the rock, where the fall of the water began, lest the sweet singer (espying me) should be alarmed, and flee away. But presently I ventured to look forth, where a bush was; and then I beheld the loveliest sight – one glimpse of which was enough to make me kneel in the coldest water.

By the side of the stream, she was coming to me, even among the primroses, as if she loved them all; and every flower looked the brighter, as her eyes were on them. I could not see what her face was, my heart so awoke, and trembled; only that her hair was flowing from a wreath of white violets, and the grace of her coming was like the appearance of the first wind-flower. The pale gleam over the western cliffs threw a shadow of light behind her, as if the sun were lingering. Never do I see that light from the closing of the west, even in these my aged days, without thinking of her. Ah me, if it comes to that, what do I see of earth or heaven, without thinking of her?

The tremulous thrill of her song was hanging on her open lips; and she glanced around, as if the birds were accustomed to make answer. To me it was a thing of terror to behold such beauty, and feel myself the while to be so very low and common. But scarcely knowing what I did, as if a rope were drawing me, I came from the dark mouth of the chasm; and stood, afraid to look at her.

She was turning to fly, not knowing me, and frightened, perhaps, at my stature; when I fell on the grass (as I fell before her seven years agone that day), and I just said, 'Lorna Doone!'

She knew me at once, from my manner and ways, and a smile broke through her trembling, as sunshine comes through willow leaves; and being so clever she saw, of course, that she needed not to fear me.

'Oh, indeed,' she cried, with a feint of anger (because she had shown her cowardice, and yet in her heart she was laughing); 'oh, if you please, who are you, sir, and how do you know my name?'

'I am John Ridd,' I answered; 'the boy who gave you those beautiful fish, when you were only a little thing, seven years ago to-day.'

'Yes, the poor boy who was frightened so, and obliged to hide here in the water.'

'And do you remember how kind you were, and saved my life by your quickness, and went away riding upon a great man's shoulder, as if you had never seen me, and yet looked back through the willow-trees?'

'Oh, yes, I remember everything! because it was so rare to see any, except – I mean, because I happen to remember. But you seem not to remember, sir, how perilous this place is.'

For she had kept her eyes upon me; large eyes, of a softness, a brightness, and a dignity, which made me feel as if I must for ever love, and yet for ever know myself unworthy. Unless themselves should fill with love, which is the spring of all things. And so I could not answer her, but was overcome with thinking, and feeling, and confusion. Neither could I look again; only waited for the melody, which made every word like a poem to me, the melody of her voice. But she had not the least idea of what was going on with me, any more than I myself had.

'I think, Master Ridd, you cannot know,' she said, with her eyes taken from me, 'what the dangers of this place are, and the nature of the people.'

'Yes, I know enough of that; and I am frightened greatly, all the time when I do not look at you.'

She was too young to answer me, in the style some maidens would have used; the manner, I mean, which now we call from a foreign word 'coquettish.' And more than that, she was trembling, from real fear of violence, lest strong hands might be laid on me, and a miserable end of it. And to tell the truth, I grew afraid; perhaps from a kind of sympathy, and because I knew that evil comes more readily than good to us.

Therefore, without more ado, or taking any advantage – although I would have been glad at heart, if needs had been, to kiss her (without any thought of rudeness) – it struck me that I had better go, and have no more to say to her until next time of coming. So would she look the more for me, and think the more about me, and not grow weary of my words, and the want of change there is in me. For, of course, I knew what a churl I was compared to her birth and appearance; but meanwhile I might improve myself, and learn a musical instrument. 'The wind hath a draw after flying straw' is a saying we have in Devonshire, made, peradventure, by somebody who had seen the ways of women.

'Mistress Lorna, I will depart' – mark you, I thought that a powerful word – 'in fear of causing disquiet. If any rogue shot me, it would grieve you; I make bold to say it; and it would be the death of mother. Few mothers have such a son as me. Try to think of me, now and then; and I will bring you some new-laid eggs, for our young blue hen is beginning.'

'I thank you heartily,' said Lorna; 'but you need not come to see me. You can put them in my little bower, where I am almost always – I mean whither daily I repair; to think, and to be away from them.'

'Only show me where it is. Thrice a day, I will come and stop – '

'Nay, Master Ridd, I would never show thee – never, because of peril – only that so happens it, thou hast found the way already.'

And she smiled, with a light that made me care to cry out for no other way, only the way to her dear heart. But only to myself I cried for anything at all, having enough of man in me, to be bashful with young maidens. So I touched her white hand softly, when she gave it to me; and (fancying that she had sighed) was touched at heart about it, and resolved to yield her all my goods, although my mother was living;

and then grew angry with myself (for a mile or more of walking) to think she would condescend so; and then, for the rest of the homeward road, was mad with every man in the world, who would dare to think of looking at her.

10

Another Dangerous Interview

To forget one's luck of life, to forget the cark of care, and withering of young fingers; not to feel, or not be moved by, all the change of thought and heart, from large young heat to the sinewy lines, and dry bones of old age – this is what I have to do, ere ever I can make you know (even as a dream is known) how I loved my Lorna. I myself can never know; never can conceive, or treat it as a thing of reason; never can behold myself dwelling in the midst of it, and think that this was I; neither can I wander far from perpetual thought of it. Perhaps I have two farrows of pigs ready for the chapman; perhaps I have ten stones of wool waiting for the factor. It is all the same: I look at both, and what I say to myself is this: 'Which would Lorna choose of them?' Of course, I am a fool for this; any man may call me so, and I will not quarrel with him, unless he guess my secret. By and by, I fetch my wit, so far as it be worth the fetching, back again to business. But there my heart is, and must be; and all who like to try can cheat me, except upon parish matters.

That week, I could do little more than dream and dream, and rove about, seeking by perpetual change to find the way back to myself. I cared not for the people round me, neither took delight in victuals; but made believe to eat and drink, and blushed at any questions. And being called the master now, head-farmer, and chief yeoman, it irked me much that any one should take advantage of me; yet everybody did so, as soon as ever it was known that my wits were gone moonraking. For that was the way they looked at it, not being able to comprehend the greatness and the loftiness. Neither do I blame them much; for the wisest thing is to laugh at people, when we cannot understand them. I, for my part, took no notice; but in my heart despised them, as beings of a lesser nature, who never had seen Lorna.

When the weather changed in earnest, and the frost was gone, and the south-west wind blew softly, and the lambs were at play with the daisies, it was more than I could do to keep from thought of Lorna. For now the fields were spread with growth, and the waters clad with sunshine; and light and shadow, step by step, wandered over the furzy cleves. As no Lorna came to me, except in dreams or fancy, and as my life was not worth living without constant sign of her, forth I must again to find her, and say more than a man can tell. Therefore, without waiting longer for the moving of the spring, dressed I was in grand attire (so far as I had gotten it), and thinking my appearance good, although with doubts about it (being forced to dress in the hay-tallat), round the corner of the wood-stack, went I very knowingly – for Lizzie's eyes were wondrous sharp – and thus I was sure of meeting none, who would care or dare to speak of me.

This time I longed to take my gun, and was half resolved to do so; because it seemed so hard a thing to be shot at, and have no chance of shooting; but when I came to remember the steepness, and the slippery nature of the waterslide, there seemed but little likelihood of keeping dry the powder. Therefore I was armed with nothing, but a good stout holly staff, seasoned well for many a winter, in our back-kitchen chimney.

Although my heart was leaping high, with the prospect of some adventure, and the fear of meeting Lorna, I could not but be gladdened by the softness of the weather, and the welcome way of everything. There was that power all around, that power and that goodness, which make us come, as it were, outside our bodily selves, to share them. Over, and beside us, breathes the joy of hope and promise; under foot are troubles past; in the distance, bowering newness tempts us ever forward. We rise into quick sense of life, and spring through clouds of mystery.

And, in good sooth, I had to spring, and no mystery about it, ere ever I got to the top of the rift leading into Doone-glade. For the stream was rushing down in strength, and raving at every corner; a mort of rain having fallen last night, and no wind come to wipe it. However, I reached the head ere dark, with more difficulty than danger; and sat in a place, which comforted my back and legs desirably.

Hereupon I grew so happy, at being on dry land again, and come to look for Lorna, with pretty trees around me, that what did I do but fall asleep with the holly-stick in front of me, and my best coat sunk in a bed of moss, among wetness and wood-sorrel. Mayhap I had not done so, nor yet enjoyed the spring so much, if so be I had not taken three-parts of a gallon of cider, at home at Plover's Barrows.

There was a little runnel, going softly down beside me, falling from the upper rock, by the means of moss and grass, as if it feared to make a noise, and had a mother sleeping. Now and then it seemed to stop, in fear of its own dropping, and waiting for some orders; and the blades of grass that straightened to it turned their points a little way, and offered their allegiance to wind instead of water. Yet, before their carkled edges bent more than a driven saw, down the water came again, with heavy drops, and pats of running, and bright anger at neglect.

This was very pleasant to me, now and then, to gaze at; blinking as the water blinked, and falling back to sleep again. Suddenly my sleep was broken by a shade cast over me; between me and the low sunlight, Lorna Doone was standing.

'Master Ridd, are you mad?' she said, and took my hand to move me.

'Not mad, but half asleep,' I answered, feigning not to notice her, that so she might keep hold of me.

'Come away, come away, if yon care for life. The patrol will be here directly. Be quick, Master Ridd, let me hide thee.'

'I will not stir a step,' said I, though being in the greatest fright that might be well imagined; 'unless you call me "John."'

'Well, John, then – Master John Ridd; be quick, if you have any to care for you.'

'I have many to care for me,' I said, just to let her know; 'and I will follow you, Mistress Lorna; albeit without any hurry, unless there be peril to more than me.'

Without another word, she led me, though with many timid glances towards the upper valley, to, and into, her little bower, where the inlet through the rock was. Inside the niche of native stone, the plainest thing of all to see, at any rate by daylight, was a stairway hewn from rock, and leading up to the mountain. To the right side of this was the mouth of a pit, looking very formidable; though Lorna laughed at my fear of it, for she drew her water thence. But on the left was a narrow crevice, very difficult to espy, and having a sweep of grey ivy laid, like a slouching beaver, over it. A man here coming from the brightness of the outer air, with eyes dazed by the twilight, would never think of seeing this, and following it to its meaning.

Lorna raised the screen for me, but I had much ado to pass, on account of bulk and stature. Instead of being proud of my size (as it seemed to me she ought to be) Lorna laughed so quietly, that I was ready to knock my head or elbows against anything, and say no more about it. However, I got through at last, without a word of compliment, and broke into the pleasant room, the lone retreat of Lorna.

The chamber was of unhewn rock, round, as near as might be, eighteen or twenty feet across, and gay with rich variety of fern, and moss, and lichen. The fern was in its winter still, or coiling for the spring-tide; but moss was in abundant life, some feathering, and some gobleted, and some with fringe of red to it. Overhead there was no ceiling but the sky itself, flaked with little clouds of April whitely wandering over it. The floor was made of soft, low grass, mixed with moss and primroses; and in a niche of shelter moved the delicate wood-sorrel. Here and there, around the sides, were 'chairs of living stone,' as some Latin writer says, whose name has quite escaped me; and in the midst a tiny spring arose, with crystal beads in it, and a soft voice as of a laughing dream, and dimples like a sleeping babe. Then, after going round a little, with surprise of daylight, the water overwelled the edge, and softly went through lines of light, to shadows and an untold bourne.

While I was gazing at all these things, with wonder and some sadness, Lorna turned upon me lightly (as her manner was) and said, –

'Where are the new-laid eggs, Master Ridd? Or hath blue hen ceased laying?'

I did not altogether like the way in which she said it, with a sort of a dialect, as if my speech could be laughed at.

'Here be some,' I answered, speaking as if in spite of her. 'I would have brought thee twice as many, but that I feared to crush them in the narrow ways, Mistress Lorna.'

And so I laid her out two dozen upon the moss of the rock ledge, unwinding the wisp of hay from each, as it came safe out of my pocket. Lorna looked with growing wonder, as I added one to one; and when I had placed them side by side, and bidden her now to tell them, to my amazement what did she but burst into a flood of tears!

'What have I done?' I asked, with shame, scarce daring even to look at her, because her grief was not like Annie's – a thing that could be coaxed away, and left a joy in going – 'oh, what have I done to vex you so?'

'It is nothing done by you, Master Ridd,' she answered, very proudly, as if nought I did could matter; 'it is only something that comes upon me, with the scent of the pure true clover-hay. Moreover, you have been too kind; and I am not used to kindness.'

Some sort of awkwardness was on me, at her words and weeping, as if I would like to say something, but feared to make things worse perhaps than they were already. Therefore I abstained from speech, as I would in my own pain. And as it happened, this was the way to make her tell me more about it. Not that I was curious, beyond what pity urged me, and the strange affairs around her; and now I gazed upon the floor, lest I should seem to watch her; but none the less for that I knew all that she was doing.

Lorna went a little way, as if she would not think of me, nor care for one so careless; and all my heart gave a sudden jump, to go like a mad thing after her; until she turned of her own accord, and with a little sigh came back to me. Her eyes were soft with trouble's shadow, and the proud lift of her neck was gone, and beauty's vanity borne down by woman's want of sustenance.

'Master Ridd,' she said in the softest voice that ever flowed between two lips, 'have I done aught to offend you?'

Hereupon it went hard with me, not to catch her up and kiss her, in the manner in which she was looking; only it smote me suddenly, that this would be a low advantage of her trust and helplessness. She seemed to know what I would be at, and to doubt very greatly about it, whether as a child of old she might permit the usage. All sorts of things went through my head, as I made myself look away from her, for fear of being tempted beyond what I could bear. And the upshot of it was, that I said, within my heart and through it, 'John Ridd, be on thy very best manners with this lonely maiden.'

Lorna liked me all the better for my good forbearance; because she did not love me yet, and had not thought about it; at least so far as I knew. And though her eyes were so beauteous, so very soft and kindly, there was (to my apprehension) some great power in them, as if she would not have a thing, unless her judgment leaped with it.

But now her judgment leaped with me, because I had behaved so well; and being of quick urgent nature – such as I delight in, for the change from mine own slowness she, without any let or hindrance, sitting over against me, now raising and now dropping fringe, over those sweet eyes that were the road-lights of her tongue, Lorna told me all about everything I wished to know, every little thing she knew, except indeed that point of points, how Master Ridd stood with her.

Although it wearied me no whit, it might be wearisome for folk who cannot look at Lorna, to hear the story all in speech, exactly as she told it; therefore let me put it shortly, to the best of my remembrance.

Nay, pardon me, whosoever thou art, for seeming fickle and rude to thee; I have tried to do as first proposed, to tell the tale in my own words, as of another's fortune. But, lo! I was beset at once with many heavy obstacles, which grew as I went onward, until I knew not where I was, and mingled past and present. And two of these difficulties only were enough to stop me; the one that I must coldly speak, without the force of pity, the other that I, off and on, confused myself with Lorna, as might be well expected.

Therefore let her tell the story, with her own sweet voice and manner; and if ye find it wearisome, seek in yourselves the weariness.

11

Lorna Tells her Story

'I cannot go through all my thoughts, so as to make them clear to you, nor have I ever dwelt on things, to shape a story of them. I know not where the beginning was, nor where the middle ought to be, nor even how at the present time I feel, or think, or ought to think. If I look for help to those around me, who should tell me right and wrong (being older and much wiser), I meet sometimes with laughter, and at other times with anger.

'There are but two in the world, who ever listen and try to help me; one of them is my grandfather, and the other is a man of wisdom, whom we call the Counsellor. My grandfather, Sir Ensor Doone, is very old and harsh of manner (except indeed to me); he seems to know what is right and wrong, but not to want to think of it. The Counsellor, on the other hand, though full of life and subtleties, treats my questions as of play, and not gravely worth his while to answer, unless he can make wit of them.

'And among the women, there are none with whom I can hold converse, since my Aunt Sabina died, who took such pains to teach me. She was a lady of high repute, and lofty ways, and learning, but grieved and harassed more and more, by the coarseness, and the violence, and the ignorance, around her. In vain she strove, from year to year, to make the young men hearken, to teach them what became their birth, and give them sense of honour. It was her favourite word, poor thing! and they called her "Old Aunt Honour."

Very often she used to say, that I was her only comfort, and I am sure she was my only one; and when she died, it was more to me than if I had lost a mother.

'For I have no remembrance now of father, or of mother; although they say that my father was the eldest son of Sir Ensor Doone, and the bravest, and the best of them. And so they call me heiress to this little realm of violence; and in sorry sport sometimes, I am their Princess, or their Queen.

'Many people living here, as I am forced to do, would perhaps be very happy, and perhaps I ought to be so. We have a beauteous valley, sheltered from the cold of winter, and power of the summer sun, untroubled also by the storms and mists that veil the mountains; although I must acknowledge that it is apt to rain too often. The grass moreover is so fresh, and the brook so bright and lively, and flowers of so many hues come after one another, that no one need be dull, if only left alone with them.

'And so, in the early day perhaps, when morning breathes around me, and the sun is going upward, and light is playing everywhere, I am not so far beside them all, as to live in shadow. But when the evening gathers down, and the sky is spread with sadness, and the day has spent itself; then a cloud of lonely trouble falls, like night, upon me. I cannot see the things I quest for of a world beyond me; I cannot join the peace, and quiet, of the depth above me; neither have I any pleasure in the brightness of the stars.

'What I want to know is something none of them can tell me – what am I, and why set here, and when shall I be with them? I see that you are surprised a little, at this my curiosity. Perhaps such questions never spring, in any wholesome spirit. But they are in the depths of mine, and I cannot be quit of them.

'Meantime, all around me is violence and robbery, coarse delight and savage pain, reckless joke and hopeless death. Is it any wonder, that I cannot sink with these, that I cannot so forget my soul, as to live the life of brutes, and die the death more horrible, because it dreams of waking? There is none to lead me forward, there is none to teach me right; young as I am, I live beneath a curse that lasts for ever.'

Here Lorna broke down for awhile, and cried so very piteously, that doubting of my knowledge, and my right or power to comfort, I did my best to hold my peace, and tried to look very cheerful. Then thinking that might be bad manners, I went to wipe her eyes for her.

'Master Ridd,' she began again, 'I am both ashamed and vexed, at my own childish folly. But you, who have a mother, who thinks (you say) so much of you, and sisters, and a quiet home; you cannot tell (it is not likely) what a lonely nature is. How it leaps in mirth sometimes, with only heaven touching it; and how it falls away desponding, when the dreary weight creeps on.

'We should not be so quiet here, and safe from interruption, but that I have begged one privilege, rather than commanded it. This was, that the lower end, just this narrowing of the valley, where it is most hard to come at, might be looked upon as mine, except for purposes of guard. Therefore none, beside the sentries, ever trespass on me here, unless it be my grandfather, or the Counsellor, or Carver.

'By your face, Master Ridd, I see that you have heard of Carver Doone. For strength, and courage, and resource, he bears the first repute among us, as might well be expected from the son of the Counsellor. But he differs from his father, in being very hot and savage, and quite free from argument. The Counsellor, who is my uncle, gives his son the best advice; commending all the virtues, with eloquence and wisdom; yet himself abstaining from them, accurately and impartially.

'You must be tired of this story, and the time I take to think, and the weakness of my telling; but my life from day to day shows so little variance. Among the riders there is none whose safe return I watch for – I mean none more than other – and indeed there seems no risk; all are now so feared of us. Neither of the old men is there, whom I can revere or love (except alone my grandfather, whom I love with trembling); neither of the women any whom I like to deal with, unless it be a little maiden, whom I saved from starving.

'A little Cornish girl she is, and shaped in western manner; not so very much less in width, than if you take her lengthwise. Her father seems to have been a miner, a Cornishman (as she declares) of more than average excellence, and better than any two men to be found in Devonshire, or any four in Somerset. Very few things can have been beyond his power of performance; and yet he left his daughter to starve upon a peat-rick. She does not know how this was done, and looks upon it as a mystery, the meaning of which will some day be clear, and redound to her father's honour. His name was Simon Carfax, and he came as the captain of a gang, from one of the Cornish stannaries. Gwenny Carfax, my young maid, well remembers how her father was brought up from Cornwall. Her mother had been buried, just a week or so, before; and he was sad about it, and had been off his work, and was ready for another job. Then people came to him by night, and said he must want a change, and everybody lost their wives, and work was the way to mend it. So what with grief, and overthought, and the inside of a square bottle, Gwenny says they brought him off, to become a mighty captain, and choose the country round. The last she saw of him was this, that he went down a ladder somewhere on the wilds of Exmoor, leaving her with bread and cheese, and his travelling-hat to see to. And from that day to this, he never came above the ground again; so far as we can hear of.

'But Gwenny, holding to his hat, and having eaten the bread and cheese (when he came no more to help her), dwelt three days near the mouth of the hole, and then it was closed over, the while that she was sleeping. With weakness, and with want of food, she lost herself distressfully, and went away, for miles or more, and lay upon a peat-rick, to die before the ravens.

'That very day, I chanced to return from Aunt Sabina's dying place; for she would not die in Glen Doone, she said, lest the angels feared to come for her; and so she was taken to a cottage in a lonely valley. I was allowed to visit her, for even we durst not refuse the wishes of the dying; and if a priest had been desired, we should have made bold with him. Returning very sorrowful, and caring now for nothing, I found this little stray thing lying, with her arms upon her, and not a sign of life, except the way that she was biting. Black root-stuff was in her mouth, and a piece of dirty sheep's wool, and at her feet an old egg-shell of some bird of the moorland.

'I tried to raise her, but she was too square and heavy for me; and so I put food in her mouth, and left her to do right with it. And this she did in a little time; for the victuals were very choice and rare, being what I had taken over, to tempt poor Aunt Sabina. Gwenny ate them without delay, and then was ready to eat the basket, and the ware that had contained them.

'Gwenny took me for an angel – though I am little like one, as you see, Master Ridd; and she followed me, expecting that I would open wings and fly, when we came to any difficulty. I brought her home with me, so far as this can be a home; and she made herself my sole attendant, without so much as asking me.

'Ah me! We are to be pitied greatly, rather than condemned, by people whose things we have taken from them; for I have read, and seem almost to understand about it, that there are places on the earth where gentle peace, and love of home, and knowledge of one's neighbours, prevail, and are, with reason, looked for as the usual state of things. There honest folk may go to work, in the glory of the sunrise, with hope of coming home again, quite safe in the quiet evening, and finding all their children; and even in the darkness, they have no fear of lying down, and dropping off to slumber, and hearken to the wind at night, not as to an enemy trying to find entrance, but a friend, who comes to tell the value of their comfort.

'Of all this golden ease I hear, but never saw the like of it.'

12

A Royal Invitation

After hearing that tale from Lorna, I went home in sorry spirits, having added fear for her, and misery about her, to all my other ailments. But the worst of all was this, that I had promised not to cause her any further trouble from anxiety and fear of harm. And this, being brought to practice, meant that I was not to show myself within the precincts of Glen Doone, for at least another month. Unless indeed (as I contrived to edge into the agreement) anything should happen to increase her present trouble and every day's uneasiness. In that case, she was to throw a dark mantle, or covering of some sort, over a large white stone, which hung within the entrance to her retreat – I mean the outer entrance – and which, though unseen from the valley itself, was (as I had observed) conspicuous from the height where I stood with Uncle Reuben.

One afternoon, when work was over, I had seen to the horses, for now it was foolish to trust John Fry, because he had so many children, and his wife had taken to scolding; and just as I was saying to myself, that in five days more my month would be done, and myself free to seek Lorna, a man came riding up from the ford where the road goes through the Lynn stream. As soon as I saw that it was not Tom Faggus, I went no further to meet him, counting that it must be some traveller bound for Brendon or Cheriton, and likely enough he would come and beg for a draught of milk or cider; and then on again, after asking the way.

But instead of that, he stopped at our gate, and stood up from his saddle, and holloed, as if he were somebody; and all the time he was flourishing a white thing in the air, like the bands our parson weareth. So I crossed the court-yard to speak with him.

'Service of the King!' he saith; 'service of our lord the King! Come hither, thou great yokel, at risk of fine and imprisonment.'

Although not pleased with this, I went to him, as became a loyal man; quite at my leisure, however, for there is no man born who can hurry me, though I hasten for any woman.

'Plover Barrows farm!' said he; 'God only knows how tired I be. Is there anywhere in this cursed country a cursed place called "Plover Barrows farm?" For last twenty mile at least they told me, 'twere only half-a-mile further, or only just round corner. Now tell me that, and I fain would thwack thee, if thou wert not thrice my size.'

'Sir,' I replied, 'you shall not have the trouble. This is Plover's Barrows farm, and you are kindly welcome. Sheep's kidneys is for supper, and the ale got bright from the tapping. But why do you think ill of us? We like not to be cursed so.'

'Nay, I think no ill,' he said; 'sheep's kidneys is good, uncommon good, if they do them without burning. But I be so galled in the saddle ten days, and never a comely meal of it. And when they hear "King's service" cried, they give me the worst of everything. Hungry I am, and sore of body, from my heels right upward, and sorest in front of my doublet; yet may I not rest, nor bite barley-bread, until I have seen and touched John Ridd. God grant that he be not far away; I must eat my saddle, if it be so. '

'Have no fear, good sir,' I answered; 'you have seen and touched John Ridd. I am he, and not one likely to go beneath a bushel.'

'It would take a large bushel to hold thee, John Ridd. In the name of the King, His Majesty, Charles the Second, these presents!'

He touched me with the white thing which I had first seen him waving, and which I now beheld to be sheepskin, such as they call parchment. It was tied across with cord, and fastened down in every corner with unsightly dabs of wax. By order of the messenger (for I was over-frightened now to think of doing anything), I broke enough of seals to keep an Easter ghost from rising; and there I saw my name in large; God grant such another shock may never befall me in my old age.

'Read, my son; read, thou great fool, if indeed thou canst read,' said the officer to encourage me; 'there is nothing to kill thee, boy, and my supper will be spoiling. Stare not at me so, thou fool; thou art big enough to eat me; read, read, read.'

'If you please, sir, what is your name?' I asked: though why I asked him I know not, except from fear of witchcraft.

'Jeremy Stickles is my name, lad, nothing more than a poor apparitor of the worshipful Court of King's Bench. And at this moment a starving one, and no supper for me unless thou wilt read.'

Being compelled in this way, I read pretty nigh as follows; not that I give the whole of it, but only the gist and the emphasis: –

'To our good subject, John Ridd, &c.' – describing me ever so much better than I knew myself – 'by these presents, greeting. These are to require thee, in the name of our lord the King, to appear in person before the Right Worshipful the Justices of His Majesty's Bench at Westminster, laying aside all thine own business, and there to deliver such evidence as is within thy cognizance, touching certain matters whereby the peace of our said lord the King, and the well-being of this realm, is, are, or otherwise may be impeached, impugned, imperilled, or otherwise detrimented. As witness these presents.' And then there were four seals, and then a signature I could not make out, only that it began with a J, and ended with some other writing, done almost in a circle. Underneath was added in a different handwriting, 'Charges will be borne. The matter is full urgent.'

The messenger watched me, while I read so much as I could read of it; and he seemed well-pleased with my surprise, because he had expected it.

Now though my mother was so willing that I should go to London, expecting great promotion and high glory for me, I myself was deeply gone into the pit of sorrow. For what would Lorna think of me? Here was the long month just expired, after worlds of waiting; there would be her lovely self, peeping softly down the glen, and fearing to encourage me; yet there would be nobody else, and what an insult to her! Dwelling upon this, and seeing no chance of escape from it, I could not find one wink of sleep; though Jeremy Stickles (who slept close by) snored loud enough to spare me some. For I felt myself to be, as it were, in a place of some importance; in a situation of trust, I may say; and bound not to depart from it. For who could tell what the King might have to say to me about the Doones – and I felt that they were at the bottom of this strange appearance – or what His Majesty might think, if after receiving a message from him (trusty under so many seals) I were to violate his faith in me as a churchwarden's son, and falsely spread his words abroad?

My only chance of seeing Lorna, before I went, lay in watching from the cliff and espying her, or a signal from her. This, however, I did in vain, until my eyes were weary, and often would delude themselves with hope of what they ached for. But though I lay hidden behind the trees upon the crest of the stony fall, and waited so quiet that the rabbits and squirrels played around me, and even the keen-eyed weasel took me for a trunk of wood – it was all as one; no cast of colour changed the white stone, whose whiteness now was hateful to me; nor did wreath or skirt of maiden break the loneliness of the vale.

A journey to London seemed to us, in those bygone days, as hazardous and dark an adventure as could be forced on any man.

By dinner-time we arrived at Porlock, and dined with my old friend, Master Pooke, now growing rich and portly. For though we had plenty of victuals with us, we were not to begin upon them, until all chance of victualling among our friends was left behind. And during that first day we had no need to meddle with our store at all; for as had been settled before we left home, we lay that night at Dunster in the house of a worthy tanner, first cousin to my mother, who received us very cordially, and undertook to return old Smiler to his stable at Plover's Barrows, after one day's rest.

Thence we hired to Bridgwater; and from Bridgwater on to Bristowe, breaking the journey between the two. The night was falling very thick by the time we were come to Tyburn, and here the King's officer decided that it would be wise to halt; because the way was unsafe by night across the fields to Charing village. I for my part was nothing loth, and preferred to see London by daylight.

Now this being the year of our Lord 1683, more than nine years and a half since the death of my father, and the beginning of this history, all London was in a great ferment, about the dispute between the Court of the King and the City. The King, or rather perhaps his party (for they said that His Majesty cared for little, except to have plenty of money and spend it), was quite resolved to be supreme in the appointment of the chief officers of the corporation. But the citizens maintained that (under their charter) this right lay entirely with themselves; upon which a writ was issued against them for forfeiture of their charter; and the question was now being tried in the court of His Majesty's bench.

This seemed to occupy all the attention of the judges, and my case (which had appeared so urgent) was put off from time to time, while the Court and the City contended. And so hot was the conflict and hate between them, that a sheriff had been fined by the King in £100,000, and a former lord mayor had even been sentenced to the pillory, because he would not swear falsely. Hence the courtiers and the citizens scarce could meet in the streets with patience, or without railing and frequent blows. The officers of the King's Bench, to whom I daily applied myself, were in counsel with their fellows, and put me off from day to day.

Now I had heard of the law's delays, which the greatest of all great poets (knowing much of the law himself, as indeed of every thing) has specially mentioned, when not expected, among the many ills of life. But I never thought at my years to have such bitter experience of the evil; and it seemed to me that if the lawyers failed to do their duty, they ought to pay people for waiting upon them, instead of making them pay for it. But here I was, now in the second month, living at my own charges, in the house of a worthy fellmonger at the sign of the Seal and Squirrel, abutting upon the Strand road, which leads from Temple Bar to Charing.

At length, being quite at the end of my money, and seeing no other help for it, I determined to listen to clerks no more, but force my way up to the Justices, and insist upon being heard by them, or discharged from my recognizance. For so they had termed the bond or deed, which I had been forced to execute, in the presence of a chief clerk or notary, the very day after I came to London. And the purport of it was, that on pain of a heavy fine or escheatment, I would hold myself ready and present, to give evidence when called upon. Having delivered me up to sign this, Jeremy Stickles was quit of me, and went upon other business; not but what he was kind and good to me, when his time and pursuits allowed of it.

In Westminster Hall I found nobody; not even the crowd of crawling varlets, who used to be craving evermore for employment or for payment. I knocked at three doors, one after other, of lobbies going out of it, where I had formerly seen some officers and people pressing in and out; but for my trouble I took nothing, except some thumps from echo. And at last an old man told me, that all the lawyers were gone to see the result of their own works, in the fields of Lincoln's Inn.

However, in a few days' time, I had better fortune; for the court was sitting and full of business, to clear off the arrears of work before the lawyers' holiday. The crier of the Court (as they told me) came out, and wanted to know who I was. I told him, as shortly as I could, that my business lay with His Majesty's bench, and was very confidential; upon which he took me inside with warning, and showed me to an underclerk, who showed me to a higher one, and the higher clerk to the head one.

When this gentleman understood all about my business (which I told him without complaint) he frowned at me very heavily, as if I had done him an injury.

'John Ridd,' he asked me with a stern glance, 'is it your deliberate desire to be brought into the presence of the Lord Chief Justice?'

'Surely, sir, it has been my desire, for the last two months and more.'

'Then, John, thou shalt be. But mind one thing, not a word of thy long detention, or thou mayest get into trouble.'

'How, sir? For being detained against my own wish?' I asked him; but he turned away, as if that matter were not worth his arguing, as, indeed, I suppose it was not, and led me through a little passage to a door with a curtain across it.

'Now, if my Lord cross-question you,' the gentleman whispered to me, 'answer him straight out truth at once, for he will have it out of thee. And mind, he loves not to be contradicted, neither can he bear a hang-dog look. Take little heed of the other two; but note every word of the middle one; and never make him speak twice.'

I thanked him for his good advice, as he moved the curtain and thrust me in, but instead of entering withdrew, and left me to bear the brunt of it.

His Lordship Judge Jeffreys was busy with some letters, and did not look up for a minute or two, although he knew that I was there. Meanwhile I stood waiting to make my bow; afraid to begin upon him, and wondering at his great bull-head. Then he closed his letters, well-pleased with their import, and fixed his bold stare on me, as if I were an oyster opened, and he would know how fresh I was.

'May it please your worship,' I said, 'here I am according to order, awaiting your good pleasure.'

'Now, John Ridd,' he said, 'having hauled thee hard, we will proceed to examine thee. '

'I am ready to answer my lord,' I replied, 'if he asks me nought beyond my knowledge, or beyond my honour.'

'Hadst better answer me every thing, lump. What hast thou to do with honour? Now is there in thy neighbourhood a certain nest of robbers, miscreants, and outlaws, whom all men fear to handle?'

'Yes, my lord. At least I believe some of them be robbers; and all of them are outlaws.'

'And what is your high sheriff about, that he doth not hang them all? Or send them up for me to hang, without more to-do about them? '

'I reckon that he is afraid, my lord; it is not safe to meddle with them. They are of good birth, and reckless; and their place is very strong.'

'Good birth! What was Lord Russell of, Lord Essex, and this Sidney? 'Tis the surest heirship to the block, to be the chip of an old one. What is the name of this pestilent race, and how many of them are there?'

'They are the Doones of Bagworthy forest, may it please your worship. And we reckon there be about forty of them, beside the women and children.'

'Forty Doones, all forty thieves! and women and children! Thunder of God! How long have they been there then?'

'They may have been there thirty years, my lord; and indeed they may have been forty. Before the great war broke out they came, longer back than I can remember.'

'Ay, long before thou wast born, John. Good, thou speakest plainly. Woe betide a liar, whenso I get hold of him. Ye want me on the Western Circuit; by God, and ye shall have me, when London traitors are spun and swung. There is a family called De Whichehalse living very nigh thee, John?'

This he said in a sudden manner, as if to take me off my guard, and fixed his great thick eyes on me. And in truth I was much astonished.

'Yes, my lord, there is. At least, not so very far from us Baron de Whichehalse, of Ley Manor.'

'Now hast thou ever heard or thought, that De Whichehalse is in league with the Doones of Bagworthy?'

Saying these words rather slowly, he skewered his great eyes into mine, so that I could not think at all, neither look at him, or yet away. The idea was so new to me, that it set my wits all wandering; and looking into me, he saw that I was groping for the truth.

'John Ridd, thine eyes are enough for me. I see thou hast never dreamed of it. Now hast thou ever seen a man, whose name is Thomas Faggus?'

'Yes, sir, many and many a time. He is my own worthy

cousin; and I fear that he hath intentions' – here I stopped, having no right there to speak about our Annie.

'Tom Faggus is a good man,' he said; and his great square face had a smile which showed he had met my cousin; 'Master Faggus hath made mistakes as to the title to property, as lawyers oftentimes may do; but take him all for all, he is a thoroughly straightforward man; presents his bill, and has it paid, and makes no charge for drawing it. Nevertheless, we must tax his costs, as of any other solicitor.'

'To be sure, to be sure, my lord!' was all that I could say, not understanding what all this meant.

'I fear he will come to the gallows,' said the Lord Chief Justice, sinking his voice below the echoes; 'tell him this from me, Jack. He shall never be condemned before me; but I cannot be everywhere; and some of our Justices may keep short memory of his dinners. Tell him to change his name, turn parson, or do something else, to make it wrong to hang him. Parson is the best thing; he hath such command of features, and he might take his tithes on horseback. Now a few more things, John Ridd; and for the present I have done with thee.'

All my heart leaped up at this, to get away from London so: and yet I could hardly trust to it.

'Is there any sound round your way of disaffection to His Majesty, His most gracious Majesty?'

'No, my lord: no sign whatever. We pray for him in church perhaps; and we talk about him afterwards, hoping it may do him good, as it is intended. But after that we have nought to say, not knowing much about him – at least till I get home again.'

'That is as it should be, John. And the less you say the better. But I have heard of things in Taunton, and even nearer to you in Dulverton, and even nigher still upon Exmoor; things which are of the pillory kind, and even more of the gallows. I see that you know nought of them. Nevertheless, it will not be long before all England hears of them. Now, John, I have taken a liking to thee; for never man told me the truth, without fear or favour, more thoroughly and truly than thou hast done. Keep thou clear of this, my son. It will come to nothing; yet many shall swing high for it. Even I could not save thee, John Ridd, if thou wert mixed in this affair. Keep from the Doones, keep from De Whichehalse, keep from every thing which leads beyond the sight of thy knowledge. I meant to use thee as my tool; but I see thou art too honest and simple. I will send a sharper down; but never let me find thee, John, either a tool for the other side, or a tube for my words to pass through.'

Here the Lord Justice gave me such a glare, that I wished myself well rid of him, though thankful for his warnings; and seeing how he had made upon me a long abiding mark of fear, he smiled again in a jocular manner, and said, –

'Now, get thee gone, Jack. I shall remember thee; and I trow, thou wilt'st not for many a day forget me.'

13

John has Hope of Lorna

It was the beginning of wheat-harvest, when I came to Oare, having walked all the way from London, and being somewhat footsore. But how shall I tell you the things I felt, and the swelling of my heart within me, as I drew nearer, and more near, to the place of all I loved and owned, to the haunt of every warm remembrance, the next of all the fledgeling hopes – in a word, to home? It would take me all the afternoon to lay before you one-tenth of the things which came home to me as the sun was sinking, in the real way he ought to sink.

What mother thought I cannot tell; and indeed I doubt if she thought at all for more than half-an-hour, but only managed to hold me tight, and cry, and thank God now and then; but with some fear of His taking me, if she should be too grateful. And though I could see they were disappointed at my failure of any promotion, they all declared how glad they were, and how much better they liked me to be no more than what they were accustomed to. At least, my mother and Annie said so, without waiting to hear any more; but Lizzie did not answer to it, until I had opened my bag and shown the beautiful present I had for her. And then she kissed me, almost like Annie, and vowed that she thought very little of captains.

For Lizzie's present was the best of all, I mean of course except Lorna's (which I carried in my breast all the way, hoping that it might make her love me, from having lain so long, close to my heart). For I had brought Lizzie something dear, and a precious heavy book it was, and much beyond my understanding: whereas I knew well that to both the others my gifts would be dear for mine own sake. And happier people could not be found, than the whole of us were that evening.

Much as I longed to know more about Lorna, and though all my heart was yearning, I could not reconcile it yet with my duty to mother and Annie, to leave them on the following day, which happened to be a Sunday.

I felt much inclined to tell dear mother all about Lorna, and how I loved her, yet had no hope of winning her. Often and often I had longed to do this, and have done with it. But the thought of my father's terrible death, at the hands of the Doones, prevented me. And it seemed to me foolish and mean to grieve mother, without any chance of my suit ever speeding. If once Lorna loved me, my mother should know it; and it would be the greatest happiness to me to have no concealment from her, though at first she was sure to grieve terribly. But I saw no more chance of Lorna loving me, than of the man in the moon coming down; or rather of the moon coming down to the man, as related in old mythology.

Now, what did I do but take my chance; reckless whether any one heeded me or not, only craving Lorna's heed, and time for ten words to her. Therefore I left the men of the farm as far away as might be, after making them work with me (which no man round our parts could do, to his own satisfaction) and then knowing them to be well weary, very unlike to follow me – and still more unlike to tell of me, for each had his London present – I strode right away, in good trust of my speed, without any more misgivings; but resolved to face the worst of it, and to try to be home for supper.

And first I went, I know not why, to the crest of the broken highland, whence I had agreed to watch for any mark or signal. And sure enough at last I saw (when it was too late to see) that the white stone had been covered over with a cloth or mantle, – the sign that something had arisen to make Lorna want me. For a moment, I stood amazed at my evil fortune; that I should be too late, in the very thing of all things on which my heart was set! Then after eyeing sorrowfully every crick and cranny, to be sure that not a single flutter of my love was visible, off I set, with small respect either for my knees or neck, to make the round of the outer cliffs, and come up my old access.

Nothing could stop me; it was not long, although to me it seemed an age, before I stood in the niche of rock at the head of the slippery watercourse, and gazed into the quiet glen, where my foolish heart was dwelling. Notwithstanding doubts of right, notwithstanding sense of duty, and despite all manly striving, and the great love of my home, there my heart was ever dwelling, knowing what a fool it was, and content to know it.

At last, a little figure came, not insignificant (I mean), but looking very light and slender in the moving shadows, gently here and softly there, as if vague of purpose, with a gloss of tender movement, in and out the wealth of trees, and liberty of the meadow. Who was I to crouch, or doubt, or look at her from a distance; what matter if they killed me now, an one tear came to bury me? Therefore I rushed out at once, as if shot-guns were unknown yet; not from any real courage, but from prisoned love burst forth.

I know not whether my own Lorna was afraid of what I looked, or what I might say to her, or of her own thoughts of me: all I know is that she looked frightened, when I hoped for gladness. Perhaps the power of my joy was more than maiden liked to own, or in any way to answer to; and to tell the truth, it seemed as if I might now forget myself; while she would take good care of it. This makes a man grow thoughtful; unless as some low fellows do, he believe all women hypocrites.

Therefore I went slowly towards her, taken back in my impulse; and said all I could come to say, with some distress in doing it.

'Mistress Lorna, I had hope that you were in need of me.'

'Oh, yes; but that was long ago; two months ago, or more, sir.' And saying this she looked away, as if it all were over. But I was now so dazed and frightened, that it took my breath away, and I could not answer, feeling sure that I was robbed, and some one else had won her. And I tried to turn away, without another word, and go.

But I could not help one stupid sob, though mad with myself for allowing it, but it came too sharp for pride to stay it, and it told a world of things. Lorna heard it, and ran to me, with her bright eyes full of wonder, pity, and great kindness, as if amazed that I had more than a simple liking for her. Then she held out both hands to me; and I took and looked at them.

'Master Ridd, I did not mean,' she whispered, very softly, 'I did not mean to vex you.'

'If you would be loth to vex me, none else in this world can do it,' I answered out of my great love, but fearing yet to look at her, mine eyes not being strong enough.

'Come away from this bright place,' she answered, trembling in her turn; 'I am watched and spied of late. Come beneath the shadows, John.'

She led me to her own rich bower, which I told of once before; and if in spring it were a sight, what was it in summer glory? But although my mind had notice of its fairness and its wonder, not a heed my heart took of it, neither dwelt it in my presence more than flowing water. All that in my presence dwelt, all that in my heart was felt, was the maiden moving gently, and afraid to look at me.

For now the power of my love was abiding on her, new to her, unknown to her; not a thing to speak about, nor even to think clearly; only just to feel and wonder, with a pain of sweetness. She could look at me no more, neither could she look away, with a studied manner – only to let fall her eyes, and blush, and be put out with me, and still more with herself.

I left her quite alone; though close, though tingling to have hold of her. Even her right hand was dropped, and lay among the mosses. Neither did I try to steal one glimpse below her eyelids. Life and death were hanging on the first glance I should win; yet I let it be so.

After long or short – I know not, yet ere I was weary, ere I yet began to think or wish for any answer – Lorna slowly raised her eyelids, with a gleam of dew below them, and looked at me doubtfully. Any look with so much in it never met my gaze before.

'Darling, do you love me?' was all that I could say to her.

'Yes, I like you very much,' she answered, with her eyes gone from me, and her dark hair falling over, so as not to show me things.

'But do you love me, Lorna; Lorna, do you love me more than all the world?'

'No, to be sure not. Now why should I?'

'In truth, I know not why you should. Only I hoped that you did, Lorna. Either love me not at all, or as I love you, for ever.'

'John, I love you very much; and I would not grieve you. You are the bravest, and the kindest, and the simplest of all men – I mean of all people – I like you very much, Master Ridd, and I think of you almost every day.'

'That will not do for me, Lorna. Not almost every day I think, but every instant of my life, of you. For you I would give up my home, my love of all the world beside, my duty to my dearest ones; for you I would give up my life, and hope of life beyond it. Do you love me so?'

'Not by any means,' said Lorna; 'no; I like you very much, when you do not talk so wildly; and I like to see you come as if you would fill our valley up, and I like to think that even Carver would be nothing in your hands – but as to liking you like that, what should make it likely? especially when I have made the signal, and for some two months or more, you have never even answered it! If you like me so ferociously, why do you leave me for other people to do just as they like with me?'

'To do as they like! Oh, Lorna, not to make you marry Carver?'

'No, Master Ridd, be not frightened so; it makes me fear to look at you.'

'But you have not married Carver yet? Say quick! Why keep me waiting so?'

'Of course I have not, Master Ridd. Should I be here if I had, think you, and allowing you to like me so, and to hold my hand, and make me laugh, as I declare you almost do sometimes? And at other times you frighten me.'

'Did they want you to marry Carver? Tell me all the truth of it.'

'Not yet, not yet. They are not half so impetuous as you are, John. I am only just seventeen, you know, and who is to think of marrying? But they wanted me to give my word, and be formally betrothed to him in the presence of my grandfather. It seems that something frightened them. There is a youth named Charleworth Doone, every one calls him "Charlie;" a headstrong and gay young man, very gallant in his looks and manner; and my uncle, the Counsellor, chose to fancy that Charlie looked at me too much, coming by my grandfather's cottage.'

Here Lorna blushed so that I was frightened, and began to hate this Charlie more, a great deal more, than even Carver Doone.

'He had better not,' said I; 'I will fling him over it, if he dare. He shall see thee through the roof, Lorna, if at all he see thee.'

'Master Ridd, you are worse than Carver! I thought you were so kind-hearted. Well, they wanted me to promise, and even to swear a solemn oath (a thing I have never done in my life) that I would wed my eldest cousin, this same Carver Doone, who is twice as old as I am, being thirty-five and upwards. That was why I gave the token that I wished to see you, Master Ridd. They pointed out how much it was for the peace of all the family, and for mine own benefit; but I would not listen for a moment, though the Counsellor was most eloquent, and my grandfather begged me to consider, and Carver smiled his pleasantest, which is a truly frightful thing. Then both he and his crafty father were for using force with me; but Sir Ensor would not hear of it; and they have put off that extreme, until he shall be past its knowledge, or, at least, beyond preventing it. And now I am watched, and spied, and followed, and half my little liberty seems to be taken from me. I could not be here speaking with you, even in my own nook and refuge, but for the aid, and skill, and courage of dear little Gwenny Carfax. She is now my chief reliance, and through her alone I hope to baffle all my enemies, since others have forsaken me.'

Tears of sorrow and reproach were lurking in her soft dark eyes, until in fewest words I told her, that my seeming negligence was nothing but my bitter loss and wretched absence far away; of which I had so vainly striven to give any tidings – without danger to her. When she heard all this, and saw what I had brought from London (which was nothing less than a ring of pearls with a sapphire in the midst of them, as pretty as could well be found), she let the gentle tears flow fast, and came and sat so close beside me, that I trembled like a folded sheep at the bleating of her lamb. But recovering comfort quickly, without more ado, I raised her left hand, and observed it with a nice regard, wondering at the small blue veins, and curves, and tapering whiteness, and the points it finished with. My wonder seemed to please her much, herself so well accustomed to it, and not fond of watching it. And then, before she could say a word, or guess what I was up to, as quick as ever I turned hand at a bout of wrestling, on her finger was my ring – sapphire for the veins of blue, and pearls to match white fingers.

'Oh, you crafty Master Ridd!' said Lorna, looking up at me, and blushing now a far brighter blush than when she spoke of Charlie; 'I thought that you were much too simple ever to do this sort of thing. No wonder you can catch the fish, as when first I saw you.'

'Have I caught you, little fish? Or must all my life be spent in hopeless angling for you? '

'Neither one, nor the other, John! You have not caught me yet altogether, though I like you dearly, John; and if you will only keep away, I shall like you more and more. As for hopeless angling, John – that all others shall have until I tell you otherwise.'

With the large tears in her eyes – tears which seemed to me to rise partly from her want to love me with the power of my love – she put her pure bright lips, half smiling, half prone to reply to tears, against my forehead lined with trouble, doubt, and eager longing. And then she drew my ring from off that snowy twig her finger, and held it out to me; and then, seeing how my face was falling, thrice she touched it with her lips, and sweetly gave it back to me. 'John, I dare not take it now else I should be cheating you. I will try to love you dearly, even as you deserve and wish. Keep it for me just till then. Something tells me I shall earn it, in a very little time. Perhaps you will be sorry then, sorry when it is all too late, to be loved by such as I am.'

What could I do at her mournful tone, but kiss a thousand times the hand which she put up to warn me, and vow that I would rather die with one assurance of her love, than without it live for ever, with all beside that the world could give?

'Now, John,' said Lorna, being so quick that not even a lover could cheat her, and observing my confusion more intently than she need have done. 'Master John Ridd, it is high time for you to go home to your mother. I love your mother very much, from what you have told me about her, and I will not have her cheated.'

'If you truly love my mother,' said I, very craftily, 'the only way to show it is by truly loving me.'

Upon that, she laughed at me in the sweetest manner, and with such provoking ways, and such come-and-go of glances and beginning of quick blushes, which she tried to laugh away; that I knew, as well as if she herself had told me, by some knowledge (void of reasoning, and the surer for it), I knew quite well, while all my heart was burning hot within me, and mine eyes were shy of hers, and her eyes were shy of mine; for certain and for ever this I knew – as in a glory – that Lorna Doone had now begun, and would go on, to love me.

Although I was under interdict for two months from my darling – 'one for your sake, one for mine,' she had whispered, with her head withdrawn, yet not so very far from me – lighter heart was not on Exmoor than I bore for half the time, and even for three quarters. For she was safe; I knew that daily by a mode of signals, well-contrived between us now, on the strength of our experience. 'I have nothing now to fear, John,' she had said to me, as we parted; 'it is true that I am spied and watched, but Gwenny is too keen for them. While I have my grandfather to prevent all violence;

and little Gwenny to keep watch on those who try to watch me; and you above all others, John, ready at a moment, if the worst comes to the worst – this neglected Lorna Doone was never in such case before. Therefore do not squeeze my hand, John; I am safe without it, and you do not know your strength.'

Ah, I knew my strength right well. Hill and valley scarcely seemed to be step and landing for me; fiercest cattle I would play with, making them go backward, and afraid of hurting them, like John Fry with his terrier; even rooted trees seemed to me but as sticks I could smite down, except for my love of every thing. The love of all things was upon me, and a softness to them all, and a sense of having something even such as they had.

14

Annie Gets the Best of It

I had long outgrown unwholesome feeling as to my father's death; and so had Annie; though Lizzie (who must have loved him least) still entertained some evil will, and longing for a punishment. Therefore I was surprised (and indeed, startled would not be too much to say, the moon being somewhat fleecy) to see our Annie sitting there as motionless as the tombstone, and with all her best fal-lals upon her, after stowing away the dishes.

'What are you doing here, Annie?' I enquired rather sternly, being vexed with her for having gone so very near to frighten me.

'Nothing at all,' said our Annie shortly.

'Why, how so?' said I; 'Miss Annie, what business have you here, doing nothing at this time of night? And leaving me with all the trouble to entertain our guests!'

'You seem not to me to be doing it, John,' Annie answered softly; 'what business have you here doing nothing, at this time of night?

I was taken so aback with this, and the extreme impertinence of it, from a mere young girl like Annie, that I turned round to march away and have nothing more to say to her. But she jumped up, and caught me by the hand, and threw herself upon my bosom, with her face all wet with tears.

'Oh, John, I will tell you. I will tell you. Only don't be angry, John.'

'Angry! no indeed, 'said I; 'what right have I to be angry

with you, because you have your secrets? Every chit of a girl thinks now that she has a right to her secrets.'

'And you have none of your own, John; of course you have none of your own? All your going out at night – '

'We will not quarrel here, poor Annie,' I answered, with some loftiness; 'there are many things upon my mind, which girls can have no notion of.'

'And so there are upon mine, John. Oh, John, I will tell you everything, if you will look at me kindly, and promise to forgive me. Oh, I am so miserable! You are very hard on me, John; but I know you mean it for the best. If somebody else – I am sure I don't know who, and have no right to know no doubt, but she must be a wicked thing – if somebody else had been taken so with a pain all round the heart, John, and no power of telling it, perhaps you would have coaxed, and kissed her, and come a little nearer, and made opportunity to be very loving.'

Now this was so exactly what I had tried to do to Lorna, that my breath was almost taken away at Annie's so describing it. For a while I could not say a word, but wondered if she were a witch, which had never been in our family: and then, all of a sudden, I saw the way to beat her, with the devil at my elbow.

'From your knowledge of these things, Annie, you must have had them done to you. I demand to know this very moment who has taken such liberties.'

'Then, John, you shall never know, if you ask in that manner. Besides it was no liberty in the least at all. Cousins have a right to do things – and when they are one's god-father – ' Here Annie stopped quite suddenly, having so betrayed herself; but met me in the full moonlight, being resolved to face it out, with a good face upon it.

'Alas, I feared it would come to this,' I answered very sadly; 'I know he has been here many a time, without showing himself to me. There is nothing meaner than for a man to sneak, and steal a young maid's heart, without her people know it.'

'You are not doing anything of that sort yourself, then, dear John, are you!'

'Only a common highwayman!' I answered, without heeding her; 'a man without an acre of his own, and liable to hang upon any common, and no other right of common over it – '

'John,' said my sister, 'are the Doones privileged not to be hanged upon common land?'

At this I was so thunderstruck, that I leaped in the air like a shot rabbit, and rushed as hard as I could through the gate and across the yard, and back into the kitchen; and there I asked Farmer Nicholas Snowe to give me some tobacco, and to lend me a spare pipe.

This he did with a graceful manner, being now some five-fourths gone; and so I smoked the very first pipe that ever had entered my lips till then; and beyond a doubt it did me good, and spread my heart at leisure.

Now by the time I had almost finished smoking that pipe of tobacco, and wondering at myself for having so despised it hitherto, and making up my mind to have another trial tomorrow night, it began to occur to me that although dear Annie had behaved so very badly and rudely, and almost taken my breath away with the suddenness of her allusion, yet it was not kind of me to leave her out there at that time of night, all alone, and in such distress.

Therefore I went forth at once, bearing my pipe in a skilful manner, as I had seen Farmer Nicholas do; and marking, with a new kind of pleasure, how the rings and wreaths of smoke hovered and fluttered in the moonlight, like a lark upon his carol. Poor Annie was gone back again to our father's grave; and there she sat upon the turf, sobbing very gently, and not wishing to trouble any one. So I raised her tenderly, and made much of her, and consoled her, for I could not scold her there; and perhaps after all she was not to be blamed so much as Tom Faggus himself was. Annie was very grateful to me, and kissed me many times, and begged my pardon ever so often for her rudeness to me. And then having gone so far with it, and finding me so complaisant, she must needs try to go a little further, and to lead me away from her own affairs, and into mine concerning Lorna. But although it was clever enough of her, she was not deep enough for me there; and I soon discovered that she knew nothing, not even the name of my darling; but only suspected from things she had seen, and put together like a woman. Upon this I brought her back again to Tom Faggus and his doings.

'My poor Annie, have you really promised him to be his wife?'

'I to marry before my brother, and leave him with none to take care of him! Who can do him a red deer collop, except Sally Snowe herself, as I can? – Come home, dear, at once, and I will do one for you; for you never ate a morsel of supper, with all the people you had to attend upon.'

This was true enough; and seeing no chance of anything more than cross questions and crooked purposes, at which a girl was sure to beat me, I even allowed her to lead me home, with the thoughts of the collop uppermost. But I never counted upon being beaten so thoroughly as I was; for knowing me now to be off my guard, the young hussy stopped at the farmyard gate, as if with a briar entangling her, and while I was stooping to take it away, she looked me full in the face by the moonlight, and jerked out quite suddenly, –

'Can your love do a collop, John?'

'No, I should hope not,' I answered rashly; 'she is not a mere cook-maid I should hope.'

'She is not half so pretty as Sally Snowe; I will answer for that,' said Annie.

'She is ten thousand times as pretty as ten thousand Sally Snowes,' I replied with great indignation.

'Oh, but look at Sally's eyes!' cried my sister rapturously.

'Look at Lorna Doone's,' said I; 'and you would never look again at Sally's.'

'Oh, Lorna Doone, Lorna Doone!' exclaimed our Annie, half-frightened, yet clapping her hands with triumph, at having found me out so: 'Lorna Doone is the lovely maiden, who has stolen poor somebody's heart so. Ah, I shall remember it; because it is so queer a name. But stop, I had better write it down. Lend me your hat, poor boy, to write on.'

'I have a great mind to lend you a box on the ear,' I answered her in my vexation; 'and I would, if you had not been crying so, you sly good-for-nothing baggage. As it is, I shall keep it for Master Faggus, and add interest for keeping.'

'Oh no, John; oh no, John,' she begged me earnestly, being sobered in a moment. 'Your hand is so terribly heavy, John; and he never would forgive you; although he is so good-hearted, he cannot put up with an insult. Promise me, dear John, that you will not strike him; and I will promise you faithfully to keep your secret, even from mother, and even from Cousin Tom himself.'

'And from Lizzie; most of all, from Lizzie,' I answered, very eagerly, knowing too well which one of my family would be hardest with me.

'Of course from little Lizzie,' said Annie, with some contempt; 'a young thing like her cannot be kept too long, in my opinion, from the knowledge of such subjects. And besides, I should be very sorry if Lizzie had the right to know your secrets, as I have, dearest John. Not a soul shall be the wiser for your having trusted me, John; although I shall be very wretched when you are late away at night, among these dreadful people.'

'Well, 'I replied, 'it is no use crying over spilt milk, Annie. You have my secret, and I have yours; and I scarcely know which of the two is likely to have the worst time of it, when it comes to mother's ears. I could put up with perpetual scolding; but not with mother's sad silence.'

'That is exactly how I feel, John;' and as Annie said it she brightened up, and her soft eyes shone upon me. We entered the house quite gently thus, and found farmer Nicholas Snowe asleep.

And dear Annie gave me a little push into the parlour, where I entered to meet Sally Snowe. And I made up my mind to examine her well, and try a little courting with her, if she should lead me on, that I might be in practice for Lorna. But when I perceived how grandly and richly the damsel was apparelled; and how, in her courtesies to me, she retreated, as if I were making up to her, in a way she had learned from Exeter; and how she began to talk of the Court, as if she had been there all her life, and the latest mode of the Duchess of this, and the profile of the Countess of that, and the last good saying of my Lord something; instead of butter, and cream, and eggs, and things which she understood; I knew there must be somebody in the room besides me to talk at.

And so there was; for behind the curtain drawn across the window-seat, no less a man than Uncle Ben was sitting half asleep and weary; and by his side a little girl, very quiet and very watchful. My mother led me to Uncle Ben, and he took my hand without rising, muttering something not over-polite, about my being bigger than ever. I asked him heartily how he was, and he said, 'Well enough, for that matter; but none the better for the noise you great clods have been making.'

'I am sorry if we have disturbed you, sir,' I answered very civilly; 'but I knew not that you were here even; and you must allow for harvest time.'

'So it seems, 'he replied; 'and allow a great deal, including waste and drunkenness. Now (if you can see so small a thing, after emptying flagons much larger) this is my granddaughter, and my heiress' – here he glanced at mother – 'my heiress, little Ruth Huckaback.'

'I am very glad to see you, Ruth,' I answered, offering her my hand, which she seemed afraid to take; 'welcome to Plover's Barrows, my good cousin Ruth.'

However, my good cousin Ruth only arose, and made me a courtesy, and lifted her great brown eyes at me, more in fear, as I thought, than kinship. And if ever any one looked unlike the heiress to great property, it was the little girl before me.

15

An Early-Morning Call

We kept up very late that night, mother being in such wonderful spirits, that she would not hear of our going to bed: while she glanced from young Squire Marwood, very deep in his talk with our Annie, to me and Ruth Huckaback, who were beginning to be very pleasant company. Alas, poor mother, so proud as she was, how little she dreamed that her good schemes already were hopelessly going awry!

Being forced to be up before daylight next day, in order to begin right early, I would not go to my bedroom that night, for fear of disturbing my mother, but determined to sleep in the tallat awhile, that place being cool, and airy, and refreshing with the smell of sweet hay. Moreover, after my dwelling in town, where I had felt like a horse on a lime-kiln, I could not for a length of time have enough of country life. The mooing of a calf was music, and the chuckle of a fowl was wit, and the snore of the horses was news to me.

'Wult have thee own wai, I rackon,' said Betty, being cross with sleepiness, for she had washed up everything; 'slape in hog-pound, if thee laikes, Jan.'

Letting her have the last word of it (as is the due of women) I stood in the court, and wondered awhile at the glory of the harvest moon, and the yellow world it shone upon. Then I saw, as sure as I was standing there in the shadow of the stable, I saw a short wide figure glide across the foot of the courtyard, between me and the six-barred gate. Instead of running after it, as I should have done, I began to consider who it could be, and what on earth it was doing there, when all our people were in bed, and the reapers gone home, or to the linhay close against the wheatfield.

Having made up my mind at last, that it could be none of our people – though not a dog was barking – and also that it must have been either a girl or a woman, I ran down with all speed to learn what might be the meaning of it. But I came too late to learn, through my own hesitation; for this was the lower end of the courtyard, not the approach from the parish highway, but the end of the sledd-way across the fields where the brook goes down to the Lynn stream. And here the dry channel of the brook, being scarcely any water now, afforded plenty of place to hide, leading also to a little coppice, beyond our cabbage-garden, and so further on to the parish highway.

I saw at once that it was vain to make any pursuit by moonlight; and resolving to hold my own counsel about it (though puzzled not a little) and to keep watch there another night, back I returned to the tallat-ladder, and slept without leaving off till morning.

Now many people may wish to know, as indeed I myself did very greatly, what had brought Master Huckaback over from Dulverton, at that time of year, when the clothing business was most active on account of harvest wages.

He seemed in no hurry to take his departure, though his visit was so inconvenient to us, as himself indeed must have noticed: and presently Lizzie, who was the sharpest among us, said in my hearing that she believed he had purposely timed his visit so that he might have liberty to pursue his own object, whatsoever it were, without interruption from us. Mother gazed hard upon Lizzie at this, having formed a very different opinion; but Annie and myself agreed that it was worth looking into.

For his mode was directly after breakfast to pray to the Lord a little (which used not to be his practice), and then to go forth upon Dolly, the which was our Annie's pony, very quiet and respectful, with bag of good victuals hung behind him, and two great cavalry pistols in front. He never returned until dark or more, just in time to be in before us, who were coming home from the harvest. And then Dolly always seemed very weary, and stained with a muck from beyond our parish.

But I refused to follow him, not only for the loss of a day's work to myself and at least half a day to the other men, but chiefly because I could not think that it would be upright and manly. It was all very well to creep warily into the valley of the Doones, and heed every thing around me, both because they were public enemies, and also because I risked my life at every step I took there. But as to tracking a feeble old man (however subtle he might be), a guest moreover of our own, and a relative through my mother – 'Once for all,' I said, 'it is below me, and I won't do it.'

Before I could quite make up my mind how to act in this difficulty, and how to get at the rights of it (for I would not spy after Uncle Reuben, though I felt no great fear of the Wizard's Slough, and none of the man with white night-cap), a difference came again upon it, and a change of chances. For Uncle Ben went away, as suddenly as he first had come to us, giving no reason for his departure.

By this time, the harvest being done, and the thatching of the ricks made sure against south-western tempests, and all the reapers being gone, with good money and thankfulness, I began to burn in spirit for the sight of Lorna.

Inasmuch as there are two sorts of month well recognised by the calendar, to wit the lunar and the solar, I made bold to regard both my months, in the absence of any provision, as intended to be strictly lunar. Therefore upon the very day when the eight weeks were expiring, forth I went in search of Lorna, taking the pearl ring hopefully, and all the new-laid eggs I could find, and a dozen and a half of small trout from our brook. And the pleasure it gave me to catch those trout, thinking as every one came forth and danced upon the grass, how much she would enjoy him, is more than I can now describe, although I well remember it. And it struck me, that after accepting my ring, and saying how much she loved me, it was possible that my sweet might invite me even to stay and sup with her; and so I arranged with dear Annie beforehand, who now was the greatest comfort to me, to account for my absence if I should be late.

But alas, I was utterly disappointed; for although I waited and waited for hours, with an equal amount both of patience and peril, no Lorna ever appeared at all, nor even the faintest sign of her. Having waited until there was no chance whatever of my love appearing, I hastened homeward very sadly; and the wind of early autumn moaned across the moorland.

Now that same night I think it was, or at any rate the next one, that I noticed Betty Muxworthy going on most strangely. She made the queerest signs to me, when nobody was looking, and laid her fingers on her lips, and pointed over her shoulder. But I took little heed of her, being in a kind of dudgeon, and oppressed with evil luck; believing too that all she wanted, was to have some little grumble about some petty grievance.

But presently she poked me with the heel of a fire-bundle, and passing close to my ear whispered, so that none else could hear her, 'Larna Doo-un.'

By these words I was so startled, that I turned round and stared at her; but she pretended not to know it, and began with all her might to scour an empty crock with a besom.

'Oh, Betty, let me help you! That work is much too hard for you,' I cried with a sudden chivalry, which only won rude answer.

'Zeed me adooing of thic, every naight last ten year, Jan, wiout vindin' out how hard it wor. But if zo bee thee wants to help, carr pegs' bucket for me. Massy, if I ain't forgotten to fade the pegs till now.'

Favouring me with another wink, to which I now paid the keenest heed, Betty went and fetched the lanthorn from the hook inside the door. Then when she had kindled it, not allowing me any time to ask what she was after, she went outside, and pointed to the great bock of wash, and riddlings, and brown hulkage (for we ground our own corn always), and though she knew that Bill Dadds and Jem Slocombe had full work to carry it on a pole (with another to help to sling it), she said to me as quietly as a maiden might ask one to carry a glove, 'Jan Ridd, carr thic thing for me.'

So I carried it for her, without any words; wondering what

she was up to next, and whether she had ever heard of being too hard on the willing horse. And when we came to hog-pound, she turned upon me suddenly, with the lanthorn she was bearing, and saw that I had the bock by one hand very easily.

'Jan Ridd,' she said, 'there be no other man in England cud a'dood it. Now thee shalt have Larna.'

Then she whispered in my ear, 'Goo of a marning, thee girt soft. Her can't get out of an avening now, her hath zent word to me, to tull 'ee.'

In the glory of my delight at this, I bestowed upon Betty a chaste salute, and she took it not amiss, considering how long she had been out of practice. But she fell back then, like a broom on its handle, and stared at me, feigning anger.

'Oh fai, oh fai! Lunnon impudence, I doubt. I vear thee hast gone on zadly, Jan.'

Of course I was up the very next morning before the October sunrise, and away through the wild and the wood-land towards the Bagworthy water, at the foot of the long cascade. The rising of the sun was noble in the cold and warmth of it; peeping down the spread of light, he raised his shoulder heavily over the edge of grey mountain, and waver-ing length of upland. Beneath his gaze the dew-fogs dipped, and crept to the hollow places; then stole away in line and column, holding skirts, and clinging subtly at the sheltering corner where rock hung over grass-land; while the brave lines of the hills came forth, one beyond other gliding.

I saw my Lorna coming, purer than the morning dew, than the sun more bright and clear. That which made me love her so, that which lifted my heart to her, as the Spring wind lifts the clouds, was the gayness of her nature, and its inborn playfulness. And yet all this with maiden shame, a conscious dream of things unknown, and a sense of fate about them.

Down the valley still she came, not witting that I looked at her, having ceased (through my own misprision) to expect me yet awhile; or at least she told herself so. In the joy of awakened life, and brightness of the morning, she had cast all care away, and seemed to float upon the sunrise, like a buoyant silver wave. Suddenly at sight of me, for I leaped forth at once, in fear of seeming to watch her unawares, the bloom upon her cheeks was deepened, and the radiance of her eyes; and she came to meet me gladly.

'At last then, you are come, John. I thought you had forgotten me. I could not make you understand – they have kept me prisoner every evening: but come into my house; you are in danger here.'

Meanwhile I could not answer, being overcome with joy; but followed to her little grotto, where I had been twice before. I knew that the crowning moment of my life was coming – that Lorna would own her love for me.

She made for awhile as if she dreamed not of the meaning of my gaze, but tried to speak of other things, faltering now and then, and mantling with a richer damask below her long eyelashes.

'This is not what I came to know,' I whispered very softly; 'you know what I am come to ask.'

'If you are come on purpose to ask anything, why do you delay so?' She turned away very bravely, but I saw her lips were trembling.

'I delay so long, because I fear; because my whole life hangs in balance on a single word; because what I have near me now may never more be near me after, though more than all the world, or than a thousand worlds, to me.' As I spoke these words of passion in a low soft voice, Lorna trembled more and more; but she made no answer, neither yet looked up at me.

'I have loved you long and long,' I pursued, being reckless now; 'when you were a little child, as a boy I worshipped you: then when I saw you a comely girl, as a stripling I adored you: now that you are a full-grown maiden, all the rest I do, and more, – I love you, more than tongue can tell, or heart can hold in silence. I have waited long and long; and though I am so far below you, I can wait no longer; but must have my answer.'

'You have been very faithful, John,' she murmured to the fern and moss; 'I suppose I must reward you.'

'That will not do for me,' I said; 'I will not have reluctant liking, nor assent for pity's sake; which only means endurance.

I must have all love, or none; I must have your heart of hearts; even as you have mine, Lorna.'

While I spoke, she glanced up shyly through her fluttering lashes, to prolong my doubt one moment, for her own delicious pride. Then she opened wide upon me all the glorious depth and softness of her loving eyes, and flung both arms around my neck, and answered with her heart on mine –

'Darling, you have won it all. I shall never be my own again. I am yours, my own one, for ever and for ever.'

I am sure I know not what I did, or what I said thereafter, being overcome with transport by her words and at her gaze. Only one thing I remember, when she raised her bright lips to me, like a child, for me to kiss, such a smile of sweet temptation met me through her flowing hair, that I almost forgot my manners, giving her no time to breathe.

'That will do,' said Lorna gently, but violently blushing; 'for the present that will do, John. And now remember one thing, dear. All the kindness is to be on my side; and you are to be very distant, as behoves to a young maiden; except when I invite you. But you may kiss my hand, John; oh yes, you may kiss my hand, you know. Ah to be sure! I had forgotten; how very stupid of me!'

For by this time I had taken one sweet hand and gazed on it, with the pride of all the world to think that such a lovely thing was mine; and then I slipped my little ring upon the wedding finger; and this time Lorna kept it, and looked with fondness on its beauty, and clung to me with a flood of tears.

'Every time you cry,' said I, drawing her closer to me, 'I shall consider it an invitation not to be too distant. There now, none shall make you weep. Darling, you shall sigh no more, but live in peace and happiness, with me to guard and cherish you: and who shall dare to vex you?' But she drew a long sad sigh, and looked at the ground with the great tears rolling, and pressed one hand upon the trouble of her pure young breast.

'It can never, never, be,' she murmured to herself alone: 'Who am I, to dream of it? Something in my heart tells me, it can be so never, never.'

16

Two Negatives Make an Affirmative

There was, however, no possibility of depressing me at such a time. To be loved by Lorna, the sweet, the pure, the playful one, the fairest creature on God's earth and the most enchanting, the lady of high birth and mind; that I, a mere clumsy blundering yeoman, without wit, or wealth, or lineage, should have won that loving heart to be my own for ever, was a thought no fears could lessen, and no chance could steal from me.

Therefore, at her own entreaty taking a very quick adieu, and by her own invitation an exceeding kind one, I hurried home with deep exulting, yet some sad misgivings, for Lorna had made me promise to tell my mother every thing; as indeed I always meant to do, when my suit should be gone too far to stop.

Unluckily for my designs, who should be sitting down at breakfast with my mother and the rest but Squire Faggus, as everybody now began to entitle him? I noticed something odd about him, something uncomfortable in his manner, and a lack of that ease and humour, which had been wont to distinguish him. He took his breakfast as it came, without a single joke about it, or preference of this to that; but with sly soft looks at Annie, who seemed unable to sit quiet, or to look at any one steadfastly. I feared in my heart what was coming on, and felt truly sorry for poor mother. After breakfast it became my duty to see to the ploughing of a barley-stubble ready for the sowing of French grass, and I asked Tom Faggus to come with me; but he refused, and I knew the reason. Being resolved to allow him fair field to himself, though with great displeasure that a man of such illegal repute should marry into our family, which had always been counted so honest, I carried my dinner upon my back, and spent the whole day with the furrows.

When I returned, Squire Faggus was gone; which appeared to me but a sorry sign, inasmuch as if mother had taken kindly to him and to his intentions, she would surely have made him remain awhile to celebrate the occasion. And presently no doubt was left: for Lizzie came running to meet me, at the bottom of the woodrick, and cried, –

'Oh John, there is such a business. Mother is in such a state of mind, and Annie crying her eyes out. What do you think? You never would guess; though I have suspected it, ever so long.'

'No need for me to guess,' I replied, as though with some indifference, because of her self-important air; 'I knew all about it long ago. You have not been crying much, I see. I should like you better, if you had.'

'Why should I cry? I like Tom Faggus. He is the only one I ever see with the spirit of a man.'

This was a cut, of course, at me. Mr Faggus had won the good will of Lizzie by his hatred of the Doones, and vows that if he could get a dozen men of any courage to join him, he would pull their stronghold about their ears without any more ado. This malice of his seemed strange to me, as he had never suffered at their hands, so far at least as I knew; was it to be attributed to his jealousy of outlaws who excelled him in his business? Not being good at repartee, I made no answer to Lizzie, having found this course more irksome to her than the very best invective: and so we entered the house together; and mother sent at once for me.

I would regret to write down what mother said about Lorna, in her first surprise and tribulation; not only because I was grieved by the gross injustice of it, and frightened mother with her own words (repeated deeply after her); but rather because it is not well, when people repent of hasty speech, to enter it against them.

However, by the afternoon, when the sun began to go down upon us, our mother sat on the garden bench, with her head on my great otter-skin waistcoat (which was waterproof), and her right arm round our Annie's waist, and scarcely knowing which of us she ought to make the most of, or which deserved most pity. Not that she had forgiven yet the rivals to her love – Tom Faggus, I mean, and Lorna, – but that she was beginning to think a little better of them now, and a vast deal better of her own children.

And it helped her much in this regard, that she was not thinking half so well as usual of herself, or rather of her own judgement; for in good truth she had no self, only as it came home to her, by no very distant road, but by way of her children. A better mother never lived; and can I, after searching all things, add another word to that?

Now, while we sate on the garden bench, under the great ash-tree, we left dear mother to take her own way, and talk at her own pleasure. Children almost always are more wideawake than their parents. The fathers and the mothers laugh; but the young ones have the best of them. And now both Annie knew, and I, that we had gotten the best of mother; and therefore we let her lay down the law, as if we had been two dollies.

'Darling John,' my mother said, 'your case is a very hard one. A young and very romantic girl – God send that I be right in my charitable view of her – has met an equally simple boy, among great dangers and difficulties, from which my son has saved her, at the risk of his life at every step. Of course, she became attached to him, and looked up to him in every way, as a superior being – '

'Come now, mother,' I said; 'if you only saw Lorna, you would look upon me as the lowest dirt – '

'No doubt I should,' my mother answered; 'and the king, and queen, and all the royal family. Well, this poor angel, having made up her mind to take compassion on my son, when he had saved her life so many times, persuades him to marry her out of pure pity, and throw his poor mother overboard. And the saddest part of it all is this – '

'That my mother will never, never, never understand the truth,' said I.

'That is all I wish,' she answered; 'just to get at the simple truth from my own perception of it. John, you are very wise in kissing me; but perhaps you would not be so wise in bringing Lorna for an afternoon, just to see what she thinks of me. There is a good saddle of mutton now; and there are some very good sausages left, on the blue dish with the anchor, Annie, from the last little sow we killed.'

'As if Lorna would eat sausages!' said I, with appearance of high contempt, though rejoicing all the while that mother seemed to have her name so pat; and she pronounced it in a manner which made my heart leap to my ears: 'Lorna to eat sausages!'

'I don't see why she shouldn't,' my mother answered smiling; 'if she means to be a farmer's wife, she must take to farmer's ways, I think. What do you say, Annie?'

'She will eat whatever John desires, I should hope,' said Annie gravely; 'particularly as I made them.'

'Oh that I could only get the chance of trying her!' I answered; 'if you could once behold her, mother, you would never let her go again. And she would love you with all her heart, she is so good and gentle.'

'That is a lucky thing for me;' saying this my mother wept, as she had been doing off and on, when no one seemed to look at her; 'otherwise I suppose, John, she would very soon turn me out of the farm, having you so completely under her thumb, as she seems to have. I see now that my time is over. Lizzie and I will seek our fortunes. It is wiser so.'

'Now, mother,' I cried; 'will you have the kindness not to talk any nonsense? Every thing belongs to you; and so, I hope, your children do. And you, in turn, belong to us; as you have proved ever since, – oh, ever since we can remember. Why do you make Annie cry so? You ought to know better than that.'

Mother upon this went over again all the things she had said before; how many times I know not; neither does it matter. Only she seemed to enjoy it more, every time of doing it. And then she said she was an old fool; and Annie (like a thorough girl) pulled her one grey hair out.

Although by our mother's reluctant consent a large part of the obstacles between Annie and her lover appeared to be removed, on the other hand Lorna and myself gained little, except as regarded comfort of mind, and some ease to the conscience.

After this, for another month, nothing worthy of notice happened, except perhaps that I found it needful, according to the strictest good sense and honour, to visit Lorna, immediately after my discourse with mother, and to tell her all about it. My beauty gave me one sweet kiss with all her heart (as she always did, when she kissed at all) and I begged for one more to take to our mother, and before leaving, I obtained it. It is not for me to tell all she said, even supposing (what is not likely) that any one cared to know it, being more and more peculiar to ourselves and no one else. But one thing that she said was this, and I took good care to carry it, word for word, to my mother and Annie: –

'I never can believe, dear John, that after all the crime and outrage wrought by my reckless family, it ever can be meant for me to settle down to peace and comfort in a simple household. With all my heart I long for home; any home, however dull and wearisome to those used to it, would seem a paradise to me, if only free from brawl and tumult, and such as I could call my own. But even if God would allow me this, in lieu of my wild inheritance, it is quite certain that the Doones never can, and never will.'

Again, when I told her how my mother and Annie, as well as myself, longed to have her at Plover's Barrows, and teach her all the quiet duties in which she was sure to take such delight, she only answered with a bright blush, that while her grandfather was living she would never leave him; and that even if she were free, certain ruin was all she should bring to any house that received her, at least within the utmost reach of her amiable family. This was too plain to be denied, and seeing my dejection at it, she told me bravely that we must hope for better times, if possible, and asked how long I would wait for her.

'Not a day if I had my will,' I answered very warmly; at which she turned away confused, and would not look at me for awhile; 'but all my life,' I went on to say, 'if my fortune is so ill. And how long would you wait for me, Lorna?'

'Till I could get you,' she answered slily, with a smile which was brighter to me than the brightest wit could be. 'And now,' she continued, 'you bound me, John, with a very beautiful ring to you, and when I dare not wear it, I carry it always on my heart. But I will bind you to me, you dearest, with the very poorest and plainest thing that ever you set eyes on. I could give you fifty fairer ones, but they would not be honest; and I love you for your honesty, and nothing else of course, John; so don't you be conceited. Look at it, what a queer old thing! There are some ancient marks upon it, very grotesque and wonderful; it looks like a cat in a tree almost; but never mind what it looks like. This old ring must have been a giant's; therefore it will fit you perhaps, you enormous John. It has been on the front of my old glass necklace (which my grandfather found them taking away, and very soon made them give back again) ever since I can remember; and long before that, as some woman told me. Now you seem very greatly amazed; pray what thinks my lord of it?'

'That it is worth fifty of the pearl thing which I gave you, you darling; and that I will not take it from you.'

'Then you will never take me, that is all. I will have nothing to do with a gentleman – '

'No gentleman, dear, – a yeoman.'

'Very well, a yeoman – nothing to do with a yeoman who will not accept my love-gage. So, if you please, give it back again, and take your lovely ring back.'

She looked at me in such a manner, half in earnest, half in jest, and three times three in love, that in spite of all good resolutions, and her own faint protest, I was forced to abandon all firm ideas, and kiss her till she was quite ashamed, and her head hung on my bosom, with the night of her hair shed over me. Then I placed the pearl ring back on the soft elastic bend of the finger she held up to scold me; and on my own smallest finger drew the heavy hoop she had given me. I considered this with satisfaction, until my darling recovered herself; and then I began very gravely about it, to keep her (if I could) from chiding me: –

'Mistress Lorna, this is not the ring of any giant. It is nothing more nor less than a very ancient thumb-ring, such as once in my father's time was ploughed up out of the ground in our farm, and sent to learned doctors, who told us all about it, but kept the ring for their trouble. I will accept it, my own one love; and it shall go to my grave with me.' And so it shall, unless there be villains who would dare to rob the dead.

Now I have spoken about this ring (though I scarcely meant to do so, and would rather keep to myself things so very holy) because it holds an important part in the history of my Lorna. I asked her where the glass necklace was, from which the ring was fastened, and which she had worn in her childhood, and she answered that she hardly knew, but remembered that her grandfather had begged her to give it up to him, when she was ten years old or so, and had promised to keep it for her, until she could take care of it; at the same time giving her back the ring, and fastening it from her pretty neck and telling her to be proud of it. And so she always had been, and now from her sweet breast she took it, and it became John Ridd's delight.

17

John Returns to Business

Now November was upon us, and we had kept Allhallowmass, with roasting of skewered apples (like so many shuttlecocks), and after that, the day of Fawkes, as became good Protestants, with merry bonfires and burned batatas, and plenty of good feeding in honour of our religion; and then while we were at wheat-sowing, another visitor arrived.

This was Master Jeremy Stickles, who had been a good friend to me (as described before) in London, and had earned my mother's gratitude, so far as ever he chose to have it. And he seemed inclined to have it all; for he made our farm-house his head-quarters, and kept us quite at his beck and call, going out at any time of the evening, and coming back at any time of the morning, and always expecting us to be ready, whether with horse, or man, or maidens, or fire, or provisions. We knew that he was employed somehow upon the service of the King, and had at different stations certain troopers and order-lies, quite at his disposal; also we knew that he never went out, nor even slept in his bedroom, without heavy firearms well loaded, and a sharp sword nigh his hand; and that he held a great commission, under royal signet, requiring all good subjects, all officers of whatever degree, and especially justices of the peace, to aid him to the utmost, with person, beast, and chattel, or to answer it at their peril.

Master Stickles was going forth upon his usual night journey, when he met me coming home, and I said something half in jest, about his zeal and secrecy; upon which he looked all around the yard, and led me to an open space in the clover field adjoining.

'John,' he said, 'you have some right to know the meaning of all this, being trusted as you were by the Lord Chief Justice. But he found you scarcely supple enough, neither gifted with due brains.'

'Thank God for that same,' I answered, while he tapped his head, to signify his own much larger allowance. Then he made me bind myself, which in an evil hour I did, to retain his secret; and after that he went on solemnly, and with much importance, –

'There be some people fit to plot, and others to be plotted against, and others to unravel plots, which is the highest gift of all. This last hath fallen to my share, and a very thankless gift it is, although a rare and choice one. Much of peril too attends it; daring courage and great coolness are as needful for the work as ready wit and spotless honour. Therefore His Majesty's advisers have chosen me for this high task, and they could not have chosen a better man. Although you have been in London, Jack, much longer than you wished it, you are wholly ignorant, of course, in matters of state, and the public weal. Now, heard you much in London town about the Duke of Monmouth?'

'Not so very much,' I answered; 'not half so much as in Devonshire: only that he was a hearty man, and a very handsome one, and now was banished by the Tories; and most people wished he was coming back, instead of the Duke of York, who was trying boots in Scotland.'

'Things are changed since you were in town. The Whigs are getting up again, through the folly of the Tories in killing poor Lord Russell; and now this Master Sidney (if my Lord condemns him) will make it worse again. There is much disaffection everywhere, and it must grow to an outbreak. Now, in ten words (without parties, or trying thy poor brain too much), I am here to watch the gathering of a secret plot, not so much against the King as against the due succession. Now hearken to one who wishes thee well, and plainly sees the end of it, – stick thou to the winning side, and have nought to do with the other one.'

'That,' said I, in great haste and hurry, 'is the very thing I want to do, if I only knew which was the winning side, for the sake of Lorna – that is to say, for the sake of my dear mother and sisters, and the farm.'

'Ha!' cried Jeremy Stickles, laughing at the redness of my face – 'Lorna, saidst thou; now what Lorna? Is it the name of a maiden, or a light-o'-love?'

'Keep to your own business,' I answered very proudly; 'spy as much as e'er thou wilt, and use our house for doing it, without asking leave or telling; but if I ever find thee spying into my affairs, all the King's lifeguards in London, and the dragoons thou bringest hither, shall not save thee from my hand – or one finger is enough for thee.'

Being carried beyond myself by his insolence about Lorna, I looked at Master Stickles so, and spake in such a voice, that all his daring courage and his spotless honour quailed within him, and he shrank – as if I would strike so small a man.

Then I left him, and went to work at the sacks upon the corn-floor, to take my evil spirit from me, before I should see mother.

But now my own affairs were thrown into such disorder, that I could think of nothing else, and had the greatest difficulty in hiding my uneasiness. For suddenly, without any warning, or a word of message, all my Lorna's signals ceased, which I had been wont to watch for daily, and as it were to feed upon them, with a glowing heart. The first time I stood on the wooded crest, and found no change from yesterday, I could hardly believe my eyes, or thought at least that it must be some great mistake on the part of my love. However, even that oppressed me with a heavy heart, which grew heavier, as I found from day to day no token.

Three times I went, and waited long at the bottom of the valley, where now the stream was brown and angry with the rains of autumn, and the weeping trees hung leafless. But though I waited at every hour of day and far into the night, no light footstep came to meet me, no sweet voice was in the air; all was lonely, drear, and drenched with sodden desolation. It seemed as if my love was dead, and the winds were at her funeral.

Once I sought far up the valley, where I had never been before, even beyond the copse, where Lorna had found and lost her brave young cousin. Following up the river channel, in the shelter of the evening fog, I gained a corner within stone's throw of the last outlying cot. This was a gloomy, low, square house, without any light in the windows, roughly built of wood and stone, as I saw when I drew nearer. For knowing it to be Carver's dwelling (or at least suspecting so, from some words of Lorna's), I was led by curiosity, and perhaps by jealousy, to have a closer look at it. Therefore, I crept up the stream, losing half my sense of fear, by reason of anxiety. And in truth there was not much to fear, the sky being now too dark for even a shooter of wild fowl to make good aim. And nothing else but guns could hurt me; as in the pride of my strength I thought, and in my skill of single-stick.

Nevertheless, I went warily, being now almost among this nest of cockatrices. The back of Carver's house abutted on the waves of the rushing stream; and seeing a loop-hole, vacant for muskets, I looked in, but all was quiet. So far as I could judge by listening, there was no one now inside, and my heart for a moment leaped with joy, for I had feared to find Lorna there. Then I took a careful survey of the dwelling, and its windows, and its door, and aspect, as if I had been a robber meaning to make privy entrance. It was well for me that I did this, as you will find hereafter.

Having impressed upon my mind (a slow but, perhaps, retentive mind) all the bearings of the place, and all its opportunities, and even the curve of the stream along it, and the bushes near the door, I was much inclined to go further up, and understand all the village. But a bar of red light across the river, some forty yards on above me, and crossing from the opposite side like a chain, prevented me. In that second house there was a gathering of loud and merry outlaws, making as much noise as if they had the law upon their side. Some indeed, as I approached, were laying down both right and wrong, as purely, and with as high a sense, as if they knew the difference. Cold and troubled as I was, I could hardly keep from laughing.

Before I betook myself home that night, and eased dear mother's heart so much, and made her sad face spread with smiles, I had resolved to penetrate Glen Doone from the upper end, and learn all about my Lorna. Not but what I might have entered from my unsuspected channel, as so often I had done; but that I saw fearful need for knowing something more than that. Here was every sort of trouble gathering upon me; here was Jeremy Stickles stealing upon every one in the dark; here was Uncle Reuben plotting, Satan only could tell what; here was my own sister Annie committed to a highwayman, and mother in distraction; most of all, – here, there, and where, – was my Lorna, stolen, dungeoned, perhaps outraged. It was no time for shilly shally, for the balance of this and that, or for a man, with blood and muscle, to pat his nose and ponder. If I left my Lorna so; if I let those black-soul'd villains work their pleasure on my love; if the heart that crave to mine could find no vigour in it – then let maidens cease from men, and rest their faith in tabby-cats.

Rudely rolling these ideas in my heavy head and brain, I resolved to let the morrow put them into form and order, but not contradict them. And then, as my constitution willed (being like that of England), I slept; and there was no stopping me.

18

A Very Desperate Venture

The enterprise now resolved upon was far more dangerous than any hitherto attempted by me.

The journey was a great deal longer to fetch around the Southern hills, and enter by the Doone-gate, than to cross the lower land, and steal in by the water-slide. However, I durst not take a horse (for fear of the Doones, who might be abroad upon their usual business), but started betimes in the evening, so as not to hurry, or waste any strength upon the way. And thus I came to the robbers' highway, walking circumspectly, scanning the sky-line of every hill, and searching the folds of every valley, for any moving figure.

Although it was now well on towards dark, and the sun was down an hour or so, I could see the robbers' road before me, in a trough of the winding hills, where the brook ploughed down from the higher barrows, and the coving banks were roofed with furze. At present, there was no one passing, neither post nor sentinel, so far as I could descry; but I thought it safer to wait a little, as twilight melted into night; and then I crept down a seam of the highland, and stood upon the Doone-track.

As the road approached the entrance, it became more straight and strong, like a channel cut from rock, with the water brawling darkly along the naked side of it. Not a tree or bush was left, to shelter a man from bullets: all was stern, and stiff, and rugged, as I could not help perceiving, even through the darkness; and a smell as of churchyard mould, a sense of being boxed in and cooped, made me long to be out again.

And here I was, or seemed to be, particularly unlucky; for as I drew near the very entrance, lightly of foot, and warily, the moon (which had often been my friend) like an enemy broke upon me, topping the eastward ridge of rock, and filling all the open spaces with the play of wavering light. I shrank back into the shadowy quarter, on the right side of the road; and gloomily employed myself to watch the triple entrance, on which the moonlight fell askew.

All across and before the three rude and beetling archways, hung a felled oak overhead, black, and thick, and threatening. This, as I heard before, could be let fall in a moment, so as to crush a score of men, and bar the approach of horses. Behind this tree, the rocky mouth was spanned, as by a gallery, with brushwood and piled timber, all upon a ledge of stone, where thirty men might lurk unseen, and fire at any invader. From that rampart it would be impossible to dislodge them, because the rock fell sheer below them twenty feet, or it may be more; while overhead it towered three hundred, and so jutted over that nothing could be cast upon them; even if a man could climb the height. And the access to this portcullis place – if I may so call it, being no portcullis there – was through certain rocky chambers known to the tenants only.

But the cleverest of their devices, and the most puzzling to an enemy, was that, instead of one mouth only, there were three to choose from, with nothing to betoken which was the proper access; all being pretty much alike, and all unfenced and yawning. And the common rumour was that in times of any danger, when any force was known to be on muster in their neighbourhood, they changed their entrance every day, and diverted the other two, by means of sliding doors to the chasms and dark abysses.

Now I could see those three rough arches, jagged, black, and terrible; and I knew that only one of them could lead me to the valley; neither gave the river any further guidance; but dived underground with a sullen roar, where it met the crossbar of the mountain. Having no means at all of judging which was the right way of the three, and knowing that the other two would lead to almost certain death, in the ruggedness and darkness, – for how could a man, among precipices and bottomless depths of water, without a ray of light, have any chance to save his life? – I do declare that I was half inclined to go away, and have done with it.

However, I knew one thing for certain, to wit, that the longer I stayed debating, the more would the enterprise pall upon me, and the less my relish be. And it struck me that, in times of peace, the middle way was the likeliest; and the others diverging right and left in their further parts might be made to slide into it (not far from the entrance), at the pleasure of the warders. Also I took it for good omen that I remembered (as rarely happened) a very fine line in the Latin grammar, whose emphasis and meaning is 'middle road is safest.'

Therefore, without more hesitation, I plunged into the middle way, holding a long ash staff before me, shodden at the end with iron. Presently I was in black darkness, groping along the wall, and feeling a deal more fear than I wished to feel; especially when upon looking back I could no longer see the light, which I had forsaken. Then I stumbled over something hard, and sharp, and very cold, moreover so grievous to my legs, that it needed my very best doctrine and humour to forbear from swearing, in the manner they use in London. But when I arose, and felt it, and knew it to be a culverin, I was somewhat reassured thereby, inasmuch as it was not likely that they would plant this engine, except in the real and true entrance.

Therefore I went on again, more painfully and wearily, and presently found it to be good that I had received that knock, and borne it with such patience; for otherwise I might have blundered full upon the sentries, and been shot without more ado. As it was, I had barely time to draw back, as I turned a corner upon them; and if their lanthorn had been in its place, they could scarce have failed to descry me, unless indeed I had seen the gleam before I turned the corner.

There seemed to be only two of them, of size indeed and

stature as all the Doones must be, but I need not have feared to encounter them both, had they been unarmed, as I was. It was plain, however, that each had a long and heavy carbine, not in his hands (as it should have been), but standing close beside him. Therefore it behoved me now to be exceeding careful; and even that might scarce avail, without luck in proportion. So I kept well back at the corner, and laid one cheek to the rock face, and kept my outer eye round the jut, in the wariest mode I could compass, watching my opportunity: and this is what I saw.

The two villains looked very happy – which villains have no right to be, but often are, meseemeth – they were sitting in a niche of rock, with the lanthorn in the corner, quaffing something from glass measures, and playing at push-pin, or shepherd's chess, or basset; or some trivial game of that sort. Each was smoking a long clay pipe, quite of new London shape I could see, for the shadow was thrown out clearly; and each would laugh from time to time, as he fancied he got the better of it. One was sitting with his knees up, and left hand on his thigh; and this one had his back to me, and seemed to be the stouter. The other leaned more against the rock, half sitting and half astraddle, and wearing leathern overalls, as if newly come from riding. I could see his face quite clearly by the light of the open lanthorn, and a handsomer or a bolder face I had seldom, if ever, set eyes upon; insomuch that it made me very unhappy to think of his being so near my Lorna.

'How long am I to stay crouching here?' I asked of myself at last, being tired of hearing them cry, 'score one,' 'score two,' 'No, by – , Charlie,' 'By – I say it is, Phelps.' And yet my only chance of slipping by them unperceived was to wait till they quarrelled more, and came to blows about it. Presently, as I made up my mind to steal along towards them (for the cavern was pretty wide, just there), Charlie, or Charleworth Doone, the younger and taller man, reached forth his hand to seize the money, which he swore he had won that time. Upon this, the other jerked his arm, vowing that he had no right to it; whereupon Charlie flung at his face the contents of the glass he was sipping, but missed him and hit the candle, which spluttered with a flare of blue flame (from the strength perhaps of the spirit) and then went out completely. At this, one swore, and the other laughed; and before they had settled what to do, I was past them and round the corner.

And then, like a giddy fool as I was, I needs must give them a startle – the whoop of an owl, done so exactly, as John Fry had taught me, and echoed by the roof so fearfully, that one of them dropped the tinder box, and the other caught up his gun and cocked it, at least as I judged by the sounds they made. And then, too late, I knew my madness, for if either of them had fired, no doubt but what all the village would have risen, and rushed upon me. However, as the luck of the matter went, it proved for my advantage; for I heard one say to the other, –

'Curse it, Charlie, what was that? It scared me so, I have dropped my box; my flint is gone, and every thing. Will the brimstone catch from your pipe, my lad?'

'My pipe is out, Phelps, ever so long. Damn it, I am not afraid of an owl, man. Give me the lanthorn, and stay here. I'm not half done with you yet, my friend.'

'Well said, my boy, well said! Go straight to Carver's, mind you. The other sleepy-heads be snoring, as there is nothing up to-night. No dallying now under Captain's window. Queen will have nought to say to you; and Carver will punch your head into a new wick for your lanthorn.'

'Will he though? Two can play at that.' And so after some rude jests, and laughter, and a few more oaths, I heard Charlie (or at any rate somebody) coming toward me, with a loose and not too sober footfall. As he reeled a little in his gait, and I would not move from his way one inch, after his talk of Lorna, but only longed to grasp him (if common sense permitted it), his braided coat came against my thumb, and his leathern gaiters brushed my knee. If he had turned or noticed it, he would have been a dead man in a moment; but his drunkenness saved him.

So I let him reel on unharmed; and thereupon it occurred to me that I could have no better guide, passing as he would exactly where I wished to be; that is to say under Lorna's window. Therefore I followed him, without any especial caution; and soon I had the pleasure of seeing his form against the moonlit sky. Down a steep and winding path, with a hand-rail at the corners (such as they have at Ilfracombe), Master Charlie tripped along – and indeed there was much tripping, and he must have been an active fellow to recover as he did – and after him walked I, much hoping (for his own poor sake) that he might not turn, and espy me.

But Bacchus (of whom I read at school with great wonder about his meaning – and the same I may say of Venus) that great deity preserved Charlie, his pious worshipper, from regarding consequences. So he led me very kindly to the top of the meadow land, where the stream from underground broke forth, seething quietly with a little hiss of bubbles. Hence I had a fair view and outline of the robbers' township, spread with bushes here and there, but not heavily overshadowed. The moon, approaching now the full, brought the forms in manner forth, clothing each with character, as the moon (more than the sun) does, to an eye accustomed.

I knew that the Captain's house was first, both from what Lorna had said of it, and from my mother's description, and now again from seeing Charlie halt there for a certain time, and whistle on his fingers, and hurry on, fearing consequences. The tune that he whistled was strange to me, and lingered in my ears, as having something very new and striking, and fantastic in it. And I repeated it softly to myself, while I marked the position of the houses and the beauty of the village.

Master Charlie went down the village, and I followed him carefully, keeping as much as possible in the shadowy places, and watching the windows of every house, lest any light should be burning. As I passed Sir Ensor's house, my heart leaped up, for I spied a window, higher than the rest above the ground, and with a faint light moving. This could hardly fail to be the room wherein my darling lay; for here that impudent young fellow had gazed while he was whistling. And here my courage grew tenfold, and my spirit feared no evil – for lo, if Lorna had been surrendered to that scoundrel, Carver, she would not have been at her grandfather's house, but in Carver's accursed dwelling.

Warm with this idea, I hurried after Charleworth Doone, being resolved not to harm him now, unless my own life required it. And while I watched from behind a tree, the door of the furthest house was opened; and sure enough it was Carver's self, who stood bare-headed, and half undressed, in the doorway. I could see his great black chest, and arms, by the light of the lamp he bore.

'Who wants me, this time of night?' he grumbled in a deep gruff voice; 'any young scamp prowling after the maids shall have sore bones for his trouble.'

'All the fair maids are for thee, are they, Master Carver?' Charlie answered laughing; 'we young scamps must be well-content with coarser stuff than thou wouldst have.'

'Would have? Ay, and will have,' the great beast muttered angrily. 'I bide my time; but not very long. Only one word for thy good, Charlie. I will fling thee senseless into the river, if ever I catch thy girl-face here again.'

'Mayhap, Master Carver, it is more than thou couldst do. But I will not keep thee; thou art not pleasant company tonight. All I want is a light for my lanthorn, and a glass of schnapps, if thou hast it.'

'What is become of thy light, then? Good for thee I am not on duty.'

'A great owl flew between me and Phelps, as we watched beside the culverin, and so scared was he at our fierce bright eyes, that he fell, and knocked the light out.'

'Likely tale, or likely lie, Charles! We will have the truth to-morrow. Here take thy light, and be gone with thee. All virtuous men are in bed now.'

'Then so will I be, and why art thou not? Ha, have I earned my schnapps now?'

'If thou hast, thou hast paid a bad debt: there is too much in thee already. Be off! my patience is done with.'

Then he slammed the door in the young man's face, having kindled his lanthorn by this time: and Charlie went up to the watch-place again, muttering as he passed me, 'Bad look-out for all of us, when that surly old beast is Captain. No gentle blood in him, no hospitality, not even pleasant language, nor a good new oath in his frowsy pate! I've a mind to cut the whole of it; and but for the girls I would so.'

My heart was in my mouth, as they say, when I stood in the shade by Lorna's window, and whispered her name gently. The house was of one storey only, as the others were, with pine-ends standing forth the stone, and only two rough windows upon that western side of it, and perhaps both of them were Lorna's. The Doones had been their own builders, for no one should know their ins and outs; and of course their work was clumsy. As for their windows, they stole them mostly from the houses round about. But though the window was not very close, I might have whispered long enough, before she would have answered me; frightened as she was, no doubt, by many a rude overture. And I durst not speak aloud, because I saw another watchman posted on the western cliff, and commanding all the valley. And now this man (having no companion for drinking or for gambling) espied me against the wall of the house, and advanced to the brink, and challenged me.

'Who are you there? Answer! One, two, three; and I fire at thee.'

The nozzle of his gun was pointed full upon me, as I could see, with the moonlight striking on the barrel; he was not more than fifty yards off, and now he began to reckon. Being almost desperate about it, I began to whistle, wondering how far I should get before I lost my windpipe: and as luck would have it, my lips fell into that strange tune I had practised last; the one I had heard from Charlie. My mouth would scarcely frame the notes, being parched with terror; but to my surprise, the man fell back, dropped his gun, and saluted. Oh sweetest of all sweet melodies!

That tune was Carver Doone's passport (as I heard long afterwards), which Charleworth Doone had imitated, for decoy of Lorna. The sentinel took me for that vile Carver; who was like enough to be prowling there, for private talk with Lorna; but not very likely to shout forth his name, if it might be avoided. The watchman, perceiving the danger perhaps of intruding on Carver's privacy, not only retired along the cliff, but withdrew himself to good distance.

Meanwhile he had done me the kindest service; for Lorna came to the window at once, to see what the cause of the shout was, and drew back the curtain timidly. Then she opened the rough lattice; and then she watched the cliff and trees; and then she sighed very sadly.

'Oh Lorna, don't you know me?' I whispered from the side, being afraid of startling her by appearing over suddenly.

Quick though she always was of thought, she knew me not from my whisper, and was shutting the window hastily, when I caught it back, and showed myself.

'John!' she cried, yet with sense enough not to speak aloud: 'oh, you must be mad, John.'

'As mad as a March hare,' said I, 'without any news of my darling. You knew I would come: of course you did.'

'Well, I thought, perhaps – you know: now, John, you need not eat my hand. Do you see they have put iron bars across?'

'To be sure. Do you think I should be contented, even with this lovely hand, but for these vile iron bars. I will have them out before I go. Now, darling, for one moment – just the other hand, for a change, you know.'

So I got the other, but was not honest; for I kept them both, and felt their delicate beauty trembling, as I laid them to my heart.

'Oh, John, you will make me cry directly' – she had been crying long ago – 'if you go on in that way. You know we can never have one another; every one is against it. Why should I make you miserable? Try not to think of me any more.'

'And will you try the same of me, Lorna?'

'Oh yes, John; if you agree to it. At least I will try to try it.'

'Then you won't try any thing of the sort,' I cried with great enthusiasm, for her tone was so nice and melancholy: 'the only thing we will try to try, is to belong to one another. And if we do our best, Lorna, God alone can prevent us.'

She crossed herself, with one hand drawn free, as I spoke

so boldly; and something swelled in her little throat, and prevented her from answering.

'Now tell me,' I said; 'what means all this? Why are you so pent up here? Why have you given me no token? Has your grandfather turned against you? Are you in any danger? '

'My poor grandfather is very ill: I fear that he will not live long. The Counsellor and his son are now the masters of the valley; and I dare not venture forth, for fear of any thing they might do to me. When I went forth, to signal for you, Carver tried to seize me; but I was too quick for him. Little Gwenny is not allowed to leave the valley now; so that I could send no message. I have been so wretched, dear, lest you should think me false to you. The tyrants now make sure of me. You must watch this house, both night and day, if you wish to save me. There is nothing they would shrink from, if my poor grandfather – oh, I cannot bear to think of myself, when I ought to think of him only; dying without a son to tend him, or a daughter to shed a tear.'

'But surely he has sons enough; and a deal too many,' I was going to say, but stopped myself in time: 'why do none of them come to him?'

'I know not. I cannot tell. He is a very strange old man; and few have ever loved him. He was black with wrath at the Counsellor, this very afternoon – but I must not keep you here – you are much too brave, John; and I am much too selfish: there, what was that shadow?'

'Nothing more than a bat, darling, come to look for his sweetheart. I will not stay long; you tremble so: yet for that very reason, how can I leave you, Lorna?'

'You must – you must,' she answered; 'I shall die if they hurt you. I hear the old nurse moving. Grandfather is sure to send for me. Keep back from the window.'

However, it was only Gwenny Carfax, Lorna's little hand-maid: my darling brought her to the window, and presented her to me, almost laughing through her grief.

'Oh, I am so glad, John; Gwenny, I am so glad you came. I have wanted long to introduce you to my "young man," as you call him. It is rather dark, but you can see him. I wish you to know him again, Gwenny.'

'Whoy!' cried Gwenny, with great amazement, standing on tiptoe to look out, and staring as if she were weighing me: 'her be bigger nor any Doone! Heared as her have bate our Carnish champion awrastling. 'Twadn't fair play nohow: no, no; don't tell me, 'twadn't fair play nahow.'

'True enough, Gwenny,' I answered her; for the play had been very unfair indeed on the side of the Bodmin champion: 'it was not a fair bout, little maid; I am free to acknowledge that.' By that answer, or rather by the construction she put upon it, the heart of the Cornish girl was won, more than by gold and silver.

'I shall knoo thee again, young man; no fear of that,' she answered, nodding with an air of patronage. 'Now, missis, gae on coortin', and I wall gee outside and watch for 'ee.' Though expressed not over delicately, this proposal arose, no doubt, from Gwenny's sense of delicacy; and I was very thankful to her for taking her departure.

'She is the best little thing in the world,' said Lorna, softly laughing; 'and the queerest, and the truest. Nothing will bribe her against me. If she seems to be on the other side, never, never doubt her. Now no more of your "coortin'," John! I love you far too well for that. Yes, yes, ever so much! If you will take a mean advantage of me. As much as ever you like to imagine; and then you may double it, after that. Only go, do go, good John; kind, dear, darling John; if you love me, go.'

'How can I go, without settling any thing?' I asked, very sensibly. 'How shall I know of your danger now? Hit upon something; you are so quick. Anything you can think of; and then I will go, and not frighten you.'

'I have been thinking long of something,' Lorna answered rapidly, with that peculiar clearness of voice, which made every syllable ring like music of a several note, 'you see that tree with the seven rooks' nests, bright against the cliffs there? Can you count them, from above, do you think? From a place where you will be safe, dear – '

'No doubt, I can; or if I cannot, it will not take me long to find a spot whence I can do it.'

'Gwenny can climb like any cat. She has been up there in

the summer, watching the young birds, day by day, and daring the boys to touch them. There are neither birds, nor eggs there now, of course, and nothing doing. If you see but six rooks' nests, I am in peril, and want you. If you see but five, I am carried off by Carver.'

'Good God!' said I, at the mere idea, in a tone which frightened Lorna.

'Fear not, John,' she whispered sadly, and my blood grew cold at it: 'I have means to stop him; or at least to save myself. If you can come within one day of that man's getting hold of me, you will find me quite unharmed. After that you will find me dead, or alive, according to circumstances, but in no case such that you need blush to look at me.'

Her dear sweet face was full of pride, as even in the gloom I saw: and I would not trespass on her feelings, by such a thing, at such a moment, as an attempt at any caress. I only said, 'God bless you, darling!' and she said the same to me, in a very low sad voice. And then I stole below Carver's house, in the shadow from the eastern cliff; and knowing enough of the village now to satisfy all necessity, betook myself to my well-known track in returning from the valley; which was neither down the waterslide (a course I feared in the darkness) nor up the cliffs at Lorna's bower; but a way of my own inventing, which there is no need to dwell upon.

A weight of care was off my mind; though much trouble hung there still. One thing was quite certain – if Lorna could not have John Ridd, no one else should have her. And my mother, who sat up for me, and with me long time afterwards, agreed that this was comfort.

19

Two Fools Together

Stickles took me aside the next day, and opened all his business to me, whether I would or not. But I gave him clearly to understand that he was not to be vexed with me, neither to regard me as in any way dishonest, if I should use for my own purpose, or for the benefit of my friends, any part of the knowledge, and privity, thus enforced upon me. To this he agreed quite readily; but upon the express provision that I should do nothing to thwart his schemes, neither unfold them to any one; but otherwise be allowed to act according to my own conscience, and as consisted with the honour of a loyal gentleman – for so he was pleased to term me. Now what he said lay in no great compass, and may be summed in smaller still; especially as people know the chief part of it already. Disaffection to the King, or rather dislike to his brother, James, and fear of Roman ascendancy, had existed now for several years, and of late were spreading rapidly; partly through the downright arrogance of the Tory faction, the cruelty and austerity of the Duke of York, the corruption of justice, and confiscation of ancient rights and charters; partly through jealousy of the French king, and his potent voice in our affairs; and partly (or perhaps one might even say, mainly) through that natural tide in all political channels, which verily moves as if it has the moon itself for its mistress.

And so there was, at the time I speak of, a great surge in England, not rolling yet, but seething: and one which a thousand Chief Justices, and a million Jeremy Stickles, should never be able to stop or turn, by stringing up men in front of it; any more than a rope of onions can repulse a volcano. But the worst of it was, that this great movement took a wrong channel at first; not only missing legitimate line, but roaring out that the back ditchway was the true and established course of it.

Now, – to reduce high figures of speech into our own little numerals, – all the towns of Somersetshire and half the towns of Devonshire were full of pushing eager people, ready to swallow any thing, or to make others swallow it. Whether they believed the folly about the black box, and all that stuff, is not for me to say; only one thing I know, they pretended to do so, and persuaded the ignorant rustics. Taunton, Bridgwater, Minehead, and Dulverton took the lead of the other towns in utterance of their discontent, and threats of what they meant to do, if ever a Papist dared to climb the Protestant throne of England. On the other hand, the Tory leaders were not as yet under apprehension of an immediate outbreak, and feared to damage their own cause by premature coercion, for the struggle was not very likely to begin in earnest, during the life of the present King; unless he should (as some people hoped) be so far emboldened as to make public profession of the faith which he held (if any). So the Tory policy was to watch, not indeed permitting their opponents to gather strength, and muster in armed force or with order, but being well apprised of all their schemes and intended movements, to wait for some bold overt act, and then to strike severely. And as a Tory watchman – or spy, as the Whigs would call him – Jeremy Stickles was now among us; and his duty was three-fold.

First, and most ostensibly, to see to the levying of poundage in the little haven of Lynmouth, and further up the coast, which was now becoming a place of resort for the folk whom we call smugglers, that is to say, who land their goods without regard to King's revenue, as by law established. And indeed there had been no officer appointed to take toll, until one had been sent to Minehead, not so very long before. The excise as well (which had been ordered in the time of the

Long Parliament) had been little heeded by the people hereabouts.

Second, his duty was (though only the Doones had discovered it) to watch those outlaws narrowly, and report of their manners (which were scanty), doings (which were too manifold), reputation (which was execrable), and politics, whether true to the King and the Pope, or otherwise.

Jeremy Stickles' third business was entirely political; to learn the temper of our people and the gentle families, to watch the movements of the trained bands (which could not always be trusted), to discover any collecting of arms and drilling of men among us, to prevent (if need were, by open force) any importation of gunpowder, of which there had been some rumour; in a word, to observe and forestall the enemy.

Now in providing for this last-mentioned service, the Government had made a great mistake, doubtless through their anxiety to escape any public attention. For all the disposable force at their emissary's command amounted to no more than a score of musketeers, and these so divided along the coast as scarcely to suffice for the duty of sentinels. He held a commission, it is true, for the employment of the train-bands, but upon the understanding that he was not to call upon them (except as a last resource) for any political object; although he might use them against the Doones as private criminals, if found needful; and supposing that he could get them.

'So you see, John,' he said, in conclusion, 'I have more work than tools to do it with. I am heartily sorry I ever accepted such a mixed and meagre commission. At the bottom of it lies (I am well convinced) not only the desire to keep things quiet, but the paltry jealousy of the military people. Because I am not a Colonel, forsooth, or a Captain in His Majesty's service, it would never do to trust me with a company of soldiers! And yet they would not send either Colonel or Captain, for fear of a stir in the rustic mind. The only thing that I can do, with any chance of success, is to rout out these vile Doone fellows, and burn their houses over their heads. Now what think you of that, John Ridd?'

'Destroy the town of the Doones,' I said, 'and all the Doones inside it! Surely, Jeremy, you would never think of such a cruel act as that!'

'A cruel act, John! It would be a mercy for at least three counties. No doubt you folk, who live so near, are well accustomed to them, and would miss your liveliness in coming home after nightfall, and the joy of finding your sheep and cattle right, when you had not expected it. But after awhile you might get used to the dulness of being safe in your beds, and not losing your sisters and sweethearts. Surely, on the whole, it is as pleasant not to be robbed as to be robbed?'

'I think we should miss them very much,' I answered, after consideration; for the possibility of having no Doones had never yet occurred to me, and we all were so thoroughly used to them, and allowed for it in our year's reckoning; 'I am sure we should miss them very sadly; and something worse would come of it.'

'Thou art the staunchest of all staunch Tories,' cried Stickles, laughing, as he shook my hand; 'thou believest in the divine right of robbers, who are good enough to steal thy own fat sheep. I am a jolly Tory, John; but thou art ten times jollier: oh! the grief in thy face at the thought of being robbed no longer!'

'Master Stickles, once for all, I will have nought to do with it. The reason why is no odds of thine, nor in any way disloyal. Only in thy plans remember, that I will not strike a blow, neither give any counsel, neither guard any prisoners.'

'Not strike a blow,' cried Jeremy, 'against thy father's murderers, John!'

'Not a single blow, Jeremy; unless I knew the man who did it, and he gloried in his sin. It was a foul and dastard deed, yet not done in cold blood; neither in cold blood will I take the Lord's task of avenging it.'

'Very well, John,' answered Master Stickles, 'I know thine obstinacy. When thy mind is made up, to argue with thee is pelting a rock with peppercorns.'

I made bold to ask Master Stickles, at what time he intended to carry out this great and hazardous attempt. He answered that he had several things requiring first to be set in order, and that he must make an inland journey, even as far as Tiverton, and perhaps Crediton and Exeter, to collect his forces and ammunition for them.

All this made me very uncomfortable, for many and many reasons, the chief and foremost being of course my anxiety about Lorna.

There was however, or seemed to be, one comfort. Tom Faggus returned from London very proudly and very happily, with a royal pardon in black and white, which everybody admired the more, because no one could read a word of it.

And now a thing came to pass which tested my adoration pretty sharply, inasmuch as I would far liefer have faced Carver Doone and his father, nay even the roaring lion himself, with his hoofs and flaming nostrils, than have met, in cold blood, Sir Ensor Doone, the founder of all the colony, and the fear of the very fiercest.

But that I was forced to do at this time, and in the manner following. When I went up one morning to look for my seven rooks' nests, behold there were but six to be seen; for the topmost of them all was gone, and the most conspicuous. I looked, and looked, and rubbed my eyes and turned to try them by other sights; and then I looked again; yes, there could be no doubt about it; the signal was made for me to come, because my love was in danger. For me to enter the valley now, during the broad daylight, could have brought no comfort, but only harm to the maiden, and certain death to myself. Yet it was more than I could do to keep altogether at distance; therefore I ran to the nearest place where I could remain unseen, and watched the glen from the wooded height, for hours and hours, impatiently.

However no impatience of mine made any difference in the scene upon which I was gazing. In the part of the valley which I could see there was nothing moving, except the water, and a few stolen cows, going sadly along, as if knowing that they had no honest right there. It sank very heavily into my heart, with all the beds of dead leaves around it, and there was nothing I cared to do, except blow on my fingers, and long for more wit.

For a frost was beginning, which made a great difference to Lorna and to myself, I trow; as well as to all the five million people who dwell in this island of England; such a frost as never I saw before, neither hope ever to see again; a time when it was impossible to milk a cow for icicles, or for a man to shave some of his beard (as I liked to do for Lorna's sake, because she was so smooth) without blunting his razor on hard grey ice.

It was lucky for me, while I waited here, that our very best sheep-dog, old Watch, had chosen to accompany me that day. For otherwise I must have had no dinner, being unpersuaded, even by that, to quit my survey of the valley. However, by aid of poor Watch, I contrived to obtain a supply of food; for I sent him home with a note to Annie fastened upon his chest; and in less than an hour back he came, proud enough to wag his tail off, with his tongue hanging out from the speed of his journey, and a large lump of bread and of bacon fastened in a napkin around his neck. I had not told my sister, of course, what was toward; for why should I make her anxious?

When it grew towards dark, I was just beginning to prepare for my circuit around the hills; but suddenly Watch gave a long low growl; I kept myself close as possible, and ordered the dog to be silent, and presently saw a short figure approaching from a thickly-wooded hollow on the left side of my hiding-place. It was the same figure I had seen once before in the moonlight, at Plover's Barrows; and proved, to my great delight, to be the little maid Gwenny Carfax. She started a moment, at seeing me, but more with surprise than fear; and then she laid both her hands upon mine, as if she had known me for twenty years.

'Young man,' she said, 'you must come with me. I was gwain' all the way to fetch thee. Old man be dying; and her can't die, or least her won't, without first considering thee.'

'Considering me!' I cried: 'what can Sir Ensor Doone want with considering me? Has Mistress Lorna told him?'

'All concerning thee, and thy doings; when she knowed old man were so near his end. That vexed he was about thy low blood, a' thought her would come to life again, on purpose for to bate 'ee. But after all, there can't be scarcely such bad luck as that. Now, if he strook thee, thou must take it; there be no denying of 'un. Fire I have seen afore, hot and red, and raging, but I never seen cold fire afore, and it maketh me burn and shiver.'

And in truth, it made me both burn and shiver, to know that I must either go straight to the presence of Sir Ensor Doone, or give up Lorna, once for all, and rightly be despised by her.

Therefore, with great misgiving of myself, but no ill thought of my darling, I sent Watch home, and followed Gwenny; who led me along very rapidly, with her short broad form gliding down the hollow, from which she had first appeared. Here at the bottom, she entered a thicket of grey ash stubs and black holly, with rocks around it gnarled with roots, and hung with masks of ivy. Soon in a dark and lonely corner, with a pixie ring before it, she came to a narrow door, very brown and solid, looking like a trunk of wood at a little distance. This she opened, without a key, by stooping down and pressing it, where the threshold met the jamb; and then she ran in very nimbly, but I was forced to be bent in two, and even so without comfort. The passage was close and difficult, and as dark as any black pitch; but it was not long (be it as it might), and in that there was some comfort. We came out soon at the other end, and were at the top of Doone valley. In the chilly dusk air it looked most untempting, especially during that state of mind under which I was labouring. As we crossed towards the Captain's house, we met a couple of great Doones lounging by the water-side. Gwenny said something to them, and although they stared very hard at me, they let me pass without hindrance. It is not too much to say that, when the little maid opened Sir Ensor's door, my heart thumped, quite as much with terror as with hope of Lorna's presence.

But in a moment the fear was gone, for Lorna was trembling in my arms, and my courage rose to comfort her. The darling feared, beyond all things else, lest I should be offended with her, for what she had said to her grandfather, and for dragging me into his presence; but I told her almost a falsehood (the first, and the last, that ever I did tell her), to wit, that I cared not that much – and showed her the tip of my thumb as I said it – for old Sir Ensor, and all his wrath, so long as I had his granddaughter's love.

Now I tried to think this as I said it, so as to save it from being a lie; but somehow or other it did not answer, and I was vexed with myself both ways. But Lorna took me by the hand as bravely as she could, and led me into a little passage, where I could hear the river moaning and the branches rustling.

Here I passed as long a minute as fear ever cheated time of, saying to myself continually that there was nothing to be frightened at, yet growing more and more afraid by reason of so reasoning. At last my Lorna came back very pale, as I saw by the candle she carried, and whispered, 'Now be patient, dearest. Never mind what he says to you; neither attempt to answer him. Look at him gently and steadfastly, and, if you can, with some show of reverence; but above all things, no compassion; it drives him almost mad. Now come; walk very quietly.'

She led me into a cold dark room, rough and very gloomy, although with two candles burning. I took little heed of the things in it, though I marked that the window was open. That which I heeded was an old man, very stern and comely, with death upon his countenance; yet not lying in his bed, but set upright in a chair, with a loose red cloak thrown over him. Upon this his white hair fell, and his pale fingers lay in a ghastly fashion, without a sign of life or movement, or of the power that kept him up; all rigid, calm, and relentless. Only in his great black eyes, fixed upon me solemnly, all the power of his body dwelt, all the life of his soul was burning.

I could not look at him very nicely, being afeared of the death in his face, and most afeared to show it. And to tell the truth, my poor blue eyes fell away from the blackness of his, as if it had been my coffin-plate. Therefore I made a low obeisance, and tried not to shiver. Only I groaned that Lorna thought it good manners to leave us two together.

'Ah,' said the old man, and his voice seemed to come from a cavern of skeletons; 'are you that great John Ridd?'

'John Ridd is my name, your honour,' was all that I could answer; 'and I hope your worship is better.'

'Child, have you sense enough to know what you have been doing?'

'Yes, I know right well,' I answered, 'that I have set mine eyes far above my rank.'

'Are you ignorant that Lorna Doone is born of the oldest families remaining in North Europe?'

'I was ignorant of that, your worship; yet I knew of her high descent from the Doones of Bagworthy.'

The old man's eyes, like fire, probed me whether I was jesting; then perceiving how grave I was, and thinking that I could not laugh (as many people suppose of me), he took on himself to make good the deficiency with a very bitter smile.

'And know you of your own low descent, from the Ridds, of Oare?'

'Sir,' I answered, being as yet unaccustomed to this style of speech, 'the Ridds, of Oare, have been honest men, twice as long as the Doones have been rogues.'

'I would not answer for that, John,' Sir Ensor replied, very quietly, when I expected fury. 'If it be so, thy family is the very oldest in Europe. Now hearken to me, boy, or clown, or honest fool, or whatever thou art; hearken to an old man's words, who has not many hours to live. There is nothing in this world to fear, nothing to revere or trust, nothing even to hope for; least of all, is there ought to love.'

'I hope your worship is not quite right,' I answered, with great misgivings; 'else it is a sad mistake for anybody to live, sir.'

'Therefore,' he continued, as if I had never spoken, 'though it may seem hard for a week or two, like the loss of any other toy, I deprive you of nothing, but add to your comfort, and (if there be such a thing) to your happiness, when I forbid you ever to see that foolish child again. All marriage is a wretched farce even when man and wife belong to the same rank of life, have temper well assorted, similar likes and dislikes, and about the same pittance of mind. But when they are matched, the farce would become a long dull tragedy, if anything were worth lamenting. There, I have reasoned enough with you; I am not in the habit of reasoning. Though I have little confidence in man's honour, I have some reliance in woman's pride. You will pledge your word in Lorna's presence, never to see or to seek her again; never even to think of her more. Now call her, for I am weary.'

He kept his great eyes fixed upon me with their icy fire (as if he scorned both life and death), and on his haughty lips some slight amusement at my trouble; and then he raised one hand (as if I were a poor dumb creature), and pointed to the door. Although my heart rebelled and kindled at his proud disdain, I could not disobey him freely; but made a low salute, and went straightway in search of Lorna.

I found my love (or not my love; according as now she should behave; for I was very desperate, being put upon so sadly). Lorna Doone was crying softly at a little window, and listening to the river's grief. I laid my heavy arm around her, not with any air of claiming, or of forcing her thoughts to me, but only just to comfort her, and ask what she was thinking of. To my arm she made no answer, neither to my seeking eyes; but to my heart, once for all, she spoke with her own upon it. Not a word, nor sound between us; not even a kiss was interchanged; but man, or maid, who has ever loved hath learned our understanding.

Therefore it came to pass, that we saw fit to enter Sir Ensor's room, in the following manner. Lorna, with her right hand swallowed entirely by the palm of mine, and her waist retired from view by means of my left arm. All one side of her hair came down, in a way to be remembered, upon the left and fairest part of my favourite otter-skin waistcoat; and her head as well would have lain there doubtless, but for the danger of walking so. I, for my part, was too far gone to lag behind in the matter: but carried my love bravely, fearing neither death nor hell, while she abode beside me.

Old Sir Ensor looked much astonished. For forty years he had been obeyed and feared by all around him; and he knew that I had feared him vastly, before I got hold of Lorna. And indeed I was still afraid of him; only for loving Lorna so, and having to protect her.

Then I made him a bow, to the very best of all I had learned both at Tiverton and in London; after that I waited for him to begin, as became his age and rank in life.

'Ye two fools!' he said at last, with a depth of contempt which no words may utter: 'ye two fools!'

'May it please your worship,' I answered softly; 'may be we are not such fools as we look. But though we be, we are well content, so long as we may be two fools together.'

'Why, John,' said the old man, with a spark, as of smiling in his eyes; 'thou art not altogether the clumsy yokel, and the clod, I took thee for.'

'Oh, no, grandfather; oh dear grandfather,' cried Lorna, with such zeal and flashing, that her hands went forward; 'nobody knows what John Ridd is, because he is so modest. I mean, nobody except me, dear.' And here she turned to me again, and rose upon tiptoe, and kissed me.

'I have seen a little of the world,' said the old man, while I was half ashamed, although so proud of Lorna; 'but this is beyond all I have seen, and nearly all I have heard of. It is more fit for southern climates, than for the fogs of Exmoor.'

'It is fit for all the world, your worship; with your honour's good leave, and will,' I answered in humility, being still ashamed of it; 'when it happens so to people, there is nothing that can stop it, sir.'

Now Sir Ensor Doone was leaning back upon his brown chair-rail, which was built like a triangle, as in old farm-houses (from one of which it had come, no doubt, free from expense or gratitude); and as I spoke he coughed a little; and he sighed a good deal more; and perhaps his dying heart desired to open time again, with such a lift of warmth and hope as he descried in our eyes, and arms. I could not understand him then; any more than a baby playing with his grandfather's spectacles; nevertheless I wondered whether, at his time of life, or rather on the brink of death, he was thinking of his youth and prime.

'Fools you are; be fools for ever,' said Sir Ensor Doone at last; while we feared to break his thoughts, but let each other know our own, with little ways of pressure: 'it is the best thing I can wish you; boy and girl, be boy and girl, until you have grandchildren.'

Partly in bitterness he spoke, and partly in pure weariness, and then he turned so as not to see us; and his white hair fell, like a shroud, around him.

20

Not Too Soon

It takes a man but a little while, his instinct being of death perhaps, at least as much as of life (which accounts for his slaying his fellow men so, and every other creature), it does not take a man very long to enter into another man's death, and bring his own mood to suit it. He knows that his own is sure to come; and nature is fond of the practice. Hence it came to pass that I, after easing my mother's fears, and seeing a little to business, returned (as if drawn by a polar needle) to the death-bed of Sir Ensor.

There was some little confusion, people wanting to get away, and people trying to come in, from downright curiosity (of all things the most hateful), and others making great to-do, and talking of their own time to come, telling their own age, and so on. But every one seemed to think, or feel, that I had a right to be there; because the women took that view of it. As for Carver and Counsellor, they were minding their own affairs, so as to win the succession; and never found it in their business (at least so long as I was there) to come near the dying man.

He, for his part, never asked for any one to come near him, not even a priest, nor a monk or friar; but seemed to be going his own way, peaceful, and well contented. Only the chief of the women said, that from his face she believed and knew, that he liked to have me at one side of his bed, and Lorna upon the other. An hour or two ere the old man died, when only we two were with him, he looked at us both very dimly and softly, as if he wished to do something for us, but had left it now too late. Lorna hoped that he wanted to bless us; but he only frowned at that, and let his hand drop downward, and crooked one knotted finger.

'He wants something out of the bed, dear,' Lorna whispered to me; 'see what it is, upon your side, there.'

I followed the bent of his poor shrunken hand, and sought among the pilings; and there I felt something hard and sharp, and drew it forth and gave it to him. It flashed, like the spray of a fountain upon us, in the dark winter of the room. He could not take it in his hand, but let in hang, as daisies do; only making Lorna see that he meant her to have it.

'Why, it is my glass necklace!' Lorna cried, in great surprise; 'my necklace he always promised me; and from which you have got the ring, John. But grandfather kept it, because the children wanted to pull it from my neck. May I have it now, dear grandfather? Not unless you wish, dear.'

Darling Lorna wept again, because the old man could not tell her (except by one very feeble nod) that she was doing what he wished. Then she gave to me the trinket, for the sake of safety; and I stowed it in my breast. He seemed to me to follow this, and to be well content with it.

In the very night which followed old Sir Ensor's funeral, such a storm of snow began, as never have I heard nor read of, neither could have dreamed it. At what time of night it first began is more than I can say, at least from my own knowledge, for we all went to bed soon after supper, being cold, and not inclined to talk. At that time the wind was moaning sadly, and the sky as dark as a wood, and the straw in the yard swirling round and round, and the cows huddling into the great cowhouse, with their chins upon one another. But we, being blinder than they, I suppose, and not having had a great snow for years made no preparation against the storm, except that the lambing ewes were in shelter.

It must have snowed most wonderfully to have made that depth of covering in about eight hours. For one of Master Stickles' men, who had been out all night, said that no snow began to fall until nearly midnight. And here it was, blocking up the doors, stopping the ways, and the water courses, and making it very much worse to walk than in a saw-pit newly used.

Therefore I fell to at once and being used to thatching-work, and the making of traps, and so on, before very long I built myself a pair of strong and light snow-shoes, framed with ash and ribbed of withy, with half-tanned calf-skin stretched across, and an inner sole to support my feet. At first I could not walk at all, but floundered about most piteously, catching one shoe in the other, and both of them in the snow-drifts, to the great amusement of the maidens, who were come to look at me. But after a while I grew more expert, discovering what my errors were, and altering the inclination of the shoes themselves, according to a plan which Lizzie found in a book of old adventures. And this made such a difference, that I crossed the farm-yard and came back again (though turning was the worst thing of all) without so much as falling once, or getting my staff entangled.

Upon the following day, I held some council with my mother; not liking to go without her permission, yet scarcely daring to ask for it. But here she disappointed me, on the right side of disappointment; saying that she had seen my pining (which she never could have done; because I had been too hard at work), and rather than watch me grieving so, for somebody or other, who now was all in all to me, I might go upon my course, and God's protection go with me! And so I took her at her word, which she was not prepared for; and telling her how proud I was of her trust in Providence, and how I could run in my new snow-shoes, I took a short pipe in my mouth, and started forth accordingly.

When I started on my road across the hills and valleys (which now were pretty much alike), the utmost I could hope to do was to gain the crest of hills, and look into the Doone Glen. Hence I might at least descry whether Lorna still was safe, by the six nests still remaining, and the view of the Captain's house.

At last I got to my spy-hill (as I had begun to call it), although I never should have known it, but for what it looked on. And even to know this last again required all the eyes of love, soever sharp and vigilant.

Seeing no Doones now about, and doubting if any guns would go off, in this state of the weather, and knowing that no man could catch me up (except with shoes like mine), I even resolved to slide the cliffs, and bravely go to Lorna.

It helped me much in this resolve, that the snow came on again, thick enough to blind a man who had not spent his time among it, as I had done for days and days. Therefore I took my neatsfoot oil, which now was clogged like honey, and rubbed it hard into my leg-joints, so far as I could reach them. And then I set my back and elbows well against a snow-drift, hanging far adown the cliff, and saying some of the Lord's Prayer, threw myself on Providence. Before there was time to think or dream, I landed very beautifully upon a ridge of run-up snow in a quiet corner. My good shoes, or boots, preserved me from going far beneath it; though one of them was sadly strained, where a grub had gnawed the ash, in the early summer-time. Having set myself aright, and being in good spirits, I made boldly across the valley (where the snow was furrowed hard), being now afraid of nobody.

If Lorna had looked out of the window, she would not have known me, with those boots upon my feet, and a well-cleaned sheepskin over me, bearing my own (J.R.) in red, just between my shoulders, but covered now in snow-flakes. The house was partly drifted up, though not so much as ours was; and I crossed the little stream almost without knowing that it was under me. At first, being pretty safe against interference from the other huts, by virtue of the blinding snow, and the difficulty of walking, I examined all the windows; but these were coated so with ice, like ferns and flowers and dazzling stars, that no one could so much as guess what might be inside of them. Moreover I was afraid of prying narrowly into them, as it was not a proper thing where a maiden might be: only I wanted to know just this, whether she were there, or not.

Taking nothing by this movement, I was forced, much against my will, to venture to the door and knock, in a hesitating manner, not being sure but what my answer might be the mouth of a carbine. However it was not so, for I heard a pattering of feet and a whispering going on, and then a shrill voice through the keyhole, asking, 'Who's there?'

'Only me, John Ridd,' I answered; upon which I heard a little laughter, and a little sobbing, or something that was like it; and then the door was opened about a couple of inches, with a bar behind it still; and then the little voice went on, –

'Put thy finger in, young man, with the old ring on it. But mind thee, if it be the wrong one, thou shalt never draw it back again.'

Laughing at Gwenny's mighty threat I showed my finger in the opening: upon which she let me in, and barred the door again like lightning.

'What is the meaning of all this, Gwenny?' I asked, as I slipped about on the floor, for I could not stand there firmly with my great snow-shoes on.

'Maning enough, and bad maning too,' the Cornish girl made answer. 'Us be shut in here, and starving, and durstn't let any body in upon us. I wish thou wer't good to eat, young man: I could manage most of thee.'

I was so frightened by her eyes, full of wolfish hunger, that I could only say, 'Good God!' having never seen the like before. Then drew I forth a large piece of bread, which I had brought in case of accidents, and placed it in her hands. She leaped at it, as a starving dog leaps at sight of his supper, and she set her teeth in it, and then withheld it from her lips, with something very like an oath at her own vile greediness; and then away round the corner with it, no doubt for her young mistress. I meanwhile was occupied, to the best of my ability, in taking my snow-shoes off, yet wondering much within myself, why Lorna did not come to me.

But presently I knew the cause; for Gwenny called me, and I ran, and found my darling quite unable to say so much as, 'John, how are you?' Between the hunger, and the cold, and the excitement of my coming, she had fainted away, and lay back on a chair, as white as the snow around us. In betwixt her delicate lips, Gwenny was thrusting with all her strength the hard brown crust of the rye-bread, which she had snatched from me so.

'Get water, or get snow,' I said; 'don't you know what fainting is, you very stupid child?'

'Never heered on it, in Carnwall,' she answered, trusting still to the bread: 'be un the same as bleeding?'

'It will be directly, if you go on squeezing away with that crust so. Eat a piece: I have got some more. Leave my darling now to me.'

Hearing that I had some more, the starving girl could resist no longer, but tore it in two, and had swallowed half, before I had coaxed my Lorna back to sense, and hope, and joy, and love.

'I never expected to see you again. I had made up my mind to die, John; and to die without your knowing it.'

As I repelled this fearful thought in a manner highly fortifying, the tender hue flowered back again to her famished cheeks and lips, and a softer brilliance glistened from the depth of her dark eyes. She gave me one little shrunken hand, and I could not help a tear for it.

'After all, Mistress Lorna,' I said, pretending to be gay, for a smile might do her good; 'you do not love me as Gwenny does; for she even wanted to eat me.'

'And shall, afore I have done, young man,' Gwenny answered, laughing; 'you come in here with they red chakes, and make us think o' sirloin.'

'Eat up your bit of brown bread, Gwenny. It is not good enough for your mistress. Bless her heart, I have something here such as she never tasted the like of, being in such appetite. Look here, Lorna; smell it first. I have had it ever since Twelfth-day, and kept it all the time for you. Annie made it. That is enough to warrant it good cooking.'

And then I showed my great mince-pie in a bag of tissue paper, and I told them how the mincemeat was made of golden pippins finely shred, with the undercut of the sirloin, and spice and fruit accordingly and far beyond my knowledge. But Lorna would not touch a morsel, until she had thanked God for it, and given me the kindest kiss, and put a piece in Gwenny's mouth. And then I begged to know the meaning of this state of things.

'The meaning is sad enough,' said Lorna; 'and I see no

way out of it. We are both to be starved until I let them do what they like with me.'

'That is to say, until you choose to marry Carver Doone, and be slowly killed by him.'

'Slowly! No, John, quickly. I hate him with such bitterness, that less than a week would kill me.'

'Not a doubt of that,' said Gwenny: 'oh, she hates him nicely then: but not half so much as I do.'

I told them both that this state of things could be endured no longer; on which point they agreed with me, but saw no means to help it. For even if Lorna could make up her mind to come away with me, and live at Plover's Barrows farm, under my good mother's care, as I had urged so often, behold the snow was all around us, heaped as high as mountains, and how could any delicate maiden ever get across it?

Then I spoke, with a strange tingle upon both sides of my heart, knowing that this undertaking was a serious one for all, and might burn our farm down, –

'If I warrant to take you safe, and without much fright or hardship, Lorna, will you come with me?'

'To be sure I will, dear,' said my beauty with a smile, and a glance to follow it; 'I have small alternative, to starve, or go with you, John.'

'Gwenny, have you courage for it? Will you come with your young mistress?'

'Will I stay behind?' cried Gwenny, in a voice that settled it. And so we began to arrange about it; and I was much excited. It was useless now to leave it longer: if it could be done at all, it could not be too quickly done. It was the Counsellor who had ordered, after all other schemes had failed, that his niece should have no food until she would obey him. He had strictly watched the house, taking turns with Carver, to ensure that none came nigh it bearing food or comfort. But this evening, they had thought it needless to remain on guard; and it would have been impossible, because themselves were busy, offering high festival to all the valley, in right of their own commandership. And Gwenny said that nothing made her so nearly mad with appetite as the account she received, from a woman, of all the dishes preparing. Nevertheless she had answered bravely, –

'Go and tell the Counsellor, and go and tell the Carver, who sent you to spy upon us, that we shall have a finer dish than any set before them.' And so in truth they did, although so little dreaming it; for no Doone that was ever born, however much of a Carver, might vie with our Annie for mincemeat.

Now while we sat, reflecting much, and talking a good deal more, in spite of all the cold, – for I never was in a hurry to go, when I had Lorna with me, – she said, in her silvery voice, which always led me so along, as if I were slave to a beautiful bell, –

'Now, John, we are wasting time, dear. You have praised my hair till it curls with pride, and my eyes till you cannot see them, even if they are brown diamonds, which I have heard for the fiftieth time at least; though I never saw such a jewel. Don't you think that it is high time to put on your snow-shoes, John?'

'Certainly not,' I answered, 'till we have settled something more. I was so cold when I came in; and now I am as warm as a cricket. And so are you, you lively soul; though you are not upon my hearth yet.'

'Remember, John,' said Lorna, nestling for a moment to me; 'the severity of the weather makes a great difference between us. And you must never take advantage.'

'I quite understand all that, dear. And the harder it freezes the better, while that understanding continues. Now do try to be serious.'

'I try to be serious! And I have been trying fifty times, and could not bring you to it, John! Although I am sure the situation, as the Counsellor always says, at the beginning of a speech, the situation, to say the least, is serious enough for anything.'

'Come to this frozen window, John, and see them light the stack-fire. They will little know who looks at them. Now be very good, John. You stay in that corner, dear, and I will stand on this side; and try to breathe yourself a peep-hole through the lovely spears and banners.'

And then I saw, far down the stream (or rather down the bed of it, for there was no stream visible), a little form of fire rising, red, and dark, and flickering. Presently it caught on something, and went upward boldly; and then it struck into many forks, and then it fell, and rose again.

'Do you know what all that is, John?' asked Lorna, smiling cleverly at the manner of my staring.

'How on earth should I know? Papists burn Protestants in the flesh; and Protestants burn Papists in effigy, as we mock them. Lorna, are they going to burn any one to-night?'

'No, you dear. I must rid you of these things. I see that you are bigoted. The Doones are firing Dunkery Beacon, to celebrate their new captain.'

'But how could they bring it here, through the snow? If they have sledges, I can do nothing.'

'They brought it before the snow began. The moment poor grandfather was gone, even before his funeral, the young men, having none to check them, began at once upon it.'

The fire went up very merrily, blazing red and white and yellow, as it leaped on different things. And the light danced on the snowdrifts with a misty lilac hue. I was astonished at its burning in such mighty depths of snow; but Gwenny said that the wicked men had been three days hard at work, clearing, as it were, a cockpit, for their fire to have its way. And now they had a mighty pile, which must have covered five land-yards square, heaped up to a goodly height, and eager to take fire.

In this I saw great obstacle to what I wished to manage. For when this pyramid should be kindled thoroughly, and pouring light and blazes round, would not all the valley be like a white room full of candles? Thinking thus, I was half inclined to abide my time for another night; and then my second thoughts convinced me that I would be a fool in this. For lo, what an opportunity! All the Doones would be drunk of course, in about three hours' time, and getting more and more in drink, as the night went on. As for the fire, it must sink in about three hours or more, and only cast uncertain shadows friendly to my purpose. And then the outlaws must cower round it, as the cold increased on them, helping the weight of the liquor; and in their jollity any noise would be cheered as a false alarm. Most of all, and which decided once for all my action, – when these wild and reckless villians should be hot with ardent spirits, what was door, or wall, to stand betwixt them and my Lorna?

This thought quickened me so much that I touched my darling reverently, and told her in a few short words how I hoped to manage it.

'Sweetest, in two hours' time, I shall be again with you. Keep the bar up and have Gwenny ready to answer any one. You are safe while they are dining, dear, and drinking healths, and all that stuff; and before they have done with that, I shall be again with you. Have every thing you care to take in a very little compass; and Gwenny must have no baggage. I shall knock loud, and then wait a little; and then knock twice, very softly.'

With this, I folded her in my arms; and she looked frightened at me; not having perceived her danger: and then I told Gwenny over again what I had told her mistress: but she only nodded her head and said, 'Young man, go and teach thy grandmother.'

21

Brought Home at Last

To my great delight, I found that the weather, not often friendly to lovers, and lately seeming so hostile, had in the most important matter done me a signal service. For when I had promised to take my love from the power of those wretches, the only way of escape apparent lay through the main Doone-gate. For though I might climb the cliffs myself, especially with the snow to aid me, I durst not try to fetch Lorna up them, even if she were not half-starved, as well as partly frozen; and as for Gwenny's door, as we called it (that is to say, the little entrance from the wooded hollow), it was snowed up long ago to the level of the hills around. Therefore I was at my wit's end, how to get them out; the passage by the Doone-gate being long, and dark, and difficult, and leading to such a weary circuit among the snowy moors and hills.

But now, being homeward-bound by the shortest possible track, I slipped along between the bonfire and the boundary cliffs, where I found a caved way of snow behind a sort of avalanche: so that if the Doones had been keeping watch (which they were not doing, but revelling) they could scarcely have discovered me. And when I came to my old ascent, where I had often scaled the cliff and made across the mountains, it struck me that I would just have a look at my first and painful entrance, to wit, the water-slide. I never for a moment imagined that this could help me now; for I never had dared to descend it, even in the finest weather; still I had a curiosity to know what my old friend was like, with so much snow upon him. But, to my very great surprise, there was scarcely any snow there at all, though plenty curling high over head from the cliff, like bolsters over it. Probably the sweeping of the north-east wind up the narrow chasm had kept the showers from blocking it, although the water had no power under the bitter grip of frost. All my water-slide was now less a slide than path of ice; furrowed where the waters ran over fluted ridges; seamed where wind had tossed and combed them, even while congealing; and crossed with little steps wherever the freezing torrent lingered. And here and there the ice was fibred with the trail of sludge-weed, slanting from the side, and matted, so as to make resting-place.

Lo, it was easy track and channel, as if for the very purpose made, down which I could guide my sledge, with Lorna sitting in it. There were only two things to be feared; one lest the rolls of snow above should fall in and bury us; the other lest we should rush too fast, and so be carried headlong into the black whirlpool at the bottom, the middle of which was still unfrozen, and looking more horrible by the contrast. Against this danger I made provision, by fixing a stout bar across; but of the other we must take our chance, and trust ourselves to Providence.

I hastened home at my utmost speed, and told my mother for God's sake to keep the house up till my return, and to have plenty of fire blazing, and plenty of water boiling, and food enough hot for a dozen people, and the best bed aired with the warming-pan. Dear mother smiled softly at my excitement, though her own was not much less, I am sure, and enhanced by sore anxiety. Then I gave very strict directions to Annie, and praised her a little, and kissed her; and I even endeavoured to flatter Eliza, lest she should be disagreeable.

After this I took some brandy, both within and about me; the former, because I had sharp work to do; and the latter in fear of whatever might happen, in such great cold, to my comrades. Also I carried some other provisions, grieving much at their coldness; and then I went to the upper linhay, and took our new light pony-sledd, which had been made almost as much for pleasure as for business; though God only knows how our girls could have found any pleasure in bumping along so. On the snow, however, it ran as sweetly as if it had been made for it; yet I durst not take the pony with it; in the first place, because his hoofs would break through the ever-shifting surface of the light and piling snow; and secondly, because those ponies, coming from the forest, have a dreadful trick of neighing, and most of all in frosty weather.

Therefore I girded my own body with a dozen turns of hay-rope, twisting both the ends in under at the bottom of my breast, and winding the hay on the skew a little, that the hempen thong might not slip between, and so cut me in the drawing. I put a good piece of spare rope in the sledd, and the cross-seat with the back to it, which was stuffed with our own wool, as well as two or three fur coats: and then just as I was starting, out came Annie, in spite of the cold, panting for fear of missing me, and with nothing on her head, but a lanthorn in one hand.

'Oh, John, here is the most wonderful thing! Mother has never shown it before; and I can't think how she could make up her mind. She had gotten it in a great well of a cupboard with camphor, and spirits, and lavender. Lizzie says it is a most magnificent sealskin cloak, worth fifty pounds, or a farthing.'

'At any rate it is soft and warm,' said I, very calmly flinging it into the bottom of the sledd. 'Tell mother I will put it over Lorna's feet.'

'Lorna's feet! Oh, you great fool;' cried Annie, for the first time reviling me: 'over her shoulders; and be proud, you very stupid John.'

'It is not good enough for her feet;' I answered, with strong emphasis; 'but don't tell mother I said so, Annie. Only thank her very kindly.'

With that I drew my traces hard, and set my ashen staff into the snow, and struck out with my best foot foremost (the best one at snow-shoes, I mean), and the sledd came after me as lightly as a dog might follow; and Annie with the lanthorn seemed to be left behind and waiting, like a pretty lamp-post.

The full moon rose as bright behind me as a patin of pure silver, casting on the snow long shadows of the few things left above, burdened rock, and shaggy foreland, and the labouring trees. In the great white desolation, distance was a mocking vision: hills looked nigh, and valleys far; when hills were far and valleys nigh. And the misty breath of frost, piercing through the ribs of rock, striking to the pith of trees, creeping to the heart of man, lay along the hollow places, like a serpent sloughing. Even as my own gaunt shadow (travestied as if I were the moonlight's daddy-longlegs) went before me down the slope; even I, the shadow's master, who had tried in vain to cough, when coughing brought good liquorice, felt a pressure on my bosom, and a husking in my throat.

However, I went on quietly, and at a very tidy speed; being only too thankful that the snow had ceased, and no wind as yet arisen. And from the ring of low white vapour girding all the verge of sky, and from the rosy blue above, and the shafts of starlight set upon a quivering bow, as well as from the moon itself and the light behind it, having learned the signs of frost from its bitter twinges, I knew that we should have a night as keen as ever England felt. Nevertheless, I had work enough to keep me warm if I managed it. The question was, could I contrive to save my darling from it?

Daring not to risk my sledd by any fall from the valley-cliffs, I dragged it very carefully up the steep incline of ice, through the narrow chasm, and so to the very brink and verge where first I had seen my Lorna, in the fishing-days of boyhood. As then I had a trident fork, for sticking of the loaches, so now I had a strong ash stake, to lay across from rock to rock, and break the speed of descending. With this I moored the sledd quite safe, at the very lip of the chasm, where all was now substantial ice, green and black in the moonlight; and then I set off up the valley, skirting along one side of it.

The stack-fire still was burning strongly, but with more of heat than blaze; and many of the younger Doones were playing on the verge of it, the children making rings of fire, and their mothers watching them. All the grave and reverend warriors, having heard of rheumatism, were inside of log and stone, in the two lowest houses, with enough of candles burning to make our list of sheep come short.

All these I passed, without the smallest risk or difficulty, walking up the channel of drift which I spoke of once before. And then I crossed, with more of care, and to the door of Lorna's house, and made the sign, and listened, after taking my snow-shoes off.

But no one came, as I expected, neither could I espy a light. And I seemed to hear a faint low sound, like the moaning of the snow-wind. Then I knocked again more loudly, with a knocking at my heart; and receiving no answer set all my power at once against the door. In a moment it flew inwards, and I glided along the passage with my feet still slippery. There in Lorna's room I saw, by the moonlight flowing in, a sight which drove me beyond sense.

Lorna was behind a chair, crouching in the corner, with her hands up, and a crucifix, or something that looked like it. In the middle of the room lay Gwenny Carfax, stupid, yet with one hand clutching the ankle of a struggling man. Another man stood above my Lorna, trying to draw the chair away. In a moment I had him round the waist, and he went out of the window with a mighty crash of glass; luckily for him that window had no bars like some of them. Then I took the other man by the neck; and he could not plead for mercy. I bore him out of the house as lightly as I would bear a baby, yet squeezing his throat a little more than I fain would do to an infant. By the bright moonlight I saw that I carried Marwood de Whichehalse. For his father's sake I spared him, and because he had been my schoolfellow: but with every muscle of my body strung with indignation, I cast him, like a skittle, from me into a snowdrift, which closed over him. Then I looked for the other fellow, tossed through Lorna's window; and found him lying stunned and bleeding, neither able to groan yet. Charleworth Doone, if his gushing blood did not much mislead me.

It was no time to linger now: I fastened my shoes in a

moment, and caught up my own darling with her head upon my shoulder, where she whispered faintly; and telling Gwenny to follow me, or else I would come back for her, if she could not walk the snow, I ran the whole distance to my sledd, caring not who might follow me. Then by the time I had set up Lorna, beautiful and smiling, with the sealskin cloak all over her, sturdy Gwenny came along, having trudged in the track of my snow-shoes, although with two bags on her back. I set her in beside her mistress, to support her, and keep warm; and then with one look back at the glen, which had been so long my home of heart, I hung behind the sledd, and launched it down the steep and dangerous way.

Though the cliffs were black above us, and the road unseen in front, and a great white grave of snow might at a single word come down, Lorna was as calm and happy as an infant in its bed. She knew that I was with her; and when I told her not to speak, she touched my hand in silence. Gwenny was in a much greater fright, having never seen such a thing before, neither knowing what it is to yield to pure love's confidence. I could hardly keep her quiet, without making a noise myself. With my staff from rock to rock, and my weight thrown backward, I broke the sledd's too rapid way, and brought my grown love safely out, by the self-same road which first led me to her girlish fancy, and my boyish slavery.

Unpursued, yet looking back as if some one must be after us, we skirted round the black whirling pool, and gained the meadows beyond it. Here there was hard collar work, the track being all uphill and rough; and Gwenny wanted to jump out to lighten the sledd and to push behind. But I would not hear of it; because it was now so deadly cold, and I feared that Lorna might get frozen, without having Gwenny to keep her warm. And after all, it was the sweetest labour I had ever known in all my life, to be sure that I was pulling Lorna, and pulling her to our own farm-house.

Gwenny's nose was touched with frost, before we had gone much further, because she would not keep it quiet and snug beneath the sealskin. And here I had to stop in the moonlight (which was very dangerous) and rub it with a clove of snow, as Eliza had taught me; and Gwenny scolding all the time, as if myself had frozen it. Lorna was now so far oppressed with all the troubles of the evening, and the joy that followed them, as well as by the piercing cold and difficulty of breathing, that she lay quite motionless, like the fairest wax in the moonlight – when we stole a glance at her, beneath the dark folds of the cloak; and I thought that she was falling into the heavy snow-sleep, whence there is no awaking.

Therefore I drew my traces tight, and set my whole strength to the business; and we slipped along at a merry pace, although with many joltings, which must have sent my darling out into the cold snow-drifts, but for the short strong arm of Gwenny. And so in about an hour's time, in spite of many hindrances, we came home to the old courtyard, and all the dogs saluted us. My heart was quivering, and my cheeks as hot as the Doones' bonfire, with wondering both what Lorna would think of our farm-yard, and what my mother would think of her. Upon the former subject my anxiety was wasted, for Lorna neither saw a thing, nor even opened her heavy eyes. And as to what mother would think of her, she was certain not to think at all, until she had cried over her.

And so indeed it came to pass. Even at this length of time, I can hardly tell it, although so bright before my mind, because it moves my heart so. The sledd was at the open door, with only Lorna in it: for Gwenny Carfax had jumped out, and hung back in the clearing, giving any reason rather than the only true one – that she would not be intruding. At the door were all our people; first of course Betty Muxworthy, teaching me how to draw the sledd, as if she had been born in it, and flourishing with a great broom, wherever a speck of snow lay. Then dear Annie, and old Molly (who was very quiet, and counted almost for nobody), and behind them mother, looking as if she wanted to come first, but doubted how the manners lay. In the distance Lizzie stood, fearful of encouraging, but unable to keep out of it.

Betty was going to poke her broom right in under the sealskin cloak, where Lorna lay unconscious, and where her precious breath hung frozen, like a silver cobweb; but I caught up Betty's broom, and flung it clean away over the corn chamber; and then I put the others by, and fetched my mother forward.

'You shall see her first,' I said; 'is she not your daughter? Hold the light there, Annie.'

Dear mother's hands were quick and trembling, as she opened the shining folds; and there she saw my Lorna sleeping, with her black hair all dishevelled, and she bent and kissed her forehead, and only said, 'God bless her, John!' And then she was taken with violent weeping, and I was forced to hold her.

'Us may tich of her now, I rackon,' said Betty in her most jealous way: 'Annie, tak her by the head, and I'll tak her by the toesen. No taime to stand here like girt gawks. Don'ee tak on zo, missus. Ther be vainer vish in the zea – Lor, but her be a booty!'

With this, they carried her into the house, Betty chattering all the while, and going on now about Lorna's hands, and the others crowding round her, so that I thought I was not wanted among so many women, and should only get the worst of it, and perhaps do harm to my darling. Therefore I went and brought Gwenny in, and gave her a potful of bacon and peas, and an iron spoon to eat it with, which she did right heartily.

Then I asked her how she could have been such a fool as to let those two vile fellows enter the house where Lorna was; and she accounted for it so naturally, that I could only blame myself. For my agreement had been to give one loud knock (if you happen to remember) and after that two little knocks. Well, these two drunken rogues had come; and one, being very drunk indeed, had given a great thump; and then nothing more to do with it; and the other, being three-quarters drunk, had followed his leader (as one might say) but feebly, and making two of it. Whereupon up jumped Lorna, and declared that her John was there.

All this Gwenny told me shortly, between the whiles of eating, and even while she licked the spoon: and then there came a message for me, that my love was sensible, and was seeking all around for me. Then I told Gwenny to hold her tongue (whatever she did, among us), and not to trust to women's words; and she told me they all were liars, as she had found out long ago; and the only thing to believe in was an honest man, when found. Thereupon I could have kissed her, as a sort of tribute, liking to be appreciated; yet the peas upon her lips made me think about it; and thought is fatal to action. So I went to see my dear.

That sight I shall not forget; till my dying head falls back, and my breast can lift no more. I know not whether I were then more blessed, or harrowed by it. For in the settle was my Lorna, propped with pillows round her, and her clear hands spread sometimes to the blazing fire-place. In her eyes no knowledge was of anything around her, neither in her neck the sense of leaning towards anything. Only both her lovely hands were entreating something, to spare her or to love her; and the lines of supplication quivered in her sad white face.

'All go away except my mother,' I said very quietly, but so that I would be obeyed; and everybody knew it. Then mother came to me alone; and she said, 'The frost is in her brain: I have heard of this before, John.' 'Mother, I will have it out,' was all that I could answer her; 'leave her to me altogether: only you sit there and watch.' For I felt that Lorna knew me, and no other soul but me; and that if not interfered with, she would soon come home to me. Therefore I sat gently by her, leaving nature, as it were, to her own good time and will. And presently the glance that watched me, as at distance and in doubt, began to flutter and to brighten, and to deepen into kindness, then to beam with trust and love, and then with gathering tears to falter, and in shame to turn away. But the small entreating hands found their way, as if by instinct, to my great protecting palms; and trembled there, and rested there.

For a little while we lingered thus, neither wishing to move away, neither caring to look beyond the presence of the other; both alike so full of hope, and comfort, and true happiness; if only the world would let us be. And then a little sob disturbed us, and mother tried to make believe that she was only coughing. But Lorna, guessing who she was, jumped up so very rashly that she almost set her frock on fire from the great ash-log; and away she ran to the old oak chair, where mother was by the cloak-case pretending to be knitting, and she took the work from mother's hands, and laid them both upon her head, kneeling humbly, and looking up.

'God bless you my fair mistress!' said mother, bending nearer, and then as Lorna's gaze prevailed, 'God bless you, my sweet child!'

And so she went to mother's heart, by the very nearest road, even as she had come to mine; I mean the road of pity, smoothed by grace, and youth, and gentleness.

22

Squire Faggus Makes Some Lucky Hits

Jeremy Stickles was gone south, ere ever the frost set in, for the purpose of mustering forces to attack the Doone Glen. But now this weather had put a stop to every kind of movement; for even if men could have borne the cold, they could scarcely be brought to face the perils of the snow-drifts. And to tell the truth, I cared not how long this weather lasted, so long as we had enough to eat, and could keep ourselves from freezing.

But now, in March, the sky at length began to come to its true manner, which we had not seen for months, a mixture (if I so may speak) of various expressions. And soon the dappled softening sky gave some earnest of its mood; for a brisk south wind arose, and the blessed rain came driving; cold indeed, yet most refreshing to the skin, all parched with snow, and the eyeballs so long dazzled.

Now when the first of the rain began, and the old familiar softness spread upon the window glass, and ran a little way in channels (though from the coldness of the glass it froze before reaching the bottom), knowing at once the difference from the short sharp thud of snow, we all ran out, and filled our eyes, and filled our hearts, with gazing.

Then Lorna came, and glorified me, for I had predicted a change of weather, more to keep their spirits up, than with real hope of it. But as the rain came down upon us, from the south-west wind, and we could not have enough of it, even putting our tongues to catch it, as little children might do, and beginning to talk of primroses; the very noblest thing of all was to hear, and see, the gratitude of the poor beasts yet remaining, and the few surviving birds.

It was now high time to work very hard; both to make up for the farm-work lost during the months of frost and snow, and also to be ready for a great and vicious attack from the Doones, who would burn us in our beds, at the earliest opportunity. Of farm-work there was little yet for even the most zealous man to begin to lay his hand to: because when the ground appeared through the crust of bubbled snow (as at last it did, though not as my Lorna had expected, at the first few drops of rain) it was all so soaked and sodden, and, as we call it, 'mucksy,' that to meddle with it in any way was to do more harm than good. Nevertheless, there was yard-work, and house-work, and tendance of stock, enough to save any man from idleness.

Now in spite of the floods, and the sloughs being out, and the state of the roads most perilous, Squire Faggus came at last, riding his famous strawberry mare. There was a great ado between him and Annie, as you may well suppose, after some four months of parting. And so we left them alone awhile, to coddle over their raptures. But when they were tired of that, or at least had time enough to be so, mother and I went in, to know what news Tom had brought with him. Though he did not seem to want us yet, he made himself agreeable; and so we sent Annie to cook the dinner, while her sweetheart should tell us everything.

Tom Faggus had very good news to tell, and he told it with such force of expression as made us laugh very heartily. He had taken up his purchase from old Sir Roger Basset of a nice bit of land, to the south of the moors, and in the parish of Molland.

Now this farm of Squire Faggus (as he truly now had a right to be called) was of the very finest pasture, when it got good store of rain. Tom saw at once what it was fit for – the breeding of fine cattle.

Being such a hand as he was, at making the most of every-thing, both his own and other people's (although so free in scattering, when the humour lay upon him), he had actually turned to his own advantage that extraordinary weather, which had so impoverished every one around him. For he taught his Winnie (who knew his meaning as well as any child could, and obeyed not only his word of mouth, but every glance he gave her), to go forth in the snowy evenings, when horses are seeking everywhere (be they wild or tame) for fodder and for shelter; and to whinny to the forest ponies, miles away from home perhaps, and lead them all, with rare appetite and promise of abundance, to her master's homestead. He shod good Winnie in such a manner, that she could not sink in the snow; and he clad her over the loins with a sheep-skin, dyed to her own colour, which the wild horses were never tired of coming up and sniffing at; taking it for an especial gift, and proof of inspiration. And Winnie never came home at night without at least a score of ponies trotting shyly after her, tossing their heads and their tails in turn, and making believe to be very wild, although hard pinched by famine. Of course, Tom would get them all into his pound in about five minutes; for he himself could neigh in a manner which went to the heart of the wildest horse. And then he fed them well, and turned them into his great cattle-pen, to abide their time for breaking, when the snow and frost should be over.

He had gotten more than three hundred now, in this sagacious manner.

I asked him what he meant to do with all that enormous lot of horses. He said that as for disposing of his stud, it would give him little difficulty. He would break them, when the spring weather came on, and deal with them as they required, and keep the handsomest for breeding. The rest he would despatch to London where he knew plenty of horse-dealers; and he doubted not that they would fetch him as much as ten pounds apiece all round, being now in great demand. I told him I wished that he might get it: but as it proved afterwards, he did.

Then he pressed us both on another point, the time for his marriage to Annie: and mother looked at me to say when, and I looked back at mother. However, knowing something of the world, and unable to make any further objection, by reason of his prosperity, I said that we must even do as the fashionable people did, and allow the maid herself to settle, when she would leave home and all. And this I spoke with a very bad grace, being perhaps of an ancient cast, and over fond of honesty – I mean, of course, among lower people.

But Tom paid little heed to this, knowing the world a great deal better than ever I could pretend to do; and being ready to take a thing, upon which he had set his mind, whether it came with a good grace, or whether it came with a bad one. And seeing that it would be awkward to provoke my anger, he left the room before more words, to submit himself to Annie.

Lorna had some curiosity to know what this famous man was like. And truth to tell, when she came to dinner, every thing about her was the neatest, and the prettiest, that can possibly be imagined.

My mother could not help remarking, though she knew that it was not mannerly, how like a princess Lorna looked, now she had her best things on; but two things caught Squire Faggus' eyes, after he had made a most gallant bow, and received a most graceful courtesy; and he kept his bright bold gaze upon them, first on one and then on the other, until my darling was hot with blushes, and I was ready to knock him down, if he had not been our visitor. But here again I should have been wrong, as I was apt to be in those days; for Tom intended no harm whatever, and his gaze was of pure curiosity; though Annie herself was vexed with it. The two objects of his close regard were, first, and most worthily, Lorna's face, and secondly, the ancient necklace restored to her by Sir Ensor Doone.

Now when the young maidens were gone – for we had quite a high dinner of fashion that day, with Betty Muxworthy waiting, and Gwenny Carfax at the gravy, – and only mother, and Tom, and I remained at the white deal table, with brandy, and schnapps, and hot water jugs; Squire Faggus said quite suddenly, and perhaps on purpose to take us aback, in case of our hiding anything –

'What do you know of the history of that beautiful maiden, good mother?'

'Not half so much as my son does,' mother answered, with a soft smile at me: 'and when John does not choose to tell a thing, wild horses will not pull it out of him.'

'Come, come,' said Master Faggus, smiling very pleasantly, 'you two understand each other, if any two on earth do. Ah, if I had only had a mother, how different I might have been!' And with that he sighed, in the tone which always overcame mother upon that subject, and had something to do with his getting Annie; and then he produced his pretty box, full of rolled tobacco, and offered me one, as I now had joined the goodly company of smokers.

But when our cylinders were both lighted, and I enjoying mine wonderfully, and astonishing mother by my skill, Tom Faggus told us that he was sure he had seen my Lorna's face before, many and many years ago, when she was quite a little child, but he could not remember where it was, or any thing more about it at present; though he would try to do so afterwards. He could not be mistaken, he said, for he had noticed her eyes especially; and had never seen such eyes before, neither again, until this day. I asked him if he had ever ventured into the Doone-valley; but he shook his head, and replied that he valued his life a deal too much for that. Then we put it to him, whether anything might assist his memory; but he said that he knew not of aught to do so, unless it were another glass of schnapps.

This being provided, he grew very wise, and told us clearly and candidly that we were both very foolish. For he said that we were keeping Lorna, at the risk not only of our stock, and the house above our heads, but also of our precious lives; and after all was she worth it, although so very beautiful? Upon which I told him, with indignation, that her beauty was the least part of her goodness, and that I would thank him for his opinion, when I had requested it.

'Bravo, our John Ridd!' he answered: 'fools will be fools till the end of the chapter: and I might be as big a one, if I were in thy shoes, John. Nevertheless, in the name of God, don't let that helpless child go about, with a thing worth half the county on her.'

'She is worth all the county herself,' said I, 'and all England put together: but she has nothing worth half a rick of hay upon her; for the ring I gave her cost only' – and here I stopped, for mother was looking, and I never would tell her how much it had cost me; though she had tried fifty times to find out.

'Tush, the ring!' Tom Faggus cried, with a contempt that moved me; 'I would never have stopped a man for that. But the necklace, you great oaf, the necklace is worth all your farm put together, and your Uncle Ben's fortune to the back of it; ay, and all the town of Dulverton.'

'What,' said I, 'that common glass thing, which she has had from her childhood!'

'Glass indeed! They are the finest brilliants ever I set eyes on: and I have handled a good many.'

'Surely,' cried mother, now flushing as red as Tom's own cheeks, with excitement, 'you must be wrong, or the young mistress would herself have known it.'

To prove herself right in that conclusion, she went herself to fetch Lorna, that the trinket might be examined, before the day grew dark. My darling came in, with a very quick glance and smile at my cigarro (for I was having the third by this time, to keep things in amity); and I waved it towards her, as much as to say, 'you see that I can do it.' And then mother led her up to the light, for Tom to examine her necklace.

On the shapely curve of her neck it hung, like dewdrops upon a white hyacinth; and I was vexed that Tom should have the chance to see it there. But even as if she had read my thoughts, or outrun them with her own, Lorna turned away, and softly took the jewels from the place which so much adorned them. And as she turned away, they sparkled through the rich dark, waves of hair. Then she laid the glittering circlet in my mother's hands; and Tom Faggus took it eagerly, and bore it to the window.

'Do you think it is worth five pounds, now?'

'Oh no! I never had so much money as that in all my life. It is very bright, and very pretty; but it cannot be worth five pounds, I am sure.'

'What a chance for a bargain! Oh, if it were not for Annie, I could make my fortune.'

'But, sir, I would not sell it to you, not for twenty times five pounds. My grandfather was so kind about it; and I think it belonged to my mother.'

'There are twenty-five rose diamonds in it, and twenty-five large brilliants that cannot be matched in London. How say you, Mistress Lorna, to a hundred thousand pounds?'

'Dear, kind mother, I am so glad,' she said in a whisper, coaxing mother out of sight of all but me; 'now you will have it, won't you, dear? And I shall be so happy; for a thousandth part of your kindness to me no jewels in the world can match.'

I cannot lay before you the grace with which she did it, all the air of seeking favour, rather than conferring it, and the high-bred fear of giving offence, which is of all fears the noblest. Mother knew not what to say. Of course she would never dream of taking such a gift as that; and yet she saw how sadly Lorna would be disappointed. Therefore mother did, from habit, what she almost always did, she called me to help her. But knowing that my eyes were full – for anything noble moves me so, quite as rashly as things pitiful – I pretended not to hear my mother, but to see a wild cat in the dairy.

Therefore I cannot tell what mother said in reply to Lorna; for when I came back, behold Tom Faggus had gotten again the necklace which had such charms for him, and was delivering all around (but especially to Annie, who was wondering at his learning) a dissertation on precious stones, and his sentiments about those in his hand. He said that the work was very ancient, but undoubtedly very good; that a trinket of this kind never could have belonged to any ignoble family, but to one of the very highest and most wealthy in England. And looking at Lorna, I felt sure that she must have come from a higher source than the very best of diamonds.

Tom Faggus said that the necklace was made, he would answer for it, in Amsterdam, two or three hundred years ago, long before London jewellers had begun to meddle with diamonds; and on the gold clasp he found some letters, done in some inverted way, the meaning of which was beyond him; also a bearing of some kind, which he believed was a mountain-cat.

We said no more about the necklace, for a long time afterwards; neither did my darling wear it, now that she knew its value, but did not know its history. She came to me the very next day, trying to look cheerful, and begged me if I loved her (never mind how little) to take charge of it again, as I once had done before, and not even to let her know in what place I restored it. I told her that this last request I could not comply with; for having been round her neck so often, it was now a sacred thing, more than a million pounds could be. Therefore it should dwell for the present in the neighbourhood of my heart; and so could not be far from her. At this she smiled her own sweet smile, and touched my forehead with her lips, and wished that she could only learn how to deserve such love as mine.

Tom Faggus took his good departure, which was a kind farewell to me, on the very day I am speaking of, the day after his arrival. Tom was a thoroughly upright man, according to his own standard; and you might rely upon him always, up to a certain point I mean, to be there or thereabouts. But sometimes things were too many for Tom, especially with ardent spirits, and then he judged, perhaps too much, with only himself for the jury. At any rate, I would trust him fully, for candour and for honesty, in almost every case in which he himself could have no interest. And so we got on very well together; and he thought me a fool; and I tried my best not to think anything worse of him.

Scarcely was Tom clean out of sight, and Annie's tears not dry yet (for she always made a point of crying upon his departure), when in came Master Jeremy Stickles, splashed with mud from head to foot, and not in the very best of humours, though happy to get back again.

23

Every Man Must Defend Himself

Master Stickles agreed with me, that we could not hope to escape an attack from the outlaws, and the more especially now that they knew himself to be returned to us. Also he praised me for my forethought, in having threshed out all our corn, and hidden the produce in such a manner that they were not likely to find it. Furthermore, he recommended that all the entrances to the house should at once be strengthened, and a watch must be maintained at night; and he thought it wiser that I should go (late as it was) to Lynmouth, if a horse could pass the valley, and fetch every one of his mounted troopers, who might now be quartered there. Also if any men of courage, though capable only of handling a pitchfork, could be found in the neighbourhood, I was to try to summon them.

Knowing how fiercely the floods were out, I resolved to travel the higher road, by Cosgate and through Countisbury. I followed the bank of the flood to the beach, some two or three hundred yards below; and there had the luck to see Will Watcombe on the opposite side, caulking an old boat. Though I could not make him hear a word, from the deafening roar of the torrent, I got him to understand at last that I wanted to cross over. Upon this he fetched another man, and the two of them launched a boat; and paddling well out to sea, fetched round the mouth of the frantic river. The other man proved to be Stickles' chief mate; and so he went back, and fetched his comrades, bringing their weapons, but leaving their horses behind. As it happened there were but four of them; however to have even these was a help; and I started again at full speed for my home; for the men must follow afoot, and cross our river high up on the moorland.

This took them a long way round, and the track was rather bad to find, and the sky already darkening; so that I arrived at Plover's Barrows more than two hours before them. But they had done a sagacious thing, which was well worth the delay; for by hoisting their flag upon the hill, they fetched the two watchmen from the Foreland, and added them to their number.

Now, expecting a sharp attack that night, we prepared a great quantity of knuckles of pork, and a ham in full cut, and a fillet of hung mutton. For we would almost surrender, rather than keep our garrison hungry. And all our men were exceedingly brave; and counted their rounds of the house in half-pints.

We sent all the women to bed quite early, except Gwenny Carfax and our old Betty. These two we allowed to stay up, because they might be useful to us, if they could keep from quarrelling. For my part, I had little fear as to the result of the combat. It was not likely that the Doones could bring more than eight or ten men against us, and to meet these we had eight good men, including Jeremy, and myself, all well-armed and resolute, besides our three farm-servants, and the parish-clerk, and the shoemaker. I was not content to abide within the house, or go the rounds with the troopers; but betook myself to the rickyard, knowing that the Doones were likely to begin their onset there. For they had a pleasant custom, when they visited farm-houses, of lighting themselves towards picking up anything they wanted, or stabbing the inhabitants, by first creating a blaze in the rickyard. Perhaps I was wrong in heeding the ricks, at such a time as that; especially as only the clover was of much importance. But it seemed to me like a sort of triumph that they should even be able to boast of having fired our mow-yard. Therefore I stood in a nick of the clover, whence we had cut some trusses, with my club in hand, and gun close by.

The robbers rode into our yard as coolly as if they had been invited, having lifted the gate from the hinges first, on account of its being fastened. Then they actually opened our stable-doors, and turned our honest horses out, and put their own rogues in the place of them. At this my breath was quite taken away; for we think so much of our horses. By this time I could see our troopers, waiting in the shadow of the house, round the corner from where the Doones were, and expecting the order to fire. But Jeremy Stickles very wisely kept them in readiness, until the enemy should advance upon them.

'Two of you lazy fellows go,' it was the deep voice of Carver Doone, 'and make us a light to cut their throats by. Only one thing, once again. If any man touches Lorna, I will stab him where he stands. She belongs to me. There are two other young damsels here, whom you may take away if you please. And the mother, I hear, is still comely. Now for our rights. We have borne too long the insolence of these yokels. Kill every man, and every child, and burn the cursed place down.'

As he spoke thus blasphemously, I set my gun against his breast; and by the light buckled from his belt, I saw the little 'sight' of brass gleaming alike upon either side, and the sleek round barrel glimmering. The aim was sure as death itself. If I only drew the trigger (which went very lightly) Carver Doone would breathe no more. And yet – will you believe me? – I could not pull the trigger. Would to God that I had done so!

For I never had taken human life, neither done bodily harm to man; beyond the little bruises, and the trifling aches and pains, which follow a good and honest bout in the wrestling ring. Therefore I dropped my carbine, and grasped again my club, which seemed a more straightforward implement.

Presently two young men came towards me, bearing brands of resined hemp, kindled from Carver's lamp. The foremost of them set his torch to the rick within a yard of me, the smoke concealing me from him. I struck him with a back-handed blow on the elbow, as he bent it; and I heard the bone of his arm break, as clearly as ever I heard a twig snap. With a roar of pain he fell on the ground, and his torch dropped there, and singed him. The other man stood amazed at this, not having yet gained sight of me; till I caught his firebrand from his hand, and struck it into his countenance. With that he leaped at me; but I caught him, in a manner learned from early wrestling, and snapped his collar-bone, as I laid him upon the top of his comrade.

This little success so encouraged me, that I was half inclined to advance, and challenge Carver Doone to meet me; but I bore in mind that he would be apt to shoot me without ceremony; and what is the utmost of human strength against the power of powder? Moreover I remembered my promise to sweet Lorna; and who would be left to defend her, if the rogues got rid of me?

While I was hesitating thus (for I always continue to hesitate, except in actual conflict) a blaze of fire lit up the house, and brown smoke hung around it. Six of our men had let go at the Doones, by Jeremy Stickles' order, as the villains came swaggering down in the moonlight, ready for rape or murder. Two of them fell, and the rest hung back, to think at their leisure what this was. They were not used to this sort of thing: it was neither just nor courteous.

Being unable any longer to contain myself, as I thought of Lorna's excitement at all this noise of firing, I came across the yard, expecting whether they would shoot at me. However, no one shot at me; and I went up to Carver Doone, whom I knew by his size in the moonlight, and I took him by the beard, and said, 'Do you call yourself a man?'

For a moment, he was so astonished that he could not answer. None had ever dared, I suppose, to look at him in that way; and he saw that he had met his equal, or perhaps his master. And then he tried a pistol at me; but I was too quick for him.

'Now, Carver Doone, take warning,' I said to him, very soberly; 'you have shown yourself a fool, by your contempt of me. I may not be your match in craft; but I am in manhood. You are a despicable villain. Lie low in your native muck.'

And with that word, I laid him flat upon his back in our straw-yard, by a trick of the inner heel, which he could not have resisted (though his strength had been twice as great as mine), unless he were a wrestler. Seeing him down, the others ran, though one of them made a shot at me, and some of them got their horses, before our men came up; and some went away without them. And among these last was Captain Carver, who arose, while I was feeling myself (for I had a little wound), and strode away with a train of curses, enough to poison the light of the moon.

We gained six very good horses, by this attempted rapine, as well as two young prisoners, whom I had smitten by the clover-rick. And two dead Doones were left behind; whom (as we buried them in the churchyard, without any service over them) I for my part was most thankful that I had not killed.

Without waiting for any warrant, only saying something about '*captus in flagrante delicto*' – if that be the way to spell it – Stickles sent our prisoners off, bound and looking miserable, to the jail at Taunton.

24

A Visit from the Counsellor

Now while I was riding home one evening, I guessed but little that all my thoughts were needed much for my own affairs. So however it proved to be; for as I came in, soon after dark, my sister Eliza met me at the corner of the cheese-room, and she said, 'Don't go in there, John,' pointing to mother's room; 'until I have had a talk with you.'

'In the name of Moses,' I inquired, having picked up that phrase at Dulverton; 'what are you at, about me now? There is no peace for a quiet fellow.'

'It is nothing we are at,' she answered; 'neither may you make light of it. It is something very important about Mistress Lorna Doone.'

'Let us have it at once;' I cried: 'I can bear anything about Lorna, except that she does not care for me.'

'Your Lorna is with Annie, having a good cry, I believe; and Annie too glad to second her. She knows that a great man is here, and knows that he wants to see her. But she begged to defer the interview, until dear John's return.'

I was almost sure that the man who was come must be the Counsellor himself; of whom I felt much keener fear than of his son Carver. And knowing that his visit boded ill to me and Lorna, I went and sought my dear; and led her with a heavy heart, from the maiden's room to mother's, to meet our dreadful visitor.

Mother was standing by the door, making courtesies now and then, and listening to a long harangue upon the rights of state and land, which the Counsellor (having found that she was the owner of her property, and knew nothing of her title to it) was encouraged to deliver. My dear mother stood gazing at him, spell-bound by his eloquence, and only hoping that he would stop. He was shaking his hair upon his shoulders, in the power of his words, and his wrath at some little thing she had suffered, which he declared to be quite illegal.

Then I ventured to show myself, in the flesh, before him; although he feigned not to see me; but he advanced with zeal to Lorna; holding out both hands at once.

'My darling child, my dearest niece; how wonderfully well you look! Mistress Ridd, I give you credit. This is the country of good things. I never would have believed our Queen could have looked so Royal. Surely of all virtues, hospitality is the finest, and the most romantic. Dearest Lorna, kiss your uncle; it is quite a privilege.'

'Perhaps it is to you, sir,' said Lorna, who could never quite check her sense of oddity; 'but I fear that you have smoked tobacco, which spoils reciprocity.'

'You are right, my child. How keen your scent is. It is always so with us. Your grandfather was noted for his olfactory powers. Ah, a great loss, dear Mrs Ridd, a terrible loss to this neighbourhood! As one of our great writers says – I think it must be Milton – "We ne'er shall look upon his like again."'

'With your good leave, sir,' I broke in, 'Master Milton could never have written so sweet and simple a line as that. It is one of the great Shakespeare.'

'Woe is me for my neglect!' said the Counsellor, bowing airily; 'this must be your son, Mistress Ridd, the great John, the wrestler. And one who meddles with the Muses! Ah, since I was young, how everything is changed, madam! Except indeed the beauty of women, which seems to me to increase every year.' Here the old villain bowed to my mother; and she blushed, and made another courtesy, and really did look very nice.

'Now though I have quoted the poets amiss, as your son informs me (for which I tender my best thanks, and must amend my reading), I can hardly be wrong in assuming that this young armiger must be the too attractive cynosure to our poor little maiden. And for my part, she is welcome to him. I have never been one of those who dwell upon distinctions of rank, and birth, and such like; as if they were in the heart of nature, and must be eternal. In early youth, I may have thought so, and been full of that little pride. But now I have long accounted it one of the first axioms of political economy – you are following me, Mistress Ridd?'

'Well, sir, I am doing my best; but I cannot quite keep up with you.'

'Never mind, madam; I will be slower. But your son's intelligence is so quick – '

'I see, sir; you thought that mine must be. But no; it all comes from his father, sir. His father was that quick and clever – '

'Ah, I can well suppose it, madam. And a credit he is to both of you. Now to return to our muttons – a figure which you will appreciate – I may now be regarded, I think, as this young lady's legal guardian; although I have not had the honour of being formally appointed such. Her father was the eldest son of Sir Ensor Doone; and I happened to be the second son, and as young maidens cannot be baronets, I suppose I am "Sir Counsellor." Is it so, Mistress Ridd, according to your theory of genealogy? And as Lorna's guardian, I give my full and ready consent to her marriage with your son, madam.'

'O how good of you, sir, how kind! Well, I always did say, that the learnedest people were, almost always, the best and kindest, and the most simple-hearted.'

'Madam, that is a great sentiment. What a goodly couple they will be! and if we can add him to our strength – '

'Oh no, sir, oh no!' cried mother: 'you really must not think of it. He has always been brought up so honest – '

'Hem! that makes a difference. A decided disqualification for domestic life among the Doones. But, surely, he might get over those prejudices, madam?'

'Oh no, sir! he never can: he never can indeed. When he

was only that high, sir, he could not steal even an apple, when some wicked boys tried to mislead him.'

'Ah,' replied the Counsellor, shaking his white head gravely; 'then I greatly fear that his case is quite incurable. I have known such cases; violent prejudice, bred entirely of education, and anti-economical to the last degree. And when it is so, it is desperate: no man after imbibing ideas of that sort, can in any way be useful.'

'Oh yes, sir, John is very useful. He can do as much work as three other men; and you should see him load a sledd, sir.'

'I was speaking, madam, of higher usefulness, – power of the brain and heart. The main thing for us upon earth is to take a large view of things. But while we talk of the heart, what is my niece Lorna doing, that she does not come and thank me, for my perhaps too prompt concession to her youthful fancies? Ah, if I had wanted thanks, I should have been more stubborn.'

Lorna, being challenged thus, came up and looked at her uncle, with her noble eyes fixed full upon his, which beneath his white eyebrows glistened, like dormer windows piled with snow.

'For what am I to thank you, uncle?'

'My dear niece, I have told you. For removing the heaviest obstacle, which to a mind so well regulated could possibly have existed, between your dutiful self and the object of your affections.'

'Well, uncle, I should be very grateful, if I thought that you did so from love of me; or if I did not know that you have something yet concealed from me.'

'And my consent,' said the Counsellor, 'is the more meritorious, the more liberal, frank, and candid, in the face of an existing fact, and a very clearly established one; which might have appeared to weaker minds in the light of an impediment; but to my loftier view of matrimony seems quite a recommendation.'

'What fact do you mean, sir? Is it one that I ought to know?'

'My dear child, I prolong your suspense. Curiosity is the most powerful of all feminine instincts; and therefore the most delightful, when not prematurely satisfied. However, if you must have my strong realities, here they are. Your father slew dear John's father, and dear John's father slew yours.'

Having said thus much, the Counsellor leaned back upon his chair, and shaded his calm white-bearded eyes from the rays of our tallow candles. He was a man who liked to look, rather than to be looked at. But Lorna came to me for aid; and I went up to Lorna; and mother looked at both of us.

Then feeling that I must speak first (as no one would begin it), I took my darling round the waist, and led her up to the Counsellor; while she tried to bear it bravely; yet must lean on me, or did.

'Now, Sir Counsellor Doone,' I said, with Lorna squeezing both my hands, I never yet knew how (considering that she was walking all the time, or something like it); 'you know right well, Sir Counsellor, that Sir Ensor Doone gave approval.' I cannot tell what made me think of this: but so it came upon me.

'Approval to what, good rustic John? To the slaughter so reciprocal?'

'No, sir, not to that; even if it ever happened; which I do not believe. But to the love betwixt me and Lorna; which your story shall not break, without more evidence than your word. And even so, shall never break; if Lorna thinks as I do.'

The maiden gave me a little touch, as much as to say, 'you are right, darling: give it to him, again, like that.' However, I held my peace, well knowing that too many words do mischief.

Then mother looked at me with wonder, being herself too amazed to speak; and the Counsellor looked, with great wrath in his eyes, which he tried to keep from burning.

'How say you then, John Ridd,' he cried, stretching out one hand, like Elijah; 'is this a thing of the sort you love? Is this what you are used to?'

'So please your worship,' I answered; 'no kind of violence can surprise us, since first came Doones upon Exmoor. Up to that time none heard of harm; except of taking a purse, may be, or cutting a strange sheep's throat. And the poor folk who did this were hanged, with some benefit of clergy. But ever since the Doones came first, we are used to any thing.'

'Thou varlet,' cried the Counsellor, with the colour of his eyes quite changed with the sparkles of his fury; 'is this the way we are to deal with such a low-bred clod as thou? To question the doings of our people, and to talk of clergy! What, dream you not that we could have clergy, and of the right sort too, if only we cared to have them? Tush! Am I to spend my time, arguing with a plough-tail Bob?'

'You old villain,' cried my mother, shaking her fist at the Counsellor, while I could do nothing else but hold, and bend across, my darling, and whisper to deaf ears; 'What is the good of the Quality; if this is all that comes of it? Out of the way! You know the words that make the deadly mischief; but not the ways that heal them. Give me that bottle, if hands you have; what is the use of Counsellors?'

I saw that dear mother was carried away; and indeed I myself was something like it; with the pale face upon my bosom, and the heaving of the heart, and the heat and cold all through me, as my darling breathed or lay. Meanwhile the Counsellor stood back, and seemed a little sorry; although of course it was not in his power to be at all ashamed of himself.

'My sweet love, my darling child,' our mother went on to Lorna, in a way that I shall never forget, though I live to be a hundred; 'pretty pet, not a word of it is true, upon that old liar's oath: and if every word were true, poor chick, you should have our John all the more for it. You, and John, were made by God and meant for one another, whatever falls between you. Little lamb, look up and speak: here is your own John, and I; and the devil take the Counsellor.'

I was amazed at mother's words, being so unlike her; while I loved her all the more because she forgot herself so. In another moment in ran Annie, ay and Lizzie also, knowing by some mystic sense (which I have often noticed, but never could explain) that something was astir, belonging to the world of women, yet foreign to the eyes of men. And now the Counsellor, being well-born, although such a heartless miscreant, beckoned to me to come away; which I, being smothered with women, was only too glad to do, as soon as my own love would let go of me.

'That is the worst of them,' said the old man, when I had led him into our kitchen, with an apology at every step, and given him hot schnapps and water, and a cigarro of brave Tom Faggus: 'you never can say much, sir, in the way of reasoning (however gently meant and put) but what these women will fly out. It is wiser to put a wild bird in a cage, and expect him to sit and look at you, and chirp without a feather rumpled, than it is to expect a woman to answer reason reasonably.' Saying this, he looked at his puff of smoke as if it contained more reason.

'Now of this business, John,' he said, after getting to the bottom of the second glass, and having a trifle or so to eat, and praising our chimney-corner; 'taking you on the whole, you know, you are wonderfully good people: and instead of giving me up to the soldiers, as you might have done, you are doing your best to make me drunk.'

'Not at all, sir,' I answered; 'not at all, your worship. Let me mix you another glass. We rarely have a great gentleman by the side of our embers and oven. I only beg your pardon, sir, that my sister Annie (who knows where to find the good pans and the lard) could not wait upon you this evening; and I fear they have done it with dripping instead, and in a pan with the bottom burned. But old Betty quite loses her head sometimes, by dint of over-scalding.'

'My son,' replied the Counsellor, standing across the front of the fire, to prove his strict sobriety: 'I meant to come down upon you to-night; but you have turned the tables upon me. Not through any skill on your part, nor through any paltry weakness as to love (and all that stuff, which boys and girls spin tops at, or knock dolls' noses together), but through your simple way of taking me, as a man to be believed: combined with the comfort of this place, and the choice tobacco, and cordials. I have not enjoyed an evening so much: God bless me if I know when!'

'Your worship,' said I, 'makes me more proud than I well know what to do with. Of all the things that please and lead us into happy sleep at night, the first and chiefest is to think that we have pleased a visitor.'

'Then, John, thou hast deserved good sleep, for I am not pleased easily. But although our family is not so high now as it hath been, I have enough of the gentleman left to be pleased when good people try me. My father, Sir Ensor, was better than I in this great element of birth, and my son Carver is far worse. *Ætas parentum*, what is it, my boy? I hear that you have been at a grammar-school.'

'So I have, your worship, and a very good one; but I only got far enough to make more tail than head of Latin.'

'Let that pass,' said the Counsellor: 'John, thou art all the wiser.' And the old man shook his hoary locks, as if Latin had been his ruin. I looked at him sadly, and wondered whether it might have so ruined me, but for God's mercy in stopping it.

25

The Way to Make the Cream Rise

That night the reverend Counsellor, not being in such state of mind as ought to go alone, kindly took our best old bedstead, carved in panels, well enough, with the woman of Samaria. I set him up, both straight and heavy, so that he need but close both eyes, and keep his mouth just open; and in the morning he was thankful for all that he could remember.

I, for my part, scarcely knew whether he really had begun to feel good-will towards us, and to see that nothing else could be of any use to him; or whether he was merely acting, so as to deceive us. And it had struck me, several times, that he had made a great deal more of the spirit he had taken than the quantity would warrant, with a man so wise and solid. Neither did I quite understand a little story which Lorna told me, how that in the night awaking, she had heard, or seemed to hear, a sound of feeling in her room; as if there had been some one groping carefully among the things within her drawers or wardrobe-closet. But the noise had ceased at once, she said, when she sat up in bed and listened; and knowing how many mice we had, she took courage, and fell asleep again.

After breakfast, the Counsellor (who looked no whit the worse for schnapps, but even more grave and venerable) followed our Annie into the dairy, to see how we managed the clotted cream, of which he had eaten a basinful. And thereupon they talked a little; and Annie thought him a fine

184

old gentleman, and a very just one; for he had nobly condemned the people who spoke against Tom Faggus.

'Your honour must plainly understand,' said Annie, being now alone with him, and spreading out her light quick hands over the pans, like butterflies, 'that they are brought in here to cool, after being set in the basin-holes, with the wood-ash under them, which I showed you in the back-kitchen. And they must have very little heat, not enough to simmer even; only just to make the bubbles rise, and the scum upon the top set thick: and after that, it clots as firm, – oh, as firm as my two hands be.'

'Have you ever heard,' asked the Counsellor, who enjoyed this talk with Annie, 'that if you pass across the top, without breaking the surface, a string of beads, or polished glass, or any thing of that kind, the cream will set three times as solid, and in thrice the quantity?'

'No, sir; I have never heard that,' said Annie, staring with all her simple eyes; 'what a thing it is to read books, and grow learned! But it is very easy to try it: I will get my coral necklace; it will not be witchcraft, will it, sir?'

'Certainly not,' the old man replied: 'I will make the experiment myself, and you may trust me not to be hurt, my dear. But coral will not do, my child, neither will any thing coloured. The beads must be of plain common glass; but the brighter they are the better.'

'Then I know the very thing,' cried Annie; 'as bright as bright can be, and without any colour in it, except in the sun or candle-light. Dearest Lorna has the very thing, a necklace of some old glass-beads, or I think they called them jewels: she will be too glad to lend it to us. I will go for it, in a moment.'

'My dear, it cannot be half so bright as your own pretty eyes. But remember one thing, Annie, you must not say what it is for; or even that I am going to use it, or anything at all about it; else the charm will be broken. Bring it here, without a word; if you know where she keeps it.'

'To be sure I do,' she answered; 'John used to keep it for her. But she took it away from him last week, and she wore it, and when – I mean when somebody was here; and he said it was very valuable, and spoke with great learning about it, and called it by some particular name, which I forget at this moment.'

Now as luck would have it – whether good luck, or otherwise, you must not judge too hastily, – my darling had taken it into her head, only a day or two before, that I was far too valuable to be trusted with her necklace. Now that she had some idea of its price and quality, she had begun to fear that some one, perhaps even Squire Faggus (in whom her faith was illiberal), might form designs against my health, to win the bauble from me. So, with many pretty coaxings, she had led me to give it up; which, except for her own sake, I was glad enough to do, misliking a charge of such importance.

Therefore Annie found it sparkling in the little secret hole, near the head of Lorna's bed, which she herself had recommended for its safer custody; and without a word to anyone she brought it down, and danced it in the air before the Counsellor, for him to admire its lustre.

'Oh, that old thing!' said the gentleman, in a tone of some contempt; 'I remember that old thing well enough. However, for want of a better, no doubt it will answer our purpose. Three times three, I pass it over. Crinkleum, crankum, grass and clover! What are you feared of, you silly child?'

'Good sir, it is perfect witchcraft! I am sure of that, because it rhymes. Oh, what would mother say to me? Shall I ever go to heaven again? Oh, I see the cream already!'

'Now,' he said, in a deep stern whisper; 'not a word of this to living soul: neither must you, nor any other enter this place for three hours at least. By that time the charm will have done its work: the pan will be cream to the bottom; and you will bless me for a secret which will make your fortune. Put the bauble under this pannikin; which none must lift for a day and a night. Have no fear, my simple wench; not a breath of harm shall come to you, if you obey my orders.'

'Oh that I will, sir, that I will: if you only tell me what to do.'

'Go to your room, without so much as a single word to anyone. Bolt yourself in, and for three hours now, read the Lord's Prayer backwards.'

Poor Annie was only too glad to escape, upon these conditions; and the Counsellor kissed her upon the forehead, and told her not to make her eyes red, because they were much too sweet and pretty. She dropped them at this, with a sob and a courtesy, and ran away to her bedroom: but as for reading the Lord's Prayer backwards, that was much beyond her; and she had not done three words quite right, before the three hours expired.

Meanwhile the Counsellor was gone. He bade our mother adieu, with so much dignity of bearing, and such warmth and gratitude, and the high-bred courtesy of the old school (now fast disappearing), that when he was gone, dear mother fell back on the chair which he had used last night; as if it would teach her the graces. And for more than an hour, she made believe not to know what there was for dinner.

'Oh the wickedness of the world! Oh the lies that are told of people – or rather I mean the falsehoods – because a man is better born, and has better manners! Why, Lorna, how is it that you never speak about your charming uncle? Did you notice, Lizzie, how his silver hair was waving upon his velvet collar, and how white his hands were, and every nail like an acorn; only pink, like shell-fish, or at least like shells? And the way he bowed, and dropped his eyes, from his pure respect for me! And then, that he would not even speak, on account of his emotion; hut pressed my hand in silence! Oh Lizzie, you have read me beautiful things about Sir Gally-head, and the rest; but nothing to equal Sir Counsellor.'

'You had better marry him, madam,' said I, coming in very sternly; though I knew I ought not to say it: 'he can repay your adoration. He has stolen a hundred thousand pounds.'

'John,' cried my mother, 'you are mad!' And yet she turned as pale as death; for women are so quick at turning; and she inkled what it was.

'Of course, I am, mother; mad about the marvels of Sir Galahad. He has gone off with my Lorna's necklace. Fifty farms like ours can never make it good to Lorna.'

Hereupon ensued grim silence. Mother looked at Lizzie's face, for she could not look at me; and Lizzie looked at me, to know: and as for me, I could have stamped almost on the heart of any one. It was not the value of the necklace – I am not so low a hound as that – nor was it even the damned folly shown by every one of us – it was the thought of Lorna's sorrow for her ancient plaything; and even more, my fury at the breach of hospitality.

But Lorna came up to me softly, as a woman should always come; and she laid one hand upon my shoulder; and she only looked at me. She even seemed to fear to look, and dropped her eyes, and sighed at me. Without a word, I knew by that, how I must have looked like Satan; and the evil spirit left my heart; when she had made me think of it.

'Darling John, did you want me to think that you cared for my money, more than for me?'

I led her away from the rest of them, being desirous of explaining things, when I saw the depth of her nature opened, like an everlasting well, to me. But she would not let me say a word, or do any thing by ourselves, as it were: she said, 'Your duty is to your mother: this blow is on her, and not on me.'

I saw that she was right; though how she knew it is beyond me; and I asked her just to go in front, and bring my mother round a little. For I must let my passion pass: it may drop its weapons quickly; but it cannot come and go, before a man has time to think.

Then Lorna went up to my mother, who was still in the chair of elegance; and she took her by both hands, and said, –

'Dearest mother, I shall fret so, if I see you fretting. And to fret will kill me, mother. They have always told me so.'

But who shall tell of Annie's grief? The poor little thing would have staked her life upon finding the trinket, in all its beauty, lying under the pannikin. She proudly challenged me to lift it – which I had done, long ere that, of course – if only I would take the risk of the spell for my incredulity.

But when we raised the pannikin, and there was nothing under it, poor Annie fell against the wall, which had been whitened lately; and her face put all the white to scorn.

That same night Master Jeremy Stickles (of whose absence

the Counsellor must have known) came back, with all equipment ready for the grand attack.

It was very strange to hear and see, and quite impossible to account for, that now some hundreds of country people (who feared to whisper so much as a word against the Doones a year ago, and would sooner have thought of attacking a church, in service time, than Glen Doone) sharpened their old cutlasses, and laid pitchforks on the grindstone, and bragged at every village cross, as if each would kill ten Doones himself, neither care to wipe his hands afterwards. And this fierce bravery, and tall contempt, had been growing ever since the news of the attack upon our premises had taken good people by surprise; at least as concerned the issue.

Jeremy Stickles laughed heartily about Annie's new manner of charming the cream; but he looked very grave at the loss of the jewels, so soon as he knew their value.

'My son,' he exclaimed, 'this is very heavy. It will go ill with all of you to make good this loss, as I fear that you will have to do.'

'What!' cried I, with my blood running cold. 'We make good the loss, Master Stickles! Every farthing we have in the world, and the labour of our lives to boot, will never make good the tenth of it.'

'It would cut me to the heart,' he answered, laying his hand on mine, 'to hear of such a deadly blow to you, and your good mother. And this farm; how long, John, has it been in your family?'

'For at least six hundred years,' I said, with a foolish pride that was only too like to end in groans; 'and some people say, by a Royal grant, in the time of the great King Alfred. At any rate, a Ridd was with him, throughout all his hiding-time. We have always held by the King and Crown: surely none will turn us out, unless we are guilty of treason?'

'My son,' replied Jeremy very gently, so that I could love him for it, 'not a word to your good mother of this unlucky matter. Keep it to yourself, my boy, and try to think but little of it. After all, I may be wrong: at any rate, least said best mended.'

'But Jeremy, dear Jeremy, how can I bear to leave it so? Do you suppose that I can sleep, and eat my food and go about, and look at other people, as if nothing at all had happened? And all the time have it on my mind, that not an acre of all the land, nor even our old sheep-dog, belongs to us of right at all! It is more than I can do, Jeremy. Let me talk, and know the worst of it.'

'Very well,' replied Master Stickles, seeing that both the doors were closed; 'I thought that nothing could move you, John; or I never would have told you. Likely enough I am quite wrong; and God send that I be so. But what I guessed at some time back seems more than a guess, now that you have told me about those wondrous jewels. Now will you keep as close as death every word I tell you?'

'By the honour of a man, I will. Until you yourself release me.'

'That is quite enough, John. From you I want no oath; which, according to my experience, tempts a bad man to lie the more, by making it more important. I know you now too well to swear you, though I have the power. Now, my lad, what I have to say will scare your mind in one way, and ease it in another. I think that you have been hard pressed – I can read you like a book, John – by something which that old villain said, before he stole the necklace. You have tried not to dwell upon it; you have even tried to make light of it for the sake of the women: but on the whole it has grieved you more than even this dastard robbery.'

'It would have done so, Jeremy Stickles, if I could once have believed it. And even without much belief, it is so against our manners, that it makes me miserable. Only think of loving Lorna, only think of kissing her; and then remembering that her father had destroyed the life of mine!'

'Only think,' said Master Stickles, imitating my very voice, 'of Lorna loving you, John, of Lorna kissing you, John; and all the while saying to herself, "this man's father murdered mine." Now look at it in Lorna's way, as well as in your own way. How one-sided all men are!'

'I may look at it in fifty ways, and yet no good will come of it. Jeremy, I confess to you, that I tried to make the best of it; partly to baffle the Counsellor, and partly because my darling needed my help, and bore it so, and behaved to me so nobly. But to you in secret, I am not ashamed to say that a woman may look over this, easier than a man may.'

'Because her nature is larger, my son, when she truly loves; although her mind be smaller. Now if I can ease you from this secret burden, will you bear, with strength and courage, the other which I plant on you?'

'I will do my best,' said I.

'No man can do more,' said he; and so began his story.

26

Jeremy Finds
Out Something

'You know, my son,' said Jeremy Stickles, with a good pull at his pipe, because he was going to talk so much, and putting his legs well along in the settle; 'it has been my duty, for a wearier time than I care to think of (and which would have been unbearable, except for your great kindness), to search this neighbourhood narrowly, and learn every thing about every body. I was riding one afternoon from Dulverton to Watchett – '

'Dulverton to Watchett!' I cried. 'Now what does that remind me of? I am sure, I remember some thing – '

'Remember this, John, if any thing – that another word from thee, and thou hast no more of mine. Well, I was a little weary perhaps, having been plagued at Dulverton with the grossness of the people. For they would tell me nothing at all about their fellow townsman, your worthy Uncle Huckaback, except that he was a God-fearing man, and they only wished I was like him. It was late in the afternoon, and I was growing weary. The road (if road it could be called) turned suddenly down the higher land to the very brink of the sea; and rounding a little jut of cliff I met the roar of the breakers.

'Watchett town was not to be seen, on account of a little foreland, a mile or more upon my course, and standing to the right of me. There was room enough below the cliffs (which are nothing there to yours, John) for horse and man to get along, although the tide was running high with a northerly gale to back it. But close at hand and in the corner, drawn above the yellow sands and long eyebrows of wrack-weed, as snug a little house blinked on me as ever I saw, or wished to see.

'Seeing that this same inn had four windows, and no more, I thought to myself how snug it was, and how beautifully I could sleep there. And so I made the old horse draw hand, which he was only too glad to do, and we climb above the spring-tide mark, and over a little piece of turf, and struck the door of the hostelry. Some one came, and peeped at me through the lattice overhead, which was full of bulls' eyes; and then the bolt was drawn back, and a woman met me very courteously. A dark and foreign-looking woman, very hot of blood, I doubt, but not altogether a bad one. And she waited for me to be first to speak, which an Englishwoman would not have done.

' "Can I rest here for the night?" I asked, with a lift of my hat to her; for she was no provincial dame, who would stare at me for the courtesy: "my horse is weary from the sloughs, and myself but little better: besides that, we both are famished."

' "Yes, sir, you can rest and welcome. But of food, I fear, there is but little, unless of the common order. Our fishers would have drawn the nets, but the waves were violent. However, we have what you call it? I never can remember, it is so hard to say – the flesh of the hog salted."

' "Bacon!" said I; "what can be better? And half-a-dozen eggs with it, and a quart of fresh-drawn ale. You make me rage with hunger, madam. Is it cruelty, or hospitality?"

'She laughed aloud, and swung her shoulders, as your natives cannot do; and then she called a little maid, to lead my horse to stable. However I preferred to see that matter done myself, and told her to send the little maid for the frying pan and the egg-box.

'However, not to dwell too much upon our little pleasantries (for I always get on with these foreign women, better than with your Molls and Pegs), I became not inquisitive, but reasonably desirous to know, by what strange hap or hazard a clever and a handsome woman, as she must have been some day, a woman moreover with great contempt for the rustic minds around her, could have settled here in this lonely inn, with only the waves for company, and a boorish husband who slaved all day in turning a potter's wheel at Watchett. And what was the meaning of the emblem set above her doorway, a very unattractive cat sitting in a ruined tree?

'However, I had not very long to strain my curiosity; for when she found out who I was, and how I held the King's commission, and might be called an officer, her desire to tell me all was more than equal to mine of hearing it.

'By birth she was an Italian, from the mountains of Apulia, who had gone to Rome to seek her fortunes, after being badly treated in some love affair. Her Christian name was Benita; as for her surname, that could make no difference to any one. Being a quick and active girl, and resolved to work down her troubles, she found employment in a large hotel; and rising gradually, began to send money to her parents. And here she might have thriven well, and married well under sunny skies, and been a happy woman, but that some black day sent thither a rich and noble English family, eager to behold the Pope.

'They were all great people, and rich, and very liberal; so that when they offered to take her, to attend to the children, and to speak the language for them, and to comfort the lady, she was only too glad to go, little foreseeing the end of it.

'And so, in a very evil hour, she accepted the service of the noble Englishman, and sent her father an old shoe filled to the tongue with money, and trusted herself to fortune. And so they travelled through Northern Italy, and throughout the south of France, making their way anyhow; sometimes in coaches, sometimes in carts, sometimes upon mule-back, sometimes even a-foot and weary; but always as happy as could be.

'My Lord, who was quite a young man still, and laughed at English arrogance, rode on in front of his wife and friends, to catch the first of a famous view, on the French side of the Pyrenee hills. And so my Lord went round the corner, with a fine young horse leaping up at every step.

'They waited for him, long and long; but he never came

again; and within a week, his mangled body lay in a little chapel-yard; and if the priests only said a quarter of the prayers they took the money for, God only knows they can have no throats left; only a relaxation.

'My Lady dwelled for six months more – it is a melancholy tale (what true tale is not so?) – scarcely able to believe that all her fright was not a dream. She would not wear a piece, or shape, of any mourning-clothes; she would not have a person cry, or any sorrow among us. She simply disbelieved the thing, and trusted God to right it.

'When the snow came down in autumn on the roots of the Pyrenees, and the chapel-yard was white with it, many people told the lady that it was time for her to go. And the strongest plea of all was this, that now she bore another hope of repeating her husband's virtues. So at the end of October, when wolves came down to the farm-lands, the little English family went home towards their England.

'They landed somewhere on the Devonshire coast, ten or eleven years agone, and stayed some days at Exeter; and set out thence in a hired coach, without any proper attendance, for Watchett, in the north of Somerset. For the lady owned a quiet mansion in the neighbourhood of that town, and her one desire was to find refuge there, and to meet her lord, who was sure to come (she said) when he heard of his new infant. Therefore, with only two serving-men and two maids (including Benita) the party set forth from Exeter, and lay the first night at Bampton.

'On the following morning they started bravely, with earnest hope of arriving at their journey's end by daylight. But the roads were soft and very deep, and the sloughs were out in places; and the heavy coach broke down in the axle, and needed mending at Dulverton; and so they lost three hours or more, and would have been wiser to sleep there.

'Through the fog, and through the muck, the coach went on, as best it might; sometimes foundered in a slough, with half of the horses splashing it, and sometimes knuckled up on a bank, and straining across the middle, while all the horses kicked at it. However, they went on till dark, as well as might be expected. But when they came, all thanking God, to the pitch and slope of the sea-bank, leading on towards Watchett town, and where my horse had shied so, there the little boy jumped up, and clapped his hands at the water; and there (as Benita said) they met their fate, and could not fly it.

'Although it was past the dusk of day, the silver light from the sea flowed in, and showed the cliffs, and the grey sandline, and the drifts of wreck, and wrack-weed. It showed them also a troop of horsemen, waiting under a rock hard by, and ready to dash upon them. The postilions lashed towards the sea, and the horses strove in the depth of sand, and the serving-men cocked their blunderbusses, and cowered away behind them; but the lady stood up in the carriage bravely, and neither screamed nor spoke, but hid her son behind her. Meanwhile the drivers drove into the sea, till the leading horses were swimming.

'But before the waves came into the coach, a score of fierce men were round it. They cursed the postilions for mad cowards, and cut the traces, and seized the wheel-horses, all wild with dismay in the wet and the dark. Then, while the carriage was heeling over, and well-nigh upset in the water, the lady exclaimed, "I know that man! He is our ancient enemy:" and Benita (foreseeing that all their boxes would be turned inside out, and carried away) snatched the most valuable of the jewels, a magnificent necklace of diamonds, and cast it over the little girl's head, and buried it under her travelling-cloak, hoping so to save it. Then a great wave, crested with foam, rolled in, and the coach was thrown on its side, and the sea rushed in at the top and the windows, upon shrieking, and clashing, and fainting away.

'What followed Benita knew not, as one might well suppose, herself being stunned by a blow on the head, beside being palsied with terror. "See, I have the mark now," she said, "where the jamb of the door came down on me!" But when she recovered her senses, she found herself upon the sand, the robbers were out of sight, and one of the serving-men was bathing her forehead with sea water. For this she rated him well, having taken already too much of that article; and then she arose and ran to her mistress, who was sitting upright on a little rock, with her dead boy's face to her bosom, sometimes gazing upon him, and sometimes questing round for the other one.

'Before the light of the morning came along the tide to Watchett my Lady had met her husband. They took her into the town that night, but not to her own castle; and so the power of womanhood (which is itself maternity) came over swiftly upon her. The lady, whom all people loved (though at certain times, particular), lies in Watchett little church-yard, with son and heir at her right hand, and a little babe, of sex unknown, sleeping on her bosom.'

'And what was the lady's name?' I asked; 'and what became of the little girl? And why did the woman stay there?'

'Well!' cried Jeremy Stickles, only too glad to be cheerful again: 'talk of a woman after that! As we used to say at school – "Who dragged whom, how many times, in what manner, round the wall of what?" But to begin, last first, my John (as becomes a woman): Benita stayed in that blessed place, because she could not get away from it. The Doones – if Doones indeed they were, about which you of course know best – took every stiver out of the carriage: wet or dry they took it. And Benita could never get her wages: for the whole affair is in Chancery, and they have appointed a receiver.'

'Whew!' said I, knowing something of London, and sorry for Benita's chance.

'So the poor thing was compelled to drop all thought of Apulia, and settle down on the brink of Exmoor, where you get all its evils, without the good to balance them. She married a man who turned a wheel for making the blue Watchett ware, partly because he could give her a house, and partly because he proved himself a good soul towards my Lady. There they are, and have three children; and there you may go and visit them.'

'I understand all that, Jeremy, though you do tell things too quickly, and I would rather have John Fry's style; for he leaves one time for his words to melt. Now for my second question. What became of the little maid?'

'You great oaf!' cried Jeremy Stickles: 'you are rather more likely to know, I should think, than any one else in all the kingdoms.'

'If I knew, I should not ask you. Jeremy Stickles, do try to be neither conceited, nor thick-headed.'

'I will when you are neither,' answered Master Jeremy; 'but you occupy all the room, John. No one else can get in with you there.'

'Very well then, let me out. Take me down in both ways.'

'If ever you were taken down; you must have your double joints ready now. And yet in other ways you will be as proud and set up as Lucifer. As certain sure as I stand here, that little maid is Lorna Doone.'

27

Mutual Discomfiture

It must not be supposed that I was altogether so thick-headed as Jeremy would have made me out. But it is part of my character that I like other people to think me slow, and to labour hard to enlighten me, while all the time I can say to myself, 'This man is shallower than I am; it is pleasant to see his shoals come up, while he is sounding mine so!'

When he described the heavy coach, and the persons in and upon it, and the breaking down at Dulverton, and the place of their destination, as well as the time and the weather, and the season of the year, my heart began to burn within me, and my mind replaced the pictures, first of the foreign lady's-maid by the pump caressing me, and then of the coach struggling up the hill; and the beautiful dame, and the fine little boy, with the white cockade in his hat; but most of all the little girl, dark-haired and very lovely, and having even in those days the rich soft look of Lorna.

But when he spoke of the necklace thrown over the head of the little maiden, and of her disappearance, before my eyes arose at once the flashing of the beacon-fire, the lonely moors embrowned with light, the tramp of the outlaw cavalcade, and the helpless child head downward lying across the robber's saddle-bow. Then I remembered my own mad shout of boyish indignation, and marvelled at the strange long way by which the events of life come round. And while I thought of my own return, and childish attempt to hide myself from sorrow in the sawpit, and the agony of my mother's tears, it did not fail to strike me as a thing of omen, that the self-same day should be, both to my darling and myself, the blackest and most miserable of all youthful days.

The King's Commissioner thought it wise, for some good reason of his own, to conceal from me, for the present, the name of the poor lady supposed to be Lorna's mother: and knowing that I could easily now discover it, without him, I let that question abide awhile. Indeed I was half afraid to hear it, remembering that the nobler and the wealthier she proved to be, the smaller was my chance of winning such a wife for plain John Ridd. Not that she would give me up: that I never dreamed of. But that others would interfere; or indeed I myself might find it only honest to relinquish her. That last thought was a dreadful blow, and took my breath away from me.

Jeremy Stickles was quite decided – and of course the discovery being his, he had a right to be so – that not a word of all these things must be imparted to Lorna herself, or even to my mother, or any one whatever. 'Keep it tight as wax, my lad,' he cried, with a wink of great expression; 'this belongs to me, mind; and the credit, ay, and the premium, and the right of discount, are altogether mine.'

'Jeremy, you are right,' I answered; 'at least as regards the issue. Although perhaps you were not right in leading me into a bargain like this, without my own consent or knowledge. But supposing that we should both be shot in this grand attack on the valley (for I mean to go with you now, heart and soul), is Lorna to remain untold of that which changes all her life?'

'Both shot!' cried Jeremy Stickles: 'my goodness, boy, talk not like that! And those Doones are cursed good shots too. Nay, nay, the yellows shall go in front; we attack on the Somerset side, I think. I from a hill will reconnoitre, as behoves a general, you shall stick behind a tree, if we can only find one big enough to hide you. You and I to be shot, John Ridd, with all this inferior food for powder anxious to be devoured?'

I laughed, for I knew his cool hardihood, and never-flinching courage; and sooth to say no coward would have dared to talk like that.

'But when one comes to think of it,' he continued, smiling at himself; 'some provision should be made for even that unpleasant chance. I will leave the whole in writing, with orders to be opened, &c. &c. – Now no more of that, my boy; a cigarro after schnapps, and go to meet my yellow boys.'

His 'yellow boys,' as he called the Somersetshire trained hands, were even now coming down the valley from the 'London-road,' as every one since I went up to town, grandly entitled the lane to the moors, and in about an hour's time the sons of Devon appeared.

The yellows and the reds together numbered a hundred and twenty men, most of whom slept in our barns and stacks; and besides these we had fifteen troopers of the regular army. You may suppose that all the country was turned upside down about it; and the folk who came to see them drill – by no means a needless exercise – were a greater plague than the soldiers.

Therefore all of us were right glad (except perhaps Farmer Snowe, from whom we had bought some victuals at rare price) when Jeremy Stickles gave orders to march, and we began to try to do it. And I wondered where Uncle Reuben was, who ought to have led the culverins (whereof we had no less than three) if Stickles could only have found him; and then I thought of little Ruth; and without any fault on my part, my heart went down within me.

The culverins were laid on bark; and all our horses pulling them, and looking round every now and then, with their ears curved up like a squirrel'd nut, and their noses tossing anxiously, to know what sort of plough it was man had been pleased to put behind them – man, whose endless whims and wildness they could never understand, any more than they could satisfy. However, they pulled their very best – as all our horses always do – and the culverins went up the hill, without smack of whip, or swearing. It had been arranged, very justly no doubt, and quite in keeping with the spirit of the Constitution, but as it proved not too wisely, that either body of men should act in its own county only. So when we reached the top of the hill, the sons of Devon marched on, and across the track leading into Doone-gate, so as to fetch round the western side, and attack with their culverin from the cliffs, whence the sentry had challenged me on the night of my passing the entrance. Meanwhile the yellow lads were to stay upon the eastern highland, whence Uncle Reuben and myself had reconnoitred so long ago; and whence I had leaped into the valley at the time of the great snow-drifts. And here they were not to show themselves; but keep their culverin in the woods, until their cousins of Devon appeared on the opposite parapet of the glen.

The third culverin was entrusted to the fifteen troopers; who with ten picked soldiers from either trained band, making in all five-and-thirty men, were to assault the Doone-gate itself, while the outlaws were placed between two fires from the eastern cliff and the western. And with this force went Jeremy Stickles, and with it went myself, as knowing more about the passage than any other stranger did. Therefore, if I have put it clearly, as I strive to do, you will see that the Doones must repulse at once three simultaneous attacks, from an army numbering in the whole one hundred and thirty-five men, not including the Devonshire officers; fifty men on each side I mean, and thirty-five at the head of the valley.

Now we five-and-thirty men lay back, a little way round the corner, in the hollow of the track which leads to the strong Doone-gate. Our culverin was in amongst us, loaded now to the muzzle, and it was not comfortable to know that it might go off at any time.

At last, we heard the loud bang-bang, which proved that Devon and Somerset were pouring their indignation hot into the den of malefactors, or at least so we supposed; therefore at double quick march we advanced round the bend of the cliff which had hidden us, hoping to find the gate undefended, and to blow down all barriers with the fire of our cannon.

But while the sound of our cheer rang back among the crags above us, a shrill clear whistle cleft the air for a single moment, and then a dozen carbines bellowed, and all among us flew murderous lead. Several of our men rolled over, but the rest rushed on like Britons, Jeremy and myself in front, while we heard the horses plunging at the loaded gun behind us. 'Now, my lads,' cried Jeremy, 'one dash, and we are beyond them!' For he saw that the foe was overhead in the gallery of brushwood.

Our men with a brave shout answered him, for his courage was fine example; and we leaped in under the feet of the foe, before they could load their guns again. But here, when the foremost among us were past, an awful crash rang behind us, with the shrieks of men, and the din of metal, and the horrible screaming of horses. The trunk of the tree had been launched overboard, and crashed into the very midst of us. Our cannon was under it, so were two men and a horse with his poor back broken. Another horse vainly struggled to rise with his thighbone smashed and protruding.

Now I lost all presence of mind at this, for I loved both those good horses, and shouting for any to follow me, dashed headlong into the cavern. Some five or six men came after me, the foremost of whom was Jeremy, when a storm of shots whistled and pattered around me, with a blaze of light and a thunderous roar. On I leaped, like a madman, and pounced on one gunner, and hurled him across his culverin; but the others had fled, and a heavy oak door fell to with a bang, behind them. So utterly were my senses gone, and nought but strength remaining, that I caught up the Doone cannon with both hands, and dashed it, breech-first, at the doorway. The solid oak burst with the blow, and the gun stuck fast, like a builder's putlog.

But here I looked round in vain, for any to come and follow up my success. The scanty light showed me no figure moving through the length of the tunnel behind me; only a heavy groan or two went to my heart, and chilled it. So I hurried back to seek Jeremy, fearing that he must be smitten down.

And so indeed I found him, as well as three other poor fellows, struck by the charge of the culverin, which had passed so close beside me. Two of the four were as dead as stones, and growing cold already, but Jeremy and the other could manage to groan, just now and then. So I turned my attention to them, and thought no more of fighting.

Having so many wounded men, and so many dead among us, we loitered at the cavern's mouth, and looked at one another, wishing only for somebody to come and take command of us. But no one came; and I was grieved so much about poor Jeremy, besides being wholly unused to any violence of bloodshed, that I could only keep his head up, and try to stop him from bleeding. And he looked up at me pitifully, being perhaps in a haze of thought, as a calf looks at a butcher.

The shot had taken him in the mouth; about that no doubt could be, for two of his teeth were in his beard, and one of his lips was wanting. I laid his shattered face on my breast, and nursed him, as a woman might. But he looked at me with a jerk at this; and I saw that he wanted coolness.

While here we stayed, quite out of danger (for the fellows from the gallery could by no means shoot us, even if they remained there, and the oaken door whence the others fled was blocked up by the culverin), a boy who had no business there (being in fact our clerk's apprentice to the art of shoemaking) came round the corner upon us, in the manner which boys, and only boys, can use with grace and freedom; that is to say, with a sudden rush, and a sidelong step, and an impudence, –

'Got the worst of it!' cried the boy: 'better be off all of you. Zomerzett and Devon a vighting; and the Doones have drashed 'em both. Maister Ridd even thee be drashed.'

We few, who yet remained of the force which was to have won the Doone-gate, gazed at one another, like so many fools, and nothing more. For we still had some faint hopes of winning the day, and recovering our reputation, by means of what the other men might have done without us. And we could not understand at all how Devonshire and Somerset, being embarked in the same cause, should be fighting with one another.

Finding nothing more to be done in the way of carrying on the war, we laid poor Master Stickles and two more of the wounded upon the carriage of bark and hurdles, whereon our gun had laid; and we rolled the gun into the river, and harnessed the horses yet alive, and put the others out of their pain, and sadly wended homewards, feeling ourselves to be thoroughly beaten, yet ready to maintain that it was no fault of ours whatever. And in this opinion the women joined, being only too glad and thankful to see us come home alive again.

Now this enterprise having failed so, I prefer not to dwell too long upon it; only just to show the mischief which lay at the root of the failure. And this mischief was the vile jealousy betwixt red and yellow uniform. Now I try to speak impartially, belonging no more to Somerset than I do to Devonshire, living upon the borders, and born of either county. The tale was told me by one side first; and then quite to a different tune by the other; and then by both together, with very hot words of reviling, and a desire to fight it out again. And putting this with that, the truth appears to be as follows: –

The men of Devon, who bore red facings, had a long way to go round the hills, before they could get into due position on the western side of the Doone Glen. And knowing that their cousins in yellow would claim the whole of the glory, if allowed to be first with the firing, these worthy fellows waited not to take good aim with their cannon, seeing the others about to shoot; but fettled it any how on the slope, pointing in a general direction and trusting in God for aim-worthiness, laid the rope to the breech, and fired. Now as Providence ordained it, the shot, which was a casual mixture of anything considered hard – for instance jug-bottoms and knobs of doors – the whole of this pernicious dose came scattering and shattering among the unfortunate yellow men upon the opposite cliff; killing one and wounding two.

Now what did the men of Somerset do, but instead of waiting for their friends to send round and beg pardon, train their gun full mouth upon them, and with a vicious meaning shoot? Not only this, but they loudly cheered, when they saw four or five red coats lie low; for which savage feeling not even the remarks of the Devonshire men concerning their coats could entirely excuse them. Now I need not tell the rest of it; for the tale makes a man discontented. Enough that both sides waxed hotter and hotter with the fire of destruction. And but that the gorge of the cliffs lay between, very few would have lived to tell of it: for our western blood becomes stiff and firm, when churned with the sense of wrong in it.

At last the Doones (who must have laughed at the thunder passing overhead) recalling their men from the gallery, issued out of Gwenny's gate (which had been wholly overlooked) and fell on the rear of the Somerset men, and slew four beside their cannon. Then while the survivors ran away, the outlaws took the hot culverin, and rolled it down into their valley. Thus of three cannons set forth that morning, only one ever came home again, and that was the gun of the Devonshire men, who dragged it home themselves, with the view of making a boast about it.

This was a melancholy end of our brave setting out: and everybody blamed every one else: and several of us wanted to have the whole thing over again, as then we must have righted it.

28

Getting into Chancery

Two of the Devonshire officers (Captains Pyke and Dallan) now took command of the men who were left, and ordered all to go home again, commending much the bravery which had been displayed on all side, and the loyalty to the King, and the English Constitution. This last word always seems to me to settle everything when said, because nobody understands it, and yet all can puzzle their neighbours. So the Devonshire men, having beans to sow (which they ought to have done on Good Friday), went home: and our Somerset friends only stayed for two days more, to backbite them.

Jeremy Stickles lay and tossed, and thrust up his feet in agony, and bit with his lipless mouth the clothes, and was proud to see blood upon them. He looked at us ever so many times, as much as to say, 'Fools, let me die; then I shall have some comfort;' but we nodded at him sagely, especially the women, trying to convey to him, on no account to die yet. And then we talked to one another (on purpose for him to hear us), how brave he was, and not the man to knock under in a hurry, and how he should have the victory yet; and how well he looked, considering.

These things cheered him, a little now, and a little more next time; and every time we went on so, he took it with less impatience. Then once when he had been very quiet, and not even tried to frown at us, Annie leaned over, and kissed his forehead, and spread the pillows, and sheet, with a curve as delicate as his own white ears; and then he feebly lifted hands, and prayed to God to bless her. And after that he came round gently; though never to the man he had been, and never to speak loud again.

Two men appeared at our gate one day, stripped to their shirts, and void of horses, and looking very sorrowful. Now having some fear of attack from the Doones, and scarce knowing what their tricks might be, we received these strangers cautiously, desiring to know who they were, before we let them see all our premises.

However it soon became plain to us that although they might not be honest fellows, at any rate they were not Doones; and so we took them in, and fed, and left them to tell their business. And this they were glad enough to do; as men who have been maltreated almost always are. And it was not for us to contradict them, lest our victuals should go amiss.

These two very worthy fellows – nay, more than that by their own account, being downright martyrs – were come, for the public benefit, from the Court of Chancery, sitting for everybody's good, and boldly redressing evil.

Now, as it fell in a very black day (for all except the lawyers), His Majesty's Court of Chancery, if that be what it called itself, gained scent of poor Lorna's life, and of all that might be made of it. Whether through that brave young lord who ran into such peril, or through any of his friends; or whether through that deep old Counsellor, whose game none might penetrate; or through any disclosures of the Italian woman, or even of Jeremy himself; none just now could tell us; only this truth was too clear – Chancery had heard of Lorna, and then had seen how rich she was: and never delaying in one thing, had opened mouth, and swallowed her.

The Doones, with a share of that dry humour which was in them hereditary, had welcomed the two apparitors (if that be the proper name for them) and led them kindly down the valley, and told them then to serve their writ. Misliking the look of things, these poor men began to fumble among their clothes, upon which the Doones cried, 'Off with them! Let us see if your message be on your skins.' And with no more manners than that, they stripped, and lashed them out of the valley; only bidding them come to us, if they wanted Lorna Doone: and to us they came accordingly. Neither were sure at first but that we should treat them so; for they had no knowledge of west country, and thought it quite a godless place, wherein no writ was holy.

We however comforted and cheered them so considerably that, in gratitude, they showed their writs, to which they had stuck like leeches. And these were twofold: one addressed to Mistress Lorna Doone, so called, and bidding her keep in readiness to travel whenever called upon, and commit herself to nobody, except the accredited messengers of the right honourable Court; while the other was addressed to all subjects of His Majesty, having custody of Lorna Doone, or any power over her. And this last both threatened, and exhorted, and held out hopes of recompense, if she were rendered truly.

Lorna was in her favourite place, the little garden which she tended with such care and diligence.

Feeling many things, but thinking without much to guide me, over the grass-plats laid between, I went up to Lorna. She in a shower of damask roses, raised her eyes, and looked at me. And even now, in those sweet eyes, so deep with loving kindness and soft maiden dreamings, there seemed to be a slight unwilling, half-confessed withdrawal; overcome by love and duty, yet a painful thing to see.

'Darling,' I said, 'are your spirits good? Are you strong enough today, to bear a tale of cruel sorrow; but which perhaps, when your tears are shed, will leave you all the happier?'

'What can you mean?' she answered trembling, not having been very strong of late, and now surprised at my manner: 'are you come to give me up, John?'

'Now, Lorna,' said I, as she hung on my arm, willing to trust me anywhere, 'come to your little plant-house, and hear my moving story.'

'No story can move me much, dear,' she answered rather faintly, for any excitement stayed with her; 'since I know your strength of kindness, scarcely any tale can move me, unless it be of yourself, love; or of my poor mother.'

'It is of your poor mother, darling. Can you bear to hear it?' And yet I wondered why she did not say as much of her father.

'Yes, I can hear anything. But although I cannot see her, and have long forgotten, I could not bear to hear ill of her.'

'There is no ill to hear, sweet child, except of evil done to her. Lorna, you are of an ill-starred race.'

'Better that than a wicked race,' she answered with her usual quickness, leaping at conclusion: 'tell me I am not a Doone, and I will – but I cannot love you more.'

'You are not a Doone, my Lorna, for that, at least, I can answer; though I know not what your name is.'

'And my father – your father – what I mean is – '

'Your father and mine never met one another. Your father was killed by an accident in the Pyrenean mountains, and your mother by the Doones; or at least they caused her death, and carried you away from her.

All this, coming as in one breath upon the sensitive maiden, was more than she could bear all at once; as any but a fool like me must of course have known. She lay back on the garden bench, with her black hair shed on the oaken bark, while her colour went and came; and only by that, and her quivering breast, could any one say that she lived and thought. And yet she pressed my hand with hers, that now I might tell her all of it.

29

John Becomes too Popular

No flower that I have ever seen, either in shifting of light and shade, or in the pearly morning, may vie with a fair young woman's face when tender thought and quick emotion vary, enrich, and beautify it. Thus my Lorna hearkened softly, almost without word or gesture, yet with sighs and glances telling, and the pressure of my hand, how each word was moving her.

When at last my tale was done, she turned away, and wept bitterly for the sad fate of her parents. But to my surprise, she spoke not even a word of wrath or rancour. She seemed to take it all as fate.

So I led her into the house, and she fell into my mother's arms; and I left them to have a good cry of it, with Annie ready to help them.

Now instead of getting better, Colonel Stickles grew worse and worse, in spite of all our tendance of him, with simples and with nourishment, and no poisonous medicines, such as doctors would have given him. And the fault of this lay not with us, but purely with himself, and his unquiet constitution. For he roused himself up to a perfect fever, when through Lizzie's giddiness he learned the very thing which mother and Annie were hiding from him with the utmost care: namely, that Serjeant Bloxham had taken upon himself to send direct to London, by the Chancery officers, a full report of what had happened, and of the illness of his chief, together with an urgent prayer for a full battalion of King's troops, and a plenary commander.

This Serjeant Bloxham, being senior of the surviving soldiers, and a very worthy man in his way, but a trifle over zealous, had succeeded to the captaincy upon his master's disablement. Then, with desire to serve his country and show his education, he sat up most part of three nights, and wrote this wonderful report by the aid of our stable lanthorn. It was a very fine piece of work, as three men to whom he read it (but only one at a time) pronounced, being under seal of secrecy. And all might have gone well with it, if the author could only have held his tongue, when near the ears of women. But this was beyond his sense, as it seems, although so good a writer. For having heard that our Lizzie was a famous judge of literature (as indeed she told almost every one) he could not contain himself, but must have her opinion upon his work.

That great despatch was sent to London by the Chancery officers, whom we fitted up with clothes, and for three days fattened them; which in strict justice they needed much, as well as in point of equity. They were kind enough to be pleased with us, and accepted my new shirts generously: and urgent as their business was, another week (as they both declared) could do no harm to nobody, and might set them upon their legs again. And knowing, although they were London-men, that fish do live in water, these two fellows went fishing all day, but never landed anything. However their holiday was cut short; for the Serjeant, having finished now his narrative of proceedings, was not the man to let it hang fire, and be quenched perhaps by Stickles.

Therefore, having done their business, and served both citations, these two good men had a pannier of victuals put up by dear Annie, and borrowing two of our horses, rode to Dunster, where they left them, and hired on towards London. We had not time to like them much, and so we did not miss them, especially in our great anxiety about poor Master Stickles.

Jeremy lay between life and death, for at least a fortnight. At last I prevailed upon him, by argument, that he must get better, to save himself from being ignobly and unjustly superseded; and hereupon I reviled Serjeant Bloxham more fiercely than Jeremy's self could have done, and indeed to such a pitch that Jeremy almost forgave him, and became much milder. And after that his fever, and the inflammation of his wound, diminished very rapidly.

However, not knowing what might happen, or even how soon poor Lorna might be taken from our power, and, falling into lawyers' hands, have cause to wish herself most heartily back among robbers, I set forth one day for Watchett, taking advantage of the visit of some troopers from an outpost, who would make our house quite safe. I rode alone, being fully primed, and having no misgivings.

When I knocked at the little door, whose sill was gritty and grimed with sand, no one came for a very long time to answer me, or to let me in. Not wishing to be unmannerly, I waited a long time, and watched the sea, from which the wind was blowing; and whose many lips of waves – though the tide was half-way out – spoke to and refreshed me. After a while I knocked again, for my horse was becoming hungry; and a good while after that again, a voice came through the key-hole –

'Who is it that wishes to enter?'

'The boy who was at the pump,' said I, 'when the carriage broke down at Dulverton. The boy that lives at oh – ah; and some day you would come seek for him.'

'Oh yes, I remember certainly. My leetle boy, with the fair white skin. I have desired to see him, oh many, yes, many times.'

She was opening the door, while saying this; and then she started back in affright, that the little boy should have grown so.

'You cannot be that leetle boy. It is quite impossible. Why do you impose on me?'

'Not only am I that little boy, who made the water to flow for you, till the nebule came upon the glass; but also I am come to tell you all about your little girl.'

'Come in, you very great leetle boy,' she answered, with her dark eyes brightened. And I went in, and looked at her. She was altered by time, as much as I was. The slight and graceful shape was gone; not that I remembered any thing of her figure, if you please; for boys of twelve are not yet prone to note the shapes of women; but that her lithe straight gait had struck me as being so unlike our people. Now her time for walking so was past, and transmitted to her children. Yet her face was comely still, and full of strong intelligence. I gazed at her, and she at me: and we were sure of one another.

'Now what will ye please to eat?' she asked, with a lively glance at the size of my mouth: 'that is always the first thing you people ask, in these barbarous places.'

'I will tell you by-and-by,' I answered, misliking this satire upon us; 'but I might begin with a quart of ale, to enable me to speak, madam.'

'Very well. One quevart of be-or:' she called out to a little maid, who was her eldest child, no doubt.

Madame Benita Odam – for the name of the man who turned the wheel proved to be John Odam – showed me into a little room containing two chairs and a fir-wood table, and sat down on a three-legged seat and studied me very steadfastly. This she had a right to do; and I, having all my clothes on now, was not disconcerted. It would not become me to repeat her judgement upon my appearance, which she delivered as calmly as if I were a pig at market, and as proudly as if her own pig. And she asked me whether I had ever got rid of the black marks on my breast.

Not wanting to talk about myself (though very fond of doing so, when time and season favour), I led her back to that fearful night of the day when first I had seen her. She was not desirous to speak of it, because of her own little children: however, I drew her gradually to recollection of Lorna, and then of the little boy who died, and the poor mother buried with him. And her strong hot nature kindled, as she dwelled upon these things: and my wrath waxed within me; and we forgot reserve and prudence under the sense of so vile a wrong. She told me (as nearly as might be) the very same story which she had told to Master Jeremy Stickles; only she dwelled upon it more, because of my knowing the outset. And being a woman, with an inkling of my situation, she enlarged upon the little maid, more than to dry Jeremy.

'Would you know her again?' I asked, being stirred by these accounts of Lorna, when she was five years old: 'would you know her as a full-grown maiden?'

'I think I should,' she answered; 'it is not possible to say, until one sees the person: but from the eyes of the little girl, I think that I must know her. Oh, the poor young creature! Is it to be believed that the cannibals devoured her? What a people you are in this country! Meat, meat, meat!'

'The little maid has not been devoured,' I said to Mistress Odam: 'and now she is a tall young lady, and as beautiful as can be. If I sleep in your good hostel to-night, will you come with me to Oare to-morrow, and see your little maiden?'

'I would like – and yet I fear. This country is so barbarous. And I am good to eat – my God, there is much picking on my bones!'

215

30

Lorna Knows Her Nurse

We set out pretty early, three of us, and a baby, who could not well be left behind. The wife of the man who owned the cart had undertaken to mind the business and the other babies, upon condition of having the keys of all the taps left with her.

As the manner of journeying over the moor has been described oft enough already, I will say no more, except that we all arrived, before dusk of the summer's day, safe at Plover's Barrows. Mistress Benita was delighted with the change from her dull hard life; and she made many excellent observations, such as seem natural to a foreigner looking at our country.

As luck would have it, the first who came to meet us at the gate was Lorna, with nothing whatever upon her head (the weather being summerly), but her beautiful hair shed round her; and wearing a sweet white frock tucked in, and showing her figure perfectly. In her joy she ran straight up to the cart; and then stopped and gazed at Benita. At one glance her old nurse knew her: 'Oh the eyes, the eyes!' she cried, and was over the rail of the cart in a moment, in spite of all her substance. Lorna, on the other hand, looked at her with some doubt and wonder; as though having right to know much about her, and yet unable to do so. But when the foreign woman said something in Roman language, and flung new hay from the cart upon her, as if in a romp of childhood, the young maid cried, 'Oh, Nita, Nita!' and fell upon her breast, and wept; and after that looked round at us.

This being so, there could be no doubt as to the power of proving Lady Lorna's birth, and rights, both by evidence and token. For though we had not the necklace now – thanks to Annie's wisdom – we had the ring of heavy gold, a very ancient relic, with which my maid (in her simple way) had pledged herself to me. And Benita knew this ring as well as she knew her own fingers, having heard a long history about it; and the effigy on it of the wild cat was the bearing of the house of Lorne.

For though Lorna's father was a nobleman of high and goodly lineage, her mother was of yet more ancient and renowned descent, being the last in line direct from the great and kingly chiefs of Lorne. A wild and headstrong race they were, and must have everything their own way. Hot blood was ever among them, even of one household; and their sovereignty (which more than once had defied the King of Scotland) waned and fell among themselves, by continual quarrelling. And it was of a piece with this, that the Doones (who were an offset, by the mother's side, holding in co-partnership some large property, which had come by the spindle, as we say) should fall out with the Earl of Lorne, the last but one of that title.

The daughter of this nobleman had married Sir Ensor Doone but this, instead of healing matters, led to fiercer conflict. I never could quite understand all the ins and outs of it; which none but a lawyer may go through, and keep his head at the end of it. The motives of mankind are plainer than the motions they produce. Especially when charity (such as found among us) sits to judge the former, and is never weary of it: while reason does not care to trace the latter complications, except for fee or title.

Therefore it is enough to say, that knowing Lorna to be direct in heirship to vast property, and bearing especial spite against the house of which she was the last, the Doones had brought her up with full intention of lawful marriage; and had carefully secluded her from the wildest of their young gallants.

While we were full of all these things, and wondering what would happen next, or what we ought ourselves to do, another very important matter called for our attention. This was no less than Annie's marriage to the Squire Faggus.

When the time for the wedding came, there was such a stir and commotion as had never been known in the parish of Oare since my father's marriage. For Annie's beauty and kindliness had made her the pride of the neighbourhood; and the presents sent her, from all around, were enough to stock a shop with. Master Stickles, who now could walk, and who certainly owed his recovery, with the blessing of God, to Annie, presented her with a mighty Bible, silver-clasped, and very handsome, beating the parson's out and out, and for which he had sent to Taunton. Even the common troopers, having tasted her cookery many times (to help out their poor rations), clubbed together, and must have given at least a week's pay apiece, to have turned out what they did for her. This was no less than a silver pot, well designed, but suited surely rather to the bridegroom's taste than bride's. In a word, everybody gave her things.

And now my Lorna came to me, with a spring of tears in appealing eyes – for she was still somewhat childish, or rather, I should say, more childish now than when she lived in misery – and she placed her little hands in mine, and she was half afraid to speak, and dropped her eyes for me to ask.

'What is it, little darling?' I asked, as I saw her breath come fast; for the smallest excitement moved her form.

'You don't think, John, you don't think, dear, that you could lend me any money?'

'All I have got,' I answered: 'how much do you want, dear heart?'

'I have been calculating; and I fear that I cannot do any good with less than ten pounds, John.'

'Oh dear, yes!' I replied. 'You want to give that stupid Annie, who has lost you a hundred thousand pounds, and who is going to be married before us, dear – God only can tell why, being my younger sister – you want to give her a wedding present. And you shall do it, darling; because it is so good of you.'

'What can I get her good enough? I am sure I do not know,' she asked: 'she had been so kind and good to me, and she is such a darling. How I shall miss her, to be sure! By-the-by, you seem to think, John; that I shall be rich some day.'

'Of course you will. As rich as the French King, who keeps ours. Would the Lord Chancellor trouble himself about you, if you were poor?'

'Then if I am rich, perhaps you would lend me twenty pounds, dear John. Ten pounds would be very mean for a wealthy person to give her.'

To this I agreed, upon condition that I should make the purchase myself, whatever it might be. For nothing could be easier than to cheat Lorna about the cost, until time should come for her paying me. And this was better than to cheat her for the benefit of our family. For this end, and for many others, I set off to Dulverton, bearing more commissions, more messages, and more questions, than a man of thrice my memory might carry so far as the corner where the sawpit is. And to make things worse, one girl, or other, would keep on running up to me, or even after me (when started), with something or other she had just thought of, which she could not possibly do without, and which I must be sure to remember as the most important of the whole.

To my dear mother, who had partly outlived the exceeding value of trifles, the most important matter seemed to ensure Uncle Reuben's countenance and presence at the marriage. And if I succeeded in this, I might well forget all the maidens' trumpery. This she would have been wiser to tell me when they were out of hearing; for I left her to fight her own battle with them; and laughing at her predicament, promised to do the best I could for all, so far as my wits would go.

Uncle Reuben was not at home; but Ruth, who received me very kindly, although without any expressions of joy, was sure of his return in the afternoon and persuaded me to wait for him. And by the time that I had finished all I could recollect of my orders, even with paper to help me, the old gentleman rode into the yard, and was more surprised than pleased to see me. But if he was surprised, I was more than that – I was utterly astonished at the change in his appearance since the last time I had seen him. From a hale, and rather heavy man, grey-haired, but plump, and ruddy, he was altered to a shrunken, wizened, trembling, and almost decrepit figure. Instead of curly and comely locks, grizzled indeed, but plentiful, he had only a few lank white hairs scattered and flattened upon his forehead. But the greatest change of all was in the expression of his eyes, which had been so keen, and restless, and bright, and a little sarcastic. Bright indeed they still were, but with a slow unhealthy lustre; their keenness was turned to perpetual outlook, their restlessness to a haggard want. As for the humour which once gleamed there (which people who fear it call sarcasm), it had been succeeded by stares of terror, and then mistrust, and shrinking. There was none of the interest in mankind, which is needful even for satire.

'Now what can this be?' thought I to myself: 'has the old man lost all his property, or taken too much to strong waters?'

'Come inside, John Ridd,' he said: 'I will have a talk with you. It is cold out here: and it is too light. Come inside, John Ridd, boy.'

I followed him into a little dark room, quite different from Ruth Huckaback's. It was closed from the shop by an old division of boarding, hung with tanned canvas; and the smell was very close and faint. Here there was a ledger-desk, and a couple of chairs, and a long-legged stool.

'Take the stool,' said Uncle Reuben, showing me in very quietly, 'it is fitter for your height, John. You are my next of kin, except among the womenkind; and you are just the man I want to help me in an enterprise.'

'And I will help you, sir,' I answered, fearing some conspiracy, 'in anything that is true, and loyal, and according to the laws of the realm.'

'Ha, ha!' cried the old man, laughing until his eyes ran over, and spreading out his skinny hands upon his shining breeches, 'thou hast gone the same fool's track as the rest; even as spy Stickles went, and all his precious troopers. Landing of arms at Glenthorne and Lynmouth, waggons escorted across the moor, sounds of metal, and booming noises! Ah, but we managed it cleverly, to cheat even those so near to us. Disaffection at Taunton, signs of insurrection at Dulverton, revolutionary tanner at Dunster! We set it all abroad, right well. And not even you to suspect our work; though we thought at one time that you watched us. Now who, do you suppose, is at the bottom of all this Exmoor insurgency, all this western rebellion – not that I say there is none, mind – but who is at the bottom of it?'

'Either Mother Melldrum,' said I, being now a little angry, 'or else old Nick himself.'

'Nay, old Uncle Reuben!' Saying this, Master Huckaback cast back his coat, and stood up, and made the most of himself.

'Well!' cried I, being now quite come to the limits of my intellect, 'then after all Captain Stickles was right in calling you a rebel, sir!'

'Of course he was: could so keen a man be wrong, about an old fool like me? But come, and see our rebellion, John. I will trust you now with everything. I will take no oath from you; only your word to keep silence; and most of all from your mother.'

'I will give you my word,' I said, although liking not such pledges; which make a man think before he speaks in ordinary company, against his usual practice. However, I was now so curious, that I thought of nothing else; and scarcely could believe at all that Uncle Ben was quite right in his head.

'Take another glass of wine, my son,' he cried, with a cheerful countenance, which made him look more than ten years younger; 'you shall come into partnership with me: your strength will save us two horses, and we always fear the horse work. Come and see our rebellion, my boy; you are a made man from to-night.'

'But where am I to come and see it? Where am I to find it, sir?'

'Meet me,' he answered, yet closing his hands, and wrinkling with doubt his forehead; 'come alone, of course; and meet me at the Wizard's Slough, at ten to-morrow morning.'

31

Master Huckaback's Secret

Knowing Master Huckaback to be a man of his word, as well as one who would have others so, I was careful to be in good time the next morning, by the side of the Wizard's Slough. I am free to admit that the name of the place bore a feeling of uneasiness, and a love of distance, in some measure to my heart. But I did my best not to think of this: only I thought it a wise precaution, and due for the sake of my mother and Lorna, to load my gun with a dozen slugs made from the lead of the old church-porch, laid by, long since, against witchcraft.

A man on horseback appeared as suddenly as if he had risen out of the earth, on the other side of the great black slough. At first I was a little scared, my mind being in the tune for wonders; but presently the white hair, whiter from the blackness of the bog between us, showed me that it was Uncle Reuben come to look for me, that way. Then I left my chair of rock, and waved my hat, and shouted to him, and the sound of my voice among the crags and lonely corners frightened me.

Old Master Huckaback made no answer, but (so far as I could guess) beckoned me to come to him. There was just room between the fringe of reed and the belt of rock around it, for a man going very carefully to escape that horrible pit-hole. And so I went round to the other side, and there found open space enough, with stunted bushes, and starveling trees, and straggling tufts of rushes.

Uncle Reuben clutched the mane of his horse, and came down, as a man does when his legs are old; and as I myself begin to do, at this time of writing. I offered a hand, but he was vexed, and would have nought to do with it.

'Now follow me, step for step,' he said, when I had tethered his horse to a tree; 'the ground is not death (like the wizard's hole), but many parts are treacherous. I know it well by this time.'

Without any more ado, he led me, in and out the marshy places, to a great round hole or shaft, bratticed up with timber. I never had seen the like before, and wondered how they could want a well, with so much water on every side. Around the mouth were a few heaps of stuff unused to the daylight; and I thought at once of the tales I had heard concerning mines in Cornwall, and the silver cup at Combe-Martin, sent to the Queen Elizabeth.

'We had a tree across it, John,' said Uncle Reuben, smiling grimly at my sudden shrink from it: 'but some rogue came spying here, just as one of our men went up. He was frightened half out of his life, I believe, and never ventured to come again. But we put the blame of that upon you. And I see that we were wrong, John.' Here he looked at me with keen eyes, though weak.

'You were altogether wrong;' I answered. 'Am I mean enough to spy upon any one dwelling with us? And more than that, Uncle Reuben, it was mean of you to suppose it.'

He said no more, but signed to me to lift a heavy wooden corb, with an iron loop across it, and sunk in a little pit of earth, a yard or so from the mouth of the shaft. I raised it, and by his direction dropped it into the throat of the shaft, where it hung and shook from a great cross-beam laid at the level of the earth. A very stout thick rope was fastened to the handle of the corb, and ran across a pulley hanging from the centre of the beam, and thence out of sight in the nether places.

'I will first descend,' he said; 'your weight is too great for safety. When the bucket comes up again, follow me, if your heart is good.'

Then he whistled down, with a quick sharp noise, and a whistle from below replied: and he clomb into the vehicle, and the rope ran through the pulley, and Uncle Ben went merrily down, and was out of sight before I had time to think of him.

Now being left on the bank like that, and in full sight of the goodly heaven, I wrestled hard with my flesh and blood, about going down into the pit-hole. And but for the pale shame of the thing, that a white-headed man should adventure so, and green youth doubt about it, never could I have made up my mind; for I do love air and heaven. However, at last up came the bucket; and, with a short sad prayer, I went into whatever might happen.

The scoopings of the side grew black, and the patch of sky above more blue, as, with many thoughts of Lorna, a long way underground I sank. Then I was fetched up at the bottom, with a jerk and rattle; and but for holding by the rope so, must have tumbled over. Two great torches of bale-resin showed me all the darkness, one being held by Uncle Ben and the other by a short square man with a face which seemed well known to me.

'Hail to the world of gold, John Ridd,' said Master Huckaback, smiling in the old dry manner: 'bigger coward never came down the shaft, now did he, Carfax?'

'They be all alike,' said the short square man, 'fust time as they does it.'

Uncle Ben led the way along a narrow passage, roofed with rock, and floored with slate-coloured shale and shingle, and winding in and out, until we stopped at a great stone block or boulder, lying across the floor, and as large as my mother's best oaken wardrobe. Beside it were several sledge-hammers, some battered, and some with broken helves.

'Thou great villain!' cried Uncle Ben, giving the boulder a little kick; 'I believe thy time has come at last. Now, John, give us a sample of the things they tell of thee. Take the biggest of them sledge-hammers and crack this rogue in two for us. We have tried at him for a fortnight, and he is a nut worth cracking. But we have no man who can swing that hammer, though all in the mine have handled it.'

'This little tool is too light,' I cried; 'one of you give me a piece of strong cord.'

Then I took two more of the weightiest hammers, and lashed them fast to the back of mine, not so as to strike, but to burden the fall. Having made this firm, and with room to grasp the handle of the largest one only – for the helves of the others were shorter – I smiled at Uncle Ben, and whirled the mighty implement round my head, just to try whether I could manage it. Upon that, the miners gave a cheer, being honest men, and desirous of seeing fair play between this 'shameless stone' (as Dan Homer calls it) and me with my hammer hammering.

Then I swung me on high, to the swing of the sledge, as a thresher bends back to the rise of his flail, and with all my power descending delivered the ponderous onset. Crashing and crushed the great stone fell over, and threads of sparkling gold appeared in the jagged sides of the breakage.

'How now, Simon Carfax?' cried Uncle Ben triumphantly; 'wilt thou find a man in Cornwall can do the like of that?'

'Ay, and more,' he answered: 'however, it be pretty fair for a lad of these outlandish parts. Get your rollers, my lads, and lead it to the crushing engine.'

I was glad to have been of some service to them: for it seems that this great boulder had been too large to be drawn along the gallery, and too hard to crack. But now they moved it very easily, taking piece by piece, and carefully picking up the fragments.

'Thou hast done us a good turn, my lad,' said Uncle Reuben, as the others passed out of sight at the corner; 'and now I will show thee the bottom of a very wondrous mystery. But we must not do it more than once, for the time of day is the wrong one.'

The whole affair being a mystery to me, and far beyond my understanding, I followed him softly, without a word, yet thinking very heavily, and longing to be above ground again. He led me through small passages, to a hollow place near the descending-shaft, where I saw a most extraordinary monster fitted up. In form it was like a great coffee-mill, such as I had seen in London, only a thousand times larger, and with a heavy windlass to work it.

'Put in a barrow-load of the smoulder,' said Uncle Ben to

Carfax; 'and let them work the crank, for John to understand a thing or two.'

'At this time of day!' cried Simon Carfax; 'and the watching as has been o' late!'

However, he did it without more remonstrance; pouring into the scuttle at the top of the machine about a basketful of broken rock; and then a dozen men went to the wheel, and forced it round, as sailors do. Upon that such a hideous noise arose, as never should have believed any creature capable of making: and I ran to the well of the mine for air, and to ease my ears, if possible.

'Enough, enough!' shouted Uncle Ben, by the time I was nearly deafened; 'we will digest our goodly boulder, after the devil is come abroad for his evening work. Now, John, not a word about what you have learned: but henceforth you will not be frightened by the noise we make at dusk.'

I could not deny but what this was very clever management. If they could not keep the echoes of the upper air from moving, the wisest plan was to open their valves during the discouragement of the falling evening; when folk would rather be driven away, than drawn into the wilds and quagmires, by a sound so deep and awful coming through the darkness.

32

Lorna Gone Away

Although there are very ancient tales of gold being found upon Exmoor, in lumps and solid hummocks, and of men who slew one another for it, this deep digging and great labour seemed to me a dangerous and unholy enterprise. And Master Huckaback confessed that, up to the present time, his two partners and himself (for they proved to be three adventurers) had put into the earth more gold than they had taken out of it. Nevertheless he felt quite sure that it must in a very short time succeed, and pay them back an hundred-fold; and he pressed me with great earnestness to join them, and work there as much as I could, without moving my mother's suspicions. I asked him how they had managed so long to carry on, without discovery; and he said that this was partly through the wildness of the neighbourhood, and the legends that frightened people of a superstitious turn; partly through their own great caution, and manner of fetching both supplies and implements by night; but most of all, they had to thank the troubles of the period, the suspicions of rebellion, and the terror of the Doones, which (like the wizard I was speaking of) kept folk from being too inquisitive where they had no business. The slough, moreover, had helped them well, both by making their access dark, and yet more by swallowing up and concealing all that was cast from the mouth of the pit. Once, before the attack on Glen Doone, they had a narrow escape from the King's Commissioner: for Captain Stickles, having heard no doubt the story of John

Fry, went with half-a-dozen troopers, on purpose to search the neighbourhood. Now if he had ridden alone, most likely he would have discovered everything, but he feared to venture so, having suspicion of a trap. Coming as they did in a company, all mounted and conspicuous, the watchman (who was posted now on the top of the hill, almost every day, since John Fry's appearance) could not help espying them, miles distant, over the moorland. He watched them under the shade of his hand, and presently ran down the hill, and raised a great commotion. Then Simon Carfax and all his men came up and made things natural, removing every sign of work; and finally, sinking underground, drew across the mouth of the pit a hurdle thatched with sedge and heather. Only Simon himself was left behind, ensconced in a hole of the crags, to observe the doings of the enemy.

Captain Stickles rode very bravely, with all his men clattering after him, down the rocky pass, and even to the margin of the slough. And there they stopped, and held council; for it was a perilous thing to risk the passage upon horseback between the treacherous brink and the cliff, unless one knew it thoroughly. Stickles, however, and one follower carefully felt their way along, having their horses well in hand, and bearing a rope to draw them out, in case of being foundered. Then they spurred across the rough boggy land further away than the shaft was. Here the ground lay jagged and shaggy, wrought up with high tufts of reed, or scragged with stunted brushwood. And between the ups and downs (which met anybody anyhow) green covered places tempted the foot, and black bog-holes discouraged it. It is not to be marvelled at that amid such place as this, for the first time visited, the horses were a little skeary; and their riders partook of the feeling, as all good riders do. In and out the tufts they went, with their eyes dilating; wishing to be out of harm if conscience were but satisfied. And of this tufty flaggy ground, pocked with bogs and boglets, one especial nature is that it will not hold impressions.

Seeing thus no track of men, nor anything but marshwork, and storm work, and of the seasons, these two honest men rode back, and were glad to do so. For above them hung the mountains, cowled with fog, and seamed with storm; and around them desolation; and below their feet the grave. Hence they went with all good will; and vowed for ever afterwards that fear of a simple place like that was only too ridiculous. So they all rode home with mutual praises, and their courage well-approved; and the only result of the expedition was to confirm John Fry's repute as a bigger liar than ever.

Now I had enough of that underground work, as before related, to last me for a year to come; neither would I, for sake of gold, have ever stepped into that bucket of my own good will again. But when I told Lorna – whom I could trust in any matter of secrecy, as if she had never been a woman – all about my great descent, and the honeycombing of the earth, and the mournful noise at eventide, when the gold was under the crusher, and bewailing the mischief it must do, then Lorna's chief desire was to know more about Simon Carfax.

'It must be our Gwenny's father,' she cried; 'the man who disappeared underground, and whom she has ever been seeking. How grieved the poor little thing will be, if it should turn out, after all, that he left his child on purpose! I can hardly believe it; can you, John?'

'Well,' I replied; 'all men are wicked, more or less, to some extent: and no man may say otherwise.'

For I did not wish to commit myself to an opinion about Simon, lest I might be wrong, and Lorna think less of my judgement.

But being resolved to seek this out, and do a good turn, if I could, to Gwenny, who had done me many a good one, I begged my Lorna to say not a word of this matter to the handmaiden, until I had further searched it out. And to carry out this resolve, I went again to the place of business, where they were grinding gold as freely as an apothecary at his pills.

At the bottom Master Carfax met me, being captain of the mine, and desirous to know my business. He wore a loose sack round his shoulders, and his beard was two feet long.

'My business is to speak with you,' I answered rather

sternly; for this man, who was nothing more than Uncle Reuben's servant, had carried things too far with me, showing no respect whatever; and though I do not care for much, I liked to receive a little, even in my early days.

'Coom into the muck-hole, then,' was his gracious answer; and he led me into a filthy cell, where the miners changed their jackets.

'Simon Carfax,' I began, with a manner to discourage him; 'I fear you are a shallow fellow, and not worth my trouble.'

'Then don't take it,' he replied; 'I want no man's trouble.'

'For your sake I would not,' I answered; 'but for your daughter's sake I will: the daughter whom you left to starve so pitifully in the wilderness.'

The man stared at me with his pale grey eyes, whose colour was lost from candle-light; and his voice as well as his body shook, while he cried, –

'It is a lie, man. No daughter and no son have I. Nor was ever child of mine left to starve in the wilderness. You are too big for me to tackle, and that makes you a coward for saying it.' His hands were playing with a pickaxe-helve, as if he longed to have me under it.

'Perhaps I have wronged you, Simon,' I answered very softly; for the sweat upon his forehead shone in the smoky torchlight: 'if I have, I crave your pardon. But did you not bring up from Cornwall a little maid named "Gwenny," and supposed to be your daughter?'

'Ay, and she was my daughter, my last and only child of five; and for her I would give this mine, and all the gold will ever come from it.'

'You shall have her, without either mine or gold; if you only prove to me that you did not abandon her.'

'Abandon her! I abandon Gwenny!' he cried, with such a rage of scorn, that I at once believed him. 'They told me she was dead, and crushed, and buried in the drift here; and half my heart died with her. The Almighty blast their mining-work, if the scoundrels lied to me!'

'The scoundrels must have lied to you,' I answered, with a spirit fired by his heat of fury: 'the maid is living, and with us. Come up; and you shall see her.'

'Rig the bucket,' he shouted out along the echoing gallery; and then he fell against the wall, and through the grimy sack I saw the heaving of his breast, as I have seen my opponent's chest, in a long hard bout of wrestling. For my part, I could do no more than hold my tongue, and look at him.

Without another word, we rose to the level of the moors and mires; neither would Master Carfax speak, as I led him across the barrows. In this he was welcome to his own way, for I do love silence; so little harm can come of it. And though Gwenny was no beauty, her father might be fond of her.

So I put him in the cow-house (not to frighten the little maid), and the folding shutters over him, such as we used at the beestings; and he listened to my voice outside, and held on, and preserved himself. For now he would have scooped the earth, as cattle do at yearning-time, and as meekly and as patiently, to have his child restored to him. Not to make a long tale of it – for this thing is beyond me, through want of true experience – I went and fetched his Gwenny forth from the back kitchen, where she was fighting, as usual, with our Betty.

'Come along, you little Vick,' I said, for so we called her; 'I have a message to you, Gwenny, from the Lord in heaven.'

'Don't 'ee talk about He,' she answered: 'Her have long forgatten me.'

'That He has never done, you stupid. Come, and see who is in the cow-house.'

Gwenny knew; she knew in a moment. Looking into my eyes, she knew; and hanging back from me to sigh, she knew it even better.

She had not much elegance of emotion, being flat and square all over; but none the less for that her heart came quick, and her words came slowly.

'Oh, Jan, you are too good to cheat me. Is it joke you are putting upon me?'

I answered her with a gaze alone; and she tucked up her clothes and followed me, because the road was dirty. Then I opened the door just wide enough for the child to go to her father; and left those two to have it out, as might be most natural. And they took a long time about it.

Meanwhile I needs must go and tell my Lorna all the matter; and her joy was almost as great as if she herself had found a father.

Without intending any harm, and meaning only good indeed, I had now done serious wrong to Uncle Reuben's prospects. For Captain Carfax was full as angry at the trick played on him, as he was happy in discovering the falsehood and the fraud of it. Nor could I help agreeing with him, when he told me all of it, as with tears in his eyes he did, and ready to be my slave henceforth; I could not forbear from owning that it was a low and heartless trick, unworthy of men who had families; and the recoil whereof was well deserved, whatever it might end in.

For when this poor man left his daughter, (asleep as he supposed, and having his food, and change of clothes, and Sunday hat to see to), he meant to return in an hour or so, and settle about her sustenance in some house of the neighbourhood. But this was the very thing of all things which the leaders of the enterprise, who had brought him up from Cornwall, for his noted skill in metals, were determined, whether by fair means or foul, to stop at the very outset. Secrecy being their main object, what chance could there be of it, if the miners were allowed to keep their children in the neighbourhood? Hence, on the plea of feasting Simon, they kept him drunk for three days and three nights, assuring him (whenever he had gleams enough to ask for her) that his daughter was as well as could be, and enjoying herself with the children. Not wishing the maid to see him tipsy, he pressed the matter no further; but applied himself to the bottle again, and drank her health with pleasure.

However, after three days of this, his constitution rose against it, and he became quite sober; with a certain lowness of heart moreover, and a sense of error. And his first desire to right himself, and easiest way to do it, was by exerting parental authority upon Gwenny. Possessed with this intention (for he was not a sweet-tempered man, and his head was aching sadly), he sought for Gwenny high and low; first with threats, and then with fears, and then with tears and wailing. And so he became to the other men a warning and great annoyance. Therefore they combined to swear what seemed a very likely thing, and might be true for all they knew; to wit, that Gwenny had come to seek for her father down the shaft-hole, and peering too eagerly into the dark, had toppled forward, and gone down, and lain at the bottom as dead as a stone.

'And thou being so happy with drink,' the villains finished up to him, 'and getting drunker every day, we thought it shame to trouble thee, and we buried the wench in the lower drift; and no use to think more of her; but come and have a glass, Sim.'

But Simon Carfax swore that drink had lost him his wife, and now had lost him the last of his five children, and would lose him his own soul, if further he went on with it; and from that day to his death he never touched strong drink again. Nor only this; but being soon appointed captain of the mine, he allowed no man on any pretext to bring cordials thither; and to this and his stern hard rule, and stealthy secret management (as much as to good luck and place) might it be attributed that scarcely any but themselves had dreamed about this Exmoor mine.

As for me, I had no ambition to become a miner; and the state to which gold-seeking had brought poor Uncle Ben was not at all encouraging. My business was to till the ground, and tend the growth that came of it, and store the fruit in Heaven's good time, rather than to scoop and burrow, like a weasel or a rat, for the yellow root of evil. Moreover, I was led from home, between the hay and corn harvests (when we often have a week to spare), by a call there was no resisting; unless I gave up all regard for wrestling, and for my county.

Now here many persons may take me amiss, and there always has been some confusion; which people who ought to have known better have wrought into subject of quarrelling. By birth, it is true, and cannot be denied, that I am a man of Somerset; nevertheless by breed I am, as well as by education, a son of Devon also. And just as both our two counties vowed that Glen Doone was none of theirs, but belonged to the other one; so now, each with hot claim and jangling (leading even to blows sometimes), asserted and would swear to it (as I became more famous) that John Ridd was of its own producing, bred of its own true blood, and basely stolen by the other.

Now I have not judged it in any way needful, or even becoming and delicate, to enter into my wrestling adventures, or describe my progress. The whole thing is so different from Lorna, and her gentle manners, and her style of walking; moreover I must seem (even to kind people) to magnify myself so much, or at least attempt to do it, that I have scratched out written pages, through my better taste and sense.

Neither will I, upon this head, make any difference even now; being simply betrayed into mentioning the matter, because bare truth requires it, in the tale of Lorna's fortunes.

For a mighty giant had arisen in a part of Cornwall; and his calf was twenty-five inches round, and the breadth of his shoulders two feet and a quarter; and his stature seven feet and three quarters. Round the chest he was seventy inches, and his hand a foot across, and there were no scales strong enough to judge of his weight in the market-place. Now this man – or I should say, his backers and his boasters, for the giant himself was modest – sent me a brave and haughty challenge, to meet him in the ring at Bodmin-town, on the first day of August, or else to return my champion's belt to them by the messenger.

It is no use to deny that I was greatly dashed and scared at first. For my part, I was only, when measured without clothes on, sixty inches round the breast, and round the calf scarce twenty-one, only two feet across the shoulders, and in height not six and three quarters. However, my mother would never believe that this man could beat me; and Lorna being of the same mind, I resolved to go and try him, as they would pay all expenses, and a hundred pounds, if I conquered him; so confident were those Cornishmen.

Now this story is too well-known for me to go through it again and again. Every child in Devonshire knows, and his grandson will know, the song which some clever man made of it, after I had treated him to water, and to lemon, and a little sugar, and a drop of eau-de-vie. Enough that I had found the giant quite as big as they had described him, and enough to terrify anyone. But trusting in my practice and study of the art, I resolved to try a back with him; and when my arms were round him once, the giant was but a farthingale put into the vice of a blacksmith. The man had no bones; his frame sank in, and I was afraid of crushing him. He lay on his back, and smiled at me; and I begged his pardon.

Now this affair made a noise at the time, and redounded so much to my credit, that I was deeply grieved at it, because deserving none. For I do like a good strife and struggle; and the doubt makes the joy of victory; whereas in this case I might as well have been sent for a match with a haymow. However, I got my hundred pounds, and made up my mind to spend every farthing in presents for mother and Lorna.

For Annie was married by this time, and long before I went away; as need scarcely be said perhaps, if any one follows the weeks and the months. The wedding was quiet enough, except for everybody's good wishes; and I desire not to dwell upon it, because it grieved me in many ways.

But now that I had tried to hope the very best for dear Annie, a deeper blow than could have come, even through her, awaited me. For after that visit to Cornwall, and with my prize-money about me, I came on foot from Okehampton to Oare, so as to save a little sum towards my time of marrying. For Lorna's fortune I would not have; small or great I would not have it; only if there were no denying, we would devote the whole of it to charitable uses, as Master Peter Blundell had done; and perhaps the future ages would endeavour to be grateful. Lorna and I had settled this question, at least twice a day, on the average; and each time with more satisfaction.

Now coming into the kitchen, with all my cash in my breeches pocket (golden guineas, with an elephant on them, for the stamp of the guinea company), I found dear mother most heartily glad to see me safe and sound again – for she had dreaded that giant, and dreamed of him – and she never asked me about the money. Lizzie also was softer, and more gracious than usual; especially when she saw me pour guineas, like pepper-corns, into the pudding-basin. But by the way they hung about, I knew that something was gone wrong.

'Where is Lorna?' I asked at length, after trying not to ask it: 'I want her to come, and see my money. She never saw so much before.'

'Alas!' said mother, with a heavy sigh; 'she will see a great deal more, I fear; and a deal more than is good for her. Whether you ever see her again will depend upon her nature, John.'

'What do you mean, mother? Have you quarrelled? Why does not Lorna come to me? Am I never to know?'

'Now, John, be not so impatient,' my mother replied, quite calmly, for in truth she was jealous of Lorna: 'you could wait now very well, John, if it were till this day week, for the coming of your mother, John. And yet your mother is your best friend. Who can ever fill her place?'

Thinking of her future absence, mother turned away and cried; and the box-iron singed the blanket.

'Now,' said I, being wild by this time; 'Lizzie, you have a little sense; will you tell me where is Lorna?'

'The Lady Lorna Dugal,' said Lizzie, screwing up her lips, as if the title were too grand, 'is gone to London, brother John; and not likely to come back again. We must try to get on without her.'

'You little' – [something] I cried, which I dare not write down here, as all you are too good for such language; but Lizzie's lips provoked me so – 'my Lorna gone, my Lorna gone! And without good-bye to me even! It is your spite has sickened her.'

'You are quite mistaken there,' she replied; 'how can folk of low degree have either spite or liking towards the people so far above them? The Lady Lorna Dugal is gone, because she could not help herself; and she wept enough to break ten hearts – if hearts are ever broken, John.'

'Darling Lizzie, how good you are!' I cried, without noticing her sneer: 'tell me all about it, dear; tell me every word she said.'

'That will not take long,' said Lizzie, quite as unmoved by

soft coaxing as by urgent cursing: 'the lady spoke very little to any one, except indeed to mother, and to Gwenny Carfax: and Gwenny is gone with her, so that the benefit of that is lost. But she left a letter for "poor John," as in charity she called him. How grand she looked to be sure, with the fine clothes on that were come for her!'

'Where is the letter, you utter vixen? Oh, may you have a husband!'

'Who will thrash it out of you, and starve it, and swear it out of you;' was the meaning of my imprecation: but Lizzie, not dreaming as yet of such things, could not understand me, and was rather thankful; therefore she answered quietly, –

'The letter is in the little cupboard, near the head of Lady Lorna's bed, where she used to keep the diamond necklace, which we contrived to get stolen.'

Without another word, I rushed (so that every board in the house shook) up to my lost Lorna's room, and tore the little wall-niche open, and espied my treasure. It was as simple, and as homely, and loving, as even I could wish. Part of it ran as follows – the other parts it behoves me not to open out to strangers: 'My own love, and sometime lord, – Take it not amiss of me, that even without farewell, I go; for I cannot persuade the men to wait! your return being doubtful. My great uncle, some grand lord, is awaiting me at Dunster, having fear of venturing too near this Exmoor country. I, who have been so lawless always, and the child of outlaws, am now to atone for this, it seems, by living in a court of law, and under special surveillance (as they call it, I believe) of His Majesty's Court of Chancery. My uncle is appointed my guardian and master; and I must live beneath his care, until I am twenty-one years old. To me this appears a dreadful thing, and very unjust, and cruel; for why should I lose my freedom, through heritage of land and gold? I offered to abandon all, if they would only let me go: I went down on my knees to them, and said I wanted titles not, neither land, nor money; only to stay where I was, where first I had known happiness. But they only laughed, and called me "child," and said I must talk of that to the King's High Chancellor. Their orders they had, and must obey them; and Master Stickles was ordered too to help, as the King's Commissioner. And then, although it pierced my heart not to say one "Good-bye, John," I was glad upon the whole that you were not here to dispute it. For I am almost certain that you would not, without force to yourself, have let your Lorna go to people who never, never can care for her.'

Here my darling had wept again, by the tokens on the paper; and then there followed some sweet words, too sweet for me to chatter them. But she finished with these noble lines, which (being common to all humanity, in a case of steadfast love) I do no harm, but rather help all true love, by repeating: 'Of one thing rest you well assured – and I do hope that it may prove of service to your rest, love, else would my own be broken – no difference of rank, or fortune, or of life itself, shall ever make me swerve from truth to you. We have passed through many troubles, dangers, and dispartments, but never yet was doubt between us; neither ever shall be. Each has trusted well the other; and still each must do so. Though they tell you I am false, though your own mind harbours it, from the sense of things around, and your own under-valuing, yet take counsel of your heart, and cast such thoughts away from you; being unworthy of itself, they must be unworthy also of the one who dwells there: and that one is, and ever shall be, your own Lorna Dugal.'

Some people cannot understand that tears should come from pleasure; but whether from pleasure or from sorrow (mixed as they are in the twisted strings of a man's heart, or a woman's), great tears fell from my stupid eyes, even on the blots of Lorna's.

'No doubt it is all over!' my mind said to me bitterly: 'Trust me, all shall yet be right!' my heart replied very sweetly.

33

John is Worsted by
the Women

All our neighbourhood was surprised, that the Doones had
not ere now attacked, and probably made an end of us. For
we lay almost at their mercy now, having only Serjeant
Bloxham, and three men, to protect us, Captain Stickles
having been ordered southwards with all his force, except
such as might be needful for collecting toll, and watching the
imports at Lynmouth, and thence to Porlock.

Now the reason, why the Doones did not attack us, was
that they were preparing to meet another, and more powerful
assault, upon their fortress; being assured that their repulse
of King's troops could not be looked over when brought
before the authorities. And no doubt they were right; for
although the conflicts in the government during that summer,
and autumn, had delayed the matter, yet positive orders had
been issued, that these outlaws and malefactors should at
any price be brought to justice; when the sudden death of
King Charles the Second threw all things into confusion, and
all minds into a panic.

Almost before we had put off the mourning, which as
loyal subjects we kept for the King, three months and a
week; rumours of disturbances, of plottings, and of outbreak
began to stir among us. We heard of fighting in Scotland,
and buying of ships on the continent, and of arms in Dorset
and Somerset; and we kept our beacon in readiness to give
signals of a landing; or rather the soldiers did so. For we,
having trustworthy reports that the new King had been to

high mass himself in the Abbey of Westminster, making all the bishops go with him, and all the guards in London, and then tortured all the Protestants who dared to wait outside, moreover had received from the Pope a flower grown in the Virgin Mary's garden, and warranted to last for ever, we of the moderate party, hearing all this and ten times as much, and having no love for this sour James, such as we had for the lively Charles, were ready to wait for what might happen, rather than care about stopping it.

For the next fortnight, we were daily troubled with conflicting rumours, each man relating what he desired, rather than what he had right, to believe. We were told that the Duke of Monmouth had been proclaimed King of England, in every town of Dorset and of Somerset; that he had won a great battle at Axminster, and another at Bridport, and another somewhere else; that all the western counties had risen as one man for him, and all the militia joined his ranks; that Taunton, and Bridgwater, and Bristowe, were all mad with delight, the two former being in his hands, and the latter craving to be so. And then, on the other hand, we heard that the Duke had been vanquished, and put to flight, and upon being apprehended had confessed himself an impostor, and a papist, as bad as the King was.

We longed for Colonel Stickles (as he always became in time of war, though he fell back to Captain, and even Lieutenant, directly the fight was over), for then we should have won trusty news, as well as good consideration. But even Sergeant Bloxham, much against his will, was gone, having left his heart with our Lizzie, and a collection of all his writings. All the soldiers had been ordered away at full speed for Exeter, to join the Duke of Albemarle, or if he were gone, to follow him. As for us, who had fed them so long (although not quite for nothing), we must take our chances of Doones, or any other enemies.

One day at the beginning of July, I came home from mowing about noon, or a little later, to fetch some cider for all of us, and to eat a morsel of bacon.

In the courtyard I saw a little cart, with iron breaks underneath it, such as fastidious people use to deaden the jolting of the road; but few men under a lord or baronet would be so particular. Therefore I wondered who our noble visitor could be. But when I entered the kitchen-place, brushing up my hair for somebody, behold it was no one greater than our Annie, with my godson in her arms, and looking pale and tear-begone.

'Tell me what it is, my dear. Any grief of yours will vex me greatly; but I will try to bear it.'

'Then, John, it is just this. Tom has gone off with the rebels: and you must, oh, you must go after him.'

'I will go seek your husband,' I said, 'but only upon condition that you ensure this house, and people, from the Doones meanwhile. Even for the sake of Tom, I cannot leave all helpless. The oat-ricks and the hay-ricks, which are my only love, they are welcome to make cinders of. But I will not have mother treated so; nor even little Lizzie, although you scorn your sister so.'

'Oh, John, I do think you are the hardest, as well as the softest, of all the men I know. Not even a woman's bitter word but what you pay her out for. Will you never understand that we are not like you, John? We say all sorts of spiteful things, without a bit of meaning. John, for God's sake, fetch Tom home; and then revile me as you please, and I will kneel and thank you.'

'I will not promise to fetch him home,' I answered, being ashamed of myself, for having lost command so: 'but I will promise to do my best, if we can only hit on a plan for leaving mother harmless.'

Annie thought for a little while, trying to gather her smooth clear brow into maternal wrinkles, and then she looked at her child, and said, 'I will risk it, for daddy's sake, darling; you precious soul, for daddy's sake.' I asked her what she was going to risk. She would not tell me; but took upper hand, and saw to my cider-cans and bacon, and went from corner to cupboard, exactly as if she had never been married; only without an apron on. And then she said, 'Now to your mowers, John; and make the most of this fine afternoon: kiss your godson, before you go.' And I, being used to obey her, in little things of that sort, kissed the baby, and took my cans, and went back to my scythe again.

By the time I came home it was dark night, and pouring again with a foggy rain, such as we have in July, even more than in January. Being soaked all through and through, and with water quelching in my boots, like a pump with a bad bucket, I was only too glad to find Annie's bright face, and quick figure, flitting in and out of the firelight, instead of Lizzie sitting grandly, with a feast of literature, and not a drop of gravy. Mother was in the corner also, with her cherry-coloured ribbons glistening very nice by candle light, looking at Annie now and then, with memories of her baby-hood; and then at her having a baby; yet half afraid of praising her much, for fear of that young Lizzie. But Lizzie showed no jealousy: she truly loved our Annie (now that she was gone from us), and she wanted to know all sorts of things, and she adored the baby. Therefore Annie was allowed to attend to me, as she used to do.

'Now, John, you must start the first thing in the morning,' she said, when the others had left the room, but somehow she stuck to the baby, 'to fetch me back my rebel, according to your promise.'

'Not so,' I replied, misliking the job; 'all I promised was to go, if this house were assured against any onslaught of the Doones.'

'Just so; and here is that assurance.' With these words she drew forth a paper, and laid it on my knee with triumph, enjoying my amazement. This, as you may suppose, was great; not only at the document, but also at her possession of it. For in truth it was no less than a formal undertaking, on the part of the Doones, not to attack Plover's Barrows farm, or molest any of the inmates, or carry off any chattels, during the absence of John Ridd upon a special errand. This document was signed not only by the Counsellor, but by many other Doones: whether Carver's name were there, I could not say for certain; as of course he would not sign it under his name of 'Carver,' and I had never heard Lorna say to what (if any) he had been baptized.

In the face of such a deed as this, I could no longer refuse to go; and having received my promise, Annie told me (as was only fair) how she had procured that paper. It was both a clever and courageous act; and would have seemed to me, at first sight, far beyond Annie's power. But none may gauge a woman's power, when her love and faith are moved.

The first thing Annie had done was this: she made herself look ugly. This was not an easy thing; but she had learned a great deal from her husband, upon the subject of disguises. It hurt her feelings not a little to make so sad a fright of herself, but what could it matter? – if she lost Tom, she must be a far greater fright in earnest, than now she was in seeming. And then she left her child asleep under Betty Muxworthy's tendance – for Betty took to that child, as if there never had been a child before – and away she went in her own 'springcart' (as the name of that engine proved to be), without a word to any one, except the old man who had driven her from Molland parish that morning; and who coolly took one of our best horses, without 'by your leave' to any one.

Annie made the old man drive her within easy reach of the Doone-gate, whose position she knew well enough, from all our talk about it. And there she bade the old man stay, until she should return to him. Then with her comely figure hidden by a dirty old woman's cloak, and her fair young face defaced by patches and by liniments, so that none might covet her, she addressed the young men at the gate in a cracked and trembling voice; and they were scarcely civil to the 'old hag,' as they called her. She said that she bore important tidings for Sir Counsellor himself, and must be conducted to him. To him accordingly she was led, without even any hood-winking; for she had spectacles over her eyes, and made believe not to see ten yards.

She found Sir Counsellor at home, and when the rest were out of sight, threw off all disguise to him, flashing forth as a lovely young woman, from all her wraps and disfigurements. She flung her patches on the floor, amid the old man's laughter, and let her tucked-up hair come down; and then went up and kissed him.

'Worthy and reverend Counsellor, I have a favour to ask,' she began.

'So I should think from your proceedings,' the old man interrupted; 'ah, if I were half my age – '

'If you were, I would not sue so. But most excellent Counsellor, you owe me some amends, you know, for the way in which you robbed me.'

'Beyond a doubt I do, my dear. You have put it rather strongly; and it might offend some people. Nevertheless I own my debt, having so fair a creditor.'

'And do you remember how you slept, and how much we made of you, and would have seen you home, sir; only you did not wish it?'

'And for excellent reasons, child. My best escort was in my cloak, after we made the cream to rise. Ha ha! The unholy spell. My pretty child, has it injured you?'

'Yes, I fear it has,' said Annie; 'or whence can all my ill luck come?' And here she showed some signs of crying knowing that the Counsellor hated it.

'You shall not have ill luck, my dear. I have heard all about your marriage to a very noble highwayman. Ah, you made a mistake in that; you were worthy of a Doone, my child; your frying was a blessing meant for those who can appreciate.'

'My husband can appreciate,' she answered very proudly; 'but what I wish to know is this, will you try to help me?'

The Counsellor answered that he would do so, if her needs were moderate; whereupon she opened her meaning to him, and told of all her anxieties. Considering that Lorna was gone, and her necklace in his possession, and that I (against whom alone of us the Doones could bear any malice) would be out of the way all the while, the old man readily undertook that our house should not be assaulted, nor our property molested, until my return. And to the promptitude of his pledge, two things perhaps contributed, namely, that he knew not how we were stripped of all defenders, and that some of his own forces were away in the rebel camp. For (as I learned thereafter) the Doones being now in direct feud with the present Government, and sure to be crushed if that prevailed, had resolved to drop all religious questions, and cast in their lot with Monmouth. And the turbulent youths, being long restrained from their wonted outlet for vehemence, by the troopers in the neighbourhood, were only too glad to rush forth upon any promise of blows and excitement.

However, Annie knew little of this, but took the Counsellor's pledge as a mark of especial favour in her behalf (which it may have been, to some extent), and thanked him for it most heartily, and felt that he had earned the necklace; while he, like an ancient gentleman, disclaimed all obligation, and sent her under an escort safe to her own cart again. But Annie, repassing the sentinels, with her youth restored, and blooming with the flush of triumph, went up to them very gravely, and said, 'The old hag wishes you good evening, gentlemen;' and so made her best courtesy.

Now look at it as I would, there was no excuse left for me, after the promise given. Dear Annie had not only cheated the Doones, but also had gotten the best of me by a pledge to a thing impossible. And I bitterly said, 'I am not like Lorna: a pledge once given, I keep it.'

'I will not have a word against Lorna,' cried Annie; 'I will answer for her truth, as surely as I would for my own, or yours, John.' And with that she vanquished me.

Right early in the morning I was off, without word to any one; knowing that mother, and sister mine, had cried each her good self to sleep; relenting when the light was out, and sorry for hard words and thoughts; and yet too much alike in nature to understand each other. Therefore I took good Kickums, who (although with one eye spoiled) was worth ten sweet-tempered horses, to a man who knew how to manage him; and being well charged both with bacon and powder, forth I set on my wild-goose chase.

We went away in merry style; my horse being ready for any thing, and I only glad of a bit of change, after months of working and brooding; with no content to crown the work; no hope to hatch the brooding, or without hatching to reckon it. Who could tell but what Lorna might be discovered, or at any rate heard of, before the end of this campaign; if campaign it could be called of a man who went to fight nobody, only to redeem a runagate?

34

Slaughter in the Marshes

Now if I tried to set down at length all the things that happened to me, upon this adventure, every in and out, and up and down, and to and fro, that occupied me, together with the things I saw, and the things I heard of – however much the wiser people might applaud my narrative, it is likely enough that idle readers might exclaim, 'What ails this man? Knows he not that men of parts, and of real understanding, have told us all we care to hear of that miserable business. Let him keep to his farm, and bacon, his wrestling, and constant feeding.'

Fearing to meet with such rebuffs (which after my death would vex me), I will try to set down only what is needful for my story, and the clearing of my character, and the good name of our parish. But the manner in which I was bandied about, by false information, from pillar to post, or at other times driven quite out of my way by the presence of the King's soldiers, may be known by the names of the following towns, to which I was sent in succession, Bath, Frome, Wells, Wincanton, Glastonbury, Shepton, Bradford, Axbridge, Somerton, and Bridgwater.

This last place I reached on a Sunday night, the fourth or fifth of July, I think – or it might be the sixth, for that matter; inasmuch as I had been too much worried to get the day of the month at church. Only I know that my horse and myself were glad to come to a decent place, where meat, and corn, could be had for money; and being quite weary of wandering about, we hoped to rest there a little.

Of this, however, we found no chance, for the town was full of the good Duke's soldiers; if men may be called so, the half of whom had never been drilled, nor had fired a gun. And it was rumoured among them, that the 'popish army,' as they called it, was to be attacked that very night, and with God's assistance beaten. However, by this time I had been taught to pay little attention to rumours; and having sought vainly for Tom Faggus, among these poor rustic warriors, I took to my hostel, and went to bed, being as weary as weary can be.

Falling asleep immediately, I took heed of nothing; although the town was all alive, and lights had come glancing, as I lay down, and shouts making echo all round my room. But all I did was to hug my pillow; not an inch would I budge, unless the house, and even my bed, were on fire. And so for several hours I lay, in the depth of the deepest slumber, without even a dream on its surface; until I was roused and awakened at last, by a pushing, and pulling, and pinching, and a plucking of hair out by the roots. And at length, being able to open mine eyes, I saw the old landlady, with a candle, heavily wondering at me.

'Can't you let me alone?' I grumbled: 'I have paid for my bed, mistress; and I won't get up, for any one.'

'Would to God, young man,' she answered, shaking me as hard as ever, 'that the popish soldiers may sleep, this night, only half as strong as thou dost! Fie on thee, fie on thee! Get up, and go fight; we can hear the battle already; and a man of thy size mought stop a cannon.'

I was by this time wide awake, though much aggrieved at feeling so, and through the open window heard the distant roll of musketry, and the beating of drums, with a quick rub-a-dub, and the 'come round the corner,' of trumpet-call. And perhaps Tom Faggus might be there, and shot at any moment, and my dear Annie left a poor widow, and my godson Jack an orphan, without a tooth to help him.

Therefore I reviled myself for all my heavy laziness; and partly through good honest will, and partly through the stings of pride, and yet a little perhaps by virtue of a young man's love of riot, up I arose, and dressed myself, and woke

Kickums (who was snoring), and set out to see the worst of it. The sleepy hostler scratched his poll, and could not tell me which way to take; what odds to him who was King, or Pope, so long as he paid his way, and got a bit of bacon on Sunday? And would I please to remember, that I had roused him up at night, and the quality always made a point of paying four times over, for a man's loss of his beauty-sleep. I replied that his loss of beauty-sleep was rather improving to a man of so high complexion; and that I, being none of the quality, must pay half-quality prices: and so I gave him double fee, as became a good farmer; and he was glad to be quit of Kickums; as I saw by the turn of his eye, while going out at the archway.

All this was done by lanthorn light, although the moon was high and bold; and in the northern heaven, flags and ribbons of a jostling pattern; such as we often have in autumn, but in July very rarely. Of these Master Dryden has spoken somewhere, in his courtly manner; but of him I think so little – because by fashion preferred to Shakespeare – that I cannot remember the passage; neither is it a credit to him.

Therefore I was guided mainly by the sound of guns and trumpets, in riding out of the narrow ways, and into the open marshes. And thus I might have found my road, in spite of all the spread of water, and the glaze of moonshine; but that, as I followed sound (far from hedge or causeway), fog (like a chestnut-tree in blossom, touched with moonlight) met me. Now fog is a thing that I understand, and can do with well enough, where I know the country: but here I had never been before. It was nothing to our Exmoor fogs; not to be compared with them; and all the time one could see the moon; which we cannot do in our fogs; nor even the sun, for a week together. Yet the gleam of water always makes a fog more difficult: like a curtain on a mirror; none can tell the boundaries.

Here the King's troops had been quite lately, and their fires were still burning; but the men themselves had been summoned away by the night attack of the rebels. Hence I procured for my guide a young man who knew the district thoroughly, and who led me by many intricate ways to the rear of the rebel army. We came upon a broad open moor, striped with sullen water-courses, shagged with sedge, and yellow iris, and in the dried part with bilberries. For by this time it was four o'clock, and the summer sun, arising wanly, showed us all the ghastly scene.

Would that I had never been there! Often in the lonely hours, even now it haunts me: would, far more, that the piteous thing had never been done in England! Flying men, flung back from dreams of victory and honour, only glad to have the luck of life and limbs to fly with, mud-bedraggled, foul with slime, reeking both with sweat and blood, which they could not stop to wipe, cursing, with their pumped-out lungs, every stick that hindered them, or gory puddle that slipped the step, scarcely able to leap over the corpses that had dragged to die. And to see how the corpses lay; some, as fair as death in sleep; with the smile of placid valour, and of noble manhood, hovering yet on the silent lips. Upon these things I cannot dwell; and none, I bow, would ask me: only if a plain man saw what I saw that morning, he (if God had blessed him with the heart that is in most of us) must have sickened of all desire to be great among mankind.

Seeing me riding to the front (where the work of death went on, among the men of true English pluck; which, when moved, no further moves), the fugitives called out to me, in half a dozen dialects, to make no utter fool of myself; for the great guns were come, and the fight was over; all the rest was slaughter.

'Arl oop wi Moonmo',' shouted one big fellow, a miner of the Mendip hills whose weapon was a pickaxe: 'na oose to vaight na moor. Wend thee hame, yoong mon, agin.'

Upon this I stopped my horse, desiring not to be shot for nothing; and eager to aid some poor sick people, who tried to lift their arms to me. And this I did to the best of my power, though void of skill in the business; and more inclined to weep with them than to check their weeping. While I was giving a drop of cordial from my flask to one poor fellow, I felt warm lips laid against my cheek quite softly, and then a little push; and behold it was a horse leaning over me! I arose in haste, and there stood Winnie, looking at me with beseeching eyes, enough to melt a heart of stone. Then seeing my attention fixed, she turned her head, and glanced back sadly towards the place of battle, and gave a little wistful neigh: and then looked me full in the face again, as much as to say, 'Do you understand?' while she scraped with one hoof impatiently. If ever a horse tried hard to speak, it was Winnie at that moment. I went to her side and patted her; but that was not what she wanted. Then I offered to leap into the empty saddle; but neither did that seem good to her: for she ran away towards the part of the field, at which she had been glancing back, and then turned round, and shook her mane, entreating me to follow her.

I mounted my own horse again, and to Winnie's great delight, professed myself at her service. With her ringing silvery neigh, such as no other horse of all I ever knew could equal, she at once proclaimed her triumph, and told her master (or meant to tell, if death should not have closed his ears,) that she was coming to his aid, and bringing one who might be trusted, of the higher race that kill.

Nearly all were scattered now. Of the noble countrymen (armed with scythe, or pickaxe, blacksmith's hammer, or fold-pitcher), who had stood their ground for hours against blazing musketry, from men whom they could not get at, by reason of the water-dyke, and then against the deadly cannon, dragged by the Bishop's horses to slaughter his own sheep; of these sturdy Englishmen, noble in their want of sense, scarce one out of four remained for the cowards to shoot down.

The last scene of this piteous play was acting, just as I rode up. Broad daylight, and upstanding sun, winnowing fog from the eastern hills, and spreading the moors with freshness; all along the dykes they shone, glistened on the willow-trunks, and touched the banks with a hoary grey. But alas! those banks were touched more deeply with a gory red, and strewn with fallen trunks, more woeful than the wreck of trees; while howling, cursing, yelling, and the loathsome creek of carnage, drowned the scent of a new-mown hay, and the carol of the lark.

Then the cavalry of the King, with their horses at full

speed, dashed from either side upon the helpless mob of countrymen. A few pikes feebly levelled met them; but they shot the pike-men, drew swords, and helter-skelter leaped into the shattered and scattering mass. Right and left, they hacked and hewed; I could hear the snapping' of scythes beneath them, and see the flash of their sweeping swords. How it must end was plain enough, even to one like myself, who had never beheld such a battle before. But Winnie led me away to the left; and as I could not help the people, neither stop the slaughter, but found the cannon-bullets coming very rudely nigh me, I was only too glad to follow her.

35

Falling Among Lambs

That faithful creature, whom I began to admire as if she were my own (which is no little thing for a man to say of another man's horse) stopped in front of a low black shed, such as we call a 'linhay.' And here she uttered a little greeting, in a subdued and softened voice, hoping to obtain an answer, such as her master was wont to give in a cheery manner. Receiving no reply, she entered; and I (who could scarce keep up with her, poor Kickums being weary) leaped from his back, and followed. There I found her sniffing gently, but with great emotion, at the body of Tom Faggus.

He groaned very feebly, as I raised him up; and there was the wound, a great savage one (whether from pike-thrust or musket-ball), gaping and welling in his right side, from which a piece seemed to be torn away. I bound it up with some of my linen, so far as I knew how; just to staunch the flow of blood, until we could get a doctor. Then I gave him a little weak brandy and water, which he drank with the greatest eagerness, and made sign to me for more of it. After that he seemed better, and a little colour came into his cheeks; and he looked at Winnie and knew her. Then he managed to whisper, 'Is Winnie hurt?'

'As sound as a roach,' I answered. 'Then so am I,' said he: 'put me upon her back, John; she and I die together.'

While I was yet hesitating, a storm of horse at full gallop went by, tearing, swearing, bearing away all the country before them. Only a little pollard hedge kept us from their blood-shot eyes. 'Now is the time,' said my cousin Tom, so far as I could make out his words; 'on their heels, I am safe, John, if I only have Winnie under me. Winnie and I die together.'

Seeing this strong bent of his mind, stronger than any pains of death, I even did what his feeble eyes sometimes implored, and sometimes commanded. With a strong sash, from his own hot neck, bound and twisted, tight as wax, around his damaged waist, I set him upon Winnie's back, and placed his trembling feet in stirrups, with a band from one to other, under the good mare's body; so that no swerve could throw him out: and then I said, 'Lean forward, Tom; it will stop your hurt from bleeding.'

'God bless you, John; I am safe,' he whispered, fearing to open his lungs much: 'who can come near my Winnie mare? A mile of her gallop is ten years of life. Look out for yourself, John Ridd.' He sucked his lips, and the mare went off, as easy and swift as a swallow.

I resolved to abide awhile, even where fate had thrown me; for my horse required good rest, no doubt, and was taking it even while he cropped, with his hind legs far away stretched out, and his fore legs gathered under him, and his muzzle on the mole-hills; so that he had five supportings from his mother earth. Moreover the linhay itself was full of very ancient cow-dung; than which there is no balmier and more maiden soporific. Hence I resolved, upon the whole, though grieving about breakfast, to light a pipe, and go to sleep; or at least until the hot sun should arouse the flies.

I may have slept three hours, or four, or it might be even five for I never count time, while sleeping – when a shaking, more rude than the old landlady's, brought me back to the world again. I looked up with a mighty yawn; and saw twenty, or so, of foot-soldiers.

'This linhay is not yours,' I said, when they had quite aroused me, with tongue, and hand, and even sword-prick: 'what business have you here, good fellows?'

'Business bad for you,' said one, 'and will lead you to the gallows.'

'Do you wish to know the way out again?' I asked, very quietly, as being no braggadocio.

'We will show thee the way out,' said one, 'and the way out of the world,' said another: 'But not the way to heaven,' said one chap, most unlikely to know it: and thereupon they all fell wagging, like a bed of clover leaves in the morning, at their own choice humour.

'Will you pile your arms outside,' I said, 'and try a bit of fair play with me?'

'Go you first, Bob,' I heard them say; 'you are the biggest man of us; and Dick the wrestler along of you. Us will back you up, boy.'

'I'll warrant I'll draw the badger,' said Bob; 'and not a tooth will I leave him. But mind, for the honour of Kirke's lambs, every man stands me a glass of gin.' Then he, and another man, made a rush, and the others came double-quick-march on their heels. But as Bob ran at me most stupidly, not even knowing how to place his hands, I caught him with my knuckles at the back of his neck, and with all the sway of my right arm sent him over the heads of his comrades. Meanwhile Dick the wrestler had grappled me, expecting to show off his art, of which indeed he had some small knowledge; but being quite of the light weights, in a second he was flying after his companion Bob.

Now these two men were hurt so badly, the light one having knocked his head against the lintel of the outer gate, that the rest had no desire to encounter the like misfortune. So they hung back whispering; and before they had made up their minds, I rushed into the midst of them. The suddenness and the weight of my onset took them wholly by surprise; and for once in their lives, perhaps, Kirke's lambs were worthy of their name. Like a flock of sheep at a dog's attack, they fell away, hustling one another, and my only difficulty was not to tumble over them.

I had taken my carbine out with me, having a fondness for it; but the two horse-pistols I left behind; and therefore felt good title to take two from the magazine of the lambs. And with these, and my carbine, I leaped upon Kickums, who was now quite glad of a gallop again; and I bade adieu to that mongrel lot; yet they had the meanness to shoot at me.

But I fell into another fold of lambs, from which there was no exit. These, like true crusaders, met me, swaggering very heartily, and with their barrels of cider set, like so many cannon, across the road, over against a small hostel.

'We have won the victory, my lord King, and mean to enjoy it. Down from thy horse, and have a stoup of cider, thou big rebel.'

'No rebel am I. My name is John Ridd. I belong to the side of the King: and I want some breakfast.'

These fellows were truly hospitable; that much I will say for them, and I was beginning to understand a little of what they told me; when up came those confounded lambs, who had shown more tail than head to me, in the linhay, as I mentioned.

Now these men upset every thing. I foresaw a brawl, as plainly as if it were Bear Street in Barnstaple.

And a brawl these was, without any error, except of the men who hit their friends, and those who defended their enemies. My partners swore that I was no prisoner, but the best and most loyal subject, and the finest-hearted fellow they had ever the luck to meet with. Whereas the men from the linhay swore that I was a rebel miscreant; and have me they would, with a rope's-end ready.

While this fight was going on it was in my power at any moment to take horse and go. And this would have been my wisest plan, and a very great saving of money; but somehow I felt as if it would be a mean thing to slip off so. Even while I was hesitating, and the men were breaking each other's heads, a superior officer rode up, with his sword drawn, and his face on fire.

'What, my lambs, my lambs!' he cried, smiting with the flat of his sword; 'is this how you waste my time, and my purse, when you ought to be catching a hundred prisoners, worth ten pounds apiece to me? Who is this young fellow we have here? Speak up, sirrah; what art thou, and how much will thy good mother pay for thee?'

'My mother will pay naught for me,' I answered; while the

lambs fell back and glowered at one another: 'so please your worship, I am no rebel; but an honest farmer, and well-proved of loyalty.'

'Ha, ha! a farmer art thou? Those fellows always pay the best. Good farmer, come to yon barren tree; thou shalt make it fruitful.'

Colonel Kirke made a sign to his men, and before I could think of resistance, stout new ropes were flung around me; and with three men on either side, I was led along very painfully. The face of the Colonel was hard and stern as a block of bogwood oak; and though the men might pity me, and think me unjustly executed, yet they must obey their orders, or themselves be put to death.

It is not in my power to tell half the thoughts that moved me, when we came to the fatal tree, and saw two men hanging there already, as innocent perhaps as I was, and henceforth entirely harmless. Though ordered by the Colonel to look steadfastly upon them, I could not bear to do so: upon which he called me a paltry coward, and promised my breeches to any man who would spit upon my countenance. This vile thing Bob, being angered perhaps by the smarting wound of his knuckles, bravely stepped forward to do for me, trusting no doubt to the rope I was led with. But, unluckily as it proved for him, my right arm was free for a moment; and therewith I dealt him such a blow, that he never spake again. For this thing I have often grieved; but the provocation was very sore to the pride of a young man; and I trust that God has forgiven me. At the sound and sight of that bitter stroke, the other men drew back; and Colonel Kirke, now black in the face with fury and vexation, gave orders for to shoot me, and cast me into the ditch hard by. The men raised their pieces, and pointed at me, waiting for the word to fire; and I, being quite overcome by the hurry of these events, and quite unprepared to die yet, could only think all upside down about Lorna, and my mother, and wonder what each would say to it. I spread my hands before my eyes, not being so brave as some men; and hoping, in some foolish way, to cover my heart with my elbows. I heard the breath of all around, as if my skull were a sounding-board; and knew even how the different men were fingering their triggers. And a cold sweat broke all over me, as the Colonel, prolonging his enjoyment, began slowly to say, 'Fire.'

But while he was yet dwelling on the 'F,' the hoofs of a horse dashed out on the road, and horse and horseman flung themselves betwixt me and the gun-muzzles. So narrowly was I saved, that one man could not check his trigger: his musket went off, and the ball struck the horse on the withers, and scared him exceedingly. He began to lash out with his heels all around, and the Colonel was glad to keep clear of him; and the men made excuse to lower their guns, not really wishing to shoot me.

'How now, Captain Stickles?' cried Kirke, the more angry because he had shown his cowardice; 'dare you, sir, to come betwixt me and my lawful prisoner?'

'Nay, hearken one moment, Colonel,' replied my old friend Jeremy; and his damaged voice was the sweetest sound I had heard for many a day; 'for your own sake hearken.' He looked so full of momentous tidings, that Colonel Kirke made a sign to his men, not to shoot me till further orders; and then he went aside with Stickles, so that in spite of all my anxiety I could not catch what passed between them. But I fancied that the name of the Lord Chief-Justice Jeffreys was spoken more than once, and with emphasis, and deference.

'Then I leave him in your hands, Captain Stickles,' said Kirke at last, so that all might hear him; and though the news was so good for me, the smile of baffled malice made his dark face look most hideous; 'and I shall hold you answerable for the custody of this prisoner.'

'Colonel Kirke, I will answer for him,' Master Stickles replied, with a grave bow, and one hand on his breast: 'John Ridd, you are my prisoner. Follow me, John Ridd.'

Upon that, those precious lambs flocked away, leaving the rope still around me; and some were glad, and some were sorry, not to see me swinging. Being free of my arms again, I touched my hat to Colonel Kirke, as became his rank and experience; but he did not condescend to return my short salutation, having espied in the distance a prisoner, out of whom he might make money.

I wrung the hand of Jeremy Stickles, for his truth and goodness; and he almost wept (for since his wound, he had been a weakened man) as he answered, 'Turn for turn, John. You saved my life from the Doones; and by the mercy of God I have saved you from a far worse company. Let your sister Annie know it.'

36

Suitable Devotion

Now Kickums was not like Winnie, any more than a man is like a woman; and so he had not followed my fortunes, except at his own distance. No doubt but what he felt a certain interest in me; but his interest was not devotion; and man might go his way and be hanged, rather than horse would meet hardship. Therefore seeing things to be bad, and his master involved in trouble, what did the horse do but start for the ease and comfort of Plover's Barrows, and the plentiful ration of oats abiding in his own manger. For that I do not blame him. It is the manner of mankind.

But I could not help being very uneasy at the thought of my mother's discomfort and worry, when she should spy this good horse coming home, without any master, or rider, and I almost hoped that he might be caught (although he was worth at least twenty pounds) by some of the King's troopers, rather than find his way home, and spread distress among our people. Yet knowing his nature, I doubted if any could catch, or catching, would keep him.

Jeremy Stickles assured me, as we took the road to Bridgwater, that the only chance for my life (if I still refused to fly) was to obtain an order forthwith for my dispatch to London, as a suspected person indeed, but not found in open rebellion, and believed to be under the patronage of the great Lord Jeffreys. 'For,' said he, 'in a few hours' time, you would fall into the hands of Lord Feversham, who has won this fight, without seeing it, and who has returned to bed again, to have his breakfast more comfortably. Now he may not be quite so savage perhaps as Colonel Kirke, nor find so much sport in gibbeting; but he is equally pitiless, and his price no doubt would be higher.'

'I will pay no price whatever,' I answered, 'neither will I fly. An hour agone I would have fled, for the sake of my mother, and the farm. But now that I have been taken prisoner, and my name is known, if I fly, the farm is forfeited; and my mother and sister must starve. Moreover, I have done no harm; I have borne no weapons against the King, nor desired the success of his enemies. I like not that the son of a bona-roba should be King of England; neither do I count the papists any worse than we are. If they have aught to try me for, I will stand my trial.'

'Then to London thou must go, my son. There is no such thing as trial here: we hang the good folk without it, which saves them much anxiety. But quicken thy step, good John; I have influence with Lord Churchill, and must contrive to see him, ere the foreigner falls to work again. Lord Churchill is a man of sense, and imprisons nothing but his money.'

Now this good Lord Churchill – for one might call him good, by comparison with the very bad people around him – granted, without any long hesitation, the order for my safe deliverance to the Court of King's Bench at Westminster; and Stickles, who had to report in London, was empowered to convey me, and made answerable for producing me. This arrangement would have been entirely to my liking, although the time of year was bad for leaving Plover's Barrows so; but no man may quite choose his times, and on the whole I would have been quite content to visit London, if my mother could be warned that nothing was amiss with me, only a mild, and as one might say, nominal captivity. And to prevent her anxiety, I did my best to send a letter through good Serjeant Bloxham, of whom I heard as quartered with Dumbarton's regiment at Chedzuy. But that regiment was away in pursuit; and I was forced to entrust my letter to a man who said that he knew him, and accepted a shilling to see to it.

For fear of any unpleasant change, we set forth at once for

London; and truly thankful may I be that God in His mercy spared me the sight of the cruel and bloody work, with which the whole country reeked and howled, during the next fortnight.

The sight of London warmed my heart with various emotions, such as a cordial man must draw from the heart of all humanity. Here there are quick ways and manners, and the rapid sense of knowledge, and the power of understanding, ere a word be spoken. Whereas at Oare, you must say a thing three times, very slowly, before it gets inside the skull of the good man you are addressing. And yet we are far more clever there, than in any parish for fifteen miles.

But what moved me most, when I saw again the noble oil and tallow of the London lights, and the dripping torches at almost every corner, and the handsome sign-boards, was the thought that here my Lorna lived, and walked, and took the air, and perhaps thought, now and then, of the old days in the good farmhouse. Although I would make no approach to her, any more than she had done to me (upon which grief I have not dwelt, for fear of seeming selfish), yet there must be some large chance, or the little chance might be enlarged, of falling in with the maiden somehow, and learning how her mind was set. If against me, all should be over. I was not the man to sigh and cry for love, like a hot-brained Romeo: none should even guess my grief, except my sister Annie.

But if Lorna loved me still – as in my heart of hearts I hoped – then would I for no one care, except her own delicious self. Rank and title, wealth and grandeur, all should go to the winds before they scared me from my own true love.

And so I came back to my old furrier; the which was a thoroughly hearty man, and welcomed me to my room again, with two shillings added to the rent, in the joy of his heart at seeing me. Being under parole to Master Stickles, I only went out betwixt certain hours; because I was accounted as liable to be called upon; for what purpose I knew not, but hoped it might be a good one. I felt it a loss, and a hindrance to me, that I was so bound to remain at home, during the session of the courts of law; for thereby the chance of ever beholding

Lorna was greatly damaged, if not altogether done away with. For these were the very hours in which the people of fashion, and the high world, were wont to appear to the rest of mankind, so as to encourage them. And of course by this time, the Lady Lorna was high among people of fashion, and was not likely to be seen out of fashion hours. It is true that there were some places of expensive entertainment, at which the better sort of mankind might be seen and studied, in their hours of relaxation, by those of the lower order, who could pay sufficiently. But alas, my money was getting low; and the privilege of seeing my betters was more and more denied to me, as my cash drew shorter. For a man must have a good coat at least, and the pockets not wholly empty, before he can look at those whom God has created for his ensample.

Hence, and from many other causes – part of which was my own pride – it happened that I abode in London, betwixt a month and five weeks' time, ere ever I saw Lorna.

Nevertheless I heard of Lorna, from my worthy furrier, almost every day, and with a fine exaggeration. This honest man was one of those who, in virtue of their trade, and nicety of behaviour, are admitted into noble life, to take measurements, and show patterns. And while so doing, they contrive to acquire what is to the English mind at once the most important, and most interesting of all knowledge, – the science of being able to talk about the titled people. So my furrier (whose name was Ramsack), having to make robes for peers, and cloaks for their wives and otherwise, knew the great folk, sham or real, as well as he knew a fox, or skunk, from a wolverine skin.

And when, with some fencing and foils of inquiry, I hinted about Lady Lorna Dugal, the old man's face became so pleasant, that I knew her birth must be wondrous high.

From Master Ramsack I discovered that the nobleman, to whose charge Lady Lorna had been committed, by the Court of Chancery, was Earl Brandir of Lochawe, her poor mother's uncle. For the Countess of Dugal was daughter, and only child, of the last Lord Lorne, whose sister had married Sir Ensor Doone; while he himself had married the sister of Earl Brandir. This nobleman had a country house near the village of Kensington; and here his niece dwelled with him, when she was not in attendance on Her Majesty the Queen, who had taken a liking to her. Now since the King had begun to attend celebration of mass in the chapel at Whitehall, – and not at Westminster Abbey, as our gossips had averred – he had given order that the doors should be thrown open, so that all who could make interest to get into the antechamber, might see this form of worship. Master Ramsack told me that Lorna was there almost every Sunday; their Majesties being most anxious to have the presence of all the nobility of the Catholic persuasion, so as to make a goodly show. And the worthy furrier, having influence with the door keepers, kindly obtained admittance for me, one Sunday, into the antechamber.

Here I took care to be in waiting, before the Royal procession entered; but being unknown, and of no high rank, I was not allowed to stand forward among the better people, but ordered back into a corner very dark and dismal; the verger remarking, with a grin, that I could see over all other heads, and must not set my own so high.

You may suppose that my heart beat high, when the King, and Queen, appeared, and entered, followed by the Duke of Norfolk bearing the sword of state, and by several other noblemen, and people of repute.

When the King and Queen crossed the threshold, a mighty flourish of trumpets arose, and a waving of banners. The Knights of the Garter (whoever they be) were to attend that day in state; and some went in, and some stayed out, and it made me think of the difference betwixt the ewes and the wethers. For the ewes will go wherever you lead them; but the wethers will not, having strong opinions, and meaning to abide by them. And one man I noticed was of the wethers, to wit the Duke of Norfolk; who stopped outside with the sword of state, like a beadle with a rapping-rod. This has taken more time to tell than the time it happened in. For after all the men were gone, some to this side, some to that, according to their feelings, a number of ladies, beautifully dressed, being of the Queen's retinue, began to enter, and were stared at three times as much as the men had been. And indeed they were worth looking at (which men never are to my ideas, when they trick themselves with gewgaws), but none was so well worth eye-service as my own beloved Lorna. She entered modestly and shyly, with her eyes upon the ground, knowing the rudeness of the gallants, and the large sum she was priced at. Her dress was of the purest white, very sweet and simple, without a line of ornament, for she herself adorned it. The way she walked, and touched her skirt (rather than seemed to hold it up), with a white hand bearing one red rose, this, and her stately supple neck, and the flowing of her hair would show, at a distance of a hundred yards, that she could be none but Lorna Doone – Lorna Doone of my early love; in the days when she blushed for her name before me, by reason of dishonesty; but now the Lady Lorna Dugal; as far beyond reproach as above my poor affection. All my heart, and all my mind, gathered themselves upon her. Would she see me, or would she pass? Was there instinct in our love?

By some strange chance she saw me. Or was it through our destiny? While with eyes kept sedulously on the marble floor, to shun the weight of admiration thrust too boldly on them, while with shy quick steps she passed, some one (perhaps with purpose,) trod on the skirt of her clear white dress, – with the quickness taught her by many a scene of danger, she looked up, and her eyes met mine.

As I gazed upon her, steadfastly, yearningly, yet with some reproach, and more of pride than humility, she made me one of the courtly bows which I do so much detest; yet even that was sweet and graceful, when my Lorna did it. But the colour of her pure clear cheeks was nearly as deep as that of my own, when she went on for the religious work. And the shining of her eyes was owing to an unpaid debt of tears.

Upon the whole I was satisfied. Lorna had seen me, and had not (according to the phrase of the high world then) even tried to 'cut' me.

All these proud thoughts rose within me, as the lovely form of Loma went inside, and was no more seen.

While I stored up, in my memory, enough to keep our parson, going through six pipes on a Saturday night – to have it as right as could be next day – a lean man with a yellow beard, too thin for a good Catholic (which religion always fattens) came up to me, working sideways, in the manner of a female crab.

'This is not to my liking,' I said: 'if aught thou hast, speak plainly; while they make that musical roar inside.'

Nothing had this man to say; but with many sighs, because I was not of the proper faith, he took my reprobate hand to save me: and with several religious tears, looked up at me, and winked with one eye. Although the skin of my palms was thick, I felt a little suggestion there, as of a gentle leaf in spring, fearing to seem too forward. I paid the man, and he went happy; for the standard of heretical silver is purer than that of the Catholics.

Then I lifted up my little billet; and in that dark corner read it, with a strong rainbow of colours coming from the angled light. And in mine eyes there was enough to make rainbow of strongest sun, as my anger clouded off.

Not that it began so well; but that in my heart I knew (ere three lines were through me) that I was with all heart loved – and beyond that, who may need? The darling of my life went on, as if I were of her own rank, or even better than she was; and she dotted her 'i's' and crossed her 't's,' as if I were at least a schoolmaster. All of it was done in pencil; but as plain as plain could be. In my coffin it shall lie, with my ring, and something else. Therefore will I not expose it to every man who buys this book, and haply thinks that he has bought me to the bottom of my heart. Enough for men of gentle birth (who never are inquisitive) that my love told me, in her letter, just to come and see her.

I ran away, and could not stop. To behold even her, at the moment, would have dashed my fancy's joy. Yet my brain was so amiss, that I must do something. Therefore to the river Thames, with all speed, I hurried; and keeping all my best clothes on (indued for sake of Lorna,) into the quiet stream I leaped, and swam as far as London Bridge, and ate noble dinner afterwards.

37

Lorna Still is Lorna

I felt myself to be getting on better than at any time since the last wheat-harvest, as I took the lane to Kensington upon the Monday evening. For although no time was given in my Lorna's letter, I was not inclined to wait any more than decency required. And though I went and watched the house, decency would not allow me to knock on the Sunday evening, especially when I found at the corner that his lordship was at home.

When I came to Earl Brandir's house, my natural modesty forbade me to appear at the door for guests; therefore I went to the entrance for servants and retainers. Here, to my great surprise, who should come and let me in but little Gwenny Carfax, whose very existence had almost escaped my recollection. Her mistress, no doubt, had seen me coming, and sent her to save trouble. But when I offered to kiss Gwenny, in my joy and comfort to see a farmhouse face again, she looked ashamed, and turned away, and would hardly speak to me.

I followed her to a little room, furnished very daintily; and there she ordered me to wait, in a most ungracious manner. 'Well,' thought I, 'if the mistress and the maid are alike in temper, better it had been for me to abide at Master Ramsack's.' But almost ere my thought was done, I heard the light quick step which I knew as well as 'Watch,' my dog, knew mine; and my breast began to tremble, like the trembling of an arch ere the keystone is put in.

Almost ere I hoped – for fear and hope were so entangled,

that they hindered one another – the velvet hangings of the doorway parted, with a little doubt, and then a good face put on it. Lorna, in her perfect beauty, stood before the crimson folds, and her dress was all pure white, and her cheeks were rosy pink, and her lips were scarlet.

Like a maiden, with skill and sense checking violent impulse, she stayed there for one moment only, just to be admired: and then like a woman, she came to me, seeing how alarmed I was. The hand she offered me I took, and raised it to my lips with fear, as a thing too good for me. 'Is that all?' she whispered; and then her eyes gleamed up at me: and in another instant she was weeping on my breast.

'Darling Lorna, Lady Lorna,' I cried, in astonishment, yet unable but to keep her closer to me, and closer; 'surely, though I love you so, this is not as it should be.'

'Yes it is, John. Yes, it is. Nothing else should ever be. Oh, why have you behaved so?'

'I am behaving,' I replied, 'to the very best of my ability. There is no other man in the world could hold you so, without kissing you.'

'Then why don't you do it, John?' asked Lorna, looking up at me, with a flash of her old fun.

Now this matter, proverbially, is not so meet for discussion, as it is for repetition. Enough that we said nothing more than, 'Oh, John, how glad I am!' and, 'Lorna, Lorna, Lorna!' for about five minutes. Then my darling drew back proudly; with blushing cheeks, and tear-bright eyes, she began to cross-examine me.

'Master John Ridd, you shall tell the truth, the whole truth, and nothing but the truth. I have been in Chancery, sir; and can detect a story. Now why have you never, for more than a twelvemonth, taken the smallest notice of your old friend, Mistress Lorna Doone?' Although she spoke in this lightsome manner, as if it made no difference, I saw that her quick heart was moving, and the flash of her eyes controlled.

'Simply for this cause,' I answered, 'that my old friend, and true love, took not the smallest heed of me. Nor knew I where to find her.'

'What!' cried Lorna; and nothing more; being overcome with wondering; and much inclined to fall away, but for my assistance. I told her, over and over again, that not a single syllable of any message from her, or tidings of her welfare, had reached me, or any one of us, since the letter she left behind; except by soldiers' gossip.

'Oh, you poor dear John!' said Lorna, sighing at thought of my misery. 'And now for the head-traitor. I have often suspected it: but she looks me in the face, and wishes – fearful things, which I cannot repeat.'

With these words, she moved an implement such as I had not seen before, and which made a ringing noise at a serious distance. And before I had ceased wondering – for if such things go on, we might ring the church bells, while sitting in our back kitchen – little Gwenny Carfax came, with a grave and sullen face.

'Gwenny,' began my Lorna, in a tone of high rank and dignity, 'go and fetch the letters, which I gave you at various times for despatch to Mistress Ridd.'

'How can I fetch them, when they are gone? It be no use for him to tell no lies – '

'Now, Gwenny, can you look at me?' I asked very sternly; for the matter was no joke to me, after a year's unhappiness.

'I don't want to look at 'ee. What should I look at a young man for, although he did offer to kiss me?'

I saw the spite and impudence of this last remark; and so did Lorna, although she could not quite refrain from smiling.

'Now, Gwenny, not to speak of that,' said Lorna very demurely, 'if you thought it honest to keep the letters, was it honest to keep the money?'

At this the Cornish maiden broke into a rage of honesty: 'A' putt the money by for 'ee. 'Ee shall have every farden of it.' And so she flung out of the room.

'And, Gwenny,' said Lorna very softly, following under the door-hangings; 'if it is not honest to keep the money, it is not honest to keep the letters, which would have been worth more than any gold, to those who were so kind to you. Your father shall know the whole, Gwenny, unless you tell the truth.'

'Now, a' will tell all the truth,' this strange maiden

answered, talking to herself at least as much as to her mistress, while she went out of sight and hearing. And then I was so glad at having my own Lorna once again, cleared of all contempt for us, and true to me through all of it, that I would have forgiven Gwenny for treason, or even forgery.

'I trusted her so much,' said Lorna, in her old ill-fortuned way; 'and look how she has deceived me! That is why I love you, John (setting other things aside), because you never told me a falsehood; and you never could, you know.'

'Well, I am not so sure of that. I think I could tell any lie, to have you, darling, all my own.'

'Yes. And perhaps it might be right. To other people besides us two. But you could not do it to. me, John. You never could do it to me, you know.'

Before I quite perceived my way to the bottom of this distinction – although beyond doubt a valid one – Gwenny came back with a leathern bag, and tossed it upon the table. Not a word did she vouchsafe to us; but stood there, looking injured.

'Go, and get your letters, John,' said Lorna very gravely; 'or at least your mother's letters, made of messages to you. As for Gwenny, she shall go before Lord Justice Jeffreys.' I knew that Lorna meant it not; but thought that the girl deserved a frightening; as indeed she did. But we both mistook the courage of this child of Cornwall. She stepped upon a little round thing, in the nature of a stool, such as I never had seen before, and thus delivered her sentiments.

'And you may take me, if you please, before the great Lord Jeffreys. I have done no more than duty, though I did it crookedly, and told a heap of lies, for your sake. And pretty gratitude I gets.'

'Much gratitude you have shown,' replied Lorna, 'to Master Ridd, for all his kindness, and his goodness to you. Who was it that went down, at the peril of his life, and brought your father to you, when you had lost him for months and months? Who was it? Answer me, Gwenny?'

'Girt Jan Ridd,' said the handmaid, very sulkily.

'What made you treat me so, little Gwenny?' I asked, for Lorna would not ask, lest the reply should vex me.

'Because 'ee be'est below her so. Her shanna' have a poor farmering chap, not even if her were a Carnishman. All her land, and all her birth – and who be you, I'd like to know?'

'Gwenny, you may go,' said Lorna, reddening with quiet anger; 'and remember that you come not near me for the next three days. It is the only way to punish her,' she continued to me, when the maid was gone, in a storm of sobbing and weeping. 'Now, for the next three days, she will scarcely touch a morsel of food;, and scarcely do a thing but cry. Make up your mind to one thing, John; if you mean to take me, for better for worse, you will have to take Gwenny with me.'

'I would take you with fifty Gwennies,' said I, 'although every one of them hated me; which I do not believe this little maid does, in the bottom of her heart.'

'No one can possibly hate you, John,' she answered very softly; and I was better pleased with this, than if she had called me the most noble and glorious man in the kingdom.

After this, we spoke of ourselves, and the way people would regard us, supposing that when Lorna came to be her own free mistress (as she must do in the course of time) she were to throw her rank aside, and refuse her title, and caring not a fig for folk who cared less than a fig-stalk for her, should shape her mind to its native bent, and to my perfect happiness. It was not my place to say much, lest I should appear to use an improper and selfish influence. And of course to all men of common sense, and to everybody of middle age (who must know best what is good for youth), the thoughts which my Lorna entertained would be enough to prove her madness.

Not that we could not keep her well, comfortably, and with nice clothes, and plenty of flowers, and fruit, and landscape, and the knowledge of our neighbours' affairs, and their kind interest in our own. Still this would not be as if she were the owner of a county, and a haughty title; and able to lead the first men of the age, by her mind, and face, and money.

Therefore was I quite resolved not to have a word to say, while this young queen of wealth and beauty, and of nobleman's desire, made her mind up how to act for her purest happiness. But to do her justice, this was not the first thing she was thinking of: the test of her judgement was only this, 'How will my love be happiest?'

'Now, John,' she cried; for she was so quick that she always had my thoughts beforehand; 'why will you be backward, as if you cared not for me? Do you dream, that I am doubting? My mind has been made up, good John, that you must be my husband, for – well, I will not say how long, lest you should laugh at my folly. But I believe it was ever since you came, with your stockings off, and the loaches. Right early for me to make up my mind; but you know that you made up yours, John; and, of course, I knew it; and that had a great effect on me. Now, after all this age of loving, shall a trifle sever us?'

I told her that it was no trifle, but a most important thing, to abandon wealth and honour, and the brilliance of high life, and be despised by everyone for such abundant folly. Moreover that I should appear a knave for taking advantage of her youth, and boundless generosity, and ruining (as men would say) a noble maid by my selfishness. And I told her outright, having worked myself up by my own conversation, that she was bound to consult her guardian, and that without his knowledge, I would come no more to see her. Her flash of pride at these last words made her look like an empress; and I was about to explain myself better, but she put forth her hand, and stopped me.

'I think that condition should rather have proceeded from me. You are mistaken, Master Ridd, in supposing that I would think of receiving you, in secret. It was a different thing in Glen Doone, where all except yourself were thieves, and when I was but a simple child, and oppressed with constant fear. You are quite right in threatening to visit me thus no more; but I think you might have waited for an invitation, sir.'

'And you are quite right, Lady Lorna, in pointing out my presumption. It is a fault that must ever be found in any speech of mine to you.'

This I said so humbly, and not with any bitterness – for I

knew that I had gone too far – and made her so polite a bow, that she forgave me in a moment, and we begged each other's pardon.

'Now will you allow me just to explain my own view of this matter, John?' said she, once more my darling. 'It may be a very foolish view, but I shall never change it. Please not to interrupt me, dear, until you have heard me to the end. In the first place, it is quite certain, that neither you nor I can be happy without the other. Then what stands between us? Worldly position, and nothing else. I have no more education than you have, John Ridd; nay, and not so much. My birth and ancestry are not one whit more pure than yours, although they may be better known. As for difference of religion, we allow for one another, neither having been brought up in a bitterly pious manner. Oh, John, you must never forsake me, however cross I am to you. I thought you would have gone, just now, and though I would not move to stop you, my heart would have broken.'

She glanced at a jewelled timepiece, scarcely larger than an oyster, which she drew from near her waist-band; and then she pushed it away, in confusion, lest its wealth should startle me. 'My uncle will come home in less than half-an-hour, dear: and you are not the one to take a side-passage, and avoid him. I shall tell him that you have been here; and that I mean you to come again.'

As Lorna said this, with a manner as confident as need be, I saw that she had learned in town the power of her beauty, and knew that she could do with most men aught she set her mind upon. And as she stood there, flushed with pride and faith in her own loveliness, and radiant with the love itself, I felt that she must do exactly as she pleased with everyone. For now, in turn, and elegance, and richness, and variety, there was nothing to compare with her face, unless it were her figure. Therefore I gave in and said, –

'Darling, do just what you please. Only make no rogue of me.'

For that she gave me the simplest, kindest, and sweetest of all kisses; and I went down the great stairs grandly, thinking of nothing else but that.

38

John is John No Longer

Although there were no soldiers now quartered at Plover's Barrows, all being busied in harassing the country, and hanging the people, where the rebellion had thrived most, my mother, having received from me a message containing my place of abode, contrived to send me, by the pack-horses, as fine a maund as need be of provisions, and money, and other comfort. Therein I found addressed to Colonel Jeremiah Stickles, in Lizzie's best handwriting, half a side of the dried deer's flesh, in which he rejoiced so greatly. Also, for Lorna, a fine green goose, with a little salt towards the tail, and new laid eggs inside it, as well as a bottle of brandied cherries, and seven, or it may have been eight pounds of fresh home-made butter.

Lorna was greatly pleased with the goose, and the butter, and the brandied cherries; and the Earl Brandir himself declared that he never tasted better than those last, and would beg the young man from the country to procure him instructions for making them. This nobleman, being as deaf as a post, and of a very solid mind, could never be brought to understand the nature of my thoughts towards Lorna. He looked upon me as an excellent youth, who had rescued the maiden from the Doones, whom he cordially detested; and learning that I had thrown two of there out of window (as the story was told him), he patted me on the back, and declared that his doors would ever be open to me, and that I could not come too often.

I thought this very kind of his lordship, especially as it

enabled me to see my darling Lorna, not indeed as often as I wished, but at any rate very frequently, and as many times as modesty (ever my leading principle) would in common conscience approve of. And I made up my mind, that if ever I could help Earl Brandir, it would be – as we say, when with brandy and water – the 'proudest moment of my life,' when I could fulfil the pledge.

And I soon was able to help Lord Brandir, as I think, in two different ways; first of all, as regarded his mind, and then as concerned his body: and the latter perhaps was the greatest service, at his time of life. But not to be too nice about that, let me tell how these things were.

Lorna said to me one day, being in a state of excitement – whereto she was over prone, when reft of my slowness to steady her, –

'I will tell him, John; I must tell him, John. It is mean of me to conceal it.'

I thought that she meant all about our love, which we had endeavoured thrice to drill into his fine old ears; but could not make him comprehend, without the risk of bringing the house down: and so I said, 'By all means, darling: have another try at it.'

Lorna, however, looked at me – for her eyes told more than tongue – as much as to say, 'Well, you are a stupid! We agreed to let that subject rest.' And then she saw that I was vexed at my own want of quickness; and so she spoke very kindly, –

'I meant about his poor son, dearest; the son of his old age almost; whose loss threw him into that dreadful cold – for he went, without hat, to look for him – which ended in his losing the use of his dear old ears. I believe if we could only get him to Plover's Barrows for a month, he would be able to hear again. And look at his age! he is not much over seventy, John, you know; and I hope that you will be able to hear me long after you are seventy, John.'

'Well,' said I, 'God settles that. Or at any rate, He leaves us time to think about those questions, when we are over fifty. Now let me know what you want, Lorna. The idea of my being seventy! But you would still be beautiful.'

'To the one who loves me,' she answered, trying to make wrinkles in her pure bright forehead: 'but if you will have common sense, as you always will, John, whether I wish it or otherwise, I want to know whether I am bound, in honour, and in conscience, to tell my dear and good old uncle what I know about his son.'

'First let me understand quite clearly,' said I, never being in a hurry, except when passion moves me, 'what his lordship thinks at present; and how far his mind is urged with sorrow and anxiety.' This was not the first time we had spoken of the matter.

'Why, you know, John, well enough,' she answered, wondering at my coolness, 'that my poor uncle still believes that his one beloved son will come to light and life again. He has made all arrangements accordingly: all his property is settled on that supposition. He knows that young Alan always was what he calls a "feckless ne'er-do-weel"; but he loves him all the more for that. He cannot believe that he will die, without his son coming back to him; and he always has a bedroom ready, and a bottle of Alan's favourite wine cool from out the cellar; he has made me work him a pair of slippers, from the size of a mouldy boot; and if he hears of a new tobacco – much as he hates the smell of it – he will go to the other end of London, to get some for Alan. Now you know how deaf he is; but if any one say "Alan," even in the place outside the door, he will make his courteous bow to the very highest visitor, and be out here in a moment, and search the entire passage, and yet let no one know it.'

'It is a piteous thing,' I said; for Lorna's eyes were full of tears.

'And he means me to marry him. It is the pet scheme of his life. I am to grow more beautiful, and more highly taught, and graceful; until it pleases Alan to come back, and demand me. Can you understand this matter, John? Or do you think my uncle mad?'

'Lorna, I should be mad myself, to call any man mad, for hoping.'

'Then will you tell me what to do? It makes me very sorrowful. For I know that Alan came to Doone-valley once

275

and was killed before my eyes by Carver Doone, and now lies below the sod in Doone-valley.'

'And if you tell his father,' I answered softly, but clearly, 'in a few weeks he will lie below the sod in London; at least if there is any.'

'Perhaps you are right, John,' she replied: 'to lose hope must be a dreadful thing, when one is turned of seventy. Therefore I will never tell him.'

The other way in which I managed to help the good Earl Brandir was of less true moment to him; but as he could not know of the first, this was the one which moved him.

The good Earl Brandir was a man of the noblest charity. True charity begins at home, and so did his; and was afraid of losing the way, if it went abroad. So this good nobleman kept his money in a handsome pewter box, with his coat of arms upon it, and a double lid, and locks. Moreover, there was a heavy chain, fixed to a staple in the wall, so that none might carry off the pewter with the gold inside of it. Lorna told me the box was full, for she had seen him go to it, and she often thought that it would be nice for us to begin the world with.

Now one evening towards September, when the days were drawing in, looking back at the house, to see whether Lorna were looking after me, I espied (by a little glimpse, as it were) a pair of villainous fellows (about whom there could be no mistake) watching the thicket-corner, some hundred yards or so behind the good Earl's dwelling. I resolved to wait, and see what those two villains did, and save (if it were possible) the Earl of Brandir's pewter box. But, inasmuch as those bad men were almost sure to have seen me leaving the house, and looking back, and striking out on the London road, I marched along at a merry pace, until they could not discern me; and then I fetched a compass round, and refreshed myself at a certain inn, entitled 'The Cross-bones, and Buttons.'

Here I remained until it was very nearly as dark as pitch; and the house being full of foot-pads and cut-throats, I thought it right to leave them. I took up my position, two hours before midnight, among the shrubs at the eastern end of Lord Brandir's mansion. Hence, although I might not see, I could scarcely fail to hear, if any unlawful entrance, either at back or front, were made.

From my own observation, I thought it likely that the attack would be in the rear; and so indeed it came to pass. For when all the lights were quenched, and all the house was quiet, I heard a low and wily whistle from a clump of trees close by; and then three figures passed between me and a white-washed wall, and came to a window which opened into a part of the servants' basement. The window was carefully raised by someone inside the house: and after a little whispering, and something which sounded like a kiss, all the three men entered.

'Oh, you villains!' I said to myself; 'this is worse than any Doone job; because there is treachery in it.' But without waiting to consider the subject from a moral point of view, I crept along the wall, and entered very quietly after them; being rather uneasy about my life, because I bore no fire-arms, and had nothing more than my holly staff, for even a violent combat.

I went along very delicately (as a man who has learned to wrestle can do, although he may weigh twenty stone), following carefully the light, brought by the traitorous maid, and shaking in her loose dishonest hand. I saw her lead the men into a little place called a pantry; and there she gave them cordials, and I could hear them boasting.

Not to be too long over it – which they were much inclined to be I followed them from this drinking-bout, by the aid of the light they bore, as far as Earl Brandir's bedroom, which I knew, because Lorna had shown it to me, that I might admire the tapestry. But I had said that no horse could ever be shod as the horses were shod therein, unless he had the foot of a frog, as well as a frog to his foot. And Lorna had been vexed at this (as taste and high art always are, at any small accurate knowledge), and so had brought me out again, before I had time to admire things.

Now, keeping well away in the dark, yet nearer than was necessary to my own dear Lorna's room, I saw these fellows try the door of the good Earl Brandir, knowing from the maid, of course, that his lordship could hear nothing, except the name of Alan. They tried the lock, and pushed at it, and even set their knees upright; but a Scottish nobleman may be trusted to secure his door at night. So they were forced to break it open; and at this the guilty maid, or woman, ran away. These three rogues – for rogues they were, and no charity may deny it – burst into Earl Brandir's room, with a light, and a crow-bar, and fire-arms. I thought to myself that this was hard upon an honest nobleman; and if further mischief could be saved, I would try to save it.

When I came to the door of the room, being myself in shadow, I beheld two bad men trying vainly to break open the pewter box, and the third with a pistol muzzle laid to the night-cap of his lordship. With foul face, and yet fouler words, this man was demanding the key of the box, which the other men could by no means open, neither drag it from the chain. 'I tell you,' said this aged Earl, beginning to understand at last what these rogues were up for; 'I will give no key to you. It all belongs to my boy, Alan. No one else shall have a farthing.'

'Then you may count your moments, lord. The key is in your old cramped hand. One, two; and at three, I shoot you.'

I saw that the old man was abroad; not with fear, but with great wonder, and the regret of deafness. And I saw that rather would he be shot, than let these men go rob his son, buried now, but still alive to his father. Hereupon my heart was moved; and I resolved to interfere. The thief with the pistol began to count, as I crossed the floor very quietly, while the old Earl fearfully gazed at the muzzle, but clenched still tighter his wrinkled hand. The villain, with hair all over his eyes, and the great horse-pistol levelled, cried, 'three,' and pulled the trigger; but luckily, at that very moment, I struck up the barrel with my staff, so that the shot pierced the tester, and then with a spin and a thwack, I brought the good holly down upon the rascal's head, in a manner which stretched him upon the floor.

Meanwhile the other two robbers had taken the alarm, and rushed at me, one with a pistol, and one with a hanger, which forced me to be very lively. Fearing the pistol most, I flung the heavy curtain of the bed across, that he might not see where to aim at me, and then stooping very quickly, I caught up the senseless robber, and set him up for a shield and target; whereupon he was shot immediately, without having the pain of knowing it; and a happy thing it was for him. Now the other two were at my mercy, being men below the average strength; and no hanger, except in most skilful hands, as well as firm and strong ones, has any chance to a powerful man armed with a stout cudgel, and thoroughly practised in single-stick.

So I took these two rogues, and bound them together; and leaving them under charge of the butler (a worthy and shrewd Scotsman), I myself went in search of the constables, whom, after some few hours, I found; neither were they so drunk but what they could take roped men to prison. In the morning, these two men were brought before the Justices of the Peace: and now my wonderful luck appeared; for the merit of having defeated, and caught them, would never have raised me one step in the State, or in public consideration, if they had only been common robbers, or even notorious murderers. But when these fellows were recognised, by some-one in the court, as Protestant witnesses out of employment, companions and under-strappers to Oates, and Bedloe, and Carstairs, and hand-in-glove with Dangerfield, Turberville, and Dugdale – in a word, the very men against whom His Majesty the King bore the bitterest rancour, but whom he had hitherto failed to catch – when this was laid before the public (with emphasis, and admiration), at least a dozen men came up, whom I had never seen before, and prayed me to accept their congratulations, and to be sure to remember them; for all were of neglected merit, and required no more than a piece of luck.

In the course of that same afternoon, I was sent for by His Majesty.

Then forth I set, with my holly staff, wishing myself well out of it. I was shown at once, and before I desired it, into His Majesty's presence, and there I stood most humbly, and made the best bow I could think of.

As I could not advance any further – for I saw that the

Queen was present, which frightened me tenfold – His Majesty, in the most gracious manner, came down the room to encourage me. And as I remained with my head bent down, he told me to stand up, and look at him.

'I have seen thee before, young man,' he said; 'thy form is not one to be forgotten. Where was it? Thou art most likely to know.'

'May it please Your Most Gracious Majesty the King,' I answered, finding my voice in a manner which surprised myself; 'it was in the Royal Chapel.'

Now I meant no harm whatever by this. I ought to have said the 'Ante-Chapel,' but I could not remember the word, and feared to keep the King looking at me.

'I am well-pleased,' said His Majesty, with a smile which almost made his dark and stubborn face look pleasant, 'to find that our greatest subject, greatest I mean in the bodily form, is a good Catholic. Thou needest say not otherwise. The time shall be, and that right soon, when men shall be proud of the one true faith.' Here he stopped, having gone rather far; but the gleam of his heavy eyes was such, that I durst not contradict.

'This is that great Johann Reed,' said Her Majesty, coming forward because the King was in meditation; 'for whom I have so much heard, from the dear, dear Lorna. Ah, she is not of this black countree, she of the breet Italie.'

I have tried to write it, as she said it: but it wants a better scholar to express her mode of speech.

'Now, John Ridd,' said the King, recovering from his thoughts about the true Church, and thinking that his wife was not to take the lead upon me; 'thou hast done great service to the realm, and to religion. It was good to save Earl Brandir, a loyal and Catholic nobleman; but it was great service to catch two of the vilest blood-hounds ever laid on by heretics. And to make them shoot another: it was rare; it was rare, my lad. Now ask us anything in reason; thou canst carry any honours, on thy club, like Hercules. What is thy chief ambition, lad?'

'Well,' said I, after thinking a little, and meaning to make the most of it, for so the Queen's eyes conveyed to me; 'my mother always used to think that having been schooled at Tiverton, with thirty marks a year to pay, I was worthy of a coat of arms. And that is what she longs for.'

'A good lad! A very good lad;' said the King, and he looked at the Queen, as if almost in joke; 'but what is thy condition in life?'

'I am a freeholder,' I answered in my confusion, 'ever since the time of King Alfred. A Ridd was with him in the isle of Athelney, and we hold our farm by gift from him; or at least people say so. We have had three very good harvests running, and might support a coat of arms; but for myself I want it not.'

'Thou shalt have a coat, my lad,' said the King, smiling at his own humour; 'but it must be a large one to fit thee. And more than that shalt thou have, John Ridd, being of such loyal breed, and having done such service.'

And while I wondered what he meant, he called to some of the people in waiting at the farther end of the room, and they brought him a little sword, such as Annie would skewer a turkey with. Then he signified to me to kneel, which I did (after dusting the board, for the sake of my best breeches), and then he gave me a little tap very nicely upon my shoulder, before I knew what he was up to; and said, 'Arise, Sir John Ridd!'

This astonished and amazed me to such extent of loss of mind, that when I got up I looked about, and thought what the Snowes would think of it. And I said to the King, without forms of speech, –

'Sir, I am very much obliged. But what be I to do with it?'

39

A Long Account Settled

The coat of arms, devised for me by the Royal heralds was of great size, and rich colours, and full of bright imaginings. Lorna took the greatest pride in it, and thought (or at any rate said), that it quite threw into the shade, and eclipsed, all her own ancient glories. And half in fun, and half in earnest, she called me 'Sir John' so continually, that at last I was almost angry with her; until her eyes were bedewed with tears; and then I was angry with myself.

Beginning to be short of money, and growing anxious about the farm, longing also to show myself and my noble escutcheon to mother, I took advantage of Lady Lorna's interest with the Queen, to obtain my acquittance and full discharge from even nominal custody. It had been intended to keep me in waiting, until the return of Lord Jeffreys from that awful circuit of shambles, through which his name is still used by mothers to frighten their children into bed. And right glad was I – for even London shrank with horror at the news – to escape a man so blood-thirsty, savage, and even to his friends (among whom I was reckoned) malignant.

Lorna was moved with equal longing towards the country, and country ways; and she spoke quite as much of the glistening dew, as she did of the smell of our oven.

I resolved to go; and as Lorna could not come with me, it was even worse than stopping. Lorna cried, when I came away (which gave me great satisfaction), and she sent a whole trunkful of things for mother, and Annie, and even

Lizzie. And she seemed to think, though she said it not, that I made my own occasion for going, and might have stayed on till the winter. Whereas I knew well that my mother would think (and every one on the farm the same) that here I had been in London, lagging, and taking my pleasure, and looking at shops, upon pretence of King's business, and leaving the harvest to reap itself, not to mention the spending of money; while all the time there was nothing whatever, except my own love of adventure and sport, to keep me from coming home again. But I knew that my coat of arms, and title, would turn every bit of this grumbling into fine admiration.

And so it fell out, to a greater extent than even I desired: for all the parishes round about united in a sumptuous dinner, at the Mother Melldrum inn to which I was invited, so that it was as good as a summons. And if my health was no better next day, it was not from want of good wishes, any more than from stint of the liquor.

Now as the winter passed, the Doones were not keeping themselves at home, as in honour they were bound to do. Twenty sheep a week, and one fat ox, and two stout red deer (for wholesome change of diet), as well as threescore bushels of flour, and two hogsheads and a half of cider, and a hundredweight of candles, not to mention other things of almost every variety, which they got by insisting upon it – surely these might have sufficed to keep the robbers happy in their place, with no outburst of wantonness. Nevertheless, it was not so: they had made complaint about something – too much ewe-mutton, I think it was – and in spite of all the pledges given, they had ridden forth, and carried away two maidens of our neighbourhood.

Before we had finished meditating upon this loose outrage – for so I at least would call it, though people accustomed to the law may take a different view of it – we had news of a thing far worse, which turned the hearts of our women sick. This I will tell in most careful language, so as to give offence to none, if skill of words may help it.

Mistress Margery Badcock, a healthy and upright young woman, with a good rich colour, and one of the finest hen-roosts any where round our neighbourhood, was nursing her child about six of the clock, and looking out for her husband.

But she was surprised, nay astonished, when by the light of the kitchen fire (brightened up for her husband) she saw six or seven great armed men burst into the room upon her; and she screamed so that the maid in the back kitchen heard her, but was afraid to come to help. Two of the strongest and fiercest men at once seized poor young Margery; and though she fought for her child and home, she was but an infant herself in their hands. In spite of tears and shrieks and struggles, they tore the babe from the mother's arms, and cast it on the lime-ash floor; then they bore her away to their horses (for by this time she was senseless), and telling the others to sack the house, rode off with their prize to the valley. And from the description of one of those two, who carried off the poor woman, I knew beyond all doubt that it was Carver Doone himself.

The other Doones being left behind, and grieved perhaps in some respects, set to with a will to scour the house, and to bring away all that was good to eat.

'Rowland, is the bacon good?' one of them asked, with an oath or two: 'it is too bad of Carver to go off with the only prize, and leave us in a starving cottage; and not enough to eat for two of us. Fetch down the staves of the rack, my boy. What was farmer to have for supper?'

'Nought but an onion or two, and a loaf, and a rasher of rusty bacon. These poor devils live so badly, they are not worth robbing.'

'No game! Then let us have a game of loriot with the baby! It will be the best thing that could befall a lusty infant heretic. Ride a cock-horse to Banbury Cross. Bye, bye, baby Bunting; toss him up, and let me see if my wrist be steady.'

The cruelty of this man is a thing it makes me sick to speak of; enough that when the poor baby fell (without attempt at cry or scream, thinking it part of his usual play, when they tossed him up, to come down again), the maid in the oven of the back-kitchen, not being any door between, heard them say as follows: –

'If any man asketh who killed thee,
Say 'twas the Doones of Bagworthy.'

Now I think that when we heard this story, and poor Kit Badcock came all around, in a sort of half-crazy manner, not looking up at any one, but dropping his eyes, and asking whether we thought he had been well-treated, and seeming void of regard for life, if this were all the style of it; then, having known him a lusty man, and a fine singer in an ale-house, and much inclined to lay down the law, and show a high hand about women, I really think that it moved us more than if he had gone about ranting, and raving, and vowing revenge upon everyone.

The people came flocking all around me, at the black-smith's forge, and the Brendon ale-house; and I could scarce come out of church, but they got me among the tombstones. They all agreed that I was bound to take command and management. I bade them go to the magistrates, but they said they had been too often. Then I told them that I had no wits for ordering of an armament, although I could find fault enough with the one which had not succeeded. But they would hearken to none of this. All they said was, 'Try to lead us; and we will try not to run away.'

This seemed to me to be common sense, and good stuff, instead of mere bragging: moreover, I myself was moved by the bitter wrongs of Margery, having known her at the Sunday-school, ere ever I went to Tiverton; and having, in those days, serious thoughts of making her my sweetheart; although she was three years my elder.

Without any further hesitation, I agreed to take command of the honest men, who were burning to punish, ay and destroy, those outlaws, as now beyond all bearing. One condition however I made, namely, that the Counsellor should be spared, if possible: not because he was less a villain than any of the others, but that he seemed less violent: and above all, had been good to Annie. And I found hard work to make them listen to my wish upon this point; for of all the Doones, Sir Counsellor had made himself most hated, by love of law and reason.

We arranged that all our men should come, and fall into order with pike and musket, over against our dunghill; and we settled, early in the day. It was known that the Doones were fond of money, as well as strong drink, and other things; and more especially fond of gold, when they could get it pure and fine. Therefore it was agreed, that in this way we should tempt them; for we knew that they looked with ridicule upon our rustic preparations: after repulsing King's troopers, – the militia of two counties, was it likely that they should yield their fortress to a set of plough-boys? We, for our part, felt, of course, the power of this reasoning, and that where regular troops had failed, half-armed countrymen must fail, except by superior judgement and harmony of action. Though perhaps the militia would have sufficed, if they had only fought against the foe, instead of against each other. From these things we took warning: having failed through over-confidence, was it not possible now to make the enemy fail, through the self-same cause?

Hence, what we devised was this; to delude from home a part of the robbers, and fall by surprise on the other part. We caused it to be spread abroad that a large heap of gold was now collected at the mine of the Wizard's Slough. And when this rumour must have reached them, through women who came to and fro, as some entirely faithful to them were allowed to do, we sent Captain Simon Carfax, the father of little Gwenny, to demand an interview with the Counsellor by night, and as it were secretly. Then he was to set forth a list of imaginary grievances against the owners of the mine; and to offer, partly through resentment, partly through the hope of gain, to betray into their hands, upon the Friday night, by far the greatest weight of gold as yet sent up for refining. He was to have one quarter part, and they, to take the residue. But inasmuch as the convoy across the moors, under his command, would be strong, and strongly armed, the Doones must be sure to send not less than a score of men if possible. He himself at a place agreed upon, and fit for an ambuscade, would call a halt, and contrive in the darkness to pour a little water into the priming of his company's guns.

Having resolved on a night-assault we fixed upon Friday night for our venture, because the moon would be at the full; and our powder was coming from Dulverton, on the Friday afternoon.

It was settled that the yeomen, having good horses under them, should give account with the miners' help of as many Doones as might be despatched to plunder the pretended gold. And as soon as we knew that this party of robbers, be it more or less, was out of hearing from the valley, we were to fall to, ostensibly at the Doone-gate (which was impregnable now), but in reality upon their rear, by means of my old water-slide.

The moon was lifting well above the shoulder of the uplands, when we, the chosen band, set forth, having the short cut along the valleys to foot of the Bagworthy water; and therefore, having allowed the rest an hour to fetch round the moors and hills, we were not to begin our climbing until we heard a musket fired from the heights, on the left hand side, where John Fry himself was stationed, upon his own and his wife's request, to keep him out of combat. And that was the place where I had been used to sit, and to watch for Lorna. And John Fry was to fire his gun, with a ball of wool inside it, so soon as he heard the hurly-burly at the Doone-gate beginning; which we, by reason of waterfall, could not hear, down in the meadows there.

We waited a very long time, with the moon marching up heaven steadfastly, and the white fog trembling in chords and quavers, like a silver harp of the meadows. And then the moon drew up the fogs, and scarfed herself in white with them; and so being proud, gleamed upon the water, like a bride at her looking-glass; and yet there was no sound of either John Fry, or his blunderbuss.

I began to think that the worthy John, being out of all danger, and having brought a counterpane (according to his wife's directions, because one of the children had a cold), must veritably have gone to sleep; leaving other people to kill, or be killed, as might be the will of God; so that he were comfortable. But herein I did wrong to John, and am ready to acknowledge it: for suddenly the most awful noise that anything short of thunder could make, came down among the rocks, and went and hung upon the corners.

'The signal, my lads!' I cried, leaping up, and rubbing my eyes; for even now, while condemning John unjustly, I was giving him right to be hard upon me. 'Now hold on by the rope, and lay your quarter-staffs across, my lads; and keep your guns pointing to heaven, lest haply we shoot one another.'

The earliest notice the Counsellor had, or any one else, of our presence, was the blazing of the log-wood house, where lived that villain Carver. It was my especial privilege to set this house on fire; upon which I had insisted, exclusively, and conclusively. No other hand but mine should lay a brand, or strike steel on flint for it; I had made all preparations carefully for a good blaze. And I must confess that I rubbed my hands, with a strong delight and comfort, when I saw the home of that man, who had fired so many houses, having its turn of smoke, and blaze, and of crackling fury.

We took good care, however, to burn no innocent women, or children, in that most righteous destruction. For we brought them all out beforehand; some were glad, and some were sorry; according to their dispositions. For Carver had ten or a dozen wives; and perhaps that had something to do with his taking the loss of Lorna so easily. One child I noticed, as I saved him; a fair and handsome little fellow, beloved by Carver Doone, as much as anything beyond himself could be. The boy climbed on my back, and rode; and much as I hated his father, it was not in my heart to say, or do, a thing to vex him.

Leaving these poor injured people to behold their burning home, we drew aside, by my directions, into the covert beneath the cliff. But not before we had laid our brands to three other houses, after calling the women forth, and bidding them go for their husbands, to come and fight a hundred of us. In the smoke, and rush, and fire, they believed that we were a hundred; and away they ran, in consternation, to the battle at the Doone-gate.

'All Doone-town is on fire, on fire!' we heard them

shrieking as they went: 'a hundred soldiers are burning it, with a dreadful great man at the head of them!'

Presently, just as I expected, back came the warriors of the Doones; leaving but two or three at the gate, and burning with wrath to crush under foot the presumptuous clowns in their valley. Just then, the waxing fire leaped above the red crest of the cliffs, and danced on the pillars of the forest, and lapped like a tide on the stones of the slope. All the valley flowed with light, and the limpid waters reddened, and the fair young women shone, and the naked children glistened.

But the finest sight of all was to see those haughty men striding down the causeway darkly, reckless of their end, but resolute to have two lives for every one. A finer dozen of young men could not have been found in the world perhaps, nor a braver, nor a viler one.

Seeing how few there were of them, I was very loth to fire, but my followers waited for no word: they saw a fair shot at the men they abhorred, the men who had robbed them of home, or of love; and the chance was too much for their charity. At a signal from old Ikey, who levelled his own gun first, a dozen muskets were discharged, and half of the Doones dropped lifeless, like so many logs of firewood, or chopping-blocks rolled over.

All the rest of the Doones leaped at us, like so many demons. They fired wildly, not seeing us well among the hazel bushes; and then they clubbed their muskets, or drew their swords, as might be; and furiously drove at us.

For a moment, although we were twice their number, we fell back before their valorous fame, and the power of their onset. For my part, admiring their courage greatly, and counting it slur upon manliness that two should be down upon one so, I withheld my hand awhile; for I cared to meet none but Carver; and he was not among them. The whirl and hurry of this fight, and the hard blows raining down – for now all guns were empty – took away my power of seeing, or reasoning, upon anything.

Now was the reckoning come that night; and not a line we missed of it; soon as our bad blood was up. I like not to tell of slaughter, though it might be of wolves, and tigers: and that was a night of fire, and slaughter, and of very long harboured revenge. Enough that ere the day-light broke, upon that wan March morning, the only Doones still left alive were the Counsellor, and Carver. And of all the dwellings of the Doones (inhabited with luxury, and luscious taste, and licentiousness) not even one was left, but all made potash in the river.

This may seem a violent and unholy revenge upon them. And I (who led the heart of it) have in these my latter years doubted how I shall be judged, not of men – for God only knows the errors of man's judgement – but by that great God Himself, the front of whose forehead is mercy.

40

The Counsellor and
the Carver

From that great confusion – for nothing can be broken up, whether lawful or unlawful, without a vast amount of dust, and many people grumbling, and mourning for the good old times, when all the world was happiness, and every man a gentleman, and the sun himself far brighter than since the brassy idol upon which he shone was broken – from all this loss of ancient landmarks (as unrobbed men began to call our clearance of those murderers) we returned on the following day, almost as full of anxiety, as we were of triumph. In the first place, what could we frugally do with all these women and children, thrown on our hands, as one might say, with none to protect and care for them? Again, how should we answer to the Justices of the peace, or perhaps even to Lord Jeffreys, for having, without even a warrant, taken the law into our own hands, and abated our nuisance so forcibly? And then, what was to be done with the spoil, which was of great value; though the diamond necklace came not to public light? For we saw a mighty host of claimants already leaping up for booty. Every man, who had ever been robbed, expected usury on his loss; the lords of the manors demanded the whole; and so did the King's Commissioner of Revenue at Porlock; and so did the men who had fought our battle; while even the parsons, both Bowden and Powell, and another who had no parish in it, threatened us with the just wrath of the Church, unless each had tithes of the whole of it.

Now this was not as it ought to be; and it seemed as if by

burning the nest of robbers, we had but hatched their eggs: until being made sole guardian of the captured treasure (by reason of my known honesty) I hit upon a plan, which gave very little satisfaction; yet carried this advantage, that the grumblers argued against one another, and for the most part came to blows; which renewed their good-will to me, as being abused by the adversary.

And my plan was no more than this – not to pay a farthing to lord of manor, parson, or even King's Commissioner, but after making good some of the recent and proven losses – where the men could not afford to lose – to pay the residue (which might be worth some fifty thousand pounds) into the Exchequer at Westminster, and then let all the claimants file what bills they pleased in Chancery.

Now this was a very noble device; for the mere name of Chancery, and the high repute of the fees therein, and the low repute of the lawyers, and the comfortable knowledge that the woolsack itself is the golden fleece, absorbing gold for ever, if the standard be but pure; consideration of these things staved off at once the lords of the manors, and all the little farmers, and even those whom most I feared; videlicit, the parsons. And the King's Commissioner was compelled to profess himself contented, although of all he was most aggrieved; for his pickings would have been goodly.

Moreover, by this plan I made – although I never thought of that – a mighty friend, worth all the enemies whom the loss of money moved. The first man now in the kingdom (by virtue perhaps of energy, rather than of excellence) was the great Lord Jeffreys, appointed the head of the Equity, as well as of the larger law, for his kindness in hanging five hundred people, without the mere grief of trial. Nine out of ten of these people were innocent, it was true; but that proved the merit of the Lord Chief Justice so much the greater for hanging them, as showing what might be expected of him, when he truly got hold of a guilty man. Now the King had seen the force of this argument; and not being without gratitude for a high-seasoned dish of cruelty, had promoted the only man in England, combining the gifts both of butcher and cook.

But the true result of the thing was this – Lord Jeffreys being now head of the law, and almost head of the kingdom, got possession of that money, and was kindly pleased with it.

And this met our second difficulty; for the law having won and laughed over the spoil, must have injured its own title by impugning our legality.

Next, with regard to the women and children, we were long in a state of perplexity. We did our very best at the farm, and so did many others, to provide for them, until they should manage about their own subsistence. And after a while, this trouble went, as nearly all troubles go with time. Some of the women were taken back by their parents, or their husbands, or it may be their old sweethearts; and those who failed of this went forth, some upon their own account to the New World plantations, where the fairer sex is valuable; and some to English cities; and the plainer ones to field-work. And most of the children went with their mothers, or were bound apprentices; only Carver Doone's handsome child had lost his mother, and stayed with me.

This boy went about with me everywhere. He had taken as much of liking to me – first shown in his eyes by the firelight – as his father had of hatred; and I, perceiving his noble courage, scorn of lies, and high spirit, became almost as fond of Ensie, as he was of me. He told us that his name was 'Ensie,' meant for 'Ensor,' I suppose, from his father's grandfather, the old Sir Ensor Doone. And this boy appeared to be Carver's heir, having been born in wedlock, contrary to the general manner and custom of the Doones.

However, although I loved the poor child, I could not help feeling very uneasy about the escape of his father, the savage and brutal Carver. This man was left to roam the country, homeless, foodless, and desperate, with his giant strength, and great skill in arms, and the whole world to be revenged upon. For his escape the miners, as I shall show, were answerable; but of the Counsellor's safe departure the burden lay on myself alone. And, inasmuch as there are people who consider themselves ill-used, unless one tells them every thing, straightened though I am for space, I will glance at this transaction.

After the desperate charge of young Doones had been met by us, and broken, I happened to descry a patch of white on the grass of the meadow, like the head of a sheep after washing-day. Observing, with some curiosity, how carefully this white thing moved, along the bars of darkness betwixt the panels of firelight, I ran up to intercept it, before it reached the little postern which we used to call Gwenny's door. Perceiving me, the white thing stopped, and was for making back again; but I ran up at full speed; and lo, it was the flowing silvery hair of that sage the Counsellor, who was scuttling away upon all fours; but now rose, and confronted me.

'John,' he said, 'Sir John, you will not play falsely with your ancient friend, among these violent fellows, I look to you to protect me, John.'

'Honoured sir, you are right,' I replied; 'but surely that posture was unworthy of yourself, and your many resources. It is my intention to let you go free.'

'I knew it. I could have sworn to it. You are a noble fellow, John; I said so, from the very first; you are a noble fellow, and an ornament to any rank.'

'But upon two conditions,' I added, gently taking him by the arm; for instead of displaying any desire for commune with my nobility, he was edging away towards the postern: 'the first is, that you tell me truly (for now it can matter to none of you) who it was that slew my father.'

'I will tell you, truly and frankly, John; however painful to me to confess it. It was my son, Carver.'

'I thought as much, or I felt as much, all along,' I answered; 'but the fault was none of yours, sir; for you were not even present.'

'If I had been there, it would not have happened. I am always opposed to violence. Therefore, let me haste away: this scene is against my nature.'

'You shall go directly, Sir Counsellor, after meeting my other condition; which is, that you place in my hands Lady Lorna's diamond necklace.'

'Ah, how often have I wished,' said the old man, with a heavy sigh, 'that it might yet be in my power, to ease my mind in that respect, and to do a thoroughly good deed, by lawful restitution.'

'Then try to have it in your power, sir. Surely, with my encouragement, you might summon resolution.'

'Alas, John, the resolution has been ready long ago. But the thing is not in my possession. Carver, my son, who slew your father, upon him you will find the necklace. What are jewels to me, young man, at my time of life? Baubles and trash, – I detest them, from the sins they have led me to answer for. When you come to my age, good Sir John, you will scorn all jewels, and care only for a pure and bright conscience. Ah! ah! Let me go. I have made my peace with God.'

He looked so hoary, and so silvery, and serene in the moonlight, that verily I must have believed him, if he had not drawn in his breast. But I happened to have noticed, that when an honest man gives vent to noble and great sentiments, he spreads his breast, and throws it out, as if his heart were swelling; whereas I had seen this old gentleman draw his breast in, more than once, as if it happened to contain better goods than sentiment.

'Will you applaud me, kind sir,' I said, keeping him very tight, all the while, 'if I place it in your power, to ratify your peace with God? The pledge is upon your heart, no doubt; for there it lies at this moment.'

With these words, and some apology for having recourse to strong measures, I thrust my hand inside his waistcoat, and drew forth Lorna's necklace, purely sparkling in the moonlight, like the dancing of new stars. The old man made a stab at me, with a knife which I had not espied; but the vicious onset failed; and then he knelt, and clasped his hands.

'Oh, for God's sake, John, my son, rob me not, in that manner. They belong to me; and I love them so; I would give almost my life for them. There is one jewel there I can look at for hours, and see all the lights of heaven in it; which I never shall see elsewhere. All my wretched, wicked life – oh, John, I am a sad hypocrite – but give me back my jewels. Or

295

else kill me here: I am a babe in your hands: but I must have back my jewels.'

'Sir Counsellor, I cannot give you what does not belong to me. But if you will show me that particular diamond, which is heaven to you, I will take upon myself the risk, and the folly, of cutting it out for you. And with that you must go contented: and I beseech you not to starve, with that jewel upon your lips.'

Seeing no hope of better terms, he showed me his pet love of a jewel; and I thought of what Lorna was to me, as I cut it out (with the hinge of my knife severing the snakes of gold) and placed it in his careful hand. Another moment, and he was gone, and away through Gwenny's postern; and God knows what became of him.

Now as to Carver, the thing was this – so far as I could ascertain from the valiant miners, no two of whom told the same story, any more than one of them told it twice. The band of Doones, which sallied forth for the robbery of the pretended convoy, was met by Simon Carfax, according to arrangement, at the ruined house called the 'Warren,' in that part of Bagworthy Forest where the river Exe (as yet a very small stream) runs through it.

Now Simon, having met these flowers of the flock of villainy where the rising moonlight flowed through the weir-work of the wood, begged them to dismount, and led them, with an air of mystery, into the Squire's ruined hall, black with fire, and green with weeds.

'Captain, I have found a thing,' he said to Carver Doone himself, 'which may help us to pass the hour, ere the lump of gold comes by. The smugglers are a noble race; but a miner's eyes are a match for them. There lies a puncheon of rare spirit, with the Dutchman's brand upon it, hidden behind the broken hearth. Set a man to watch outside; and let us see what this be like.'

With one accord they agreed to this, and Carver pledged Master Carfax, and all the Doones grew merry. But Simon being bound, as he said, to see to their strict sobriety, drew a bucket of water from the well, and begged them to mingle it with their drink; which some of them did, and some refused.

But the water from that well was poured, while they were carousing, into the priming-pan of every gun of theirs; even as Simon had promised to do with the guns of the men they were come to kill. Then just as the giant Carver arose, with a glass of pure hollands in his hand, and by the light of the torch they had struck, proposed the good health of the Squire's ghost – in the broken doorway stood a press of men, with pointed muskets, covering every drunken Doone. How it fared upon that I know not, having none to tell me; for each man wrought, neither thought of telling, nor whether he might be alive to tell. The Doones rushed to their guns at once, and pointed them, and pulled at them; but the Squire's well had drowned their fire: and then they knew that they were betrayed; but resolved to fight like men for it. Upon fighting I can never dwell; it breeds such savage delight in me; of which I would fain have less. Enough that all the Doones fought bravely; and like men (though bad ones) died in the hall of the man they had murdered. And with them died poor young De Whichehalse, who, in spite of all his good father's prayers, had cast in his lot with the robbers. Carver Doone alone escaped. Partly through his fearful strength, and his yet more fearful face; but mainly perhaps through his perfect coolness, and his mode of taking things.

I am happy to say, that no more than eight of the gallant miners were killed in that combat, or died of their wounds afterwards; and adding to these the eight we had lost in our assault on the valley (and two of them excellent warehouse-men), it cost no more than sixteen lives to be rid of nearly forty Doones, each of whom would most likely have killed three men, in the course of a year or two. Therefore, as I said at the time, a great work was done very reasonably; here were nigh upon forty Doones destroyed (in the valley, and up at the 'Warren'), despite their extraordinary strength, and high skill in gunnery; whereas of us ignorant rustics there were only sixteen to be counted dead – though others might be lamed, or so – and of those sixteen, only two had left wives, and their wives had no trouble to marry again.

Yet, for Lorna's sake, I was vexed at the bold escape of Carver. Not that I sought for Carver's life, any more than I did for the Counsellor's; but that for us it was no light thing, to have a man of such power, and resource, and desperation, left at large and furious, like a famished wolf round the sheep-fold. Yet greatly as I blamed the yeomen, who were posted on their horses, just out of shot from the Doone-gate, for the very purpose of intercepting those who escaped the miners, I could not get them to admit that any blame attached to them.

But lo, he had dashed through the whole of them, with his horse at full gallop; and was out of range, ere ever they began to think of shooting him. Then it appears from what a boy said – for boys manage to be everywhere – that Captain Carver rode through the Doone-gate, and so to the head of the valley. There he discovered all the houses, and his own among the number, flaming with a handsome blaze, and throwing a fine light around, such as he often had revelled in, when of other people's property. Now he swore the deadliest of all oaths, and seeing himself to be vanquished (so far as the luck of the moment went), spurred his great black horse away, and passed into the darkness.

41

Blood Upon the Altar

Things at this time so befell me, that I cannot tell one half; but am like a boy who has left his lesson (to the master's very footfall) unready, except with false excuses. And as this makes no good work, so I lament upon my lingering, in the times when I might have got through a good page, but went astray after trifles. However, every man must do according to his intellect; and looking at the easy manner of my constitution, I think that most men will regard me with pity, and good will, for trying; more than with contempt, and wrath, for having tried unworthily. Even as in the wrestling ring, whatever man did his very best, and made an honest conflict, I always laid him down with softness, easing off his dusty fall.

But the thing which next betided me was not a fall of any sort; but rather a most glorious rise to the summit of all fortune. For in good truth it was no less than the return of Lorna – my Lorna, my own darling; in wonderful health and spirits, and as glad as a bird to get back again. It would have done any one good for a twelvemonth to behold her face and doings, and her beaming eyes and smile (not to mention blushes also at my salutation), when this Queen of every heart ran about our rooms again. She did love this, and she must see that, and where was her old friend the cat? All the house was full of brightness, as if the sun had come over the hill, and Lorna were his looking-glass.

My mother sat in an ancient chair, and wiped her cheeks,

and gazed at her; and even Lizzie's eyes must dance to the freshness and joy of her beauty. As for me, you might call me mad; for I ran out, and flung my best hat on the barn, and kissed mother Fry, till she made at me with the cracker of the churn. In the morning, Lorna was ready to tell her story, and we to hearken. Earl Brandir's ancient steward, in whose charge she had travelled, with a proper escort, looked upon her as a lovely maniac; and the mixture of pity, and admiration, wherewith he regarded her was a strange thing to observe; especially after he had seen our simple house and manners. On the other hand, Lorna considered him a worthy but foolish old gentleman; to whom true happiness meant no more than money and high position.

These two last she had been ready to abandon wholly, and had in part escaped from them, as the enemies of her happiness. And she took advantage of the times in a truly clever manner. For that happened to be a time – as indeed all times hitherto (so far as my knowledge extends), have, somehow or other, happened to be – when everybody was only too glad to take money for doing anything. And the greatest money-taker in the kingdom (next to the King and Queen, of course, who had due pre-eminence, and had taught the maids of honour) was generally acknowledged to be the Lord Chief Justice Jeffreys.

Upon his return from the Bloody Assizes, with triumph and great glory, after hanging every man who was too poor to help it, he pleased His Gracious Majesty so purely with the description of their delightful agonies, that the King exclaimed, 'This man alone is worthy to be at the head of the law.' Accordingly in his hand was placed the Great Seal of England.

So it came to pass that Lorna's destiny hung upon Lord Jeffreys; for at this time Earl Brandir died, being taken with gout in the heart, soon after I left London. Lorna was very sorry for him; but as he had never been able to hear one tone of her sweet silvery voice, it is not to be supposed that she wept without consolation. She grieved for him, as we ought to grieve for any good man going; and yet with a comforting sense of the benefit which the blessed exchange must bring to him.

Now the Lady Lorna Dugal appeared, to Lord Chancellor Jeffreys, so exceeding wealthy a ward, that the lock would pay for turning. Therefore he came, of his own accord, to visit her, and to treat with her; having heard (for the man was as big a gossip as never cared for anybody, yet loved to know all about everybody) that this wealthy and beautiful maiden would not listen to any young lord, having pledged her faith to the plain John Ridd.

Thereupon, our Lorna managed so to hold out golden hopes to the Lord High Chancellor, that he, being not more than three parts drunk, saw his way to a heap of money. And there and then (for he was not the man to dally long about any thing) upon surety of a certain round sum – the amount of which I will not mention, because of his kindness towards me – he gave to his fair ward permission, under sign and seal, to marry that loyal knight, John Ridd; upon condition only that the King's consent should be obtained.

His Majesty, well-disposed towards me for my previous service, and regarding me as a good Catholic, being moved moreover by the Queen, who desired to please Lorna, consented, without much hesitation, upon the understanding that Lorna, when she became of full age, and the mistress of her property (which was still under guardianship), should pay a heavy fine to the Crown, and devote a fixed portion of her estate to the promotion of the holy Catholic faith, in a manner to be dictated by the King himself. Inasmuch, however, as King James was driven out of his kingdom before this arrangement could take effect, and another king succeeded, who desired not the promotion of the Catholic religion, neither hankered after subsidies (whether French or English), that agreement was pronounced invalid, improper, and contemptible. However, there was no getting back the money once paid to Lord Chancellor Jeffreys.

But what thought we of money, at this present moment; or of position, or anything else, except indeed one another?

Everything was settled smoothly, and without any fear or fuss, that Lorna might find end of troubles, and myself of eager waiting, with the help of Parson Bowden, and the good wishes of two counties. I could scarce believe my fortune, when I looked upon her beauty, gentleness, and sweetness, mingled with enough of humour, and warm woman's feeling, never to be dull or tiring; never themselves to be weary.

For she might be called a woman now; although a very young one, and as full of playful ways, or perhaps I may say ten times as full, as if she had known no trouble. To wit, the spirit of bright childhood, having been so curbed and strait-ened, ere its time was over, now broke forth, enriched and varied with the garb of conscious maidenhood. And the sense of steadfast love, and eager love enfolding her, coloured with so many tinges all her looks, and words, and thoughts, that to me it was the noblest vision even to think about her.

But this was far too bright to last, without bitter break, and the plunging of happiness in horror, and of passionate joy in agony. My darling, in her softest moments, when she was alone with me, when the spark of defiant eyes was veiled beneath dark lashes, and the challenge of gay beauty passed into sweetest invitation; at such times of her purest love and warmest faith in me, a deep abiding fear would flutter in her bounding heart, as of deadly fate's approach. She would cling to me, and nestle to me, being scared of coyishness, and lay one arm around my neck, and ask if I could do without her.

Hence, as all emotions haply, of those who are more to us than ourselves, find within us stronger echo, and more perfect answer, so I could not be regardless of some hidden evil; and my dark misgivings deepened as the time drew nearer. I kept a steadfast watch on Lorna, neglecting a field of beans entirely, as well as a litter of young pigs, and a cow somewhat given to jaundice. And I let Jem Slocombe go to sleep in the tallat, all one afternoon, and Bill Dadds draw off a bucket of cider, without so much as a 'by your leave.' For these men knew that my knighthood, and my coat of arms, and (most of all) my love, were greatly against good farming; the sense of our country being – and perhaps it may be sensible – that a man who sticks up to be anything must allow himself to be cheated.

But I never did stick up, nor would, though all the parish bade me; and I whistled the same tunes to my horses, and held my plough-tree just the same, as if no King, nor Queen, had ever come to spoil my tune or hand. For this thing, nearly all the men around our part upbraided me, but the women praised me; and for the most part these are right, when themselves are not concerned.

However humble I might be, no one, knowing anything of our part of the country, would for a moment doubt that now here was a great to-do, and talk of John Ridd, and his wedding. The fierce fight with the Doones so lately, and my leading of the combat (though I fought not more than need be), and the vanishing of Sir Counsellor, and the galloping madness of Carver, and the religious fear of the women that this last was gone to hell – for he himself had declared that his aim, while he cut through our yeomanry; also their remorse, that he should have been made to go thither, with all his children left behind – these things, I say (if ever I can again contrive to say anything), had led to the broadest excitement about my wedding of Lorna. We heard that people meant to come from more than thirty miles around, upon excuse of seeing my stature and Lorna's beauty; but in good truth out of sheer curiosity, and the love of meddling.

Our clerk had given notice, that not a man should come inside the door of his church without shilling-fee; and women (as sure to see twice as much) must every one pay two shillings. I thought this wrong; and, as churchwarden, begged that the money might be paid into mine own hands, when taken. But the clerk said that was against all law; and he had orders from the parson to pay it to him without any delay. So as I always obey the parson, when I care not much about a thing, I let them have it their own way; though feeling inclined to believe, sometimes, that I ought to have some of the money.

Dear mother arranged all the ins and outs of the way in which it was to be done; and Annie, and Lizzie, and all the Snowes, and even Ruth Huckaback (who was there, after great persuasion), made such a sweeping of dresses, that I scarcely knew where to place my feet, and longed for a staff, to put by their gowns. Then Lorna came out of a pew half-way, in a manner which quite astonished me, and took my left hand in her right, and I prayed God that it were done with.

My darling looked so glorious, that I was afraid of glancing at her, yet took in all her beauty. She was in a fright, no doubt; but nobody should see it; whereas I said (to myself at least), 'I will go through it like a grave-digger.'

Lorna's dress was of pure white, clouded with faint lavender (for the sake of the old Earl Brandir), and as simple as need be, except for perfect loveliness. I was afraid to look at her, as I said before, except when each of us said, 'I will;' and then each dwelled upon the other.

It is impossible for any, who have not loved as I have, to conceive my joy and pride when after ring and all was done, and the parson had blessed us, Lorna turned to look at me, with her playful glance subdued, and deepened by this solemn act.

Her eyes, which none on earth may ever equal, or compare with, told me such a tale of hope, and faith, and heart's devotion, that I was almost amazed, thoroughly as I knew them. Darling eyes, the clearest eyes, the loveliest, the most loving eyes – the sound of a shot rang through the church, and those eyes were dim with death.

Lorna fell across my knees, when I was going to kiss her, as the bridegroom is allowed to do, and encouraged, if he needs it; a flood of blood came out upon the yellow wood of the altar steps; and at my feet lay Lorna, trying to tell me some last message out of her faithful eyes. I lifted her up, and petted her, and coaxed her, but it was no good; the only sign of life remaining was a drip of bright red blood.

Some men know what things befall them in the supreme time of their life – far above the time of death – but to me comes back as a hazy dream, without any knowledge in it, what I did, or felt, or thought, with my wife's arms flagging, flagging, around my neck, as I raised her up, and softly put them there. She sighed a long sigh on my breast, for her last farewell to life, and then she grew so cold, and cold, that I asked the time of year.

It was now Whit-Tuesday, and the lilacs all in blossom; and why I thought of the time of year, with the young death in my arms, God, or His angels, may decide, having so strangely given us. Enough that so I did, and looked; and our white lilacs were beautiful. Then I laid my wife in my mother's arms, and begging that no one would make a noise, went forth for my revenge.

Of course, I knew who had done it. There was but one man upon earth, or under it, where the Devil dwells, who could have done such a thing – such a thing. I used no harsher word about it, while I leaped upon our best horse, with bridle but no saddle, and set the head of Kickums towards the course now pointed out to me. Who showed me the course, I cannot tell. I only know that I took it. And the men fell back before me.

Weapon of no sort had I. Unarmed, and wondering at my strange attire (with a bridal vest, wrought by our Annie, and red with the blood of the bride), I went forth just to find out this; whether in this world there be, or be not, God of justice.

With my vicious horse at a furious speed, I came upon Black Barrow Down, directed by some shout of men, which seemed to me but a whisper. And there, about a furlong before me, rode a man on a great black horse; and I knew that the man was Carver Doone.

'Thy life, or mine,' I said to myself; 'as the will of God may be. But we two live not upon this earth, one more hour, together.'

I knew the strength of this great man; and I knew that he was armed with a gun – if he had time to load again, after shooting my Lorna, – or at any rate with pistols, and a horseman's sword as well. Nevertheless, I had no more doubt of killing the man before me, than a cook has of spitting a headless fowl.

Sometimes seeing no ground beneath me, and sometimes heeding every leaf, and the crossing of the grass blades, I followed over the long moor, reckless whether seen or not. But only once, the other man turned round, and looked back again; and then I was beside a rock, with a reedy swamp behind me.

Although he was so far before me, and riding as hard as ride he might, I saw that he had something on the horse in front of him; something which needed care, and stopped him from looking backward. In the whirling of my wits, I fancied first that this was Lorna; until the scene I had been through fell across hot brain, and heart, like the drop at the close of a tragedy. Rushing there, through crag and quag, at utmost speed of a maddened horse, I saw, as of another's fate, calmly (as on canvas laid), the brutal deed, the piteous anguish, and the cold despair.

The man turned up the gully leading from the moor to Cloven Rocks, through which John Fry had tracked Uncle Ben, as of old related. But as Carver entered it, he turned round, and beheld me not a hundred yards behind; and I saw that he was bearing his child, little Ensie, before him. Ensie also descried me, and stretched his hands, and cried to me; for the face of his father frightened him.

Carver Doone, with a vile oath, thrust spurs into his flagging horse, and laid one hand on a pistol-stock, whence I knew that his slung carbine had received no bullet, since the one that had pierced Lorna. And a cry of triumph rose from the black depths of my heart. What cared I for pistols? I had no spurs, neither was my horse one to need the rowel; I rather held him in than urged him, for he was fresh as ever; and I knew that the black steed in front, if he breasted the steep ascent, where the track divided, must be in our reach at once.

His rider knew this; and, having no room in the rocky channel to turn and fire, drew rein at the crossways sharply, and plunged into the black ravine leading to the Wizard's Slough. 'Is it so?' I said to myself, with brain and head cold as iron: 'though the foul fiend come from the slough, to save thee; thou shalt carve it, Carver.'

I followed my enemy carefully, steadily, even leisurely; for I had him, as in a pitfall, whence no escape might be. He thought that I feared to approach him, for he knew not where he was: and his low disdainful laugh came back. 'Laugh he who wins,' thought I.

A gnarled and half-starved oak, as stubborn as my own resolve, and smitten by some storm of old, hung from the crag above me. Rising from my horse's back, although I had no stirrups, I caught a limb, and tore it (like a wheat-awn) from the socket. Men show the rent even now, with wonder; none with more wonder than myself.

Carver Doone turned the corner suddenly, on the black and bottomless bog; with a start of fear he reined back his horse, and I thought he would have rushed upon me. But instead of that, he again rode on; hoping to find a way round the side.

Now there is a way between cliff and slough, for those who know the ground thoroughly, or have time enough to search it; but for him there was no road, and he lost some time in seeking it. Upon this he made up his mind; and wheeling, fired, and then rode at me.

His bullet struck me somewhere, but I took no heed of that. Fearing only his escape, I laid my horse across the way, and with the limb of the oak struck full on the forehead his charging steed. Ere the slash of the sword came nigh me, man and horse rolled over, and well-nigh bore my own horse down, with the power of their onset.

Carver Doone was somewhat stunned, and could not arise for a moment. Meanwhile I leaped on the ground, and waited, smoothing my hair back, and baring my arms, as though in the ring for wrestling. Then the little boy ran to me, clasped my leg, and looked up at me: and the terror in his eyes made me almost fear myself.

'Ensie, dear,' I said quite gently, grieving that he should see his wicked father killed, 'run up yonder round the corner, and try to find a bunch of bluebells for the pretty lady.' The child obeyed me, hanging back, and looking back, and then laughing, while I prepared for business. There and then, I might have killed mine enemy, with a single blow, while he lay unconscious; but it would have been foul play.

With a sullen and black scowl, the Carver gathered his mighty limbs, and arose, and looked round for his weapons; but I had put them well away. Then he came to me, and gazed, being wont to frighten thus young men.

'I would not harm you, lad,' he said, with a lofty style of sneering: 'I have punished you enough, for most of your impertinence. For the rest I forgive you; because you have been good, and gracious, to my little son. Go, and be contented.'

For answer, I smote him on the cheek, lightly, and not to hurt him: but to make his blood leap up. I would not sully my tongue, by speaking to a man like this.

There was a level space of sward, between us and the slough. With the courtesy derived from London, and the processions I had seen, to this place I led him. And that he might breathe himself, and have every fibre cool, and every muscle ready, my hold upon his coat I loosed, and left him to begin with me, whenever he thought proper.

I think he felt that his time was come. I think he knew from my knitted muscles, and the firm arch of my breast, and the way in which I stood; but most of all from my stern blue eyes; that he had found his master. At any rate a paleness came, an ashy paleness on his cheeks, and the vast calves of his legs bowed in, as if he were out of training.

Seeing this, villain as he was, I offered him first chance. I stretched forth my left hand, as I do to a weaker antagonist, and I let him have the hug of me. But in this I was too generous; having forgotten my pistol-wound, and the cracking of one of my short lower ribs. Carver Doone caught me round the waist, with such a grip as never yet had been laid upon me.

I heard my rib go; I grasped his arm, and tore the muscle out of it (as the string comes out of an orange); then I took him by the throat, which is not allowed in wrestling; but he had snatched at mine; and now was no time of dalliance. In vain he tugged, and strained, and writhed, dashed his bleeding fist into my face, and flung himself on me, with gnashing jaws. Beneath the iron of my strength – for God that day was with me – I had him helpless in two minutes, and his blazing eyes lolled out.

'I will not harm thee any more,' I cried, so far as I could for panting, the work being very furious: 'Carver Doone, thou art beaten: own it, and thank God for it; and go thy way, and repent thyself.'

It was all too late. Even if he had yielded in his ravening frenzy, for his beard was frothy as a mad dog's jowl; even if he would have owned that, for the first time in his life, he had found his master; it was all too late.

The black bog had him by the feet; the sucking of the ground drew on him, like the thirsty lips of death. In our fury, we had heeded neither wet nor dry, nor thought of earth beneath us. I myself might scarcely leap, with the last spring of o'er-laboured legs, from the engulfing grave of slime. He fell back, with his swarthy breast (from which my gripe had rent all clothing), like a hummock of bog-oak, standing out the quagmire; and then he tossed his arms to heaven, and they were black to the elbow, and the glare of his eyes was ghastly. I could only gaze and pant: for my strength was no more than an infant's, from the fury and the horror. Scarcely could I turn away, while, joint by joint, he sank from sight.

42

Give Away the Grandeur

When the little boy came back with the bluebells, which he had managed to find – as children always do find flowers, when older eyes see none – the only sign of his father left was a dark brown bubble, upon a new-formed patch of blackness. But to the centre of its pulpy gorge, the greedy slough was heaving, and sullenly grinding its weltering jaws among the flags, and the sedges.

With pain, and ache, both of mind and body, and shame at my own fury, I heavily mounted my horse again, and looked down at the innocent Ensie. Would this playful, loving child grow up like his cruel father, and end a godless life of hatred with a death of violence? He lifted his noble forehead towards me, as if to answer, 'Nay, I will not:' but the words he spoke were these: –

'Don' – for he never could say 'John' – 'oh Don, I am so glad, that nasty naughty man is gone away. Take me home, Don. Take me home.'

It has been said of the wicked, 'Not even their own children love them.' And I could easily believe that Carver Doone's cold-hearted ways had scared from him even his favourite child. No man would I call truly wicked, unless his heart be cold.

It hurt me, more than I can tell, even through all other grief, to take into my arms the child of the man just slain by me. The feeling was a foolish one, and a wrong one, as the thing had been – for I would fain have saved that man, after he was con-

310

quered – nevertheless my arms went coldly round that little fellow; neither would they have gone at all, if there had been any help for it. But I could not leave him there, till some one else might fetch him; on account of the cruel slough, and the ravens which had come hovering over the dead horse; neither could I, with my wound, tie him on my horse, and walk.

For now I had spent a great deal of blood, and was rather faint and weary. And it was lucky for me that Kickums had lost spirit, like his master, and went home as mildly as a lamb. For, when we came towards the farm, I seemed to be riding in a dream almost; and the voices both of men and women (who had hurried forth upon my track), as they met me, seemed to wander from a distant muffling cloud. Only the thought of Lorna's death, like a heavy knell, was tolling in the belfry of my brain.

When we came to the stable door, I rather fell from my horse than got off; and John Fry, with a look of wonder, took Kickums' head, and led him in. Into the old farm-house I tottered, like a weanling child, with mother in her common clothes, helping me along, yet fearing, except by stealth, to look at me.

'I have killed him,' was all I said; 'even as he killed Lorna. Now let me see my wife, mother. She belongs to me none the less, though dead.'

'You cannot see her now, dear John,' said Ruth Hucka-back, coming forward; since no one else had the courage. 'Annie is with her now, John.'

'What has that to do with it? Let me see my dead one; and then die.'

All the women fell away, and whispered, and looked at me, with side-glances, and some sobbing; for my face was hard as flint. Ruth alone stood by me, and dropped her eyes, and trembled. Then one little hand of hers stole into my great shaking palm, and the other was laid on my tattered coat: yet with her clothes she shunned my blood, while she whispered gently, –

'John, she is not your dead one. She may even be your living one yet, your wife, your home, and your happiness. But you must not see her now.'

'Is there any chance for her? For me, I mean; for me, I mean?'

'God in heaven knows, dear John. But the sight of you, and in this sad plight, would be certain death to her. Now come first, and be healed yourself.'

I obeyed her, like a child, whispering only as I went, for none but myself knew her goodness – 'Almighty God will bless you, darling, for the good you are doing now.'

Tenfold, ay and a thousandfold, I prayed and I believed it, when I came to know the truth. If it had not been for this little maid, Lorna must have died at once, as in my arms she lay for dead, from the dastard and murderous cruelty. But the moment I left her Ruth came forward, and took the command of every one, in right of her firmness and readiness.

She made them bear her home at once upon the door of the pulpit, with the cushion under the drooping head. With her own little hands she cut off, as tenderly as a pear is peeled, the bridal-dress so steeped and stained, and then with her dainty transparent fingers (no larger than a pencil) she probed the vile wound in the side, and fetched the reeking bullet forth; and then with the coldest water staunched the flowing of the life-blood. All this while, my darling lay insensible, and white as death; and the rest declared that she was dead, and needed nothing but her maiden shroud.

But Ruth still sponged the poor side and forehead, and watched the long eyelashes flat upon the marble cheek; and laid her pure face on the faint heart, and bade them fetch her Spanish wine. Then she parted the pearly teeth (feebly clenched on the hovering breath), and poured in wine from a christening spoon, and raised the graceful neck and breast, and stroked the delicate throat, and waited; and then poured in a little more.

Annie all the while looked on, with horror and amazement, counting herself no second-rate nurse, and this as against all theory. But the quiet lifting of Ruth's hand, and one glance from her dark bright eyes, told Annie just to stand away, and not intercept the air so. And at the very moment, when all the rest had settled that Ruth was a simple idiot, but could not harm the dead much, a little flutter in the throat, followed by a short low sigh, made them pause, and look, and hope.

For hours, however, and days, she lay at the very verge of death, kept alive by nothing but the care, the skill, the tenderness, and perpetual watchfulness of Ruth. Luckily Annie was not there very often, so as to meddle; for kind and clever nurse as she was, she must have done more harm than good. But my broken rib, which was set by a doctor, who chanced to be at the wedding, was allotted to Annie's care; and great inflammation ensuing, it was quite enough to content her. This doctor had pronounced poor Lorna dead; wherefore Ruth refused most firmly to have aught to do with him. She took the whole case on herself; and with God's help, she bore it through.

Now whether it were the light, and brightness of my Lorna's nature, or the freedom from anxiety – for she knew not of my hurt; – or, as some people said, her birthright among wounds and violence, or her manner of not drinking beer, – I leave that doctor to determine, who pronounced her dead. But anyhow, one thing is certain; sure as the stars of hope above us, Lorna recovered long ere I did.

On me lay overwhelming sorrow, having lost my love and lover, at the moment she was mine. With the power of fate upon me, and the black cauldron of the wizard's death boiling in my heated brain, I had no faith in the tales they told. I believed that Lorna was in the churchyard, while these rogues were lying to me. For with strength of blood like mine, and power of heart behind it, a broken bone must burn himself.

Mine went hard with fires of pain, being of such size and thickness; and I was ashamed of him for breaking by reason of a pistol-ball, and the mere hug of a man. And it fetched me down in conceit of strength; so that I was careful afterwards.

All this was a lesson to me. All this made me very humble; illness being a thing, as yet, altogether unknown to me. Not that I cried small, or skulked, or feared the death which some foretold: shaking their heads about mortification, and a green appearance. Only that I seemed quite fit to go to heaven, and

Lorna. For in my sick distracted mind (stirred with many tossings), like the bead in a wisp of frog-spawn drifted by the current, hung the black and worthless burden of the life before me. A life without Lorna; a tadpole life. All stupid head; and no body.

Many men may like such life; anchorites, fakirs, high-priests, and so on; but to my mind, it is not the native thing God meant for us. My dearest mother was a show, with crying, and with fretting. The Doones, as she thought, were born to destroy us. Scarce had she come to some liveliness (though sprinkled with tears, every now and then) after her great bereavement, and ten years' time to dwell on it – when lo, here was her husband's son, the pet child of her own good John, murdered like his father! Well, the ways of God were wonderful!

So they were, and so they are, and so they ever will be. Let us debate them as we will, our ways are His, and much the same; only second-hand from Him. And I expected something from Him, even in my worst of times, knowing that I had done my best.

This is not edifying talk – as the Puritans used to remind my father, when there was no more to drink – therefore let me only tell what became of Lorna. One day, I was sitting in my bedroom, for I could not get downstairs, and there was no one strong enough to carry me, even if I would have borne it.

Though it cost me sore trouble and weariness, I had put on all my Sunday clothes, out of respect for the doctor, who was coming to bleed me again (as he always did, twice a week); and it struck me, that he had seemed hurt in his mind, because I wore my worst clothes to be bled in – for lie in bed I would not, after six o'clock; and even that was great laziness.

I looked at my right hand, whose grasp had been like that of a blacksmith's vice; and it seemed to myself impossible, that this could be John Ridd's. The great frame of the hand was there, as well as the muscles, standing forth like the guttering of a candle, and the broad blue veins, going up the back, and crossing every finger. But as for colour, even

Lorna's could scarcely have been whiter; and as for strength, little Ensie Doone might have come and held it fast. I laughed, as I tried in vain to lift the basin set for bleeding me.

Then I thought of all the lovely things going on out of doors just now, concerning which the drowsy song of the bees came to me. These must be among the thyme, by the sound of their great content. Therefore the roses must be in blossom, and the woodbine, and clove-gilly-flower; the cherries on the wall must be turning red, and the first brood of thrushes come to watch them do it, wheat must be callow with a tufted quivering, and the early meadows swathed with hay.

Yet there was I, a helpless creature, quite unfit to stir among them, gifted with no sight, no scent of all the changes that move our love, and lead our hearts, from month to month, along the quiet path of life. And what was worse, I had no hope of caring ever for them more.

Presently a little knock sounded through my gloomy room, and supposing it to be the doctor, I tried to rise, and make my bow. But to my surprise, it was little Ruth, who had never once come to visit me, since I was placed under the doctor's hands. Ruth was dressed so gaily, with rosettes, and flowers, and what not, that I was sorry for her bad manners; and thought she was come to conquer me, now that Lorna was done with.

Ruth ran towards me, with sparkling eyes, being rather short of sight; then suddenly she stopped, and I saw entire amazement in her face.

'Can you receive visitors, Cousin Ridd? – why, they never told me of this!' she cried: 'I knew that you were weak, dear John; but not that you were dying. Whatever is that basin for?'

'I have no intention of dying, Ruth; and I like not to talk about it. But that basin, if you must know, is for the doctor's purpose.'

'What, do you mean bleeding you? You poor weak cousin! Is it possible that he does that still?'

'Twice a week for the last six weeks, dear. Nothing else has kept me alive.'

'Nothing else has killed you, nearly. There!' and she set her little boot across the basin, and crushed it. 'Not another drop shall they have from you. Is Annie such a fool as that? And Lizzie, like a zany, at her books! And killing their brother, between them!'

I was surprised to see Ruth excited; her character being so calm and quiet. And I tried to soothe her with my feeble hand, as now she knelt before me.

'Dear cousin, the doctor must know best. Annie says so, every day. Else what has he been brought up for?'

'Brought up for slaying, and murdering. Twenty doctors killed King Charles, in spite of all the women. Will you leave it to me, John? I have a little will of my own; and I am not afraid of doctors. Will you leave it to me, dear John? I have saved your Lorna's life. And now I will save yours; which is a far, far easier business.'

'You have saved my Lorna's life! What do you mean by talking so?'

'Only what I say, Cousin John. Though perhaps I over-prize my work. But at any rate she says so.'

'I do not understand,' I said, falling back with bewilderment, 'all women are such liars.'

'Have you ever known me tell a lie?' cried Ruth in great indignation – more feigned, I doubt, than real – 'your mother may tell a story, now and then, when she feels it right; and so may both your sisters. But so you cannot do, John Ridd; and no more than you, can I do it.'

If ever there was virtuous truth in the eyes of any woman, it was now in the eyes of Ruth Huckaback: and my brain began very slowly to move, the heart being almost torpid, from perpetual loss of blood.

'I do not understand,' was all I could say, for a very long time.

'Will you understand, if I show you Lorna? I have feared to do it, for the sake of you both. But now Lorna is well enough, if you think that you are, Cousin John. Surely you will understand, when you see your wife.'

Following her, to the very utmost of my mind and heart, I felt that all she said was truth; and yet I could not make it out. And in her last few words, there was such a power of sadness, rising through the cover of gaiety, that I said to myself, half in a dream, 'Ruth is very beautiful.'

Before I had time to listen much for the approach of footsteps, Ruth came back, and behind her Lorna; coy as if of her bridegroom; and hanging back with her beauty. Ruth banged the door, and ran away; and Lorna stood before me.

But she did not stand for an instant, when she saw what I was like. At the risk of all thick bandages, and upsetting a dozen medicine bottles, and scattering leeches right and left, she managed to get into my arms, although they could not hold her. She laid her panting warm young breast on the place where they meant to bleed me, and she set my pale face up; and she would not look at me, having greater faith in kissing.

I felt my life come back, and glow; I felt my trust in God revive; I felt the joy of living and of loving dearer things than life. It is not a moment to describe; who feels can never tell of it. But the compassion of my sweetheart's tears, and the caressing of my bride's lips, and the throbbing of my wife's heart (now at last at home on mine) made me feel that the world was good, and not a thing to be weary of.

Little more have I to tell. The doctor was turned out at once; and slowly came back my former strength, with a darling wife, and good victuals. As for Lorna, she never tired of sitting and watching me eat and eat. And such is her heart, that she never tires of being with me here and there, among the beautiful places, and talking with her arm around me – so far at least as it can go, though half of mine may go round her – of the many fears, and troubles, dangers and discouragements, and worst of all the bitter partings, which we used to undergo.

There is no need for my farming harder than becomes a man of weight. Lorna has great stores of money, though we never draw it out, except for some poor neighbour; unless I find her a sumptuous dress, out of her own perquisites. And this she always looks upon as a wondrous gift from me; and kisses me much when she puts it on, and walks like the noble woman she is. And yet I may never behold it again; for she gets back to her simple clothes, and I love her the better in them. I believe that she gives half the grandeur away, and keeps the other half for the children.

As for poor Tom Faggus, everyone knows his bitter adventures, when his pardon was recalled, because of his sally to Sedgemoor. Not a child in the county, I doubt, but knows far more than I do of Tom's most desperate doings. The law had ruined him once, he said; and then he had been too much for the law: and now that a quiet life was his object, here the base thing came after him. And such was his dread of this evil spirit, that being caught upon Barnstaple Bridge, with soldiers at either end of it (yet doubtful about approaching him), he set his strawberry mare, sweet Winnie, at the left-hand parapet, with a whisper into her dove-coloured ear. Without a moment's doubt she leaped it, into the foaming tide, and swam, and landed according to orders. Also his flight from a public-house (where a trap was set for him, but Winnie came, and broke down the door, and put two men under, and trod on them), is as well known as any ballad. It was reported for awhile that poor Tom had been caught at last, by means of his fondness for liquor, and was hanged before Taunton Gaol; but luckily we knew better. With a good wife, and a wonderful horse, and all the country attached to him, he kept the law at a wholesome distance, until it became too much for its master; and a new king arose. Upon this, Tom sued his pardon afresh; and Jeremy Stickles, who suited the times, was glad to help him getting it, as well as a compensation. Thereafter, the good and respectable Tom lived a godly and righteous (though not always sober) life; and brought up his children to honesty, as the first of all qualifications.

My dear mother was as happy as possibly need be with us; having no cause for jealousy, as others arose around her. And everybody was well pleased, when Lizzie came in one day and tossed her bookshelf over, and declared that she would have Captain Bloxham, and nobody should prevent her. For that he alone, of all the men she had ever met with, knew good writing when he saw it, and could spell a word when told. As he had now succeeded to Captain Stickles' position (Stickles going up the tree), and had the power of collecting and of keeping what he liked, there was nothing to be said against it; and we hoped that he would pay her out.

I sent little Ensie to Blundell's school, at my own cost and charges, having changed his name, for fear of what anyone might do to him. I called him 'Ensie Jones;' and I hope he will be a credit to us. For the bold adventurous nature of the Doones broke out on him, and we got him a commission, and after many scrapes of spirit, he did great things in the Low Countries. He looks upon me as his father; and without my leave, will not lay claim to the heritage, and title of the Doones, which clearly belong to him.

Ruth Huckaback is not married yet; although upon Uncle Reuben's death she came into all his property; except, indeed, £2000, which Uncle Ben, in his driest manner, bequeathed 'to Sir John Ridd, the worshipful knight, for greasing of the testator's boots.' And he left almost a mint of money, not from the mine, but from the shop, and the good use of usury. For the mine had brought in just what it cost, when the vein of gold ended suddenly; leaving all concerned much older, and some, I fear, much poorer; but no one utterly ruined, as is the case with most of them. Ruth herself was his true mine, as upon death-bed he found. I know a man even worthy of her: and though she is not very young, he loves her, as I love Lorna. More and more I hope, and think, that in the end he will win her; and I do not mean to dance again, except at dear Ruth's wedding; if a floor can be found strong enough.

Of Lorna, of my lifelong darling, of my more and more loved wife, I will not talk; for it is not seemly, that a man should exalt his pride. Year by year, her beauty grows, with the growth of goodness, kindness, and true happiness – above all with loving. For change, she makes a joke of this, and plays with it, and laughs at it; and then, when my slow nature marvels, back she comes to the earnest thing. And if I wish to pay her out for something very dreadful – as may happen once or twice, when we become too gladsome – I bring her to forgotten sadness, and to me for cure of it, by the two words, 'Lorna Doone.'

Leabharlann Contae na Mídhe

Библиотека